Love Somebody Like You

Love Somebody Like You

SUSAN FOX

ZEBRA BOOKS
KENSINGTON PUBLISHING CORP.
http://www.kensingtonbooks.com

ZEBRA BOOKS are published by

Kensington Publishing Corp.
119 West 40th Street
New York, NY 10018

All Kensington titles, imprints, and distributed lines are available at special quantity discounts for bulk purchases for sales promotion, premiums, fund-raising, educational, or institutional use.

Special book excerpts or customized printings can also be created to fit specific needs. For details, write or phone the office of the Kensington Sales Manager: Attn.: Sales Department. Kensington Publishing Corp., 119 West 40th Street, New York, NY 10018. Phone: 1-800-221-2647.

Zebra and the Z logo Reg. U.S. Pat. & TM Off.

First Printing: October 2015
ISBN-13: 978-1-4201-3578-7
ISBN-10: 1-4201-3578-3

eISBN-13: 978-1-4201-3579-4
eISBN-10: 1-4201-3579-1

10 9 8 7 6 5 4 3 2 1

Printed in the United States of America

Chapter One

Sally Ryland squeezed her eyes shut and opened them again, but the numbers on her computer screen didn't change. The mortgage payment would come out of Ryland Riding's bank account today, the feed bill was a month overdue, and her quarterly insurance premium came due in two weeks. She loved this place with all her heart, but most of the time she was treading water, desperately trying to keep the whole operation afloat.

If the bank foreclosed on this property, not only would her business go down the drain, but she'd be homeless. She'd lose her personal piece of heaven, not to mention her beloved horses and flock of chickens. She'd lose her way of life. Her independence. She'd be left with nothing.

But it wasn't going to happen. Day by day, she hung on—even if it was by fingernails bitten to the quick. And so far today was proving to be one of the good ones. The mail had brought a couple of checks from riding students, totaling enough to hang on for a while longer.

Just as well Corrie had quit two weeks ago, and that

Sally hadn't been able to find a new assistant. Even though Corrie had worked for peanuts plus a free room, Sally needed every "peanut" now. This past weekend, a married couple who boarded horses with her had told her they'd be moving from Caribou Crossing to the Fraser Valley.

She stood up from the old desk in her office in the barn, stretched, and dug her fingers into her aching lower back. It was damned hard work handling this place on her own, but she'd done it before and could do it now.

It was Tuesday afternoon and the eight kids in her beginner children's class—aged five to seven—would be here in an hour. Energy overcame the exhaustion that had dogged her footsteps since Corrie's departure, and she bustled out of the office, smiling. She loved children as much as she loved horses, this countryside, and her chickens. Life was good after all. It was great, in fact.

She'd long ago put her old dream of a happy marriage and two or three kids behind her. Or, rather, her husband, Pete, had killed that dream. The charming boyfriend who had wooed her so romantically had, once they were wed, taught her how insidiously love could tip over into fear and pain. No way would she ever put herself in that position again—which meant she'd live her life alone.

She brushed aside the negative thoughts. Pete had been dead for three years. She was safe. Her life was her own.

The lesson horses that she'd brought in from the paddock waited in stalls. As she headed for the tack room to gather grooming supplies, the sound of a powerful engine coming down the driveway outside made her change direction. Striding down the wide aisle between the banks of stalls, she spoke to the horses who hung their heads over the doors, their ears cocked. "No, I'm not expecting anyone."

She stopped in the doorway of the barn, squinting against early-July sunshine as a big silver pickup truck stopped in the parking area. Hitched to it was a battered silver and white trailer, the kind of rig that contained living quarters for humans and for horses. She'd had a smaller version in her barrel racing days. An image flashed into her mind.

A younger Sally, dressed in her brown and silver rodeo costume, leaned forward as her horse cleanly rounded the third and last barrel on the course and they sprinted for the finish line. The announcer's voice boomed, "Looks like Sally Pantages and Autumn Mist are gonna chalk up another win today, folks!"

A punch of nostalgia hit her. For the mare that had been her partner and best friend. For life on the circuit. For the woman she'd once been. Before Pete.

Outside, the engine cut off, the driver's door opened, and a man stepped down. With the sun in her eyes, she couldn't see details, only the shape of a cowboy, from hat to boots. He had the stride of one, too: easy and athletic, confident and purely male. In her early twenties, she'd found that so sexy.

Now, she drew back into the shadows. At thirty-two, it was a very long time since she'd felt sexy. Men made her feel wary, not aroused.

Pete's hands, gripping her shoulders . . . "Other men," he said, "they only want one thing from you, baby. Don't you lead them on now. Remember, I'm the one who loves you, who understands you. You're my wife."

She jerked her shoulders, banishing the memory as the man came toward her. Probably he was a prospective boarder, or a parent looking to arrange lessons for his child. Though she never felt comfortable being alone with a man, new business would sure be welcome.

"Sally?" he said as he approached, sweeping off his straw hat. "That you?" Where she stood in the shade of the barn, he wouldn't be able to see her very well.

"Yes. Do I know—"

Oh my gosh. She did know him. Now that he was close, blocking the sun's glare, she recognized that striking face with the dark skin and bold features of his aboriginal heritage. She hadn't seen him in seven years, not since she married Pete.

"Ben Traynor?" She gaped at him, remembering the wiry bronc rider three years her junior, with his cocky swagger and those dancing chestnut brown eyes framed with long black lashes. "What are you doing here?"

He was all grown up now, that was for sure. Around six feet tall, he was still lean but more solidly muscled, nicely filling out clean Wranglers and a tan Western shirt with rolled-up sleeves. His left arm was in a collar and cuff sling.

"Just passing by," he said in a husky drawl. "It's been a while."

Her gaze lifted back to his face, even more handsome with maturity. Shaggy dark hair brushed past his shirt collar, hair that glinted with chestnut highlights that matched his eyes. Those amazing eyes. Eyes that, she realized, were making their own survey of her body and face.

"Yes, it has," she agreed.

His gaze reminded her that she'd changed, too. Ben would remember her in figure-hugging pants and fancy Western shirts, with long, strawberry-blond hair and a touch of make-up. Now her clothing was loose and nondescript; she chopped off her hair with nail scissors when it got in her eyes; and the closest thing to make-up her face ever saw was lip balm. Not only didn't she have the time to fuss over her appearance, but she had learned that it was safest to be semi-invisible.

As for Ben Traynor, he couldn't be semi-invisible if he tried. She managed to tear her fascinated gaze from his face. The sling that looped around his neck and cuffed his left wrist sure did bring back the old days. And for a moment she was the old Sally, teasing, "Still can't stay on a bucking bronc, eh?"

"Fractured my damned shoulder competing at Williams Lake." The Stampede and Rodeo had been held this past weekend, the Canada Day long weekend.

"Fractured?" That was worse than she'd guessed. Grimacing in sympathy and regretting her joke, she said, "Sorry. How bad is it? Are you going to be out of commission?" Rodeo cowboys were notoriously tough to the point of being stupid. A broken bone wouldn't necessarily stop one from riding.

Ben scowled. "Yeah. The doc says if I ride before it heals some, that'd probably be the end to my season."

"Not to mention you could wind up with a serious enough injury that it ends your career. We've both seen that happen." Some cowboys were so "macho" that the word was a synonym for "idiotic."

He nodded. "And I still got a lot of good years in me."

"If your shoulder's that bad, are you supposed to be driving?"

"Nah. But what'm I gonna do? Sit on my butt in Williams Lake? Figure I'll drive back home to Alberta, and catch up with the rodeo in a bit."

"How long will you be out?"

"He says I should give it six weeks. So that means . . ." He gave a one-shoulder shrug.

"Three or four?" That must be one serious fracture.

"Worst-case scenario, I figure three. I heal quickly

and I need to get back in the game. You know how that goes."

"Yeah." You only made money if you competed and placed. Earnings also determined whether you qualified for the Canadian Finals Rodeo and the chance to win higher purses, not to mention championships.

A grin snuck across his mouth, a cousin to that old cocky one. "Just so's you know, that bronc didn't buck me off until after the buzzer. I ended up taking first."

Though she was impressed, she wasn't about to act like a buckle bunny. She'd always hated the way those rodeo groupies oohed and aahed all over the cowboys. "Guess that's some consolation."

His eyes twinkled. "You always were hard on me, Sally Pantages. But damn, it's real good to see you all the same. It's been forever."

And that brought her back to reality. She hadn't been Sally Pantages for a long time. "It has," she said stiffly. Since she'd last seen Ben, she'd given up barrel racing, married, moved from Alberta to British Columbia, bought Ryland Riding along with Pete, built up a business—

"I was sorry to hear about your husband." His gruff voice cut through her thoughts. "It's not right, a guy that young dying from a heart attack."

Wondering how Ben had heard, she ducked her head and muttered, "Thanks." She hated it when people offered sympathy. It sent sour pangs of shame and guilt through her. People assumed she was a grieving widow who'd been deeply in love with her husband. The bitter truth was, in the last year or two of her marriage she'd more than once wished Pete dead, and his death from a massive heart attack at age thirty had been partly her fault.

It was time to change the subject. Not to mention,

time to get back to work. She straightened her shoulders. "Ben, I have kids coming for a lesson and I need to get their horses ready. It's been nice seeing you, but . . ." And it had been. Not only was he awfully easy on the eyes, but for a moment he'd taken her back to the days when life was uncomplicated and fun. When *she* had been uncomplicated and fun. She'd actually relaxed with him, which was something she rarely did with a man. Now, though, she needed to get back to her routine.

"Can't get rid of me that easily."

For the first time since she'd recognized him, a shiver of anxiety rippled through her. The easy grin on his face did nothing to relieve it. A man's smile and charm didn't guarantee safety.

Ben went on. "'Sides, your sister'd have my hide."

Her heart gave a painful jerk. God, how she missed her family. "You've seen Penny?"

"At the rodeo in Wainwright. She was volunteering at one of the concessions. We got chatting. She said her sister used to barrel race and gave your name, so I said I used to know you. When I mentioned that I was heading out to Williams Lake, she told me where you were, and about Pete. She asked me to stop by if I had a chance."

"She did?" It was almost six years since Sally had spoken to her family, since they'd cut her out of their lives for marrying Pete and moving here. Once, she and her younger sister had shared confidences, ganged up on their parents, done each other's hair. Now, after all this time, Penny had asked Ben to drop by and see her? "How is she? Did she say—" Frustrated, Sally shook her head. "No, sorry, I don't have time to talk." She was desperate for news, but her students and their moms would be here soon.

"I'll help you get the horses ready."

She eyed his sling, knowing he needed to wear it so the broken bones would heal in the correct position. "What can you do with one hand?"

"I'd be real happy to show you." His low, suggestive chuckle and the gleam in his eyes left no doubt that he was talking about more than saddling a few horses.

And Lord, for one quick, astonishing moment, she felt a responding tingle of sexual heat. Turning quickly to hide the color that flamed in her cheeks, she said crisply, "If that was an attempt at flirtation, I'm not interested."

"Okay, sorry. Old habits, I guess."

Old habits? Hah! No doubt he still cut a swathe through the buckle bunnies.

"I'm right-handed," he went on. "I can help with the horses. Then how about I hang around while you give your lesson? Maybe give my horse some water and exercise. After, we can talk about Penny."

He sounded matter-of-fact, with no hint of teasing innuendo, and he'd offered her the best inducement in the world: news of her family. She shot him a glance over her shoulder. This was Ben Traynor. He might've been a cocky young charmer, moving from conquest to conquest, but she'd never heard a single word about him being mean to a woman. Or to an animal. She'd always liked the respectful way he treated horses, even including the broncs he rode, those trained buckers whose immediate mission in life was to toss him out of the saddle and onto the dirt of the arena floor.

She'd probably misinterpreted his comment about showing her what he could do with one hand. Why would a sexy guy like him be flirting with a drab, worn-out woman like her?

Though she wasn't big on trusting men, something told her she was safe with Ben.

"Sure," she said. "Thanks."

Sally had changed, Ben thought as he followed her into the barn. There were moments when she seemed like her old self, but she was less outgoing and more guarded. Like she wasn't sure whether she trusted him. But then he'd been twenty-two the last time she saw him. She didn't know what kind of man he'd turned into in the past seven years.

She was older too—must be thirty-one, thirty-two now—and it showed in a bunch of ways. She was leaner than before, in body and face, and he'd never seen her in practical work clothes before—though the sway of her hips and butt were still sexy despite the loose jeans. Her fiery copper-gold hair used to hang well past her shoulders; now it was short and curly, framing her face. She still had that cute dusting of freckles across her nose and cheeks, but her forehead and greenish gray eyes had tiny creases that suggested her life wasn't a bed of roses. She looked like she could use a weekend at a spa.

Or a weekend in bed. Which he'd be happy to provide. To be honest, that was one of the reasons he'd agreed when Penny had asked him to look up her sister. He'd always had a thing for Sally and, according to Penny, she'd been a widow for three years.

Sally shot him a glance over her shoulder, and he quickly raised his gaze from her backside as she said, "How about you groom? It'd be hard for you to do up saddle cinches and put on bridles, working with only one hand."

He could manage, but this was her turf. And a mighty

impressive operation from what he'd seen so far. "Whatever you say, boss."

"I'll pick out their hooves, though."

"That'd be good." They both knew it was a task that took two strong hands, one to support the hoof and the other to use the pick to clean out dirt, manure, and stones.

She went to the tack room and returned with a box of supplies, which he sorted through as she brought a chestnut mare from its stall and put it in cross ties. With the horse securely tied in the middle of the aisle, Ben groomed and Sally wielded the hoof pick. Then she put on the saddle pad, saddle, and bridle while Ben went into the next stall and began to groom a small pinto gelding.

Ben had been injured enough times over the years that he was pretty proficient with a single functioning arm, even if his fractured shoulder hurt like a son of a bitch. Besides, being around horses was one of his favorite things. Sally's animals weren't prime stock but they were healthy and had good manners. The tools and tack were worn but well maintained.

When he moved to the next stall, he peeked at Sally as she put the pinto in cross ties and saddled it with spare efficiency and quiet, affectionate murmurs. He figured he wasn't likely to hear her whispering sweet nothings in his ears anytime soon, not with the way she'd cold-shouldered his attempt at flirtation.

That had been kind of weird. In the old days, she'd have flung back something teasing, like how it'd take more than a fuzzy-cheeked boy's hand to satisfy a woman like her. One of those comments that'd have him waking in the middle of the night, hard and aching from dreaming about her.

Sally Pantages. The barrel racing queen, while he

was a kid honing his skills as a saddle bronc competitor. The sexy, curvy woman with fiery hair to match her sassy temperament. Yeah, he'd had a crush on her and she'd been the reason for more cold showers than any other gal he'd ever met.

As she finished with each horse, she took it out of the barn. When she came back to move the next one, a bay mare, from its stall to the cross ties, she said, "Ben, you said you have a horse in that trailer?" Her slightly raised voice carried easily into the nearby stall where he was working.

"Yeah. These days, I compete in team roping as well as saddle bronc. I'm a heeler. Got myself a great horse, Chauncey's Pride."

"Where's your header?"

He frowned, again cursing himself for having fallen wrong and broken his stupid shoulder. "That'd be Dusty Whelan. Remember him?"

"I think so. Hair to match his name, right?"

"Yeah, that's him. A good guy. He and I haul together in that rig out there. But since I've got this busted shoulder, Dusty hitched a ride for him and his horse with another cowboy who had room." Ben put some extra force behind the rubber curry comb he was using to remove loose hair and dirt from a black mare's hindquarters. "The other guy's pretty new. Competes in tie-down roping. He wants to try team roping, but couldn't find a partner. Dusty said they could see how they did together."

"You'll be fit again soon, and back roping." Her tone was consoling.

"You bet I will," he said grimly. No way was he letting some new kid take his place.

Once, he'd been the new guy. Back then, Ben had hoped to prove himself, and make Sally stop seeing him as a kid. Before it could happen, Pete Ryland had swept her off her feet. The man hadn't even been a cowboy. He'd been in construction or some such thing.

Pete and Sally had been crazy in love. So much so that she'd given up barrel racing, and done it mid-season when she'd likely have gone on to win another Canadian championship. And to compete at the National Finals Rodeo in the U.S. and maybe become world champion.

Ben shook his head. He remembered wondering what it would be like, to love and be loved in such an all-consuming way. Couldn't imagine it himself, not if it meant giving up rodeo.

His boots silent on the straw-covered floor, he walked to the stall door, ready to move on to the next horse.

Sally, with the bay mare in cross ties, had paused in her work. Her head was down and her shoulders were slumped. A hand rested on the horse's shoulder, not stroking but more as if she was holding herself up. Ben saw her body move as she heaved a silent sigh. Then she straightened, rubbed her lower back, and returned to work.

Spunky Sally Pantages had fallen in love and given up rodeo, and look how things had ended up for her. Widowed and, from what he'd seen, operating this big, successful spread on her own. Whatever combination of hard work, grief, and loneliness she was experiencing, it had bowed her shoulders and put lines of strain around her eyes.

For the first time since Ben had met her all those years ago, she brought out his protective side.

Right now, the best thing he could do for her was help out, and so he did exactly that as they readied nine horses. She'd taken eight of them outside and had just finished bridling a gray gelding when Ben heard the sound of an approaching vehicle.

"That'll be the first of my students," Sally said.

"Want to go say hi and I'll bring this guy out?" He stroked the gray's neck.

"Thanks." She took a battered straw hat from a peg and left the barn.

He put on his own hat—a nicer one than he normally wore, since he'd kind of dressed up to come see her. After untying the gray, he led it across the barnyard to the hitching rails where the other horses waited. Sally stood by a white SUV, talking to a plump brunette and a little boy and girl. The dark-haired kids wore pint-sized Western gear, though with riding helmets rather than cowboy hats.

Ben tied the reins to a hitching rail with a little assistance from his left hand and patted the horse as he watched the students arrive.

Soon they were all there: five girls and three boys around the age of six. The moms clustered around Sally, but a few of the kids came to say hello to the horses. An older boy stared at Ben. "Hey, didn't I just see you at the rodeo in Williams Lake? Aren't you Ben Traynor?"

"You bet." He flashed a grin, happy to greet a fan.

The kid eyed the sling. "You fell off."

Ben grimaced. So much for impressing a fan. "Yeah. I got the bronc until the buzzer, but then he got me." Ben had hung on for the required eight seconds, then before he could jump free or the pickup riders could help him get off, Devil's Eyes had tossed him. Ben had landed badly, on his shoulder, and felt jarring pain, but he had risen quickly and waved to signal—with his right hand—that he was okay. As he had sauntered from the arena, he'd had a bad feeling that this wasn't a run-of-the-mill injury. The sports medicine team at the rodeo had sent him to the hospital. The rest was history.

"You were in the roping, too," the boy said as some of the other children wandered over.

"Yeah. Team roping." He and Dusty had come in second. Thank God that event had been scheduled before saddle bronc.

"You're the heeler, right?" the kid asked.

"I am." The other kids, the moms, and Sally had now gathered around.

The boy turned to the others. "His partner's the header. He ropes the steer's head or horns, then Mr. Traynor ropes the hind legs." His know-it-all tone reminded Ben of how he'd been as a boy, hooked on rodeo and ready to tell the world about it.

"That's right." And, thanks to Devil's Eyes, Dusty was trying out another heeler while Ben was twiddling his thumbs waiting for his damned shoulder to heal.

"Mom?" The boy tugged on his mother's hand. "I want to take rodeo lessons. Mr. Traynor can teach me."

Flattered, Ben tapped the kid's helmet. "Sorry, not me. I'm a doer, not a teacher." He sent a smile in Sally's direction. "Takes a special person to be a good teacher." Though he had yet to see her at work, he knew that anything Sally Pantages—Ryland—did, she'd do well.

She acknowledged the compliment with a smile. "Kids, it's time for our lesson. Ben, d'you want to take your horse out of that trailer and give him some water, food, and exercise?"

"Appreciate that." Chaunce was a good traveler but, like Ben, he'd rather stretch his legs than be confined to the rig.

He walked over to the trailer as the kids mounted up, some with Sally's assistance and some using a mounting block. A couple of parents drove away; the others seated themselves on wooden bleachers at one side of the ring.

Ben gazed around, checking out Sally's spread. As well as the barn, two riding rings, and a couple of fenced paddocks with grazing horses, she had an indoor arena. It was a smart setup, allowing her to be operational year-round and to accommodate boarders as well as riding students. The farmhouse, set apart a ways, was small and attractive, but could use a fresh coat of paint and maybe a new roof. Interestingly, the chicken coop and run looked to be in better shape.

All in all, it was a mighty impressive place that she and her husband had built. Ben shouldn't be surprised that the woman who owned it wouldn't be attracted to a man like him. Maybe the truth was that Sally would always be a few steps ahead of him—steps that took her out of his league. And that was a damned shame, at least as far as he was concerned. All the same, he looked forward to sitting down together with a couple beers and catching up.

In the ring, mounted on the gray gelding, Sally had the students walking their horses, working on proper posture. She sure had a different lifestyle now, from back in her rodeo days. It was a nice life, he guessed, if a person liked settling down in one spot and having a daily routine. Hard things for a guy like him to imagine doing.

Instructing the students, she looked more like the old Sally, not guarded and stressed but relaxed and happy. Easy in her body, free with her smiles.

She'd always been a natural with kids. He remembered her patience, her smiles when children would ask for her autograph and chatter about their riding experiences and dreams. He'd expected her to have two or three little ones of her own, but so far he'd seen no sign of any. Her sister hadn't been sure, saying Sally hadn't even notified the family about Pete's death; they'd found out when an acquaintance in B.C. mentioned it to them.

He shook his head, unable to fathom being so distanced from family. It sure didn't fit with the outgoing barrel racing queen he'd once known.

Ben entered the living quarters of his rig and downed a painkiller and a glass of cold water, then he went through to the back where his horse was stabled. "Hey, Chaunce. Bet you could use a drink too, and some fresh air and a stretch."

Working one-handed with his horse's cooperation, he got Chaunce's bridle on, but skipped the saddle. The horse, smart and even-tempered, exited the trailer easily and stood while Ben used the ramp as a mounting block and eased onto his back. He urged the gelding forward, down the access road. Chaunce had a smooth gait that didn't jar Ben's shoulder, and the painkiller was starting to work.

"We'll check out the countryside," he said to his horse as he turned him onto a trail. "Then when Sally's students are gone, I'll introduce you to her. Bet she'll let you hang out in her paddock, maybe even let me park the rig here tonight."

Chaunce bobbed his head.

"Wonder if she'll offer me dinner?" Ben mused. "Nah, better if I invite her out to eat." In the old days, she'd let him buy her an occasional beer, but had refused to go on a real date.

Not that tonight would be a date. She'd made it pretty clear she wasn't interested in him that way.

Chapter Two

If Ben wasn't supposed to drive, Sally would bet he wasn't supposed to ride either. Yet, as she'd seen from her perch atop Stormy, he'd just slid onto the back of an American Paint. The horse was mighty fine: white and bay patches in an unusual, attractive pattern, stocky and muscular, yet with a graceful neck and head, strength and spring in its stride.

Memories hit her. She squeezed her eyes shut against the pain. Seven years ago, she'd sold her own quarter horse, Autumn Mist. Pete had said they needed every penny they could scrape up to make the down payment on this place. Secretly, Sally had wondered if he was a little jealous of the affection she'd lavished on her horse.

Honest to God, selling Misty had been tougher than leaving the rodeo. The horse had been more than her barrel racing partner, she'd been Sally's best friend: sweet-tempered, smart, and always happy to listen to a girl's secrets.

Not that Sally'd had a lot of heavy secrets back in those days. Just shallow stuff like thinking Mandy Kilpatrick, her closest competitor, was a prize bitch. And feeling stupidly attracted to the cocky young cowboy, Ben Traynor, at least until Pete Ryland came along and blinded her to all other men.

Sally refocused on her students. She loved working with children. It was the closest she'd ever get to having kids of her own. No matter how challenging her students were, their energy, innocence, and perspective on life always made her smile.

Yet a part of her mind drifted back to Ben. He would be almost thirty now, the man who sat his horse so easily despite having his left arm in a sling. A little cocky still, but not so much as before. Willing to take orders from a woman and to work hard despite what must be some pretty serious pain.

He was more than eye candy: he was mature, thoughtful, conscientious. And still wonderful with horses. He was . . . appealing. She had felt a small, undeniable tug. It was partly physical, which shocked her. She'd thought the part of her that could feel desire had, quite literally, been beaten out of her long ago. That tug was partly emotional too, and that scared her. That was how a guy got to you: your emotions were the most vulnerable part of you, the part he could best use to control you.

She shuddered. Yes, there were good reasons that she'd sworn off men for life.

As soon as she could free up some time, she'd ask Ben about Penny, then send him on his way. For now, she needed to concentrate fully on her students.

The lesson went well, and after the kids had dismounted and were chattering together, she took one of the moms aside. Tiffany Knight was the mother of Marty, the boy who'd spoken to Ben. "Your son is doing really well," Sally said.

"Don't tell me you think he's ready for rodeo lessons.

Have to admit, I wouldn't mind watching that cowboy teach my boy, but I do think Marty's still awfully young."

"Ben Traynor isn't teaching." She'd heard Ben's comment about being a doer, not a teacher; she'd seen his impatience to get back to the circuit. He was a competitor through and through. "I do think Marty's ready to move up to the next class: the eight- to ten-year-olds." The boy would be eight at the end of the summer. "He's turning into a fine rider and he's confident. He has the right instincts." She pressed her lips together, remembering being a child a lot like Marty. "If he really is interested in rodeo, he needs to be ten to join Little Britches."

"I know." Tiffany gave a rueful chuckle. "I'm safe for two more years."

"You don't want him getting involved in rodeo?" Sally's parents had supported her interest in barrel racing—despite the dangers, the generally low income, and the crazy lifestyle of driving from rodeo to rodeo for most of the year. Her mom and dad had both been in Little Britches as teens, though neither was good enough, or committed enough, to pursue rodeo professionally.

"Well . . . It's too early to say. We don't want him getting hurt, yet it's something he loves. Of course, kids' interests can change." With a smile, Tiffany went to collect her son.

Sally's interests hadn't changed, not from when she was tiny. She'd loved horses, the almost psychic bond that could exist with them, the challenge of learning, the thrill of competing, the excitement of winning, the companionship of other cowgirls and cowboys. Once she was a pro, she'd even enjoyed the days of driving from one rodeo to the next, seeing mile after mile of countryside unwind. It had been a fine way of life. Until

Pete had come along, and a new life began. One that brought wonderful things like living in this lovely place and teaching kids to ride—but that also slowly tore down her self-confidence and brought confusion, dependence, pain. But now Pete was gone and she had Ryland Riding to herself. She'd found another way of life that suited her completely.

Regretting the loss of her assistant, Corrie, Sally loosened cinches on the horses' saddles so they'd be more comfortable. Right now, she didn't have time to remove their tack, give them a brush, and put them out in the paddock. She needed to prepare Star of Egypt, one of the boarded horses, because her owner was coming out for a ride. Madeleine, an assistant bank manager, preferred to spend her "horse time" riding, not doing grooming and tack. Sally couldn't relate to that herself, but she was happy to do whatever the owners wanted, and she charged for the service.

When Star, a gorgeous palomino with Arabian blood, was glossy and tacked up, Sally led the horse out of the barn. Madeleine had arrived, and Ben was back from his ride. He had dismounted and stood stroking his horse's shoulder as he talked to the sleek blonde.

Madeleine wore figure-hugging jeans, tooled boots, and a long-sleeved blue tee that clung to her full breasts. She laughed at something Ben said, took off her Stetson, and tossed her head so a waterfall of golden hair rippled in the sunlight. Once upon a time, Sally had used that same hair toss.

"Hi, Madeleine," she called as she led the showy palomino toward the equally showy owner. "Want me to tie Star up, or are you ready to go?"

Madeleine glanced her way, then back at Ben. Obviously, it was a tough decision.

"You go on and enjoy your ride," Ben said.

"Want to come along and I'll show you some of our sights?" The invitation in her voice suggested she had more to show Ben than scenery.

"Thanks, but I've already had my ride. Besides, I want to talk to Sally."

Madeleine cast an appraising glance at Sally, cocked a rather pitying eyebrow, and then turned back to Ben with a smug smile. "Sure. We'll do it some other time, if you decide to stay in Caribou Crossing." Clearly, she didn't consider Sally to be competition.

Not, of course, that Sally wanted to *be* competition. She just hated having another woman look at her in that dismissive way.

Forcing a smile, Sally cupped her hands and gave Madeleine a leg up, then brushed her hands on her already grubby jeans. "Have a good ride."

When Madeleine and Star had gone, Sally turned to Ben. "I'd really like to hear about Penny, but I have a couple of private lessons. It'll be more than two hours before I can take a break." Even then, she'd have horses to deal with, but at least she could talk to him while she worked. If he was willing to wait until then. "Are you in a hurry to get on the road?" She felt a pang of guilt. He was injured, in pain, and shouldn't even be driving, and here she was, delaying his journey home.

"I'll hang around." He tapped his good hand against his sling. "It's not like I have anywhere to be."

A rodeo cowboy, grounded. Yeah, that would hurt in more ways than one. Sympathy and a sense of . . . not exactly comfort, but familiarity, overruled her normal wariness. "Okay. Thanks, Ben. I appreciate it." She stepped forward to greet his horse, who nuzzled her work-callused hand. "Hey there," she murmured as she stroked the smooth, warm neck. "Chauncey's Pride, right? Aren't you the handsome boy?"

She slanted a glance at Ben, as handsome as his horse and definitely not a boy any longer. "Do you want to let him out in the smaller paddock? The horses there are friendly."

"Sounds good. Thanks." He led his horse away, giving Sally the opportunity to enjoy a classic cowboy back: broad shoulders tapering to a narrow waist belted in leather; lean hips, a firm butt, and long, strong legs clad in denim.

Again, she felt an unfamiliar, disconcerting pulse of awareness. Awareness of him as a man. Of herself as a woman.

She tore her gaze away. She needed to prepare for thirteen-year-old Jude's barrel racing lesson.

Sally brought in the next two horses. The buckskin mare, Melody, which she'd ride herself, was her best horse. Puffin, a sturdy black-and-white gelding, was the horse Jude was learning on. The girl was keen on barrel racing and hoped to persuade her parents to buy her a horse of her own.

While Sally saddled Puffin, Ben came up to her. "The horses from the lesson," he said. "You done with them? I can bring them in."

"You don't have to do that."

He gave a rueful smile. "Got nothing better to do except feel sorry for myself."

"In that case, thanks. The horses will appreciate it, too. But don't strain your shoulder."

Things sure did run more smoothly when she had an assistant. What a pity Ben wasn't a single, strong, horse-loving female looking for a live-in job that paid minimum wage.

Of course it was impossible to imagine Ben being anything other than totally male.

* * *

Moving awkwardly and painfully, Ben got to work bringing the horses in, removing tack, and giving them a light grooming. He enjoyed being with the animals even though his shoulder ached something fierce.

He was finishing up when a middle-aged couple in casual Western clothing entered the barn. "Can I help you?" he asked them.

The pair gazed at him curiously. The man said, "We board our horses here and we're going out for a ride."

"Need help with anything?"

"No, we're good," he said.

"You're Sally's new assistant?" the woman asked.

Ah, that explained Sally's air of tiredness and strain. She'd had an employee who'd quit on her. Ben shook his head. "Just an old friend, passing through."

The couple gathered halters and left the barn. Ben gave the horses a little water. Unsure whether Sally wanted them turned out to pasture, he left them in stalls and went out to watch her lesson.

A smile lifted the corners of his mouth at the sight that met his eyes.

She'd set up three barrels in the cloverleaf pattern of a barrel racing course and she was urging a compact buckskin around the first barrel and on to the second. She looked intensely focused, yet vibrant and joyful—and years younger, like the old Sally. The horse wasn't a patch on that striking silvery quarter horse she used to own, but Sally herself looked mighty fine.

When she finished, the sound of clapping drew Ben's attention to the petite, ponytailed girl atop a black-and-white horse just outside the gate to the ring, and to the woman in the bleachers.

"You still got it, Pantages," Ben called.

Sally swung the horse around, her gaze finding him where he stood near the barn. She shook her head, took off her hat, and ran a hand through tousled red-gold curls. "It's been a long time since I was in shape to compete." She glanced away from him to the girl. "But Jude here is a rising star. Come on into the ring, Jude, and you and Puffin give it a run."

For the next ten minutes, Ben sat with the mom and enjoyed watching Sally work with her student, who did indeed show promise. Following the doc's instructions, he let his left arm hang free in the sling rather than supporting it with his other arm, which could push the broken bones into the wrong position. And he kept the fingers and wrist on his left side moving, to help prevent stiffness and swelling.

By the time the lesson ended, two more riders, a middle-aged woman and a teenaged girl, had arrived in separate vehicles. Ben caught Sally for a moment, asking, "Anything I can do to help?"

Sitting atop the buckskin, she gazed down at him. "Thanks for the offer, but I'm good. I'm using the same horses for my lesson with Margaret, and it's the last one of the day. The other rider, Chrissie, boards her horse here and she's going to work her in the small ring. She'll look after her own needs." She rolled her shoulders, loosening them. "Once I'm finished, you can tell me about Penny, okay?"

"How about I take you for dinner in town? It'll give us a chance to catch up."

Her eyebrows pulled together. "I don't go into town."

"Huh? Why not?"

A quick, dismissive flick of her head. "Takes too long. I'm too busy."

Wasn't the town of Caribou Crossing only fifteen or

twenty minutes away? Before he could ask, she had ridden away to join her new student, who was getting mounted.

As the lesson started in the ring, Ben watched for a few minutes. The teenaged student wasn't a barrel racer, just working to improve her riding skills. Sally had her trot and lope the horse in a variety of patterns around the barrels. She lacked natural talent, but had a great attitude.

His stomach growled, reminding him that lunch had been too long ago. He went to the trailer to get a handful of cherries from the fridge. Sally hadn't accepted his invitation. Nor had she invited him to stay for dinner, but it was getting late and they both needed to eat. Easy fix: he'd drive into town and pick something up. Takeout, some beer, and a bunch of flowers.

Easy, friendly stuff. Hopefully, she wouldn't be offended.

He unhitched the trailer, then climbed into the old Dodge Ram. The truck was a dually, the double set of rear tires giving it the extra strength he and Dusty needed to haul the rig. He cranked the windows down to enjoy the fresh air, and drove off, avoiding using his left hand unless absolutely necessary. On the way from Williams Lake, he'd found the local country and western station, CXNG, on the radio. Now he hummed along to some vintage Merle Haggard: "Workin' Man Blues."

Damn pretty land around here, but then horse country always was scenic, he reflected. The kind of scenic that not only pleased his eyes, but sank deep into his soul. On either side of the two-lane road, ranch land rolled away in gentle curves. On the right, low, craggy hills formed a backdrop. Traffic was light on this Tuesday afternoon, no one in a hurry. He slowed to pass a couple of riders on the gravel shoulder. When they waved, he took his right hand off the wheel for a moment to return the salutation.

He saw the turnoff to the main highway, leading back the way he'd driven earlier. He passed by, staying on the country road, and soon was greeted by a WELCOME TO CARIBOU CROSSING sign with a stylized caribou illustration. A couple of minutes later, he was in the outskirts of town.

Cruising down the main street, he noted some nicely restored heritage buildings, fresh paint on most storefronts, and flowers in planter boxes. A cute little town and yeah, it wasn't much more than fifteen minutes' drive from Sally's place. How odd that she never came here.

Seeing a parking spot across from the town square, he grabbed it.

He strolled a couple blocks. A restored old hotel called the Wild Rose Inn had a fine-looking dining room and Western-style bar; a coffee shop called Big & Small offered sandwiches, wraps, and salads; a Japanese restaurant called Arigata looked interesting. He wasn't a sushi guy, but he liked teriyaki, tempura prawns, and a few other Japanese dishes.

He settled on the Gold Pan, a diner that was two-thirds full. It had Formica tables and red leatherette booths, a long counter and red-topped stools, even a jukebox. John Denver's "Take Me Home, Country Roads" wove beneath the sound of customers chatting. On the walls hung black-and-white photos of gold miners, some looking haggard as all get-out, others beaming and holding up sizable nuggets.

Feeling right at home, Ben took a seat at the counter. The middle-aged, auburn-haired waitress gave him a plasticized menu and a big smile, which he returned.

The air smelled of frying chicken and grilling beef, and everything on the menu sounded delicious.

Thinking about what would work best for takeout, he ordered meat loaf, mashed potatoes, and coleslaw for two. Normally, as part of his fitness regimen, he took it easy on the carbs, but women liked dessert—that was his excuse and he was sticking to it—so he also asked for a couple of slices of strawberry-rhubarb pie. "That's to go," he told the woman. Terry, her name tag said.

She clipped the order slip to one of those old-fashioned carousels that hung between the diner and the kitchen, then turned back to him. "How are you liking our fair town so far?"

He figured the population was small enough, she'd know he wasn't a local. "Looks nice, but I haven't seen much of it. I've been out at Ryland Riding, visiting Sally. She's an old friend."

Her dark eyebrows arched. "You're a friend of Sally Ryland's?" Her tone held disbelief.

He eyed her quizzically. "Yeah. From way back. Before she got married."

"Huh. Didn't know she had friends except for Dave and—" She broke off, flushing. "That sounded terrible. Sorry. It's just, well . . . she keeps to herself, you know?"

No friends? The Sally he'd known had been so outgoing. But then, Pete's death had probably messed her up, not to mention left her swamped with work. "Since her husband died?"

Terry shook her head. "I've never once met Sally, and she's been here seven, eight years. I don't know if she's set foot in town more than a few times, and her husband wasn't here much more often. They built Ryland Riding and it was, like, their own little world. Just the two of them."

"You mean, except for students and people boarding horses, right?"

"Sure. But Sally and Pete didn't socialize." She took a lattice-topped fruit pie from the display case. "Seems they didn't need anyone except each other. That's true love for you. I guess. I mean, it's not how me and my hubby, Jeff, back there in the kitchen, like things." Slicing pie, she chuckled. "Well, obviously, eh, or we wouldn't own a diner. We like being in the center of what's going on in town." She put two generous slices of pie into a take-out container.

"I remember when Sally and Pete first met. It was like, *bam*, neither of them had eyes for anyone else."

"Well, I guess it stayed that way. I heard that the rare times he did come into town he'd buy flowers for Sally." An order was up, and she went to deliver it.

Maybe Ben had better not take flowers tonight. He didn't want Sally thinking he was trying to compete, or compare, with Pete.

Idly, he glanced at the write-up on the back of the menu. It said that the Gold Pan had been open for ten years, and its name was in honor of the town's history. Caribou Crossing had its origins in the 1860s gold rush. When the gold ran out, it became a ranching community.

Terry returned. "Just a couple more minutes."

"No rush."

"It was such a tragedy," she said, returning to their earlier conversation, "Pete dying that way. So young, and totally unexpected. Goes to show you never can tell, right?"

"That's the truth." He'd been riding bucking broncs for more than fifteen years and the worst he'd done was break some bones.

"It's so sad, Sally out there all alone with a broken heart. For a while, folks thought she was dating Dave

Cousins, though he denied it. But it seems he was telling the truth and they only ever were friends. Guess she's got no room in her heart for another man."

Maybe that was the reason she hadn't been receptive to his flirting. Still, a woman had to move on at some point. His grandma had learned that, after his grandpa died.

Terry turned to get Ben's order. She slipped take-out containers into a couple of string-handled paper bags with the diner's name and logo. Eyeing his sling, she asked, "You gonna be okay with these, hon?"

"Sure. Thanks, Terry." He paid, leaving a good-sized tip.

"Hope to see you again."

"Thanks, but I'm just passing through."

Unless Sally gave him a reason to stay. Which, he had to admit, didn't seem likely. Still, he'd always been an optimist. Couldn't survive long in the rodeo world if you weren't.

Chapter Three

After turning Melody and Puffin out into the large paddock, Sally walked to the small foaling paddock at the back of the barn. The grassy pasture, with a half dozen cottonwoods for shade, was away from the other horses and the hustle and bustle of students and horse owners. The sole occupant, a heavily pregnant palomino, nickered and came over to the fence, head extended and ears cocked forward.

"Hey there, girl. Yes, I have your treat." Sally pulled a carrot from her pocket and fed Sunshine Song. "You're lonely, aren't you? It won't be much longer." Song's behavior was calm and normal, and there was no waxing on her teats, but the mare was due any day.

Sally went into the office in the barn to check e-mail. The farrier confirmed an appointment in two days to shoe Campion, now that the horse's abscess had healed. That'd mean another bill, on top of the vet's for treating the abscess.

There were no new requests for lessons or horse boarding, and no applications for the assistant's position. Maybe she should pull the ad, but it was possible that the perfect person might see it and that somehow

Sally'd be able to swing a meager paycheck. So far, she'd received two applications, but both were from men. Trusting a man wasn't high on her agenda.

She stretched, thinking fondly of Dave Cousins, the one man who had won her trust. A couple of years back, one of her boarders, Karen Estevez, had mentioned to her friend Dave that Sally was struggling, running Ryland Riding on her own. He'd offered to help out. Sally's need for independence said no, as did her mistrust of men. Karen, a Royal Canadian Mounted Police officer, had sworn that Dave was a genuine good guy with no ulterior motive.

Over time, Dave had proved Karen right. He'd been a godsend, and had slowly become a friend. When he started dating Cassidy Esperanza last summer, Cassidy had turned into a friend and helper, too. The pair kept coming around even after they convinced Sally to hire an assistant. She still found it hard to believe that, after years of social isolation, she actually had friends.

But now Dave and Cassidy were on their honeymoon, Corrie had quit due to a personal matter, and Sally was on her own again. Ben's assistance this afternoon had been so welcome. She was tired now, but not totally exhausted.

And hours of waiting had sure made her anxious to hear news of her sister, and perhaps her parents. Ben had driven off a while back, though, and hadn't returned. Likely he'd gone into town for a bite to eat.

Her kitchen didn't hold much more than eggs and tinned soup and stew, though she was now getting fresh vegetables in the garden Corrie had planted in the spring. The old Sally would have invited Ben for dinner and found a way of preparing a decent meal. But she hadn't been that woman in a long time.

She began to muck out stalls. Shortly after that, she

heard a vehicle pull in and stop. A minute later, Ben's voice called, "Sally?"

"In the barn," she shouted back. She stepped out of the stall, pitchfork in hand.

He came through the door to the barn. "Hi. Still working?"

"Hi." She'd seen him off and on all afternoon, and each time it was almost like a flashback to happier days. Normally, she paid little attention to a man's looks, yet there was something about Ben that had her noticing. Now she found herself staring again. The man was born to wear Western clothing. Without that sling, he could've modeled for ads. A five o'clock shadow made his strong jaw even more masculine. Some folks might say his hair was too long, but she'd never thought a cowboy hat looked right on a man with short hair.

Forcing her gaze away from him, she gestured with her pitchfork. "I need to muck out stalls and clean tack. Why don't you tell me about Penny while I work?"

"Take a dinner break, then I'll help you."

She deliberated. After Pete died, she had realized how dependent she'd been on him—or how dependent he'd made her—and sworn she'd never rely on anyone again. It was hard accepting assistance, yet Ben had a way about him. Maybe it was a holdover from the rodeo days, when most competitors had helped each other. "I might accept some help, but I don't need a break." She was hungry, but she was also used to working late and not having a chance to grab a bite to eat until after eight. "You got dinner in town?"

"Brought back takeout for both of us. You haven't eaten already, have you?"

He'd picked up dinner to share? That was thoughtful. Or presumptuous. How was a woman supposed to read a man's motivation for doing anything? She could lie and say she'd already eaten. That was safer than letting him into her house and sitting down at the kitchen table with him. Her kitchen had been the scene of a lot of . . . unpleasantness.

A roast of beef that wasn't rare enough for Pete, hurled across the room to drip blood down the wall . . . Her hand, pressed onto the hot stove when she'd forgotten to put on her flashy engagement ring before he got home . . . His fist—

"Meat loaf."

She jumped, and returned to the present. To Ben. "Wh-what?" she stammered.

His eyebrows pulled together. "I brought meat loaf, with mashed potatoes and coleslaw." He added in a wheedling, almost seductive tone, "And the prettiest strawberry-rhubarb pie you ever did see."

Now he had her full attention. That was more food—delicious-sounding food—than she'd eaten in . . . she couldn't remember when. "Meat loaf?" Comfort food that always reminded her of her mom, who'd made the best meat loaf in the world. Yes, she not only wanted news of her estranged family, but she did want a real meal. Maybe she even wanted Ben Traynor's company, and the simple pleasure of looking at a handsome cowboy. They could eat on the deck; she didn't have to invite him in. It'd only be an hour, tops.

She rested the pitchfork against the wall and walked toward him. "You persuaded me."

He stepped back, letting her precede him out the door. There, she saw a couple of paper bags resting on the ground. She slipped her fingers through the string handle of one, and left him to take the other as she led the way toward the house.

It was built on a bit of a hill, the front on the high side. Sally never used the front door. At the back of the house, steps led up to a deck and the mudroom.

The deck had a barbecue, a cheap patio table, and four chairs—four, because occasionally Dave, Cassidy, and Dave's daughter Robin shared a bite to eat with her. The view across rolling grassland to distant hills couldn't be beat, in her opinion. When the weather permitted, she ate her quick meals here, surrounded by the wide open serenity of nature, rather than in the closed-in kitchen with its bad memories.

Leading the way up the stairs, she said, "Let's eat on the deck. Why don't you unwrap the food and I'll get plates and cutlery." Hopefully, he wouldn't think twice about her not inviting him inside.

She went into the mudroom, closing the screen door against mosquitoes and flies. Her hat went on a peg. She sat to pull off her boots and socks, stepped into battered flip-flops, and continued on to the kitchen. The young Sally would have rushed into the bathroom to brush her hair, slick on lip gloss, add a touch of mascara, and rub lotion into her skin. This one washed her hands at the kitchen sink and splashed water on her dusty face.

When she stepped out onto the deck again, Ben had removed the takeout containers from the bags, but he had disappeared. Setting the table, she decided to give him her usual seat with the best view. Not wanting to block that view—or have him look too closely at her—she didn't set her own place directly across from him, but across and to the side. Back into the kitchen she went, to run tap water into glasses and add ice.

When she took the water to the deck, Ben had returned, hatless now, to plunk a six-pack of beer on the table. He removed two bottles and said, "Want me to put the rest in the fridge?"

She grabbed the handle of the cardboard carton, which had a stylized caribou on it and the label CARIBOU

CROSSING PALE ALE. "I will." Reaching for one of the two other bottles, she said, "This one, too. I don't drink."

"Seriously?"

His disbelieving tone almost made her smile. Beer had been an intrinsic part of the scene she'd once enjoyed: Western bars, shooting pool, country songs, two-stepping with a cute cowboy. "Seriously."

"How come?"

"Alcohol makes people do foolish things," she said stiffly.

One corner of his mouth turned up. "What foolish things did it make you do, Sally?"

Laugh too loud, flaunt her body, flirt with men. At least according to Pete. The last time she'd had a drink was the champagne at her wedding reception. Later that night, her new husband had said she'd made a fool of herself and of him, and she was asking for trouble, coming on to men like that. She hadn't had a clue; she'd only been having fun, so excited about starting her life with the man she loved passionately. Pete had said that, for the sake of their marriage, they would ban alcohol from their house.

"Sally?" Ben, head cocked, was watching her.

The brown bottle's shape felt so familiar, as did the coolness, the damp condensation. Her taste buds sprang to life and saliva pooled as she remembered the taste of beer.

"Are you an alcoholic?" Ben gently asked.

"What? No! No, I just don't drink." Because Pete had said so.

Had her husband been right about the way she acted when she drank? Even when she hadn't had a drink in years, he had still got on her case for coming on to guys although she'd had no intention of doing it. Dads of students, male owners of boarding horses, the large animal vet whom Pete had fired when he caught the man and Sally hunkered down in the straw examining a horse's cracked hoof. Even three years after Pete's death, she still couldn't figure out whether she'd been a seriously flawed wife and he'd been the doting husband everyone took him for, or whether he'd turned into an abuser once they were married, and she'd been too weak, too stupid to leave him. Neither was good; both reflected badly on her.

"I promise you," Ben said, "a beer or two won't make *me* do anything foolish." There was a teasing gleam in his chestnut eyes, eyes the same color as the bottle in her hand. "And one's not going to hurt you. Or half a one. A couple swallows. Come on," he said in an exaggerated wheedling tone, "you know you wanna."

She'd have been annoyed—if his tone wasn't so funny, and if he hadn't been right. Slowly, she put the bottle down on the table beside her place mat. A swallow or two wasn't going to make her lose her mind. It wouldn't make her flirt with Ben. As for him, she remembered him as a guy who didn't drink to excess, or get out of control when he drank.

By the time she'd stored the beer carton in the fridge, Ben had opened both bottles and taken the lids off the takeout containers. "I'm starving," he said. "Driving back smelling the meat loaf made me crazy." He handed her a serving spoon and took one himself.

She put a napkin on her lap and then dished out coleslaw as Ben served himself some meat loaf. "It's nice of you to do this," she told him. Pete had never bought takeout. He'd had groceries delivered once a week and had expected her to cook. That was a wife's job, he'd said. He had, however, typically brought home a bouquet on the rare occasions when he went into town. To show her how much he loved his pretty wife, he'd said. Carnations, usually, but red roses after he'd hit her. Red roses to accompany an apology, even though the tearful expression of regret was framed as "but you shouldn't have made me do it."

She shivered, then shoved those thoughts away. She refused to let memories of Pete ruin this dinner with an old friend. Deliberately, she picked up her beer bottle and took a sip.

"You're smiling," Ben said. "You like it."

"I do," she admitted, taking a larger sip. Hoppy, slightly bitter, it hit her tongue like . . . like an old friend, she thought, this time keeping her smile to herself. Relaxed and hungry, she served herself some mashed potatoes and meat loaf, and dug in.

Oh my, this was good. She'd almost forgotten what it was like to taste food that had taken more than five minutes to prepare—much less to have someone else do the preparing. Her idea of luxury was having Dave toss burgers on the barbecue when he, Cassidy, and Robin came to help out and stayed to eat. "This is delicious. Thank you so much for bringing it."

"My pleasure."

They both ate enthusiastically, in silence, for a few minutes, though Ben made occasional *mmm-mmm* noises. Simple sounds of appreciation, but they struck her as sensual, and somehow increased her own enjoyment of the food. When she and Ben had taken the edge off their appetites, she said, "Please tell me about Penny. And did she say anything about our parents?"

He put his fork down and took a long pull from his beer bottle. "You're curious about your family, yet Penny says you've been out of touch with them for years."

Sally lowered her gaze. "Mom and Dad didn't like me marrying Pete and moving away."

"That's no excuse for cutting their daughter out of their lives," he said firmly.

Her parents had let her know they disapproved. They'd given advice or, as Pete put it, poked and pried into her and Pete's business. Sally'd felt caught in the middle, although she did agree with Pete that her first loyalty lay with him. In the end, her family had solved her dilemma; they'd simply stopped communicating.

"These things happen," she said neutrally. "And yes, I'm curious. What did Penny say?"

"To start with, she's married and expecting. Far enough along that it's like she has a watermelon under her shirt."

A pang hit Sally's heart. Her little sister, going to have a baby. She was envious, but mostly regretful that she wouldn't be there by Penny's side admiring the sonogram images, teasing her about her food cravings and constant need to pee, throwing her a baby shower. "I'm going to be an aunt," she marveled. One who might never see her niece or nephew.

Brushing that pain aside, she asked, "Who did she marry? Anyone I'd know?"

"You knew she was teaching elementary school?"

"She planned to get her teaching degree." She'd always believed that her sister, who loved kids as much as Sally did, would make a great teacher.

"One of her students had a single-parent mom whose brother helped out a lot. Penny and the brother fell for each other. He's a lawyer."

"Really? Bet our dad wasn't thrilled about that. He never had much time for lawyers."

"I dunno. Penny said your mom and dad are looking forward to being grandparents."

"What else did she say about them?" she asked, greedy for information.

"We only had a minute to chat. She said everyone was well, and that they missed you."

She bit her lip. Was that true? The only time she'd heard from them in years was months after Pete died, when she got a sympathy card. She hadn't notified them of his death, not seeing the point, but obviously word had reached them. The card had a printed message reading, "Our thoughts and prayers are with you." Below it, her mother had written: "They really are, Sally. Love, Mom, Dad, and Penny."

She'd felt a tug at her heart, and a crazy wish to be enfolded in the arms of her family, to have her sister sympathize and her parents make everything better. But she'd known it couldn't happen. They were being polite. They didn't want to see her, much less deal with her problems. Besides, how could she face them when she was such a mess of shame and guilt? She hadn't responded to the card, and they hadn't contacted her again.

"Sally?"

"Hmm?" She realized she'd been peeling away the label on her beer bottle. "What did Penny say when she asked you to look me up?"

"Something about maybe enough time has gone by." He studied her. "Time for what? She didn't say."

"I don't know," she said quietly. Enough time for her parents to forgive her for marrying Pete and moving away? Or enough time for her to admit that she'd made a mistake and they'd been right all along? Could she do that without spilling the whole nasty story and making herself look like a total loser? "When you see her again, maybe you could ask."

"If I do see her, what'll I tell her about you?"

Considering, she took another sip of beer. "That I'm well. That I love working with horses and teaching children. That the business is doing fine." Would Penny tell their parents?

He frowned slightly but said only, "Okay," then began to eat again.

She did the same. The meat loaf wasn't quite as good as her mom's, or maybe that was her memory playing tricks on her.

"Do you handle this place all on your own?" Ben asked. "One of the owners who came to ride this afternoon asked me if I was your new assistant."

"Sorry about that." To mistake a rodeo cowboy for a barn assistant was an insult.

"It's okay. I just wondered if you'd had an assistant, and he'd quit."

She gazed at his striking brown-skinned face, noted the way the fading sun gleamed off the hints of chestnut in his hair, and saw concern in those beautiful brown eyes. "I did have one. She had to leave because of a personal issue."

"So you're hiring?"

Embarrassment and the habit of privacy kept her from sharing her financial woes. "I haven't found anyone suitable yet. It has to be the right person, because they need to live here."

"Here? You mean they share the house?"

She shook her head. It was tough to let anyone, even Corrie or Dave's family, cross the doorstep of her house. No way could she have someone else living in it. "There's a little apartment in the loft of the barn. My assistant gets a free room and utilities." Because Sally couldn't afford to pay more than minimum wage, she needed someone who was willing to accept a free room as part of the compensation package. Now, though, unless she got some new business soon, she couldn't even manage minimum wage.

"Sounds like a decent arrangement. For the right person."

"Corrie liked it. And she was perfect. She loved horses and riding. She's a hard worker, quick to learn, strong, and never complains. Her previous job was at a plant nursery, and this spring she put in the vegetable garden." Which, sadly, Sally wouldn't have the time to keep up.

"She does sound ideal."

"Hard to replace." Perhaps best of all, Corrie had been private and self-sufficient, like Sally. So much so that Sally didn't even know the nature of the personal matter that had called the younger woman away. It wasn't that Sally didn't care, but you couldn't start a personal conversation without being expected to reciprocate. And talking about herself was something she didn't—couldn't—do.

"You been dating?" Ben asked. "Have some guy to help you out sometimes?"

"Dating? No, not at all." Nor would she. Ever. "I do have a couple of friends who come by from time to time, but they're away right now."

"Makes it tough."

"I manage."

"Feel like managing some pie?"

"Most definitely." In her weekly orders from the grocery store, Sally bought whichever fruit was cheapest. Apples, bananas, oranges, typically. One or two a day, that was her dessert allotment. "Want some coffee with it?" He'd only drunk the one beer, and she hoped he didn't move on to a second. As for her, she'd had a third of her bottle and, though she'd have loved to drain it, she would pour the rest down the sink.

"Coffee sounds great."

When she rose and took their plates and forks, he

stacked the now-empty takeout containers and got up, too. "I'll give you a hand."

"No!" Realizing how abrupt that had sounded, she added, "Sit and enjoy the view."

A high-pitched whine and a sting on his right forearm had Ben slapping at a mosquito, an unthinking response that sent pain radiating to his broken shoulder. Wincing, he sank back into his chair and watched Sally pile the stacked containers on top of the dirty plates. As she'd instructed, he turned his gaze toward the view where a doe and an adolescent fawn grazed, illuminated by rosy light as the sun dropped toward the hills.

Was he imagining things, or did Sally not want him going into her house? Maybe she'd been too busy to do housework and was embarrassed. Women got like that.

Or maybe she just wanted a few moments' privacy. Talking about her family had clearly upset her. Ben sure wished he knew what was going on there. Sally'd always been such a friendly, outgoing person and he'd assumed she came from a loving, supportive family.

She returned with several metal cans, which she stacked around the railing of the deck. Then she took a match to each, and he realized they were candles. Well, how about that. Had she decided on a little romance?

A pungent, lemony scent hit his nostrils. "Citronella candles? Mosquito repellant?"

"I make them myself," she confirmed.

So much for romance.

When she went inside again, he stretched as far back as he could, trying to ease the ache in his injured shoulder. It probably wouldn't have hurt so much if he could support his arm, but he didn't want the broken bones shifting into the wrong position. Following the doctor's instructions, he flexed his fingers and wrist. Two or three weeks to heal enough that he could at least get back to roping, if not bronc riding. The doc had said more, but he wasn't a sports medicine doctor and Ben would prove him wrong.

When he'd learned he had to be out of action for a while, Ben had planned to drive back to Alberta. Now, gazing out at scrubby grassland rolling in a sweet curve like a woman's hip, the sun sinking toward the hills in soothing shades of purple and pink, another idea took root. It'd sure be no hardship staying here awhile, making himself useful.

Sally came outside again, this time placing plates, small forks, and two mugs of coffee on the table. "How do you take your coffee?"

"Black."

"So do I." She sat down, then dished out the two slices of pie. "Sorry, I don't have ice cream. But this looks wonderful just as it is. Thanks again, Ben."

When she gazed at him, he realized that it was one of the few times she'd looked him directly in the eyes and held the gaze when he looked back at her. Did he make her nervous for some reason?

Her eyes sure were pretty, despite the signs of tiredness and strain around them. They'd always been special, the greens and grays changing with her mood. He'd seen them with green sparkles like sunlight on gemstones, but tonight they were a sultry gray tinged with moss green. Deep and unreadable. Drawing him in. Making him want to understand what was going on behind them. Yeah, he could see hanging around here for a while.

She glanced away, picked up her fork, and ate a bite of pie. An expression of pleasure brightened her face.

That was how Sally should look. Relaxed, happy, in the moment.

"How did you end up doing team roping?" she asked. "You used to only compete in saddle bronc."

"I grew up on a ranch and I've always roped, but not competitively. Then this trainer I work for had such a great roping horse—Chauncey's Pride—I couldn't resist buying him. Dusty and I'd always got along; his heeler had quit; we tried it out together and it stuck." He dug into his own pie.

"And now you have to travel by road, hauling a trailer with a horse."

"Yeah. Takes longer to get to events, and gas can cost near as much as flying. Dusty and his old heeler had the Ram dually and the rig, so I bought a half share. Saves on motels. And on meals. We don't eat out as much, and it's easier to stick to a decent diet." He chuckled. "And I don't run the risk of a baggage handler deciding he doesn't like dealing with saddles and leaving mine on the tarmac." It was a liability of riding saddle bronc rather than bareback bronc, needing to tote your saddle along with you. Still, he'd found out early in his rodeo days that he competed more successfully in saddle bronc, so he'd stuck with it.

She nodded. "Really sucks when they do that. Yeah, there are lots of advantages to driving yourself."

He nodded, sipped coffee, and said, "I like to drive. Like to see the country. So does Dusty. We get along pretty well."

"I enjoyed seeing the country, too. Splitting the driving would have been nice. I always traveled on my own, with Autumn Mist."

"I remember. You had the same kind of trailer as I'm hauling, one you could live in." He finished off his pie, thinking that he could happily eat a dinner like this every day. Eating it across from Sally made it especially good.

"A smaller version, yes. My home away from home." She gave a soft laugh. "Actually, that was our real home. Misty and I were in that trailer more than we were at my parents' ranch." At the mention of her parents, her mouth tightened.

He was about to ask her what had happened to that great horse of hers, but she spoke first. "How're you doing this season? D'you figure you'll make it to the CFR?"

"Damn right. I've been doing well on earnings, and even if the injury costs me and I don't qualify based on money, there's a good chance of finishing first or second in one of the last ten rodeos." The Canadian Finals Rodeo qualifiers were the ten top money winners in each event for the past season, as well as those who finished first or second in the final ten rodeos. "Both for me in saddle bronc and for Dusty and me in team roping." Assuming Dusty didn't decide to finish the season with the new guy. Ben touched his right hand to his bad shoulder. "I just need to get back at it."

"How about the NFR?" The National Finals Rodeo in the States decided the world championships. Qualification was based on total earnings.

"You haven't been following rodeo, have you?" he said, surprised.

She shook her head. "Giving it up was hard. I went cold turkey. What's going on?"

"In the past few years, only one Canadian has qualified for the NFR each year."

"It's tougher for Canadians, isn't it? Rodeo has to be your entire life. You have to be on the circuit constantly, hit a bunch of U.S. events, do multiple events in a weekend. It's crazy."

"You did it, at least for a couple of years. Even finished second one time."

Green lights danced in her eyes. "No one ever said I wasn't crazy."

Hoping she wouldn't call *him* crazy, Ben shared the idea he'd come up with when he was watching that doe and fawn. An idea that, he now realized, had probably been percolating ever since he arrived at Ryland Riding and saw Sally. "I was thinking, how about I stay here until my shoulder heals?"

"What?" The frown was back, creasing fine lines into her forehead.

That sure wasn't the reaction he'd been going for. "I could help you out." Her frown had intensified rather than eased, so he went on. "You'd give me a place to park my rig and keep Chaunce. And I could borrow your spare ring when it's not booked, and keep up with training. Seems it could be good for both of us." Best of all would be spending time with her.

"Don't you want to go back home to Alberta?"

"Not really. I kind of minimized the shoulder thing when I talked to my folks on Sunday. If Mom sees me wearing a sling, she'll fuss and drive me nuts. And the horse trainer I work for when I'm not rodeoing already hired someone for the summer. As for being useful around here"—he shrugged his good shoulder—"sure, there's some things I can't do, what with this damned fracture, but there's a lot that I can."

"You should heal, not work."

He snorted. "Sit back and do nothing? I'd go outta my freaking mind."

Her lips twitched, but she quickly straightened them and frowned again. "Have you seen a physiotherapist? Do you have exercises to do?"

"Haven't seen one yet, but I will." During his years in

rodeo, he had several times gone to a registered physio—
or physical therapist as they were called in the States—to
help with rehab after an injury. There was bound to be
one in Caribou Crossing.

He'd hoped Sally would leap at his offer. It should relieve some pressure until she could hire a new helper.
Instead, she was acting like he'd added another stress to
her life. Damned if he could figure out why. "Eat your
pie. You can think about my suggestion overnight."

"Overnight?" She flicked a wary glance at him.

"Sun's set," he pointed out. "We got chores to do after
we finish dessert. I was hoping, after that, you'd let me
and Chaunce spend the night."

Now her eyes flared wide. "What do you mean?"

Man, she was touchy. "That wasn't a proposition," he
clarified. He thought about adding "much as I'd like it
to be," but figured that'd be shooting himself in the
foot. "Like I said, I could use a place to park the rig. I
have everything I need in the trailer, so I won't have to
trouble you for anything. Chaunce sure would like
being able to roam around in your paddock rather than
be cooped up in his stall in the rig."

Her lips pressed together so tightly that they disappeared into a single thin line. When she eased them
open, tautness remained around her eyes. "A woman
living alone has to be careful."

Suddenly, her wariness made sense. She was scared.
Surely not of him? But something had made her nervous.
His heart thudded. "Did someone hurt you? Threaten
you?"

She sucked in air in a soft gasp. "N-no. But like I said,
I have to be careful."

Only halfway reassured, he said, "Having me here
would be like having a watchdog."

"That's not . . . I mean . . ."

Insulted, he said, "Sally, come on. You can't think you have anything to fear from me. I'd never hurt you."

"That's easy to say." The words burst out, then she clamped her lips shut again.

"It's easy to *do,* damn it. I'd never hurt a woman. What kind of sick bastard does that?" Of course he knew there were men like that. He'd punched out a couple who were being rough with women in bars. The idea that Sally might have met someone like that made him want to shove his fist through that guy's face.

"Ben?" she said cautiously. "You look a little, um . . ."

"Sorry." He rubbed the fingers of his right hand across his tense jaw.

"I didn't mean to upset you." Her expression was still anxious.

He could kick himself for making her feel that way. "Sorry. *I* didn't mean to upset *you.* The idea of a man abusing a woman, a kid, even a weaker man, it makes me steam."

"Okay." She didn't sound convinced.

"It's getting late. Why don't you finish up your pie? There are still chores to tend to."

She began to eat again, in small bites, casting glances up at him from under her lashes.

Musing, Ben sipped the last of his coffee. Something had happened to Sally to make her wary of men. Couldn't have been Pete; the man had clearly adored her. She'd mentioned a couple of friends who helped her out, probably including that guy Dave who the woman at the diner had mentioned, so it couldn't be them. She hadn't been dating. Maybe one of her clients had harassed her? He wanted to find out what had happened, and make sure that asshole never scared her again. But right now, it seemed she didn't trust him enough to tell him.

"I'm surprised you don't have a dog," he commented. "For protection and company."

"Some horses are nervous around dogs. Some children as well." She spoke without inflection, almost as if she was parroting someone else's words.

Ranches and farms almost always had dogs. Still, he wasn't about to argue. This was her spread, and she clearly knew how she wanted to run it. "I guess."

She finished her pie and stood, collecting the dirty dishes.

Normally, Ben would have offered to help, but his new understanding of Sally made him say instead, "How about you clear up and I'll get started in the barn?"

"I'm worried about your shoulder. You've had a long day."

Yeah, it hurt, but that was just how things were going to be until it healed a bit. He rose too and gazed at her across the table. "Sally, I'm not going to be stupid and make the fracture worse. I can handle some barn chores."

"Okay. But doing my chores, bringing me dinner . . . I don't like to be beholden."

Nor did he, but folks should help each other out. "You gave my horse a place to stay." Before she could say anything more, he turned away and took the steps down from the deck. As he strode past the vegetable garden, a light clicked on behind him, helping to illuminate the rough ground. The light outside the barn door glowed, too.

He yawned and wished the pain in his shoulder would ease up. Sure did hope that if he helped Sally out for an hour, she wouldn't make him hitch up the trailer, load his horse, and drive off looking for someplace to park for the night.

Under his breath, he gave a rueful laugh. When he'd driven here, he'd wondered what it'd be like seeing

Sally again. Whether he'd still be attracted to her. Now he knew the answer to that: he was, and might well be until the day he died. She was the first and so far the only woman who'd gotten under his skin.

Earlier today, he'd also been optimistic enough to wonder if a friendly visit might wind up with him sharing Sally's bed.

Sure looked like that wouldn't be happening anytime soon.

Chapter Four

A chorus of trills and chirps accompanied the pale dawn light that came through Sally's mosquito-screened bedroom window. After Pete's death, when she'd moved from their bedroom to the room she'd once hoped would be their child's, she hadn't bothered to put up a curtain or blinds. She always rose at or before dawn anyhow, and no one could see in the second-floor window at the back of the house.

Lying in bed, the fresh, damp scent coming in the window told her it had rained during the night. She wouldn't have to water the vegetable garden, which would save a few dollars.

Pressing her fingers against tired eyes, she wished she had slept better. The knowledge that Ben Traynor was outside in his trailer, parked in her parking lot, had kept her tossing.

He was in her space. He was in her thoughts. She wasn't used to this.

Dave Cousins had spent a lot of Sunday afternoons at Ryland Riding. He'd eased past the barriers of what he referred to as her stubborn pride, and convinced her to let him help her. He was a kind, gentle man and she'd slowly grown comfortable with him. He respected her boundaries, too; he didn't invade her personal space and he didn't ask about personal subjects.

Ben Traynor was an entirely different thing. Even though she'd sworn off men—and sex—for life, her body was aware of him. It wasn't just that he was handsome to look at. Dave was mighty easy on the eyes, too. With Ben, there was an odd spark. Maybe it was like muscle memory. The fact that she used to find him sexy now sent residual tingles through her blood.

The kind of tingles she hadn't felt in years.

And to be honest, Ben was even more attractive now than he used to be. Behind her closed lids, she thought of his bold features, shadowed jaw, and muscular frame, of the easy confidence in his movements and in those stunning chestnut eyes. And her body tingled. For the grown-up Ben. These weren't residual tingles. And that was bad. She opened her eyes and sat up.

Finding a man attractive and sexy was bad. It could get her into trouble in all sorts of ways. First of all, it was ridiculous: he was young, vital, and distinctly hot, and she was a worn-out, middle-aged woman. He might flirt a little, but that was only habit. If she let herself succumb, she'd make a fool out of herself. And, worse, if she actually fell for him, she would give him power over her. Never would she let another man have that kind of power.

This morning, she would tell Ben to go. She had to.

Yawning, she rose. She'd showered before bed, so now only did a quick face-wash, hair-comb, and tooth-brushing before pulling on clean clothes. Every day she wore the same thing: jeans and a plain T-shirt with a long-sleeved shirt over it, each item a size too large so her body was concealed rather than on display. The knees of the jeans she put on were wearing through. Hopefully, they'd hold out until she acquired a new student or boarder to ease her dire financial situation.

As she went downstairs, the welcome aroma of strong coffee told her that the coffeemaker's timer had done its job. She filled a mug and flicked on the radio, tuned to CXNG. The news never interested her much, but she enjoyed the country music.

Deciding against eggs, she poured a bowl of generic bran flakes, sliced the last banana—overripe, but edible—on top, and added milk. The milk carton was almost empty and so was the fridge, but today was grocery delivery day.

She went through the mudroom and unlocked the outside door, then settled at the deck table with her breakfast. As she ate, she surveyed her domain and sighed with pleasure. Despite her financial worries and the pressure of too much work, life was pretty wonderful. The landscape was both stunning and peaceful. A pale, gentle sun shone in a clear sky, promising a beautiful day.

Her time would be spent with her three pleasures in life: her horses, the children who came for lessons, and her flock of chickens. And her day would be free of fear. There'd be no Pete with his impossibly high standards. No Pete to make her second-guess her every move for fear she'd do something to set him off.

Breakfast finished, she rose. There would be no Ben either, because she'd send him away as soon as he woke up. Maybe she should offer him a cup of coffee first, so she wouldn't seem too rude about rejecting his offer of help. He was being gracious; he was being a cowboy. And she was turning up her nose.

For a moment, she imagined what it might be like to accept his offer. To share the workload. To have time to tend the garden. To look up from whatever activity she was engaged in and see Ben. Ben leading a horse from the barn; Ben cheering after she took Melody around the barrels; Ben on the back of his American Paint.

Stupid. She'd once let herself be seduced by an appealing man, and it had nearly destroyed her.

Briskly, she returned to the kitchen, washed her few dishes, and poured the rest of the contents of the coffeepot into her battered thermos. She always took a second cup to the barn to give her a boost as she did her morning chores. Later, when Ben was up, she'd decide if she wanted to make fresh coffee and offer him some.

In the mudroom, she slipped into her work boots and clapped her straw hat on her head. She started toward the foaling paddock, but when the parking lot came into view she stopped abruptly. Though it wasn't yet six o'clock, Ben sat on a folding chair beside his rig, a mug cradled in his right hand. He smiled and called, "Mornin.'"

Slowly, she walked toward him. "Good morning."

But for the collar and cuff sling, he looked so relaxed and comfortable. Yesterday, his jeans had been newish, but today's were faded and worn, hugging his muscled thighs. His long-sleeved Western shirt had been replaced by a faded blue short-sleeved one with a frayed collar. Comfy old work clothes, but his were so much more flattering than hers. His damp, freshly combed hair suggested that, unlike her, he'd taken the time to shower.

The shower in that trailer would be small, too small for a man his size, especially when he had a fractured shoulder. Her own old-fashioned bathroom had a tub she rarely had time to use, with a shower at one end. Loads of room for a big man. A big, muscled, naked man. Even for a big man and a slender woman.

Oh, Lord, what was she thinking? Where had these wild imaginings come from?

"I'd offer you a cup of coffee," he said, "but I'm guessing that's what's in the thermos."

"Good guess. How's your shoulder this morning?" She gazed more closely at his left arm and grimaced at the deep purple bruise that extended below his shirtsleeve. "Ouch."

"Looks like I've been rolling in blackberries, doesn't it?"

And now she was thinking of him rolling naked in blackberries. The image should have been ridiculous, but instead was so wildly sensual that it sent hot tingles of arousal through her.

Sensual? In the past years, her only experiences of sensuality came from stroking a sun-warmed horse, cuddling her hens, or crunching into a freshly picked carrot. Generic sensuality, not feminine—much less sexual—sensuality. A cold shudder chased the warm tingles away.

Pete's strong hand bruised her wrists as he forced her hands above her head, holding her captive as he pounded into her so hard that she had to bite her lip to keep from crying out in agony. If she cried, he'd backhand her across the face and—

"It's not that bad." Ben's voice broke into the memory.

Yes, it was. It was horrible. He was supposed to love me—he swore he loved me—and that's how he treated me once I was his wife.

"Really." Ben peered at her and gave a one-shouldered shrug. "It's coming along fine."

She stared at him blankly. What? Oh, his shoulder, of course. She breathed out slowly, and managed to say, "That's great."

He wasn't supposed to drive. If she sent him packing and he went home to Alberta, he'd be driving for hours.

That could be dangerous, and certainly wouldn't help his shoulder.

Not that barn chores would be good for his shoulder either. And that reminded her . . . "I need to get to work. Have you had breakfast? I can give you some eggs."

"Thanks. I've already eaten, but a fresh egg omelet for lunch sounds mighty good."

It did. That was fancier than her usual quick meal. But then he had to keep that professional athlete's body in shape.

She'd bet he was in fantastic shape. Ben with his clothes off would be a sight to behold.

No! There she went again. Shaking her head at her own foolishness, she strode away. She'd give him a few eggs as a thank-you and send him on his way. If he had any sense, he wouldn't drive far today, but what he chose to do was his business, not her responsibility.

Decision made, she checked on Sunshine Song. The pregnant palomino still seemed relaxed, not restless or sweating. From the looks of it, she wouldn't foal today. Sally then went to visit her hens. As always, the mere sight of the neatly laid-out coop made her smile.

Her family'd had chickens when she was growing up, and she'd loved them. When she'd suggested to Pete that they get some, he'd said no; they were messy and involved too much work. Last year, she'd bought an insulated storage shed and fitted it out with nesting boxes, roosts, and a workbench. With Dave's help, she had added a large run extending out from the shed, fenced on the sides and on the top to protect from predators. She'd chosen the location so that the run included a few shrubs for shade. Once the coop was complete, she'd found online ads for rescue chickens, and installed her flock.

Her dozen hens were all that she'd hoped for: cheerful and bustling, entertaining, and good company. They were her family, her friends. These early-morning visits with them were always a nice start to her workday.

Her ladies were *not* meat chickens. Even when they were past laying age, she would never slaughter them. She had named them, of course. Now she murmured greetings and stroked feathers as she filled waterers and feed cans and collected eggs. The birds clucked and chirped, keeping up their end of the conversation. She netted six eggs, which she cleaned with a sanding sponge and placed in an old basket. They looked so pretty: medium brown, light brown, and a pale pinkish egg from Lucille, one of the Barred Rocks. Sally would give them to Ben. Eggs had become a staple of her diet—cholesterol be damned—but now that Corrie wasn't around, Sally accumulated more than she could eat. "Thanks, ladies," she said as she left.

Walking toward the trailer, she saw that Ben and his chair were gone. Tentatively, she went to the door and called, "Hello?"

No response. Probably he'd gone to check on Chauncey's Pride. After putting the egg basket on his doorstep, she turned toward the paddock. As she passed the barn door, whistling came from inside: "King of the Road," an oldie. She went inside. "Ben?"

"Hey there." He stuck his head out of the door of her office.

"I thought you'd be checking on your horse."

"Did that before breakfast. I was taking a look at your schedule."

She kept a printout tacked on the wall by the desk.

"Those two horses you brought in last night are boarders, right?" he asked.

"Yes, their owners are coming for early rides."

"Do we need to get their horses ready, or do they do it themselves?"

"I need to do these two. Their owners come out before work and want to maximize their riding time. But you don't have to—"

"I can help with grooming, and muck out stalls."

She frowned skeptically. "You can't wield a pitchfork or a shovel with one hand."

"Bet I can. Though not at a blinding pace."

Wait a minute. Why was she having this conversation? She was supposed to send him on his way. "Ben, I put a basket of eggs on the doorstep of your rig. You should—" She intended to say that he should put the eggs in his fridge, load up his horse, and head away.

But he cut her off, with a smile and a "Much obliged." Striding toward the barn door, he said, "I'll put those away and be right back." And he was gone, leaving her with her mouth open.

If she really wanted him to leave, she should run after him and set him straight. So what did it mean that she instead took Rambler out of the stall where he'd spent the night, tied him in cross ties, and began to groom him? And that, when Ben came back, she let him take over the grooming while she went to get Rambler's tack?

As she saddled the horse, Ben got a wheelbarrow and a pitchfork, and stepped into the stall Rambler'd been in. "The other boarder's the dapple gray you brought in?"

"Right."

"What about the bay gelding? He's been in a stall since I got here." Ben's voice, along with the sounds of a pitchfork being wielded, came from the open stall.

"Campion's mine. He had a hoof abscess. It's been drained, the vet filled the hole with hoof putty, and the farrier will be out day after tomorrow to replace the shoe." Sally finished putting Rambler's bridle on. "There you go, pretty boy. You're all ready for a nice morning ride." She took him out to the yard and tied his reins to a hitching rail.

Returning, she saw that Ben had mucked out the stall and was laying down fresh straw. She took Smoke Signals, the dapple gray, out of her stall and into the cross ties, and got to work.

As she and Ben went about their tasks, they chatted back and forth, with him asking her about the horses and her schedule at Ryland Riding. It was companionable. Kind of like when she'd worked with Corrie, but different because Ben was a man. Because Ben was Ben.

Disturbed, she led Smoke Signals outside and was tightening his cinch when a Jeep drove up with a man and woman inside. They were a twenty-something brother and sister who, together with their parents, owned a natural foods store in Caribou Crossing. After an exchange of greetings, they mounted their horses and rode off.

Sally checked her schedule. The chicken coop could use cleaning. Did she have time now? Yes, the next riders wouldn't be here for an hour and a half. The four women, all moms who worked part-time, came for a ride at least a couple of times a week. They had nice lives, balancing work, recreation, and family.

Or at least so it seemed from the outside, from their easy smiles and the bits of conversation she heard. But Sally well knew that no one could judge the happiness of a marriage from the outer facade. Like an overly made-up face, you had no idea what lay beneath.

That reminder, that return of common sense, had her leaning on the open stall door and telling Ben, "Much as I appreciate the help, your top priority should be seeing a physiotherapist. You have one you see in Alberta, don't you?"

"Sure do. How about Caribou Crossing? Is it big enough to have a physio or two?"

Absentmindedly, she said, "One of my students goes to Monique Labelle, who's doing a great job with the girl." If Ben drove home, taking it slow, he could make an appointment for a couple of days from now. "Once you see the physio, you'll heal more quickly." And healing, getting back to the rodeo, was what mattered to him, after all.

He used the back of his right hand to shove his shaggy hair from his brow. She saw the calluses on his palm. Rodeo calluses. She used to have them, too. Now hers came from pitchforks and shovels.

"You're right," he said. "I need to make an appointment."

"Okay." He'd agreed so easily. . . . "I mean, that's good." Of course it was good. Having him here might lighten her workload, but it wreaked havoc with her peace of mind.

Ben went looking for Sally, who had disappeared after their chat. Despite what she seemed to think, he did know how to look after himself. Rodeo was his livelihood, supplemented in the off season by working for a horse trainer. Rodeo had also been his passion since he was a little kid. He and Chaunce would be back on the circuit the moment his shoulder was healed enough for roping, though bronc riding might have to wait a while longer.

In the meantime, he and Chaunce needed to keep in shape. He was glad Sally had finally accepted his help, but her next booking was a ways off, so he figured she'd have time to handle the preparation herself. This seemed like a good opportunity to take Chaunce out.

As Ben went around the barn, he heard Sally's voice coming from inside the chicken coop. Outside in the run, a few chickens pecked, scratched, and clucked. He eased the gate open and slipped inside, careful not to let any of them escape, then stood in the doorway of the neat little coop.

Sally had her back to him as, rubber-gloved, she cleaned roosts and nest boxes and chatted to another four or five chickens who seemed to be answering. He didn't alert her to his presence, just enjoyed watching her, all cheerful and relaxed the same as with the kids she taught. Treating these hens like children, too.

She had a nice-looking flock, not that he was an expert on chickens. Half of hers were a blond color and the others had charcoal and white alternating bands.

Sally turned and saw him. Her hand flew to her chest. "I didn't know you were there."

"You name your hens?"

A flush colored her cheeks, making her look young and flustered. "They lay better when they have names," she said defensively.

He suppressed a grin. It was probably true. Maybe not about the names, but that well cared for hens were contented and good producers. "They're pretty. What kinds are they?"

"The black-and-white stripy ones are Barred Rocks and the apricot ones are Buff Orpingtons."

"Buff what?"

"Orpington for the town in England where they originated. Buff for the color."

"Learn something every day. Their eggs sure looked good."

Sally folded her arms across her chest. "Are you heading off now?"

"Unless you need me to groom those horses in the barn, I thought I'd take Chaunce for a ride. He could use some exercise."

"Oh. Um, sure, that makes sense."

Her surprised expression made him think twice. "I can do it later. Want me to help with the next horses?"

"No. No, I was planning to do it. Go ahead."

Before taking that ride, Ben went to his trailer, yanking off his grubby work boots before entering. He opened his phone and got on the Internet to look up the physiotherapist Sally had mentioned. Monique Labelle's bio said that, among other things, she did rehab for sports injuries. He called her office, explained his situation, and the sympathetic receptionist said she'd squeeze him in this afternoon.

Whistling, he put on riding boots and went to get his horse. A quarter of an hour later, Chaunce strode eagerly down the road with Ben riding bareback.

"I'm seeing a physio," he told his horse. "Maybe she'll clear me to get back to roping practice, and Sally'll let us use her spare ring."

Chaunce bobbed his head like he couldn't wait.

"Sorry, pal, but for now you'll have to settle for a trail ride." It was easy on Ben's body and he did enjoy exploring the countryside. On an inside wall of Sally's barn, she had a map showing a network of farm roads and riding trails. Yesterday, a rider he crossed paths with had told him that a number of the trails were on private property, but the owners allowed public access through portions of their spreads.

Setting Chaunce into a comfortable lope, Ben took

a dirt farm road for ten minutes or so. He stopped at a gate in a fence, bent down to unlatch it, and guided his horse through. Latching it again, he noted the sign reminding passers-through to do exactly that. No farmer or rancher wanted livestock going astray. The new trail led through a grove of aspens, slim and lovely with their white bark and gently rustling leaves. At a walk, Chaunce negotiated the twists and turns until they came out at the shore of a small lake. A beaver dam cut off part of the stream that fed into the lake. There was no beach, and probably no swimming due to submerged logs the beavers had cut.

Ben swung off Chaunce's back, dropped the reins knowing his well-trained horse would neither step on them nor stray, and walked closer to the bank. His boots sank into the boggy ground as he admired white water lilies floating among heart-shaped green pads. Dragonflies stirred the air with shimmery wings and ducks bobbed their heads beneath the surface of the water, hunting for food. It would be a nice spot for a picnic.

Did Sally ever take time off and go riding for pure pleasure? Did she picnic by a lake, maybe nap under the shade of an aspen? Or how about getting together with friends for a meal, or going to a bar to listen to some music, shoot a game of pool, dance the two-step the way she used to on the rodeo circuit?

She'd said she didn't have time to go to town. Now that he was here to assist her, she ought to be able to enjoy some R&R. Preferably with him. He wanted time with the Sally who smiled at little kids, who whipped her buckskin mare around the barrels, who named her chickens and carried on conversations with them.

Why did that Sally go into hiding so often? Was it fear, because of something some jerk had done? Or might some of it be grief over Pete's death? He'd seen how beaten-down his grandma was after she was widowed. But she'd adjusted over a period of a couple of years and rediscovered her joy in life. She'd even started dating.

Sally'd been crazy in love with Pete, but she had been widowed for three years. Maybe she wasn't ready for sex with another guy—though Ben could always hope— but that was no reason she shouldn't lighten up and have some fun. With someone other than her chickens. With a guy she could trust, who would never do anything to hurt her.

"That's me," he told Chaunce as he bent to gather the reins. "Now how can I make her believe it?" He mounted, using a stump as a mounting block and hating the awkwardness of his banged-up shoulder. Yeah, he could mount bareback from the ground, one-armed, but it would jar his shoulder. Much as it pissed him off, he had to be sensible.

"Sensible," he said. "A sensible rodeo rider. Isn't that what they call an oxymoron?"

Chaunce snorted and tossed his head.

It was nearing noon, so Ben headed back to Ryland Riding. It wasn't a surprise to see Sally in the ring with a student. He remembered the schedule saying: "Amanda: lesson." The girl looked to be about twelve. He raised a hand in greeting to Sally, who stood in the middle of the ring as her student trotted a little bay mare in a circle. The mom sat in the bleachers, body slanted forward, all her attention on her daughter.

Halting Chaunce, Ben watched for a few minutes and realized that Amanda had a prosthetic leg. He read signs of pain and frustration in her squinched-up brow and tight mouth. Her body language made him think she'd lost the leg fairly recently and was still figuring out how to deal with her new reality. He'd seen rodeo competitors go through the same process after a major injury. Most cowboyed up, handling it with the same guts they'd shown when competing, but a few let catastrophe defeat them. This kid was a gutsy one, it was clear to see.

Giving the girl some privacy, he dismounted and led Chaunce away.

Working at half his normal speed, he took off his horse's bridle and groomed him, then let him out in the paddock. When Ben returned to the barnyard, Sally was saying good-bye to her student and the mom. Rather than help her with the horse, a task she could do faster than he, he decided to make lunch for both of them.

In the tiny kitchen of his trailer, he clumsily chopped onions and mushrooms and got them sautéeing, then he grated cheddar and jack cheeses. He whipped up those pretty eggs of hers, along with a splash of milk and some seasonings, and pretty soon he had an omelet cooking.

A glance out the window showed him that Sally stood outside the barn door, staring toward his trailer, looking puzzled. Probably wondering where her helper had gone.

Chapter Five

Sally stared at Ben's trailer. He'd put Chauncey's Pride in the paddock, rather than loading him into the trailer. Shouldn't he get on the road? If he interspersed driving with rest stops for himself and his horse, he could cover a fair number of miles today.

She walked toward the trailer, intending to inquire about his plans and say a final good-bye. And if the thought of saying farewell gave her a pang of sorrow, that was only because it had been fun catching up with an old rodeo friend, not to mention having a helping hand. *Hand*, singular. But Ben was right that he, even single-handed, was pretty darned impressive. Remembering his flirtatious comment yesterday, she imagined that callused palm caressing her shoulder as surely, as softly, as he stroked his horse.

But big, strong hands weren't always gentle. Men who seemed sweet, even romantic and loving, could turn mean with the slightest provocation.

Ben appeared in the open door of the trailer and, as if in answer to her unspoken question, said, "Lunchtime."

All right, he planned to eat before leaving. She needed to grab a snack, too. Her grocery delivery had come and her fridge was stocked up, so she'd have cheese and fresh fruit to add to carrots from the garden and her usual couple of hard-boiled eggs.

Ben gestured her to come closer, saying, "I need to—" The rest of his words were lost as he turned and disappeared inside.

Grumbling under her breath, she walked to the trailer door. She didn't have time for this. She needed to eat before her first afternoon booking, which was one she always enjoyed. Wenda Strom homeschooled her adolescent boy and girl and brought them out almost every week of the year for a guided trail ride. That basically meant that Sally got to go for a scenic ride with a woman who loved nature and a couple of kids who were excited about being on horseback. The clients also handled the grooming and tack themselves.

"Ben?" she said from outside the open door. "What did you want to tell me?"

"Hang on a sec."

She rolled her eyes and shifted from foot to foot. He was in the tiny kitchen, his back to her. The delicious aroma of onions and cheese cooking made her stomach growl. His lunch smelled better than what she had in mind for hers.

Curiously, she glanced around his living space. The trailer was an older model, and about half again as big as the one she used to tow. The compact interior wasn't fancy and it had seen lots of use, but it was neat. The front overhang had a bed, and the couch would flip out to make another one. A scratched dinette provided cramped seating, and there was a flat-screen TV. A tablet was propped up on the dinette table, with resistance exercise tubing beside it.

"I could pull out my folding chairs and set them up,"

he said over his shoulder, "but your deck has a much nicer view."

"What are you—" She broke off as he turned and came toward her, holding out a plate filled with a steaming serving of melted cheese-covered omelet, a fork laid beside it. Her mouth stayed open as he handed the plate down to her and turned away. "You cooked lunch for me?"

He came back carrying a second plate, and walked down the steps. "Least I could do, when you supplied the eggs. Hold this for a sec?" He handed her that plate as well, pulled on his work boots, then took the plate back. Confidently, he headed across the yard toward her house.

"Well . . . thank you." She trailed behind him. Even the rare times she'd been sick—or so beaten up she couldn't drag herself out of bed—the most Pete had done was heat a tin of soup. He didn't think cooking was a man's job, and he didn't believe in malingering in bed. Now, for no reason at all, Ben had cooked her lunch.

They walked up to the deck. Ben put his plate on the table and sank into the same chair he'd used last night. No place mats, no napkins. Pete had said there was no excuse for not laying a proper table. Sally had gathered that his ideas of male and female roles had come from his parents, who'd died when he was in his late teens. Once, frustrated but trying to joke, she'd told Pete that he wanted the two of them to live in a fifties TV rerun. Once . . .

"You think you're better than my mother?" Pete grabbed her shoulders. "You're not fit to clean her floor. You hear me?" He shook her so hard she could almost hear her bones rattle.

"I hear you," she whispered. "I'm sorry. I was wrong."

"Damn right, you were wrong. Seems like you're wrong most of the time. You're pathetic, that's what you are." He flung her

aside, so hard she cracked her head against the kitchen table as she fell to the floor.

She cowered there, vision blurred and ears ringing. Praying he wouldn't kick her.

And he didn't, that time. He stared down at her. "Damn it, Sally. I love you. I deserve better from you."

"I know. I'm sorry. I love you too, Pete." And she did, back then. He was her handsome, charming husband, the one who'd swept her off her feet and into a whole new life. The one who'd made her the center of his universe. Why was she so stupid as to get her back up over a few old-fashioned courtesies like setting a pretty table and having a meal ready on time? "I'll do better. I promise."

"What's wrong? Did I mess up? Don't you like onions?" Ben's voice. Not Pete's.

Sally realized she was staring down at the plate in her hand. Ben's words sank in. He was worried that she might not like the meal he'd prepared for her? "I do. Sorry, I just, uh, thought of something I'd forgotten to do. Lunch looks great and I really appreciate your making it." She put her plate on the table. "What would you like to drink? Water or milk? Or, uh, beer?"

"A glass of milk would be great. Thanks."

She went inside to pour milk for him and water for herself. Out of habit, she started to gather up place mats and napkins. And then, deliberately, she put them back in the drawer.

When she returned, she noted that Ben had waited for her rather than started eating. Quickly, she sat down and picked up her fork. After the first mouthful, she said, "Delicious. Thank you."

He swallowed a bite. "Ever get sick of eggs?"

"Not really. There are lots of things you can do with them." Though mostly all she had time for was boiling, frying, or scrambling. The meal he'd prepared was a treat.

"D'you eat chicken?" he asked.

She shook her head. "No." Automatically, she lowered her voice. "I used to. I used to love fried chicken. I suppose it seems foolish to you, raising hens and not eating chicken."

"More like softhearted." He grinned over a heaping forkful of omelet. "Have to confess, I can't imagine life without fried chicken."

"Sshh," she teased. "Don't say that so loud. My ladies might hear."

He laughed, and she smiled in response. Ben had a way about him. Somehow he got her to loosen up the way she hadn't done since she got married. Probably because he was an old acquaintance, and there was no personal baggage between the two of them—like there was with the family and friends she'd left behind years ago.

Penny had told Ben that the family missed Sally, and that maybe enough time had gone by. Her sister had made a first move, asking Ben to look Sally up. Did Sally dare make the next one, and get in touch? It had been so long. . . .

"What's the story on Amanda?" Ben asked, his tone sympathetic and curious.

"You noticed her leg?" When he nodded, she went on. "Amanda used to be in one of my after-school classes. Then she was in a car accident and they had to amputate her leg below the knee. She's learning how to use a prosthesis. Her parents kept her out of school, homeschooling her so she could attend all her rehab and therapy appointments and start adjusting, physically and mentally. She wanted to keep riding, so I did a bunch of online research and worked with her physiotherapist—that

LOVE SOMEBODY LIKE YOU

woman Monique Labelle who I mentioned earlier—to figure out the best way to help her."

"Poor kid." He shook his head. "That sure sucks. I could see she's frustrated and in pain, but she seems like one gutsy girl."

"She is. She won't settle for anything less than living life the way she did before. In September she'll go back to school, and she wants to re-join her riding class." She gazed across at him. "She wants to learn barrel racing."

He grinned. "Good for her. I like this kid."

"Me, too. If I'd had—" She broke off. When she was with this man, things came out of her mouth that she never intended to say.

"If you'd had what? Kids?" Ben asked quietly.

She and Pete hadn't discussed the subject of children until after they were married. She'd just assumed he wanted them as badly as she did. Instead, he said the two of them were a unit; they didn't need anyone else intruding. How could he see their own child as an intrusion? "Yes," she told Ben. "But I didn't. So that's that." She hadn't intended to open that conversational door and now she was shutting it firmly.

"I was surprised you didn't have kids. I always figured you would."

Closed door. Hadn't he got the memo, or was he deliberately ignoring it? Even her closest—okay, her only—friends Dave and Cassidy respected her boundaries and didn't pry into her personal life.

There were so many things she would never tell anyone. But right now she felt a strong need to share one small secret with an old friend, a man who would soon be gone from her life again. "I figured I would, too," she said quietly. "But it just didn't happen."

"That's too bad." Ben had finished his omelet and gazed sympathetically at her.

Pete never wanted her to see a doctor, so they'd relied on condoms. She'd wanted children so badly and hoped he'd eventually change his mind. When their birth control failed and she became pregnant, she was ecstatic. Knowing that Pete was likely to be less enthusiastic, she'd kept her pregnancy a secret for as long as she could. Morning sickness gave her away. When she'd admitted the truth, he'd gone into a rage. He'd slapped her, punched her, kicked her. Kicked her repeatedly—in the belly. When she miscarried, alone in the bathroom sobbing her heart out, he wouldn't take her to the hospital.

Sally swallowed against the lump in her throat. "Yeah. It is too bad."

Pete had followed his normal pattern afterward: flowers, tears, a plea for forgiveness, and an apology couched in "you shouldn't have made me do it" terms. As always, he'd told her he needed her and she needed him, and they didn't need anyone else.

Her body had healed, but her soul never did. She'd realized how crazy it was to think of bringing an innocent child into Pete's world.

Why had she stayed with him? What was wrong with her?

"You're only what, thirty-two?" Ben said. "There's plenty of time to have kids."

She shook her head. "Not going to happen."

"Sally, you're young and healthy. I'm sorry about Pete, but you can't mourn forever."

Or at all. What she could do, and would likely do for the rest of her life, was mistrust men. Or, perhaps more accurately, mistrust her ability to choose a man who would be a good husband and a good father.

Take right now, for example. The expression in Ben's dark-fringed chestnut eyes seemed so honest, so sympathetic. Affectionate, almost. A woman could get drawn in, could believe that this man really did care for her. And maybe he even did. But in what way? The way that Dave felt for Cassidy, where he loved her to pieces and also respected her strength and independence? Or the way Pete had loved Sally, where she and their marriage became an obsession? Where he saw something in her, some flaw that told him he could take a champion barrel racer, deconstruct her, and turn her into his idea of—

"Shit," Ben said. "I'm sorry. I didn't mean to upset you." He reached over to rest his hand on the back of hers.

She flinched, then tried to conceal the movement by quickly rising and freeing her hand to pick up her empty plate. "I'm not upset."

But her heart raced erratically. And not, she realized, just because strong hands could be dangerous but because, for a moment, that warm male flesh, the roughness of his calluses, had felt good. Because that long-forgotten sensual, feminine side of her wanted more.

She grabbed up his plate. "I'll wash these and leave them on the doorstep of your rig. Then I have to bring in some horses."

He stood and rotated his neck inside the confining collar of the sling. "I'd help, but I need to get going."

Finally. She should have been relieved, but instead felt a twinge of disappointment. Though he'd thrown her off balance, she would actually miss him. "Sure. Of course." Dishes in hand, she took a step away from the table. She was all set to wish him a safe trip, and good luck healing and making the Finals, when he spoke.

"Need anything in town? Groceries? I have a physio appointment in half an hour and—"

The plates almost slipped from her hands. "You what? You made an appointment with a physiotherapist in Caribou Crossing?"

"Monique Labelle."

"But what's the point, when you're going back to Alberta?"

"What?" He gave a puzzled frown. "I'm staying here."

"You can't do that."

"I don't have time to discuss it. They squeezed me in and I don't want to be late." He turned on booted heel and strode away, leaving her scowling after him.

As she washed the dishes, she wondered why he was doing this. Was he trying to manipulate her? If so, what did he want from her? Or was it possible that Ben Traynor was the rare type of man like Dave Cousins who was simply kindhearted? Even if that were true, she couldn't accept any more of his help.

Dave talked about her stubborn pride. He didn't understand that Pete had whipped every ounce of pride out of her. What was crucial to Sally now was that she not depend on others.

"I'll leave you!" she screamed at Pete, tears pouring down her face as she cradled her injured arm against her body.

"You can't," he said flatly. "You have no one but me. Nowhere to go."

And it was true. She'd cut all ties with her family and old friends, and made no new friends. Pete handled everything: the business, their finances. He'd said those things were the man's job and she'd let it happen. Let herself become dependent on him. So dependent that the only way she'd be free was if he died.

And she wished he would.

Sally shivered despite the warm water running over

her hands. If you depended on someone, you gave them power over you.

She dried Ben's plates and took them out to the trailer. His old Ram dually was gone.

Resisting the temptation to step into the trailer and explore, she put the plates down on a step, and then brought in the horses for the family trail ride. With ten minutes to spare, she checked e-mail. There were no students nor any boarding requests. Ryland Riding was hanging on by its fingernails. She had a website—marginal, but functional—and she'd placed ads in the local paper and online. What more could she do to generate business?

Giving in to temptation, she searched online for this year's Canadian rodeo standings. Ben was running fourth in saddle bronc, and he and his partner Dusty were sixth in team roping. They were nicely positioned to make the CFR—if Ben could get back to competing soon. Out of curiosity, she checked for videos of Ben riding, and found several.

She was viewing the second, admiring his power and ease as he seemed to read the mind of a bronc called Hurricane Force, when a female voice called, "Sally?"

Oh my gosh, she'd forgotten all about the trail ride! "Coming!" She hurried out to greet Wenda and her two kids, and they all readied their horses and got going.

Sally rode one of the boarded horses, Moonshot. The black gelding's owner was away for a couple of weeks and Sally had promised to ride the horse occasionally, to give him exercise and attention. He had a long, smooth stride, Wenda and her children were good company, and the scenery was, as always, a delight. Yet Sally's mind kept returning to the videos. Ben had matured into one hell of a competitor, and he looked mighty fine on the back of a bucking bronc.

Of course, he looked mighty fine whatever he was doing. . . .

After the ride, a couple of owners came, and then she taught a children's class. Midway through the afternoon, Ben returned and calmly lent a hand. Sally realized that she was getting used to having him around.

It wasn't until they'd turned out the last horses into the paddock that there was a spare moment to talk. She and Ben leaned side by side on the top fence rail, watching the horses graze. His right forearm rested on the rail, but his left arm hung down in the sling so his shoulder would heal correctly. "What did Monique say?" she asked.

"She gave me some light exercises. Said to do my normal leg and core exercises and stretches, but hold off on running for a couple more days."

Into her head flashed an image of Ben in running shorts and a tank top, the thin garments plastered to his body with sweat. "You run?" Knowing her cheeks had flushed, she didn't turn her head to look at him.

"And do weights, crunches, chin-ups, isometrics, stretches. As much as I can fit in when I'm traveling. Anyhow, she said the shoulder's coming along fine." He turned his head and she felt his gaze.

Determinedly, she stared out at the horses as Moonshot had himself a fine old roll and came up shaking off dust.

"See, you've got no reason to get rid of me," Ben said. "The work's not hurting me."

Maybe not, but it was making her think about all manner of things that disconcerted her. Now she did turn toward him. "Ben, I won't be beholden to you."

She forced herself to stare straight into his eyes, even though confronting a man pretty much terrified her.

"Jesus, Sally. You'd be giving me a place to park my trailer, look after my horse, and get some exercise, rather than spend the next couple days on the road. But it seems to me, it shouldn't be about who's beholden to who. Whom. Whatever. When friends help each other out, no one should be keeping score."

"But I can handle things on my own. You have no idea how important that is to me."

He gave a puzzled frown. "No, I guess I don't. I mean, you've been handling things since long before I first met you. You made it to the top of the heap as a barrel racer. I figured you could do anything you set your mind to. And do it well."

"You did?" He saw her that way, as strong and capable?

"And now I see what you've built here." He gestured around.

"That was Pete," she said automatically. Her husband had made it clear to her that she was nothing without him. He'd obtained the mortgage, persuading a business connection at a credit union to take a chance on a young couple, and he'd handled the finances. He had fixed up the old barn, built the indoor arena, and done the repairs and maintenance. All she'd done was occasionally provide a second pair of hands.

Pete could do everything, as he'd repeatedly pointed out. All she could do, aside from try to be a good wife, was ride and take care of horses. She hadn't even known how to teach; she'd figured that out as she went along.

Ben said, "Maybe it was Pete who built some of it, but the core of the operation is horses, and they're your expertise. He was never more than a weekend rider, right?"

"A weekend rider who worked in construction as a

site manager." A rodeo fan who, as Pete had told her, lost his heart to her the first time he saw her ride.

Sally, girl, when I saw you in that silver shirt, atop your silver horse, you were like a bolt of lightning. And that long fiery hair of yours, flying out from under your brown hat, was a banner of flame. Blazing right into my heart. I knew I had to make you mine.

Oh yes, Pete had been poetic when he was courting her. And every now and then after that, too. Enough to keep her confused. To make her think that he really did love her, even though his way of expressing it—of reinforcing that she was *his* after their marriage—was as often through high expectations, demeaning comments, and hard fists as through flattery and flowers.

"I'd bet," Ben went on, "that you've always been the heart and soul of Ryland Riding. Not only that, but for the past three years you've run the whole show yourself."

She'd taught herself the bookkeeping program, learned about the relevant laws and regulations, and figured out how to do the taxes. She did most of the maintenance work herself, grateful for what she'd learned by assisting Pete.

He'd always said that the two of them, together, ought to be able to do anything. They didn't need anyone interfering in their business. Driving a wedge between them. Not her family; not the residents of Caribou Crossing. He had staked a claim on her, built a fence around her, and wouldn't let anyone near. What was wrong with her that she had let him do it?

Pete would be so pissed off to see her here leaning side by side against the fence with Ben, their elbows almost touching. For her, it felt surprisingly natural. Surprisingly right.

And that kind of thinking was purely dangerous. Abruptly, she pushed away from the fence. "I'm going to check on Sunshine Song, the pregnant mare."

Sally hadn't told him not to come along, so Ben followed slowly, thinking about the thin lines that had creased her forehead. It seemed that something would trigger a memory, and she'd go off inside her head somewhere. Somewhere that made her unhappy.

Yeah, it was obvious she'd loved Pete like crazy and Ben figured she was missing him like crazy, too. But Pete was gone. That was the cold, hard truth. And Sally still had a whole lot of life ahead of her. Ben's grandma had pulled out of the sorrow, and she'd been in her seventies. Sally, barely more than thirty, should have smile lines, not ones of tension and sadness. If there was anything he could do to put them there, he wanted to do it.

Tucked away behind the barn was a small foaling paddock. Ben hung back as Sally went over to the fence, tugging a carrot from her pocket. A very pregnant palomino ambled over to take it from her hand. "How's it going, Song?" Sally murmured.

The horse ducked her head, munched, then wandered off toward a grove of cottonwoods.

"Hmm," Sally said. "Usually she stays to be stroked. I think she's getting near her time."

Ben moved up slowly beside her. "You're keeping her outside, not putting her in a stall?"

Still watching the horse, Sally said, "My vet recommends it. It's more natural and healthier, with less risk of infection."

"The trainer I work for does it that way, too. It makes sense. Let a horse do it the natural way." He glanced at her profile. "You moved her to the foaling paddock a while ago?" The mare needed time to build up antibodies against that environment in her colostrum. That first milk would contain immune cells essential to her foal's health.

Sally turned to him with a smile. "Yes. I have an excellent vet, Ben."

He gave a soft laugh. "Sorry, I don't mean to sound like I'm telling you how to do your job." And that reminded him . . . "On that subject." He pulled a scrap of paper from his shirt pocket. "I don't know if you're taking new students."

"Absolutely."

"I met this guy in the physio's waiting room. He'd like to talk to you. I realized I didn't have your phone number to give him."

"About lessons for his son or daughter?" She unfolded the paper.

"No, him. He's—"

"I don't usually teach men. Just kids and women."

Because she didn't feel safe alone with a man? "He seems like a nice guy. Used to be big into running, but now he needs to avoid high-impact exercise. He and his husband are both interested in riding lessons."

"He's gay? Married?"

"That a problem for you?" He wouldn't have taken Sally for a homophobe.

"No, not at all. That's actually better. I mean . . ." She shook her head, apparently unwilling to explain further.

Ben guessed that a gay couple was less of a threat than a single heterosexual man. He sure wanted to get his hands on whatever jerk had made her so nervous.

"Are they both beginners?" she asked.

"Andrew, the guy I met, is. His husband used to ride

a bit as a kid. They've moved here recently and his husband says they should get into riding. That's how Andrew and I got talking, when he asked how I'd hurt my shoulder. Anyhow, I told him about Ryland Riding. He says they both want to take lessons, and if it works out they'd be looking for advice on buying horses. Then they'd want to board the horses."

"That could be some nice business. Thanks, Ben."

"No sweat." Now that she'd relaxed, he figured he could tease her a bit. "But knowing how you hate to be beholden to anyone, I guess I should give you a chance to pay me back."

Her expression turned guarded. "What did you have in mind?" she asked coolly.

So much for teasing. "How about you put together a salad with some of those veggies growing in your garden, and I'll barbecue burgers? I picked up some ground beef at the butcher in town, and fresh buns at the bakery. Fudge brownies as well."

When he said "fudge brownies," her eyes gleamed. Still, she said, "I don't think that's a good idea."

"Why not?"

"I'm still not comfortable with you being here," she said stiffly. "Not that I don't appreciate the help. But if you stay, we need to work out some ground rules."

"Fair enough. Let's do that over dinner."

The corners of her mouth twitched, then straightened. "When Corrie was here, we worked really well together, but when the work was done we went our separate ways. She was a private person like me. We didn't get into each other's business."

He cocked his head. "You lived side by side, worked together all day, but didn't socialize? You each cooked and ate your meals by yourselves?" That sounded pretty strange and awfully lonely. And not at all like the Sally he used to know.

She nodded. "Neither of us are very social."

"You used to be social. On the rodeo circuit, you were the life of the party in the bars where the cowboys and cowgirls hung out."

A slight, reminiscent smile warmed her face. It died quickly. "I drank too much."

She'd said something like that before, about alcohol making her do stupid things. He searched his memories of seven years back, and shook his head. "Not that I recall. You had fun. And I don't just mean partying. You had friends; you cared about people and helped them out."

A sad, almost bleak expression darkened her pretty eyes. "I was a different person then. I can't find my way back to being her again."

That wasn't just sad, but wrong. "Sure you can. But you gotta want to. Like that little girl Amanda, determined to find a way back to being the girl she was before she lost a leg."

Sally's lips opened, but no words came out. Was she mad at him? Did she want to say that losing a husband didn't compare to losing the lower part of a leg? To his mind, loss was loss. Of course it changed you, but it didn't have to turn you into a different person.

Or was there something more going on with Sally, tying into her wariness around men?

The woman fascinated him. She always had, but back then the fascination had been superficial. *He* had been superficial, a cocky wannabe rodeo cowboy. She'd been the queen, the glittery flame that drew all the moths. Now, the fire in her was banked down so far that he barely glimpsed a glowing ember every now and then.

LOVE SOMEBODY LIKE YOU

83

Damn it, he wanted to see her come to life again. He wanted to see her fire, her warmth, her passion. But if he poked too hard, he might scare her.

"Look," he said, "you like efficiency, right? We need to talk about ground rules. And we need to prepare dinner and eat. You do salad, I do burgers, dinner's prepared in half the time. We talk while we eat, so we're multitasking. And you get to share my fudge brownies." And maybe she'd share her smile with him.

Well, damned if it didn't work.

She actually gave him a grin. "You always were persuasive, Ben Traynor."

"Hah. The most I could persuade you into was a dance now and then."

"You were too young for me."

He chuckled. "Maybe. But you put a major dent in my ego when you pointed it out."

She snorted. "Someone had to. You had enough cowgirls and buckle bunnies after you. If your ego'd gotten any more swollen, it would've burst." She studied his face, for once not looking guarded but curious. "You seem different now. Confident, but not so cocky."

"It's been a lot of years. I did some growing up."

"Not all rodeo cowboys do. What with the buckle bunnies and all," she drawled.

"Yeah, well. Different guys want different things. When you can't remember the name of the woman you wake up next to, seems to me there's something wrong."

"You think?" she said drily. "So are you in a serious relationship now?"

He shook his head, pleased that she was interested enough to ask. "Winter before last, after the rodeo season ended and I was back home, I dated a woman I'd gone to high school with. We got along pretty well, but she was looking to settle down and start a family. Didn't want to do that with a guy who spent most of the year driving from rodeo to rodeo."

"No, I can imagine not. And for you, life's all about the rodeo?"

"Yeah." That was the short, easy answer.

She nodded, apparently willing to accept that. A private person, respecting his privacy.

Damn it, that wasn't how he wanted things to be between them. So he went on, speaking slowly as he sorted out his thoughts. "For now. But that doesn't mean I haven't thought about settling down at some point. I can see the appeal, some years down the road, of being with one woman, of raising kids and teaching them to ride."

"Yeah." Something glinted in her green eyes, maybe a hint of yearning. "What kind of work would you do? Ranching?"

A lot of rodeo cowboys were into ranching, often because their families owned a spread. "Maybe, if I make enough money to buy a ranch. My folks sold theirs a while back. It was grinding them down. Or I could train horses, maybe buy into a partnership with the guy I've been working for. Do some weekend rodeo and keep my hand in. It would be okay, I guess."

"Too bad the timing was off for you and your ex-girlfriend."

"It wasn't just the timing," he admitted. "I couldn't see doing all that stuff with her. The kids; building a life."

Sally's eyes urged him to go on.

"Jana was great. We were pretty compatible, but there was something missing." For him, anyhow. "I liked her a lot, but it didn't go deeper than that." They sure hadn't had that "you're my one and only" thing that Sally'd had with Pete. Not that Ben was about to mention her husband and get her all depressed again.

Jana had made him wary about getting into another serious relationship. She'd been hurt when they broke up, even though he'd never been anything but honest. Seemed like she got some expectations into her head, and maybe felt more for him than he did for her. "The one-night stand thing's worn thin, but I'm nowhere near ready to settle down. When I do date someone, I'm real clear that it's just for fun, and I make sure she's of the same mind."

"Seems like the best approach." Sally smiled a little. "I always thought women were crazy if they figured they could rope a cowboy before he was good and ready. But I guess some of them just don't understand how rodeo can get into your blood."

"That's for sure. It's one hell of a way to try to make a living, but once it's in your blood it's hard to give up." He straightened, wincing as his shoulder twinged. "I'll get my portable barbecue out, get going on those burgers."

She raised her forearms from the fence rail she'd been leaning on and crossed her arms in front of her chest. "If you're going to stay," she said slowly, "you can move your trailer to a better location. Down where my truck and horse trailer are parked." She gestured. "You'll find some flat ground and you'll have a pretty view." Then, as if she didn't want him to think she was being too nice, she added gruffly, "And you won't clog up my parking lot."

Ben suppressed a laugh. "Thanks. I'll do that."

"There's a water tap, if you want to run a hose to it. The closest electric outlet's by the barn door, but maybe we could patch some extension cords together."

Yes, Sally knew all about life on the road. "I'll take

the water, but don't worry about power. I can run my generator every now and then. Hopefully, I'd be far enough away that the noise wouldn't bother you or the horses."

"That should be fine." She cast a final look at the pregnant mare, who was grazing. "I'll go pick salad veggies."

"Before I forget, give me your cell number. In case I run into any other prospective clients."

She did, and he input it into his phone and gave her his in exchange, and then they went their separate ways. She was so prickly nowadays, he mused. Softening every now and then, but mostly trying to keep him at a distance. Her body language was like that too: those guarded expressions, the arms crossed over her chest. Even her clothing was different. Either she'd lost weight recently, or she bought her clothes a size too large. Always a shirt over her tee, and a long-sleeved one at that. She didn't even roll up her sleeves on a hot July afternoon. The only flesh that was visible was her work-roughened hands, her unmade-up face, the stretch of her neck, and a small curve of freckled skin not covered by the high necklines of her tee and shirt. It was almost like she wanted to disappear inside her clothes.

Seven years ago, she'd been a vibrant, confident woman, a rodeo queen at the top of her game, passionately in love with the man of her dreams. Had Pete's death changed her so dramatically? Or had something else happened to create this wary, closed-in woman?

One day, she would talk to him. From what the physiotherapist had said, it would be a couple of weeks at least before he could think of rejoining Dusty. Why not spend it here? Ben knew how to be patient, although he had more experience doing it with horses than with women. Eventually, the animal trusted you. It'd be the same with Sally.

He was smart enough to realize that he might be no more successful at hooking up with her than he'd been seven years ago, but before he left Caribou Crossing, he'd get her to smile and laugh again.

Chapter Six

Ben was more subtle these days, Sally reflected as she picked leaf lettuce from the garden. More effective, because he wormed his way around her defenses with logic and teasing—as well as with those warm brown eyes and flashing white smile. He was a hard man to resist.

So had Pete been, when he'd set out to court her. She couldn't let her guard down.

She pulled green onions from the soil, the tender green stalks and white bulbs so fresh and appealing. Baby radishes, their red and white outsides hinting at the crisp, zippy taste inside. Carrots, vivid orange with those feathery green tops. This garden gave her an amazing amount of pleasure, on top of the fact that fresh-picked produce was almost free and tasted much better than grocery-delivered. If Ben stayed, as he seemed set on doing, she might have time to keep up with the garden. Maybe even figure out a way to deal with the deer and rabbits.

She should e-mail Corrie and tell her how the garden was doing. And ask if things were okay with whatever personal situation had led her to quit a job she'd seemed happy with.

Ben had pretty much come out and accused Sally of being uncaring. It wasn't true, but with Pete she'd learned to keep her life private. That meant not asking other people about their personal lives, because they might ask questions back.

Sally straightened and pressed a hand to her lower back. It ached a little, but wasn't as sore as it had been before Ben started helping out.

She took her basket of pretty vegetables into the kitchen and turned on the radio. George Strait—a rodeo cowboy himself—was singing "Check Yes or No." She hummed along as she started putting together a salad. All she had in the fridge was ranch dressing, so hopefully Ben would be fine with that.

The salad looked so fresh and colorful, it inspired her to make a dessert one too, cutting up an apple, an orange, and a banana. Something healthy to go along with the brownies.

When she went outside to put the vegetable salad on the table, Ben was walking toward the house. The straps of a recyclable bag were hooked over his right forearm, and in his right hand he carried two stacked plates with three hamburgers on top. He really was adept with just one good arm.

Adept . . . A hum of awareness rippled through her. Damn the man for having this effect on her.

He came up the steps. "Salad looks great. It must be nice having your own garden."

"Or at least as much of it as the deer and rabbits are willing to share." She relieved him of the plates, and put one of the burgers on the bottom one. "These look delicious." Big patties of seared meat rested inside whole wheat kaiser buns. "What's in the bag?"

"Didn't know what you liked." He took out a package of cheddar cheese, a tomato, an onion, and bottles of ketchup, mustard, and pickles. "I figured we could fix our own."

Considerate. As he so often was. When he wasn't poking into her private business or stirring up her long-dormant sexuality.

She went into the kitchen to get a cutting board and a couple of knives. Through the screened window, she called, "Want a beer?"

"You bet."

She took a bottle from the fridge and paused, her hand hovering beside a second one. Decisively, she closed her fingers around it. Nothing went as well with burgers as a cold beer.

Once she and Ben were both seated, they doctored their burgers, dished out salad, and dug in. Through the screen door and window, the radio provided easy background listening, so low that she recognized songs but didn't really hear the words.

"Do you like Monique?" she asked.

"Yeah, she's great. Totally gets what it's like for a professional athlete. She was a figure skater. She and her pairs partner made the Olympic team."

Sally had never met Monique, only spoken to her over the phone. The woman always sounded competent and upbeat, and she spoke English with a charming French Canadian accent. Now, hearing about the physiotherapist's skating career, Sally imagined an impossibly fit, beautiful, graceful, strong, determined, pretty much perfect woman. "Impressive."

"I know. That was back in the early nineties. They didn't medal but she said the experience was incredible. Her partner wanted to retire afterward. Rather than start all over with a new guy, she retired, too. Found a new career."

So the woman was likely to be fortyish. Probably married, with kids. There was absolutely no reason Sally should find that fact reassuring.

Ben told her more about his appointment, then asked her about her day. She told him about the trail ride with Wenda and her kids, and discussed a problem one of her barrel racing students was having. He asked good questions, listened to her, and offered suggestions but no criticism. With Pete, conversation had some-times felt like she was being grilled or lectured, but this was . . . nice. There was a back and forth, a give and take.

Why had she and Corrie never done this? Neither of them had sought it out, the way Ben had tonight. Sally knew her reasons. Now she wondered about Corrie's.

When Sally had made it three-quarters of the way through her giant burger, she shoved the plate aside. "That was delicious, but I can't eat a bite more. Want to finish it?"

"You're trying to fill me up so you'll get all the brownies." He slid the meat and tomato from her burger, but left the bun.

"You're on to me."

Ben teased and joked a lot. He pushed sometimes, but was willing to back off. He didn't set traps with his words or his actions. She could actually relax with him.

She checked her beer bottle. It was still well more than half full. Yes, her relaxation had to do with Ben, not with getting drunk and silly.

Finished eating, he stacked the two dirty plates. From his tote bag, he pulled out a bakery box. The ketchup and other condiments went back in the bag.

She stood and held out her hand. "I'll put that stuff in the fridge. Want some coffee?"

"Sounds good."

She went in to turn on the coffeemaker and fetch the fruit salad and a couple of bowls. When she put the salad on the table, he said, "Nice. I love fruit. Thanks, Sally."

"You're welcome. I'll get the coffee." How about that? A man thanking her for something as simple as tossing three kinds of fruit into a salad, rather than expecting her to produce a fancy meal. Ben was about as different from Pete as she could imagine, she mused as she poured coffee into two mugs.

Except for the fact that, as with Pete in the beginning, she found him handsome and appealing. Magnetically appealing. Sexually appealing. Not that she'd ever let Ben know that, she thought as she sat down across from him. Sex did *not* have a place in her life.

Chocolate hadn't had a place for a while either, but tonight it did. She happily took a brownie as well as a serving of fruit salad. She was so caught up in savoring the rich fudginess that she didn't notice, until she finished, that Ben hadn't taken the other treat. "No brownie? Did I succeed in filling you up?"

"I watch my carbs. Help yourself. Or save it to have with your lunch tomorrow."

When she thought about protesting, he said, "Take it and say thank you."

This was one battle she'd happily let him win. "Thank you, Ben." She took the bakery box to the kitchen and put it in the fridge, then came back and lit citronella candles.

When she sat down again, she said, "We need to discuss ground rules."

He rolled his eyes. "Thought you'd forgotten."

"I was waiting until you were mellowed out on cholesterol and alcohol." Actually, she almost had forgotten, she'd been so caught up in enjoying the company and food.

"Do I need to get a notebook and take notes?"

"Not unless you've been concussed so many times you have no memory."

When he rolled his eyes, she said, "Okay, rule number one. Your health comes first. Don't do anything that strains your shoulder. Take whatever time you need for physio appointments and exercise."

"Agreed."

That was easier than she'd expected. She opened her mouth to state rule two, but he spoke first. "My turn. My first rule is—"

"Wait a minute. You don't get to make rules."

"Sure I do," he said easily. "It's not a dictatorship. And my first rule is, your health's important, too. Don't lift anything too heavy; ask me for help. Don't work too hard without taking a break."

His rule surprised a smile out of her. "Today's been my easiest day since Corrie left," she admitted. "In fact it's been the nicest day since—" She stopped herself, then finished, "In quite a while." What she'd almost said was that it was the nicest day she'd had since the beginning of her marriage.

Now that was a disconcerting thought.

Her nicest day in quite a while? Damn, that sounded good to his ears. Ben wished he could give Sally a big hug, but was pretty sure that'd make her back off.

So he settled for saying, "I'm glad. Now, what's your second rule?"

"You're not my employee. You don't have to work regular hours. Chauncey's Pride needs exercise and you need to keep training. Take off whenever you need to. Or want to, like to go into town or take a ride in the country."

He gave her a slow smile. "Okay. On the condition that you agree to my rule two. You gotta take some time off, too." It'd be pushing his luck to suggest she come into town for a drink and some dancing, so he said, "And come for a ride with me."

"I can't just take off and go riding."

"Then I'll pay you for a guided trail ride."

"Ben! I won't let you pay me."

"Then agree with my rule two, or I won't agree with yours."

She shook her head, but her eyes danced. "You're determined to get your own way, aren't you?"

"Pretty much." At least when it came to giving her brownies and getting her to take some R&R. He studied her face, wishing he could smooth that curl of red-gold hair off her cheek and caress her skin. "You done with the rules now?"

Her lips twisted like a grin was struggling to escape. "Rule three. Don't eat chicken; don't even talk about eating chicken. If you want fried chicken, go into town."

He chuckled. "That one I can live with. That it?"

"For now." She cocked a brow. "You?"

"Me, too." He rose and stacked plates and bowls. Last night, he'd given her space and gone to do barn chores. Tonight, he cast out a feeler. "Want me to give you a hand with these?"

"No," she said quickly, grabbing the stack. "Thanks. You can get started in the barn."

Damn it, he wanted to know the truth, and to find some way of helping her. How could he convince her to trust him? Quietly, he asked, "What man scared you, Sally?"

"No one!" The dishes rattled in her grip. "I told you that."

He rescued the dishes before she dropped them, and set them back on the table. "I don't think you told me the truth. Either you think I'm a real jerk—"

"I don't."

"I figured, or you wouldn't be here with me. So it seems you're wary of men in general."

She crossed her arms in front of her chest, so tightly that her fingers bit into her upper arms. "It's sensible to be cautious."

"Sure it is. But with you it's more than that." Studying her taut, closed face, her tightly wound arms, he sighed. No way was this woman ready to open up to him. "I get that you don't want to talk about it. But I need to know if he's still a threat."

After a very long moment, she slowly shook her head.

"Okay. Good. If you ever want to talk about it, I'm here. And you need to know, I'm not like him. I will never hurt you."

"All right." She said the words, but without conviction, and her eyes were skeptical.

He had to be patient and show her he was a man she could trust. "I'll be in the barn."

As Ben turned and walked away, he pondered her behavior. One threatening incident wouldn't have made her so mistrusting. Something really awful—

like rape—might have. But Sally acted like a wounded creature who'd sustained long-term harm. . . .

His long stride hitched. Not Pete. It couldn't have been Pete, the man who was so madly in love with her.

Madly. Obsessively. Possessively.

Crap. Had it been Pete? If the man who'd swept her off her feet, romanced her, made her fall passionately in love had abused her over the course of their marriage . . .

But no. How could that have happened? Sally had been strong, independent, feisty. She'd never have let a man do that to her.

He shook his head, realizing that he was oversimplifying. The whole spousal abuse thing sickened him and made no sense. Yet he'd seen enough articles, even heard one or two stories, to know that the dynamic was anything but simple. It was wrong to blame the victim for not escaping the situation. Often, the victim was no more capable of running away than was an abused horse confined in a locked stall.

In the barn, he got to work cleaning the day's tack. Likely, his imagination was acting up on him. There must be some other explanation for the dramatic change in Sally's personality.

He heard her bring a couple of horses into the barn. She did that with boarded horses that required grooming and tacking up first thing in the morning.

She murmured to the horses as she settled them, and then she came to lean against the frame of the tack room door. "I checked on Sunshine Song. She's restless, pacing. There's wax on her teats. She may be going into labor. I'm going to bandage her tail and clean her."

Ben gazed up at her from where he sat on a stool, cleaning a bridle. "Anything I can do?"

"She'll probably foal with no problems, but I'll keep

an eye on her. With the outside light turned on low, I can see her out the office window and she'll still have privacy."

He had noticed the shabby old sofa in the barn office, set facing the window. "You're going to stay up all night, waiting to see if she foals? Sometimes it can take a couple of days."

"They usually foal at night, so it'll likely be tonight or tomorrow night. I won't worry as much during the day."

"You plan to stay up for two nights? You do this whenever you have a pregnant mare?"

"There are only a couple each year. Ben, I don't want anything happening to my mares or to their foals."

"No, of course not. I'll spell you off. We'll take shifts."

"I can't let you—"

"Gaaah! Sometimes you piss me off, Sally."

She flinched, tensing in the doorway as if she was ready to run.

He lowered his voice, but didn't hide his annoyance. "Don't look at me like I'm going to hit you. I would never do that, no matter how mad you make me."

"I'm not trying to make you mad," she said in a placating tone that grated on his nerves. He'd rather she stood up for herself than backed down.

"Could have fooled me," he grumbled. "Anyhow, I'm not going to argue. We'll take shifts so we'll both be reasonably functional tomorrow. Otherwise you'll be exhausted and I'll have to do all the heavy lifting." He raised his sling. "Which won't be good for my shoulder."

Her head tilted to one side as she thought about it. "Okay. You have a point. What is it, almost nine?" She checked her watch. "I'll take the first four hours. I'll do some work on the computer and keep an eye on Song. I'll wake you at one and you can take the second shift."

Yeah, like he trusted her to rouse him? "No, I'm wide awake." Not because he wasn't tired, more due to the pain in his shoulder. "I'll take the first shift." When she opened her mouth, he held up his hand. "Don't even think of trying to argue."

He stood. "Tack's done. I'm gonna make a thermos of coffee and get my tablet." And take a painkiller. "Then I'll settle down in the office and do some e-mail, read, entertain myself. You go on up to the house and get some sleep. Keep your cell handy. I'll call if Song goes into labor."

"No, I'll stay in the barn. If there's a problem, things can happen fast. A couple years back, we had a red bag delivery."

He'd heard the term before, but never seen one. "That's where the placenta separates from the uterus, and it's delivered first?"

"Yes. It can be fatal for the foal if you don't cut the placenta and get the foal out immediately."

"Sounds scary."

"Terrifying. But I'd seen it once before, when I was a teen, so I knew what to do."

"Okay, I hear you. Stay in the barn and I'll wake you if anything changes with Song."

She pressed her lips together and studied him solemnly.

"Sally, I won't go to sleep. I promise. You can trust me."

Chapter Seven

Trust Ben with her horses? They were the most important thing in the world to her.

But he loved horses too, and would never want to see one come to harm. "All right," Sally said. "You go and get your stuff. Oh, I put a couple of eggs on your trailer steps—my ladies' contribution to your breakfast."

"Nice. Thank them for me, will you?"

After he left, she went out to ready Song for foaling and whisper reassuring words to her. Back in the barn, she checked on Campion. His hoof showed no sign of swelling or heat. "You'll have a new shoe tomorrow, boy. I bet you'll be glad to go out in the paddock with your friends."

In the office, she checked e-mail. No new students or boarders, but she remembered the slip of paper Ben had given her. Though she was shy about calling a stranger, she forced herself to do it. Andrew's voice immediately put her at ease. He sounded excited; after he had a quick conversation with his husband they agreed on Monday morning for the first lesson.

Sally was about to shut down the computer when another e-mail popped into her Inbox. It was an application for Corrie's position, from a young man. She responded, saying that the job was no longer available. Then, with Corrie on her mind, she sent her a quick note.

> Hi, Corrie. I hope everything is okay with you. The horses and I miss you. I think Sunshine Song is almost ready to foal. The vegetable garden is doing great and I love having fresh produce. So delicious. Thanks for planting the garden. I know it was a lot of work and I'm sorry you don't get to reap the benefits. Take care, and let me know how you're doing if you have a chance. Sally

Ben stepped into the room, his size and presence making the space feel crowded.

"Guess what?" she said. "Andrew and his husband are coming for a lesson on Monday."

"Cool. Now turn off the computer and get some rest."

Could she sleep on the sofa, with him so close by? She could go up to the apartment Corrie had used, but if anything went wrong with Song, every second could be crucial. Stalling, she said, "They're software designers and work at home, so they have flexible schedules. I'm glad they can come Monday morning; it's one of my slow times."

"Good. Now curl up on the sofa. I'll use the desk chair."

The hard wooden chair with the straight back. It would kill his shoulder.

"The sofa's too small for curling up." She sat at one end, up against the armrest, and raised her booted feet to the battered coffee table. "You can sit on the other side." She'd be happier if this were a four-seater rather than a two-seater. Not that she thought Ben was going to attack her in her sleep, but being close to him was unsettling.

He clicked off the office light. It was nine-thirty. The sun had only just set and there was still some light in the sky as well as that coming from the dim outside barn light.

Gazing out, Sally said, "Song is pacing."

Ben sat down on the other side of the sofa and opened his thermos. "Coffee?" he offered.

"No, thanks."

He poured himself a cup and she almost wished she'd said yes. The brew smelled stronger and richer than the economy brand she bought. Balancing his tablet on his lap, he manipulated the touch screen. He wasn't a huge man—bronc riders usually weren't—but all his lean, muscled masculinity seemed to take up a lot of space even though their bodies didn't touch. Or maybe it was just that she was so aware of his physicality. Of his male strength—something that could be scary. Of his heat, and his scent like pine needles in summer— things that were scary in a different way, tugging at something inside her, urging her to move closer.

Instead, she turned her head away, closed her eyes, and tried to relax her neck muscles. She forced herself to take slow, deep breaths, but sleep was a long way off.

She was aware of Ben shifting position, reaching for his coffee. At first, each movement made her tense up, but gradually she got used to having him there. He was watching over Song, and it almost felt as if he was watching over her, too. . . .

"Sally?" A quiet voice drew her out of wherever she'd been floating.

"Hmm?" Her heavy eyelids didn't want to open. Her cheek rested on soft fabric, with heat and hardness beneath it. A strange pillow, but surprisingly comfortable.

Something stroked her right arm gently, up and down, and—

Her eyes flew open. Oh, Lord, she was cuddled up against Ben, her head on his good shoulder and his arm around her. She jerked away. "Sorry."

"Don't be. It was nice. But I think Song's having contractions. She's swishing her tail and nosing at her flank. She lay down then got up again."

Sally jumped up and flew to the window. The horse sank to the ground and then rose restlessly. "I think you're right." She glanced at her watch. Eleven-thirty.

Ben joined her as the palomino went down again, on her side, and fluid gushed from her body. "Her water broke. It's coming," Sally breathed, starting to count time on her watch. An uncomplicated labor went amazingly fast; the foal could be born within five minutes. "Song's pushing; I can see her muscles working." She'd lost track of how many foals she'd seen born since the first when she was five years old, but each time filled her with wonder. Excitement, fear, hope.

Not long after, Ben said, "I see the membrane—and a foot!" His tone conveyed the same sense of wonder. When he stepped closer and grasped her hand, his touch felt surprisingly right and she didn't move away.

Squinting in the dim light, she said, "Another foot. The front legs are coming out. We should see the head any second now."

But nothing happened. The two forelegs remained extended from the horse's body, but the head didn't appear. Sally checked her watch. It was four minutes since the membrane had broken. "Come on, Song," she muttered. "Come on, little baby, come out now. Please be okay."

Sally slid her cell from her shirt pocket. "I wonder if

we need to pull the foal out? Or reach in and turn the head?" She thumbed to the vet's number at the top of her contact list. It had now been five minutes. She pressed the screen and listened to the phone ring. "Pick up, Max. Please."

Only two rings, then the vet, Maxine Grey, said crisply, "Sally, what's up?"

"It's Sunshine Song." She recited exactly what had happened. "I still don't see the head."

"Its head and neck may be bent backward. Don't try to turn it or push the legs back in. Get the mare up and walking. We don't want her pushing, and we want to reduce pressure in the birth canal. Ideally, the foal will slide back into the uterus by itself and get repositioned."

Phone to her ear, Sally raced to the tack room to get a halter with a lead rope. "What if that doesn't happen?"

"I'm on my way. I may be able to reposition the foal. If not, I'll have to bring Song in and do a C-section—or do an emergency one on-site. But let's not cross that bridge yet. I'm in my truck and I'm hanging up now. If anything happens that worries you, call and I'll answer."

"Thanks." Sally rushed outside, the halter in her hand.

Ben was on her heels. Voice low, he asked, "What's the scoop? Can I help?"

"Maybe." Whispering, she filled him in.

Approaching the horse, she crooned, "Hey there, Song. I'm afraid you're going to have to take an intermission. You can't push. You've got to get up and walk. Max will be here soon."

To Ben, she said, "You talk to her, too. Stroke her, soothe her."

He obeyed, his voice low and reassuring, while Sally

put the halter on. She pulled lightly but steadily on the rope. "Up now, Song."

The palomino shifted her weight, gathered herself, and then with a grunt rose awkwardly.

"Ben, you lead her." Sally put the rope in his hand. "I'll walk beside her." She positioned herself at the horse's shoulder, resting a comforting hand on Song's sweaty coat and telling her that everything was going to be okay. As she tried to calm the horse with her touch and words, Sally realized that Ben's quiet support was having that very effect on her.

It was after two when Ben walked with Sally and the vet, Max, to the parking lot. He wondered how often Max got called out at night after putting in a full day's work. Hell of a job. One that she clearly did very well, and loved. As Max loaded her medical kit into her truck, Sally asked, "You really think Moon Song will be okay? And Sunshine Song?"

"They're looking good," Max said reassuringly. "Once the foal adjusted his position, the delivery seemed perfectly normal."

They'd been lucky. The foal's legs had slipped back into his mom's body as she walked. When the vet arrived and did an internal exam, she'd confirmed that his position was correct. They had let the restless palomino lie down again, and the foal had slid out in the space of a couple of minutes. A perfect black colt.

"Check them around dawn," Max instructed. "If Moon Song hasn't passed the meconium or isn't urinating, or if you see any other possible problems, give me a call. Don't forget to dip the umbilical stump in antiseptic solution every few hours. I'll drop by this afternoon when I get a chance."

Max glanced from Sally to Ben, and back again. "You two have had a long night. Might as well get some sleep." Her tone was neutral. Deliberately so, it seemed to him.

Sally'd been so anxious about her horse, she hadn't introduced Ben to the vet. He'd done it himself, giving Max his name and saying he was Sally's new assistant. Now he kept any hint of innuendo from his voice when he said, "Sounds good. Night, Max. Nice to meet you."

"You too, Ben."

As Max drove away, Sally plopped down on a mounting block. "Whew." She blew out air. "That was scary."

"All's well that ends well, right? Let's follow Max's advice and get some shut-eye. It'll be dawn before we know it."

"I think I should stay up." She rotated an obviously stiff neck and he heard it crunch.

"Sore neck?"

"It tightens up when I'm worried."

He could help with that, if she let him. The woman had slept in the curve of his arm. Maybe her body had just slumped over, but he wanted to believe that her instincts told her to trust him. Stepping behind her, he removed his left arm from the sling and gently rested both hands on her shoulders. Her shoulders rose, tense, but she didn't shake him off or move away. Encouraged, he massaged lightly, through her sweatshirt. She remained taut, then her muscles loosened under his hands.

His shoulder ached fiercely, but a few minutes of massage shouldn't do any real damage.

He moved from her sweatshirt to the bare skin of her neck, working his thumbs into the knots. "You're all locked up," he said quietly. His hands warmed as he worked, and so did her skin. She even tilted her head slightly, giving him better access.

It wasn't only his hands that were heating. Arousal was thick in his blood, tightening his groin. He tried to ignore his own physical sensations.

What mattered was that Sally was starting to trust him. Sharing tonight—the worry, and then the joy of a healthy foal—had helped. Slowly, she was coming to realize that he wasn't a bad guy like the man who'd hurt her. All Ben wanted to do was help, to make her life easier.

Well, really he wanted a lot more than that. He wanted to change his massaging strokes to caressing ones, to press his lips to her soft, heated skin. But he wouldn't.

"Max seems pretty smart," he murmured. Gently, he braced the left side of Sally's head in the curve of his palm so he could work the right side of her neck.

"She is." She tipped her head more snugly into his hand, stretching her neck under his fingers.

He swallowed back a groan of need and tried to sound normal. "She says the two Songs will be fine until morning. And for you, she prescribed sleep."

The inflection in her voice when she answered told him she was smiling. "She's a horse doctor, not a people one."

He didn't respond, didn't argue, just kept rubbing her neck.

"Okay," she said, "I guess she's right. We should both— wait, what are you doing?" She slipped free from his hands, rose, and turned to face him. "Ben! Put your arm back in that sling!"

Rolling his eyes, he said, "Yes, ma'am," glad that her gaze was focused on his face, not below his waist. "I'll do that, because I for one can listen to good advice. I'm heading off to bed. See you at dawn."

She nodded, her face unnaturally pale in the moonlight. "Ben?" Gazing up at him, she seemed to be considering her words. "Thank you for being there tonight. It made everything easier. Nicer."

His heart warmed. "Hey, I wouldn't have missed it for the world." He wanted to kiss her. Just one soft, light kiss. On her lips, or he'd even settle for her forehead. But they'd come a long way tonight and he didn't want to risk spoiling things. He raised his good hand in a salute and walked toward his rig, feeling her gaze on his back. Or maybe that was just wishful thinking. He wouldn't turn and find out.

Inside his cramped home, he took a pain pill, had a long drink of water, stripped off his clothes, and eased his aching body into bed. Into his mind came the image of Sally's dazzling smile when that little black colt tottered to its feet. Grinning himself, he tumbled into sleep.

Dawn light and a medley of bird trills, chirps, and twitters woke Ben what seemed like only minutes later, and he groaned. But then he remembered the events of the night.

Anxious to see how the mare and foal were doing, hopeful that the new mellowness between him and Sally would continue, he clambered out of bed.

Today, he wouldn't take the time to make a healthy breakfast. Instead, between sips of strong black coffee, he slathered a multigrain bagel with cream cheese and strawberry jam. He slipped into the annoying sling and, with the bagel in his cuffed hand and the mug in his good one, went to visit Sunshine Song and Moon Song.

Sally was already in the birthing paddock, dipping the foal's umbilical stump in antiseptic solution while Sunshine Song watched protectively. When Sally finished, she stroked the colt's shiny black neck. Then, seeing Ben, she came over, smiling. "All's well. Moon's peeing and he passed the meconium."

"That's great." Had to love the horse world, where topics like a foal's first dump were cheerful breakfast conversation. Speaking of which. "You had breakfast?"

She shook her head. "Not yet."

He set his coffee mug on a fence post and held out the bagel. "Want to share?"

"Thanks, but I'll go get some cereal now that I know these two are okay."

"I'm gonna hang out here, have my bagel and coffee, then I'll get to work."

"If you can tear yourself away," she teased.

As pretty a sight as the mare and foal were, the sparkling emerald glints in Sally's eyes and the smile on her face were even more addictive.

After she'd gone, he ate breakfast, said good morning to Chaunce, and then went into the barn and readied horses for a couple of early riders.

The actions and the scents—horse, straw, hay, manure, leather—were familiar. Growing up on a ranch, he was used to the routine involved in caring for animals. At Ryland Riding, some tasks were the same, some different, but it was easy to slip into the flow of it. Life in the country had a rhythm governed by dawn and dusk, by seasons, by cycles of animals and crops. The work was physically demanding, occasionally mentally challenging, and always satisfying. For him. His sister, older than him by ten years, had been bored to tears and had moved to the city.

When Ben had chosen rodeo, or it had chosen him, he'd figured that one day he'd come full circle, back to the ranch where he'd grown up. Now, though he understood why his parents had sold it, their decision left him feeling like he didn't have a home base. Nothing more than a spare bedroom in his parents' house in Calgary, or the bunkhouse at the horse trainer's where he worked in the off season. Strange how a guy who spent most of his life on the road could miss having a home base.

Chapter Eight

Midmorning, Sally had just turned Campion out in the paddock after the farrier's visit. Her cell rang as she walked back to the barn. "Ryland Riding," she answered.

"Hey, you," a warm male voice said.

"Dave! You're back." How wonderful to hear that familiar voice. She'd missed him and Cassidy in the month they'd been on their honeymoon.

"Yes, we got back on Sunday. Sorry I didn't call earlier, but there was so much to catch up on at the inn."

"I bet." Dave had spent years restoring the historic Wild Rose Inn, and had done a fabulous job. "But Madisun handled things okay?" Cassidy, Dave's brand-new wife, shared the assistant manager position with Madisun Joe and had persuaded Dave to leave the younger woman in charge.

"Madisun did great. It was good for both of us, me learning to delegate and her developing more confidence."

A cheeky female voice said, in the background, "Told you so."

Sally smiled. "Say hi to Cassidy."

Dave did, and his wife called, "Hi to you too, Sally."

Sally went into the office. "Did you have a wonderful honeymoon? How was Italy?" she asked Dave as she sank down on the sofa in the same spot where she'd sat last night.

"Fantastic. Next time we see you, we'll tell you all about it."

"How was Cassidy's health?" She'd been diagnosed with multiple sclerosis last year.

"Terrific. A couple of pseudo-exacerbations when we had unavoidably long days, but no new attacks and mostly she was pretty symptom-free."

Cassidy's voice came again. "Even if I did try his patience more than once."

Sally smiled. Dave was superorganized. Cassidy was a free spirit and had struggled against the structure imposed by her disease: a treatment plan, lots of rest, a regular exercise regimen, and so on. "You two are good for each other."

"That's for sure," Dave said. "Now what's this I hear about Ryland Riding? Corrie left, and you have some new guy, Ben, who's an old friend?"

She frowned. "How did you know that?" Not that it was a secret, but she hated people gossiping about her.

"Sally, it's a small town."

"Which I'm not a part of," she reminded him.

"Doesn't stop the rumor mill. I heard about Ben from, let's see, Terry at the Gold Pan diner, Madeleine at the bank, and Tiffany Knight who was in for lunch and said her son Marty was excited to meet a rodeo star."

And Ben had been around for all of two days. Sally shook her head. This was why Pete had been so adamant about keeping their lives private. "Why were they telling you?" she asked grumpily.

"They know we're friends. So what's the story, Sally? Who is this guy?"

"I told you I used to barrel race, right? Ben was riding saddle broncs. He's still competing." Not wanting to get into family stuff, she didn't mention her sister. "He was at the Williams Lake Stampede and Rodeo and came by to say hi. He's injured and needs time to heal. Rather than drive himself and his horse back to Alberta, he's helping me out in exchange for having a place to park his trailer, look after his horse, and train. We're friends, Dave. That's it."

Friends. The word popped out, a word she had previously only applied to Dave, Cassidy, and Dave's daughter, Robin. Yet it felt like the right one to describe Ben. The fact that he stirred up her blood in a disconcerting way . . . well, that was a completely separate and ridiculous thing she'd never admit to.

"I kind of figured," Dave said. "I know how you felt about Pete."

No, he didn't. She had let him believe that Pete had been the love of her life and that she'd never get over his loss. No one knew the truth about her life with Pete, nor about the way he'd died.

"You and Ben should come for dinner," Dave said.

"Oh! Thanks, but, Dave, you know I don't like going into town." Besides, going out for dinner together was the kind of thing couples did, and she and Ben most definitely weren't a couple.

"I know you're shy around people. We'll have dinner at our place. You and Ben, Cassidy, Robin, and me."

"I have lessons late in the afternoons, and horses to get ready for owners who're coming out to ride."

"Not every day. Right?"

Not on Fridays and Sundays. She tried a different

approach. "Ben's only here for a short time. I don't want to drag him into, uh . . . I mean, not that meeting you and your family would be . . . Look, Dave, I just don't see it working."

"Give me that," Cassidy said in the background and then, into the phone, "Sally?"

"Hi, Cassidy. Welcome back."

"Thanks. As for dinner, Dave's protective instinct has kicked in and he wants to check Ben out."

Of course. Sally should have known it was more than a casual dinner invitation.

Cassidy went on. "You know he won't back down when he gets like this. You might as well stop arguing. Besides, I'm dying to tell you about Italy. What nights work for you?"

Sally had been outmaneuvered, and she didn't want to be rude to her friends. Reluctantly, she said, "I'd have to check with Ben, but the best days for me are Fridays and Sundays."

"Perfect! This is Thursday, so let's do tomorrow night. What time can you come?"

"Tomorrow? Uh . . ." This was happening too fast for her to think. "Around six-thirty? Is that too late?" *Please say it's too late.*

"Great!" the other woman said. "I'll assume Ben's free unless you let me know otherwise. We're looking forward to meeting him."

Sally slowly lowered the phone. A sound made her look up as Ben stepped into the office. Sweat beaded his dark forehead, and she had the absurd urge to reach up and brush back a few strands of damp black hair. She put the phone in her pocket and clasped her hands. "Did you hear that?"

"The last part. Sorry, but you had the office door open."

"It's fine." She bit her lip. "Friends have invited us for dinner. It seems people are talking about you. Us. That's . . . I hate the idea of people gossiping about me."

"It's human nature. Especially in a small town. Besides, what's the big deal? You've got an old friend visiting, helping you out."

"But what if they think . . ." She ducked her head, embarrassed.

"That we're more than friends?"

Keeping her head down, she nodded.

"Would that be so terrible?" he asked. "You're a widow. I'm single. Consenting adults; no one getting hurt."

She tried not to flinch at the last word. When she *had* been getting hurt, she and Pete had kept their secret so well that no one suspected.

"You're allowed to date," Ben said.

"I don't want to date," she rejoined, lifting her head. She wished she hadn't, because his strong-boned face and warm chestnut eyes were too appealing, making her question the truth of her words.

No, that was crazy. She knew better than to fall for a man again—much less a rodeo star who was only in town for a couple of weeks. Besides, she had a business to run and a reputation to protect. Her private life, pitiful as it was, should remain private.

Ben's mouth had tightened. Probably, like everyone else, he figured she was still grieving Pete's death, and after three years ought to get over it. Fine. Let him think that.

"Anyhow," she said, "we're invited for dinner, but we

don't have to go. Dave can be a little overprotective, so it might be awkward."

"Macho cowboy here," Ben joked. "He doesn't scare me."

The man had a way of making her want to grin. "No, but—"

"Sally, don't overthink it. I'd like to meet your friends. What's the big deal?" A considering expression crossed his face. "Did you and this Dave guy ever date?"

"No! Never. It was never like that between us." She'd never once felt attracted to Dave, and she was sure the same was true for him.

"Did Dave and Pete get along?"

"They never met. I only got to know Dave a couple of years ago."

"Oh?" He paused. "Did you and Pete have friends in the area?"

Hah. "We didn't have time to socialize."

"Uh-huh." He studied her for a long moment, and then he turned away. "I came in to check the schedule." Gazing at the tacked-up chart, he said. "I see there's a couple of hours clear in the early afternoon. Seems like a good time to take Chaunce out."

"Of course. Anytime."

"Come with us."

"I can't—"

"Bet there's a horse that could use a nice long trail ride."

"You have the most annoying habit of not listening to me." And yet he did it in such a different way from how Pete had. Ben teased rather than threatened.

"No need to, when I already know what you're going to say."

She pressed her lips together. "How can you annoy me and amuse me at the same time?"

His grin flashed. "It's my special talent. So, how about it? Got a horse that needs exercise? Maybe the one that had the abscessed hoof?"

"Campion. Yes, he's been stall-bound for a while. The farrier just shooed him. He'd love to get out for a ride." She cocked her head and studied Ben's face, frowning slightly.

"What?"

"How do you do that? Get me to agree to things?" Pete had done it, too. He'd got her to do things that he said made her a good wife. Like always having dinner on the table when he wanted it, and being cool and businesslike with male clients. Like having sex with him whenever he was in the mood, no matter how she felt. Like covering the bruises he inflicted under long-sleeved shirts and not wincing when she moved.

"By showing you that you really want to do them."

Hmm. She did appreciate Ben's help, she enjoyed sharing meals with him, and maybe she did want an excuse to take Campion for a trail ride. But then in the beginning with Pete, she'd enjoyed making a home for them, and she'd been flattered by his possessiveness and his jealousy of other men. How could she trust her own judgment? "You confuse me," she said softly.

"If it's any consolation, you confuse me, too."

She hadn't the slightest idea what he meant by that, but wasn't going to ask.

Thursday afternoon, riding with Sally, Ben thought that a guy could get used to this. A pretty woman, good horses, fine weather. They trotted single file down a trail that followed a small, meandering river lined by cottonwoods, and then loped side by side across a rolling meadow. As they approached a bluff, a flock of grouse took off with a whir of wings.

Sally and Ben slowed their horses to a walk, and she gestured toward the bluff. "There's a spectacular view from the top." The trail was a narrow switchback. She rode ahead of him, shifting forward in the saddle to take her weight off her horse's hind legs. Ben admired her slim back, curvy butt, and the tousled sun-gilded curls below the brim of her hat.

When they reached the top, they dismounted and walked to the edge. He filled his lungs with fresh, pine-scented air and said appreciatively, "We're not in Alberta anymore." The scenery was more varied and lush than where he'd grown up. Here, the hay fields and range land were broken into an irregular patchwork by woods of hemlock, red cedar, and pine, by groves of cotton-wood and aspen, by streams and small lakes, and by hills and craggy bluffs.

"Do you figure you'll end up in Alberta?" Sally asked.

He watched a pair of hawks lazily riding thermals. "I guess. My parents are in Calgary now. So's my sister and her family. I won't live in a city, but I'll probably try to set up something nearby."

"Your own ranch or horse training business?"

"Maybe." He glanced at her, where she stood a foot away from him, her hat shading her face. "I'd like to be my own boss. But it'll depend on whether I win enough and can save enough." Maybe, years down the road, he'd achieve what Sally already had: owning a success-ful operation. But for now, rodeo was his life, and it was a good one.

"How long d'you plan on competing?"

"Haven't really thought about it. Could go another ten or so years, I guess."

"That might be pushing your luck, at least when it

comes to bronc riding." She shot a pointed glance at his sling.

Injuries did add up. "Perhaps. But not with roping. Some guys ride into their forties."

"You could go on the senior pro circuit."

He grimaced. "Don't imagine I'll think of myself as a senior when I'm forty."

"Keep falling off the broncs," she teased, "and you'll be as crippled as an eighty-year-old by the time you're forty."

"Now that's just mean." Without thinking, he reached out with his good arm, tucked it around her, and pulled her close.

Her body tensed.

He bit back a curse and released her. "Time to head back and get the horses ready for your kids' lesson."

She didn't say a word, just walked toward her bay gelding.

He sure would like to know what had happened to make Sally so jumpy. He'd like to beat up the guy who'd done this to her. Increasingly, he was coming to wonder if it might have been her husband. Little things like her not going to town, and her and Pete not having friends, were just too incongruous when Ben thought of the outgoing Sally he used to know.

Patience, he reminded himself. He had to win Sally's trust before she'd share the truth with him.

As they rode back down the bluff, he asked her about her afternoon's students and, as she shared stories, she relaxed again.

When they arrived back at Ryland Riding, they fell into their routine. As Ben got to know the horses' names, and figured out what he could do within the limitations of his injury, he and Sally became a more efficient team.

They had the horses ready by the time the first students arrived. This was another group of little kids, and once everyone was assembled, Sally told them, "We have a new arrival. My mare Sunshine Song had a baby last night. It's a colt—a boy—and his name is Moon Song. If you promise to be really quiet and not disturb them, you can have a peek."

Their faces bright with excitement, the children and their moms all promised, and Sally led them around to the foaling paddock. Ben trailed behind.

The colt and his mother were in the shade of a few cottonwoods. Moon was nursing, but released the mare's teat and turned his head to study the visitors who lined up along the fence. He looked just as curious as the children who gazed at him with hushed oohs and "Isn't he cute?" comments. Sally stood back watching, a smile on her face.

As if she felt Ben's gaze, she glanced toward him.

He gave her a smile and a nod, hoping to share the specialness of the moment. She nodded back, and held his gaze for a long moment. He liked it when the two of them connected, when she put aside whatever made her so wary.

Moon went back to nursing, and Sally herded her reluctant students to the lesson ring.

For Ben, the rest of the afternoon was pretty easy. Sally's second class was made up of adolescents and young teens, and they were responsible for grooming and tacking up their horses, then removing the tack after the lesson and currying the horses. After that, Sally had a lesson with two teenaged girlfriends.

He helped out with students and owners as needed, cleaned tack when it was finished with, and kept the barn tidy. When Max, the vet, came to check on the two Songs, he chatted briefly with her. Other than that, he did the exercises the physio had given him as well as most of his regular core, lower back, and leg exercises and stretches. It made for a pretty laid-back day, which was good since he'd had only three hours of sleep last night.

But Sally was on the go all the time, however. It was after seven when she finished, and he could see she was dragging.

"Why don't I throw together some dinner?" he offered.

She gazed at him, bleary-eyed. "I'm beat. I just want to look after my hens, grab a sandwich, and hit the sack. I'm not in the mood for company."

He studied her face. Should he say that he'd make her the sandwich, and that he didn't expect scintillating conversation? Earlier, she'd commented about him not listening, and always persuading her to agree to things. There'd been a troubled expression on her face.

Maybe this time he would not only listen, but take what she said at face value. "Okay, Sally, I hear you. You get a good sleep."

Her eyes widened slightly. "You're not going to argue?"

"Did you want me to?"

She blinked. "No, actually, I don't." A pause. "Thank you, Ben. Thank you for everything." Another blink, as if she was deciding what more to say. She settled for "See you in the morning."

Chapter Nine

What had she been thinking, letting Cassidy and Dave talk her into this? Late on Friday afternoon, Sally went into the barn where Ben was taking off Puffin's tack. "We can't go to dinner," she told him. "I don't know what I was thinking. I have to call Cassidy."

"Now?" Deftly, he slid off the saddle and pad so that they hooked over his good arm. "They'll have shopped, maybe started to cook. You can't cancel now."

"Then you go. I can't." Relief, tinged surprisingly with a little disappointment, seeped through her.

He took the saddle to the tack room and she undid the black-and-white gelding's bridle. When Ben came back carrying Puffin's halter, he asked, "Why can't you go?"

Sally slipped the bridle off as Ben put the halter on, his fingers brushing against hers. A tingle of heat rippled up her arm. She took a couple of steps backward, holding on to the bridle. "I can't leave this place unattended."

"You did when we went riding. You do it when you take people on trail rides."

"That's daytime. It's different."

"Hmm. What d'you figure might happen?" He began to give the horse a light curry.

"Anything. Fire, horse thieves, vandals. The owners who are coming in—"

"Are all ones who care for their own horses, didn't you say?" He moved around to the horse's other side.

"Yes, but they might need help with something, or have a question." She gazed at him across Puffin's back. "But I'm more worried about the other things. Fire, vandalism, and so on."

"Hmm. You've never left this place unattended at night?"

When did she ever go out at night? Only for Dave and Cassidy's wedding. "Corrie was here." Even during the day, Sally almost never left except to lead a trail ride.

Ben came back around the gelding and planted himself beside her. Right there, in her personal space, close enough that she could feel the heat he gave off. Or was that heat coming from her? "Call Heather," he said.

"Heather?" The sixteen-year-old was one of her occasional students.

"I talked to her when she came for her lesson the other day. She said she'd love to ride more often but can't afford to. I bet she'd babysit the place if you gave her a free lesson."

"I can't put a teenager in charge of Ryland Riding."

"All she has to do is watch out for fires and horse thieves and call you or 911 if something worries her. She strikes me as a responsible girl."

"I guess." Heather did seem to be mature and disciplined.

"You have a problem delegating."

"This is my place," she defended herself. "And I did

delegate to Corrie, once she proved herself." Like Dave with Madisun, Sally had been reluctant at first, but delegating had proved to be a good thing. "Heather might be okay," she admitted, "but it's Friday night. She'll be busy." And Sally could stay home, safe inside her comfort zone.

"Don't know unless you try. Want me to call?" He pulled his phone out of his pocket. "I'll look up her number on the office computer."

Sally opened her mouth to protest, but he'd gone. She shrugged. No way that a pretty, outgoing girl like Heather wouldn't have Friday night plans. Sally led Puffin out to the paddock.

When she came back, Ben shoved his phone into his pocket. "She'll be here in an hour."

"She's available at this late notice?"

"She planned to hang out with a couple friends, but she's canceling. Guess she'd rather be with horses."

"I can relate," Sally said dryly. But maybe it wouldn't be so bad. Dave, Cassidy, and Robin were nice. Ben was nice. They'd probably get along and have lots to talk about. She didn't need to stress out; she could sit back and listen.

Hard to believe that she used to love hanging out in a Western bar, chatting with rodeo colleagues and fans. Now, even a simple dinner among friends had her nerves a-jangle.

"How about I finish up here?" Ben said. "You go do whatever girly stuff you need to do."

Girly stuff? Sally's mouth fell open. "Oh, Lord, I can't go!"

"What now?" He sounded exasperated.

Despite his vow that he'd never hurt her, it made her

anxious when a man was annoyed with her. Eyeing him warily, she said, "I don't have anything to wear."

To her surprise, he chuckled. "Women always say that."

"In my case it's true. I own a dress, but it's . . ." She'd worn it to Dave and Cassidy's wedding. "It's not right for a casual dinner. Other than that, all I have are jeans and shirts."

"It's ranch country. Jeans and a shirt will be fine."

"No, I mean work jeans and shirts. The kind I wear every day."

"Sally, they won't care what you wear. They want to see *you*, not your clothes."

"Actually, it's you they want to see." And Ben, even in the most casual of work clothes, looked fantastic.

"Well, I'm wearing jeans and a shirt. You'd better do the same or I'll feel underdressed."

She twisted her mouth. Life was so much easier when she didn't socialize.

As she walked to the house, she mused that, even though she'd learned the wisdom of dressing to not be noticed by men, her vanity hadn't entirely deserted her. Just for once, it would be nice to look like Sally Pantages again rather than Sally Ryland.

She showered off the day's dust and sweat, washed her hair and dragged a comb through her tangled curls, and rubbed heavy duty lotion into her dry skin. The contents of her closet were uninspiring: everything was old, plain, and baggy. She selected the least worn pair of jeans, a tee in a pretty shade of yellow, and a green and white plaid shirt with a thin yellow stripe running through it. Wearing green brought out the green highlights in her gray eyes.

No make-up. She didn't own any.

It used to be part of her image as a barrel racer, along with the flashy silver shirt and long, fiery hair. Rodeo was performance as well as sport. But Pete had told her she was so pretty she didn't need make-up. On the flip side, he'd also said it made her look slutty.

She studied her reflection. Drab. Definitely not slutty.

Was Ben attracted to her? Sometimes his eyes gleamed in a way that sent a tug of awareness through her. If he was, it couldn't be because of her appearance.

"A lot of men will jump anything with two tits, given the opportunity," Pete said. He'd just fired the male vet. Gripping Sally's upper arm hard enough to leave bruises, he warned her, "Don't go leading them on."

Sally shook her head vigorously to get rid of his voice. Ben wasn't like that. Two or three of the female owners and students, including the beautiful Madeleine, had flirted with him. He'd been friendly, but nothing more. The only person she'd seen him look at *that way* was her. Which really didn't make sense.

"Sally?" A knock sounded downstairs.

The bedside alarm clock told her it was later than she'd thought. "Be right down." Sock-footed, she ran down the stairs and into the kitchen.

Ben leaned against the frame of the open door between the mudroom and the kitchen, a doorway she'd never invited him through. A part of her noted that fact, and appreciated that he hadn't invaded her space. But mostly, she gaped in pure appreciation of *him.*

This was just plain unfair. He hadn't lied; he wore jeans and a shirt. But while she looked like her work-day self, he was stunning. From the top of his damp, overly long hair to the toes of his gorgeous tooled cowboy boots. His blue snap-front shirt had black embroidery in a Native Canadian design and was tucked into jeans that hugged his long, muscled legs. The rodeo buckle on his belt—Calgary Stampede—drew attention to his narrow waist and hips.

Her own shirt had no embroidery and it hung loose over her jeans. Her trophy buckles for barrel racing were in a box in the storage room that used to be her and Pete's bedroom.

"You look good in green," Ben said.

"Thanks. You, uh, look good, too." *You'd look good in anything. And, I'm dead sure, in nothing at all.* The latter thought, coming out of nowhere, sent shocked heat racing through her. Why, why did he have this effect on her?

Ben stepped away from the doorway so she could enter the mudroom. "Heather's here. I made sure she has our cell numbers and the vet's number."

"Thanks." She pulled on her best boots, which were embarrassingly old and hadn't been conditioned in ages. Following Ben out of the mudroom, she closed and locked the door.

In silence they walked toward the barn. "Heather?" she called.

The girl trotted around from the back of the barn. A slim, ponytailed redhead, she was clad in jeans, work boots, and a plain gray tee. "Hi, Sally. I was admiring Moon Song. Isn't he the most handsome guy you've ever seen?"

No, that would be Ben. "He's a beauty. Thanks so much for doing this. It should be pretty quiet. There'll be some owners coming—"

"Yup. Ben showed me the schedule."

"You shouldn't have to do anything for them. Just say hi and be friendly."

She grinned. "You bet. Is there anything else I can do while I'm here? Muck out stalls, clean tack?"

"If you cleaned the tack from this afternoon, that would be great. Thanks."

"No problem, Sally." Her expression sobered. "Money's tight at home, so if I can work in exchange for a lesson or some riding time, I'll be, like, eternally grateful."

Sally glanced at Ben. "He's the person to thank." She swallowed. "I guess we both owe him a thank-you."

"Jeez, ladies," he said. "Don't make a big deal of it. Sally, we'd better get going."

"Okay. Heather, my cell's in my pocket. Call if anything, I mean *anything*, worries you the least little bit."

"You bet."

Somewhat reassured that Ryland Riding would survive the evening, and hoping she did the same, Sally walked beside Ben to where she parked her truck and horse trailer. His rig was there too, on a piece of flat ground with a view across rolling grasslands to the distant hills. As she'd suggested, he'd run a hose to the closest water tap.

"Want to take my truck?" he asked. It was unhitched from the trailer.

Her old truck almost never got used, and each time she turned the key in the ignition she said a silent prayer that the engine would turn over. Still, she eyed his sling. "Are you sure you should be driving?"

"Hasn't stopped me yet."

"Well, then, thanks." She climbed up into the passenger side of his truck.

When he got in the driver's side, a flutter of anxiety and excitement quickened her breath. This was the first time in forever that she'd been in a vehicle with a man. Even when she was married, she'd held down the fort

at Ryland Riding while Pete did the few errands that
required leaving. If she mentioned this to Ben, he'd
think she was even odder than he already did.

Ben glanced at Sally, all the way over by the passenger
window. Her hands were clasped tightly in her lap and
her face muscles looked tense as she stared straight
ahead. He wanted to touch her arm or leg to offer re-
assurance, but figured she wouldn't take it in a good
way. Besides, he needed his right hand on the steering
wheel.

Speaking over a Faith Hill song that was playing on
the radio, he said, "Stop having second thoughts."

Sally's mouth twitched, not with humor but with a
grimace.

He really didn't get her behavior. On the phone,
she'd sounded genuinely affectionate with Dave and his
new wife. Yet she'd tried to avoid this dinner. Was it because of Ben? Did she not want to introduce him to
these people? Or was her reluctance somehow linked
to her comments about not going to town and not
having clothes other than work ones?

He turned down the radio. "Tell me a little about
your friends."

"Dave Cousins was born here. He owns the Wild Rose
Inn, which he restored."

"I saw that place. He did a great job."

She nodded. "He's married to Cassidy Esperanza—
she kept her own surname—and he has a twelve-year-
old daughter, Robin, who'll be there tonight."

"*He* has a daughter? From a previous marriage?"

"Yes. He and Cassidy have just come back from their
honeymoon. He and his ex, Jess, share custody of Robin.

Jess remarried a few years ago, and she and Evan have a little boy." Sally's voice relaxed as she spoke. Now she was glancing around, taking in the hay fields and ranch land broken by occasional houses and outbuildings.

"Jess remarried quite a while before Dave did."

"Dave was engaged to a woman who was diagnosed with brain cancer. Anita died and it shattered him. He couldn't imagine ever loving another woman."

When she stopped speaking, Ben glanced over and saw that she'd pressed her lips together and was frowning. Was she remembering Pete? He sure wished he knew the truth about their marriage. Had Pete been an abuser, or the love of Sally's life? Had his death shattered her? If so, that might have forged a bond between her and Dave. "But he did move on," he said.

Her face softened; her lips curved. "Cassidy came to town last summer, intending to stay only a few months. She was a drifter with no real home. She got a job at the inn and she and Dave fell for each other. She stopped drifting and he found that he could love again."

It was a nice story, and he liked the way Sally's face warmed in telling it. "How do all of them get along?" Ben's family life was so straightforward compared to Dave's.

"Really well. I'm sure that's partly due to Dave. He's a genuine good guy." Again, Ben heard real affection in her voice.

He envied the man who'd won Sally's trust and friendship. Turning onto the now-familiar road into town, he said, "You said you and Dave were never an item?"

She shook her head. "Never. After Anita died, he was heartbroken and had absolutely no interest in dating. Neither did I."

Because she was heartbroken after Pete died? Or because her husband had taught her to mistrust relationships? He wondered if Sally had confided the truth to Dave.

After a minute or two, Sally said quietly, "I was surprised when he took up with Cassidy. I didn't think he'd ever . . ."

When she didn't finish the thought, Ben asked, "Ever what?"

"Risk that kind of heartbreak again."

Was that what Sally was afraid of, or was there something else she didn't want to risk? As a friend, Ben wanted to see this attractive, mature woman come alive with the young Sally's sparkle and confidence. As a man, he sure wouldn't mind if she took her first steps forward with him. He'd never be the right man, long term, for her. Sally owned a big spread, a successful business. She needed a guy who was settled and successful in his own right. An equal partner, not a cowboy who spent most of his year traveling from rodeo to rodeo.

But for the short term, Ben could sure handle getting to know Sally a lot more intimately. Too bad she didn't seem to share that interest.

"Take the main street," she directed. "They live at the Wild Rose."

"That's different, living at a hotel."

"It lets Dave and Cassidy be close to work. He converted some rooms on the top floor into an owner's suite."

Ben found parking near the liquor store. "Figure we should pick up a bottle of wine. Or beer?"

"I didn't think of that." She sounded subdued. Nervous again.

Together, they went into the store. Ben asked the

salesclerk for a recommendation, and bought a chilled bottle of sparkling wine from the Okanagan. While he was paying, Sally checked her phone.

"Nothing from Heather?" he asked, and she shook her head.

Five minutes later, they walked into the Wild Rose Inn. The décor matched up with the picturesque exterior. A little rustic, a little classy; mostly, it looked attractive and comfortable. Photos from gold rush days decorated the walls, as they had at the diner he'd visited a few days ago.

They took the elevator to the fourth floor and walked to the end of the hall. Ben rang the bell and a moment later the door swung open.

He gazed down at a bright-eyed, smiling adolescent girl. She wore jeans and a tee with running horses on it, and had chestnut hair pulled back in a ponytail. Beside her stood a large black poodle, its curly coat cropped close, its tail wagging.

"Hi, Sally," the girl said. Then, to him, "You're Ben Traynor. I recognize you from your pictures."

"And you must be Robin. What pictures?"

"I checked you out on the Internet. You're, like, famous!"

"Not quite. And sometimes the broncs get the best of me." He gestured toward his shoulder, which was sore but not as bad as yesterday.

"Everyone falls off a horse now and then," Robin said. "Even me."

He exchanged amused glances with Sally as Robin went on. "Come on in. Leave your boots by the door. This is Merlin, he's friendly. You're okay with dogs, right?"

"Definitely okay with dogs." He let the animal smell his hand, and then patted it.

Sally greeted Robin and stroked the dog, too. By the time she and Ben had pulled off their boots, a man and woman had joined them. Sally made the introductions, and Ben shook hands with Cassidy first, and then Dave—both of them giving him firm, straightforward shakes.

Sally's friend Dave Cousins, a tall, sandy-haired guy in jeans and a green Western shirt, was a surprise. Ben had expected an older guy, someone less fit and outdoorsy looking. Dave looked to be thirtyish, yet he'd renovated and now ran this impressive hotel, and he had a twelve-year-old daughter.

His wife, Cassidy Esperanza, was a slender, beautiful woman about Sally's height. She had Latina blood to go along with that surname. There was something a little exotic about her olive skin, the shape of her blue-gray eyes, and the shiny cap of black hair. That hint of the exotic made a nice contrast to her Western-style jeans and pale blue snap-front shirt with darker blue embroidery.

"I apologize for not dressing up more," Sally said. "But all I have is work clothes."

"No worries," Cassidy said. "But if you ever want to shop, check out Days of Your. It's a thrift shop. My friend Maribeth owns it. She has awesome clothes, amazing prices, and she supports some wonderful charities. I get almost all my clothes there."

"You do?" Sally said. "I had no idea. You always look so great."

"Women," Dave said. "One minute together and they're talking about clothes."

Ben hoped Sally would listen to the younger woman's advice. Not that Sally didn't look pretty, but he wouldn't mind seeing her in the kind of figure-flattering clothes she used to wear. What kind of woman only owned farm-work clothes?

"*I'd* rather talk about horses," Robin said. "They're way more interesting than clothes. I want to hear all about the rodeo, Mr. Traynor."

He wrinkled his nose. "I'd rather you call me Ben, if that's all right with your parents."

"We're pretty informal," Dave said. "Ben it is. Now come on in and sit down." He led the way into a fair-sized living room. The furniture was nice, but it was just a foundation that this family had built on. A vase of flowers, family photos, travel books and photos, a crocheted afghan, horse books and artwork, and other odds and ends made this a home.

The horse paintings drew Ben. The style was youthful, but he saw genuine talent and an understanding of horses. After checking the signatures, he said, "Robin, I like your art. Those are real horses. You captured the spirit, and some artists don't."

"Thanks!" She beamed. "I love horses."

"I can tell."

Sally, Ben, and Cassidy sat down and Robin curled up on the rug by her stepmom's feet. Starving, Ben eyed the large bowl of tortilla chips and smaller bowls of salsa and guacamole on the coffee table.

Dave, who'd remained standing, said, "Let's have a drink. Dinner's in the oven. Cassidy makes great baked chiles rellenos. I hope you like Mexican food."

"Love it," Ben said, and Sally agreed.

"We brought wine," Ben said, reaching over to hand Dave the bottle.

"Thanks."

Cassidy said, "Oh, yum. Bubbles! Is it chilled? Yes? Open that one now, okay?"

"Yes, ma'am," Dave said. "Dig in, everyone. I'll be back with glasses. Sally, what would you like to drink?" The man clearly knew that Sally didn't drink alcohol.

Her forehead creased as she glanced at the bottle in Dave's hand, then she said, "I'll have some of the bubbly, please."

Dave's mouth opened, and Cassidy shot a quick glance from Sally to her husband. "Sure," he said.

Ben held back a smile at this small triumph. He loved seeing Sally loosen up.

He dug a chip into the salsa, and the others followed his example. After several bites, he and Sally complimented the delicious salsa and guacamole.

Robin fielded the compliment. "We make it ourselves, the way Anita did."

Surprised by the mention of Dave's deceased fiancée, Ben glanced at Cassidy and saw her smile warmly at the girl. "We sure do."

That was actually a pretty healthy attitude. Dave had loved Anita and no doubt so had Robin. By talking about her, they kept her memory warm in their hearts. Whereas Sally avoided mentioning Pete. If memories were too painful, was it the pain of loss or another kind of pain?

Dave returned with five flute glasses. One, which he handed to Robin, was already filled with golden liquid. He fetched an ice bucket, then deftly opened the wine, poured, and passed out the other glasses. He put the bottle in the ice bucket and sat on the couch beside his wife.

Cassidy hoisted her glass. "Sally, it's great to have you here. And Ben, it's wonderful to meet you."

They all clicked glasses and drank. Although Ben was mostly a beer man, he enjoyed the fruity dryness and slight fizz of this wine. "It's kind of you to invite—" He stopped before saying "us," which might imply he and Sally were a couple. She wouldn't like that, though he sure wouldn't mind if it were true. After clearing his throat, he finished, "To invite me. Especially when you only recently got back from your honeymoon. Sally said you went to Italy?"

"Yes," Cassidy said. "I'd been there before but it was wonderful seeing it with Dave. We rented a car, which was total luxury for me. I've always traveled by bus or thumb." She made a hitchhiker's gesture.

Her husband linked fingers with her. "I've always been a planner and she's a gypsy, so we compromised. We had hotel reservations in Rome for the first two nights, and then took it from there. We'd pick a direction, stop anywhere that appealed to us, and in the late afternoon we'd hunt for an interesting place to stay."

"Which Dave then insisted on checking out online," Cassidy teased.

"And we always ended up in nice places, didn't we?" he teased back. "I even made some industry contacts."

Cassidy winked at him. "Which made for some tax deductions. He loved that part."

"I loved all of it." The gaze he turned on her made it clear that what he loved most of all was his wife.

Ben felt a twinge of envy. If he and Jana, his ex-girlfriend in Alberta, had felt that way about each other, would they have found a compromise? But then compromising on how to take a holiday was very different from compromising on how to live your life. Jana would never have given up her job and her comfortable way of life to drive around to rodeos with him, and he couldn't imagine quitting rodeo yet.

Conversation stayed on the topic of the trip as they

made significant inroads into the snacks on the table. He noticed Sally sneaking a couple of peeks at her phone.

Cassidy asked, "Have you ever been to Europe, Ben?"

"No." Nor had he had any particular desire to go. Australia, yes, because they had rodeo. "Lots of places in Canada and the States, though. Wherever there was a pro rodeo, right, Sally?" He smiled over at her.

She returned the smile, giving him an alluring flash of the old Sally Pantages. "True."

"Huh?" Robin said.

"Didn't Sally ever tell you she was a barrel racer?" he asked. Did the woman share *any* personal information with people?

"You were? Wow!" Robin gazed at Sally as if she'd hung the stars.

"Yup," Sally said. "Until I was twenty-five."

"She won an impressive number of buckles, too," Ben put in.

"That's so exciting!" the girl cried. "I want to hear all about it."

"So do I," Cassidy said. "But dinner's ready, so let's move into the dining room first. Robin, will you help me in the kitchen?" She rose and walked down the hall with Robin tagging along.

Dave stood. "The dining room's this way."

Ben followed him, but Sally hung back in the living room and Ben heard her quietly say, "Heather?"

The dining room held a rustic oak table set with colorful woven place mats and five place settings. Extra wooden chairs lined one wall, suggesting that the table must have an extension leaf that allowed it to seat more people. On the walls hung half a dozen architect's sketches and photos documenting the restoration of the hotel. Ben walked closer to study them.

"D'you mind me asking how old you are?" he asked Dave.

"Thirty-one. Why?"

"It's amazing what you've accomplished with this hotel."

"I started in my teens. I loved the beaten-up old girl and made it my mission to restore her beauty."

Teenaged Ben had made it his mission in life to win at Canadian Finals Rodeo. He'd achieved that twice, but this year his goal was the same damned thing. He had to admit, people like Sally and Dave made him feel like he hadn't done much with his life. But there was nothing wrong with loving rodeo. He just needed to get back on the circuit and hang out with like-minded folk chasing similar dreams.

Sally joined the two men in the dining room. Ben sent her a questioning glance, and she nodded to confirm that all was well.

Dave seated Ben at one end of the table and Sally to his right. Robin came in with glasses of ice water and sat beside Sally. Cassidy brought a serving dish of chiles rellenos, which smelled spicy and delicious, and took the seat across from Sally and Robin. "Help yourselves," she said, and they began to serve out the food. Dave refilled the flutes, then seated himself opposite Ben at the other end of the table.

After Ben's first bite, he said, "Man, this is good, Cassidy."

"Thanks. It's Justine's—my mom's—recipe. My dad is Mexican. They met there, then he moved to Canada and married her."

Dave stifled a snort, and Robin said cheerfully, "And married her, and married her."

"Excuse me?" Ben said.

"Three times," the girl said. "But that's it. They're staying together now."

"Amazingly enough, that seems to be true," Cassidy said. "Anyhow, Justine learned some Mexican recipes. That's the short story. With our family, it's best to stick to the short stories. The long ones are pretty convoluted."

"I want to talk about rodeo," Robin said firmly. "Everyone keeps changing the subject." She turned to Sally. "I can't believe you quit barrel racing. Why did you do that?"

Chapter Ten

Sally gazed at the bright-eyed girl who sat to her right. "I quit because I got married, Robin." And that was enough of that story. She took a sip of wine. This bubbly stuff went down far too easily.

The twelve-year-old frowned. "People don't quit jobs because they get married. Mom didn't, Cassidy didn't."

It depended on who they married.

Robin was continuing. "Grandma Sheila didn't, Gramma Brooke didn't—"

When it seemed like the girl would go on forever, Sally broke in. "Rodeo involves a lot of travel. It doesn't work so well for married people." When Pete had proposed, she hadn't known how much her life would change. But she'd quickly found out.

"Unless they're both in rodeo," Ben put in. "Otherwise, people are separated much of the year. That's real hard on a relationship."

His handsome face was serious, and Sally wondered if he was thinking of his ex-girlfriend in Alberta. She also wondered when he'd be ready to settle down and what kind of woman he'd end up with. Not a buckle bunny; someone more down-to-earth. Pretty, sexy, smart, and of course a horse lover. She'd be one lucky gal to be with a man like Ben.

"Yeah, I guess," Robin said. "And Ryland Riding is cool, too. Sally, did you and your husband start it up right after you got married?"

Sally nodded. "We wanted something we could do together." When Pete had said that, it had sounded so romantic and so grown-up. She hadn't realized he meant "alone together," with no ties to family or friends. "And yes, Ryland Riding is cool. It's as much fun as rodeo." Especially now that Pete was gone.

"And a lot safer," Dave said.

She pressed her lips together. She'd been safer on Autumn Mist pelting around barrels, or driving lonely highways in the middle of the night, than being alone with her husband.

"I'm definitely going to work with horses," Robin said. "But I haven't figured out exactly what I'll do."

"You're twelve," Sally said. "You have loads of time." Though at that age, she'd known she wanted to pursue rodeo. She was sure Ben had been just as single-minded.

"I may go into my mom's business."

"Tell Ben what your mother does." Sally turned to smile at him, seated at her left at one end of the table. "You'll love this." Happy to get the attention off herself, she forked up another yummy mouthful.

"Mom runs Riders Boot Camp," Robin told Ben. "It's an intensive riding program, and it's also a charitable foundation. We give scholarships to people who'd benefit from the experience but can't afford it."

Sally loved that "we" and knew it was true. Robin was mature for her age and was actively involved in Boots, as the family referred to it.

"Sounds great," Ben said. "Is it therapeutic riding for people with disabilities?"

"No," the girl answered. "We're not qualified to do that. But there's definitely a therapeutic effect. Mastering new skills, learning how to connect with horses, and enjoying the great outdoors are very beneficial."

Sally held back a grin. The girl sounded like a promotional brochure. No doubt she'd not only memorized that brochure, but had input in creating it.

"That's for sure," Ben said. "What a terrific idea."

"Maybe you could come see it," Robin said.

Dave asked, "How long will you be in town?"

Ben touched his left shoulder. "Until I can get back to roping. Two weeks, maybe."

He was working out rigorously. This morning, Sally had seen him come back from a run. He'd had his sling on, and wore shorts and a loose tank top, ripped at the neckline so he could get it over his injured shoulder. The tank had revealed the purple bruising on his shoulder and arm, though she'd been more interested in how the sweat-soaked cotton plastered itself to one of the most finely muscled torsos she'd ever laid eyes on.

The memory sent a ripple of heat through her. She only hoped she wasn't blushing. Oh yes, the woman Ben married would be lucky indeed. Especially if he used that fine body as effectively in lovemaking as he did in every other physical activity she'd seen him perform.

Once upon a time, Sally had enjoyed sex unreservedly. Last week, she'd have said she'd never even think about sex again. But Ben had awakened something. A sensual, womanly side of her, one that had sexy thoughts. Maybe, just maybe, it was possible she might enjoy sex again one day. If so, it would have to be with a man who was patient and gentle, one she trusted totally.

Vaguely, she was aware of Dave saying that he was

sure Sally appreciated Ben's help, especially with Corrie gone. And then Dave asked her, "But what will you do when Ben leaves?"

Be lonely again. That thought struck her first, but she shoved it away. "I'm running an ad for an assistant." She might even be able to afford one. If things worked out with Andrew and his husband, she'd have the income from lessons and perhaps down the road two new boarders.

"You know Dave and I will help out any way we can," Cassidy said, gazing at Sally across the table.

"Me, too," Robin chimed in.

"You have good friends," Ben said to Sally.

"I do." Though she hated to take their help when there was nothing she could do for them in return.

"Maybe when I'm a grown-up, I could work for you, Sally," Robin said. "Your business will get bigger and you'll need another riding teacher."

"I like your optimism," Sally told her.

"Or," the girl went on, "it would be cool to be a horse whisperer like Ty."

"Ty?" Ben asked. "Would that be Ty Ronan, down in the Fraser Valley?"

"Yeah, he's a friend of Mom's. He's a trainer and he heals rescue horses. He sends some of them to Mom for Boots. You know him, Ben?"

"From the rodeo," he said. "He's been one of my competitors since back when I started. Remember him, Sally?"

"I do." Another hot young cowboy. Almost, but not quite, as sexy as Ben. If Ty Ronan was seated to her left, she doubted she'd feel a constant hum in her blood or a tingle on her skin as if he gave off a sexy energy.

"He still rides in a few local rodeos," Ben said, "and he's still damned good. But he semi-retired several years back. Saved up his earnings, bought a spread that he and his parents run, and now he's married."

Sally gazed at him. "That's the same kind of thing you've thought about doing, right?"

"Right." The word came out a little rough, and Ben's jaw looked tight. Did the idea of giving up full time rodeo and living a life like Ty Ronan's bother him that much?

"Or you could run a rodeo school, Ben," Robin said. "This girl in my class, her older brother's at rodeo school and he had to go all the way to Alberta."

"Rodeo schools are great," Ben said. "I've gone to a couple, over the years."

"You'll decide what you want to do when the time's right," Cassidy said cheerfully, raising her glass toward him in a toast.

"That's my wife. She doesn't believe in planning," Dave said with an amused glance at her. "From my experience, it's good to have a specific goal in mind."

"I guess that does make it easier to be motivated about saving money," Ben said. He sounded a bit defensive.

"And about laying the groundwork, figuring out the details," Dave said.

Sally shot Dave a narrow-eyed gaze. Why was he on Ben's case? "Everyone does things their own way," she commented, hoping to take the pressure off Ben. "Pete and I leaped into Ryland Riding without much planning."

"And you're recommending that course of action?" Dave's tone was light.

She wrinkled her nose at him. Dave had a pretty good idea of her precarious financial situation. If she and Pete *had* planned, and saved more money ahead of time, maybe it wouldn't always be such a struggle to stay in the black. Would there ever come a time when she didn't need every penny just to keep Ryland Riding afloat from week to week?

She resisted the impulse to check her phone again. It was set to vibrate and she'd have felt that buzzing pulse if Heather had called. Instead, she took a tiny sip of wine.

"Goals, plans." Cassidy gave an exaggerated shiver. "Once upon a time, I lived my life all footloose and fancy-free." She raised her flute glass and said, with a touch of nostalgia, "Those were the days." After she took a swallow, she gazed at her husband and grinned. "Mind you, I gained way more than I lost."

"You mean, in getting married?" Ben queried, his tone more relaxed.

"Finding Dave and Robin, a whole family here in Caribou Crossing. A home. A different perspective on life." She winked at her husband. "I'm sure Dave would say a more mature one. And all it took was one earth-shattering diagnosis."

"Uh . . ." Ben glanced at her uncertainly.

"Sally didn't tell you?"

Sally shook her head. No way would she share someone else's private business.

"The diagnosis," Cassidy said, "came last September. Multiple sclerosis." She cocked her head. "Know what that is?"

He frowned slightly. "Kind of. A good friend of my mom's has it. She was diagnosed something like five years ago. Cassidy, I'm sorry you have to deal with that."

"Thanks. How's your mom's friend doing?"

"Pretty well, I think. I see her at the rodeo from time to time and she always comes to say hi. When I ask how she is, she says, 'Glad for every good day.'"

Cassidy grinned. "Ain't that the truth! It's a crazy,

unpredictable disease. But I have a great support team and my treatment plan is working well."

"That must be hard," Ben said. "The unpredictability."

Her laugh burbled. "Says the man who rides bucking broncs? Seems to me they've got a lot in common with MS. Sometimes you win, and other times you get tossed on your butt."

"Or shoulder," he agreed ruefully. "Yeah, rodeo's definitely not predictable, is it, Sally?"

When he grinned at her, she could summon only a half-hearted smile. She'd dealt fine with the unpredictability of rodeo. But later she'd learned about a much scarier kind. Like when you didn't know if your husband was going to bring you flowers or backhand you across the room. She'd never figured out how to handle that kind.

"Cassidy," she asked tentatively, "if you don't mind my asking, how do cope with the unpredictability?"

Ben shot her a startled glance, but Sally focused on the younger woman across the table.

"I put myself in control as much as I can with meds, reducing stress, and so on," Cassidy responded. "I try to be flexible so I can adjust to whatever the disease may throw at me without letting it whip me. Perhaps toughest of all, I've learned to let others help me without feeling like I'm incompetent or weak, or I'm imposing on people."

Sally frowned. There was another problem with letting people help. If you became dependent on them, then they had power over you.

"You have trouble with that too, don't you?" Cassidy asked. "You're proud and independent, and you hate it when you need help. That's how I was. But MS humbled me."

Dave talked about Sally's stubborn pride, but she'd

figured Pete had knocked the pride out of her. Was that true, or was it in part pride that made her so determined to be self-sufficient?

Cassidy went on. "Of course I could go it alone. But it's so much better when my family and friends are there for support. It took me a while to realize that they really wanted to do that." She paused, then said softly, "That they think I'm worth it, that I deserve love and support. But they finally convinced me." She reached out her hands, one to Dave on her left and one over the table to Robin. Her husband and stepdaughter grasped them.

Sally gazed at the three of them linked together. A team. A family.

Pete had taken her away from her family. He'd said he loved her, yet had hurt her. Though she'd tried to control everything that she could—like how she dressed and behaved, what she cooked, and when she put dinner on the table—somehow she often got it wrong. She was too stupid to remember the rules he'd made. Or so on edge that she made mistakes.

Most of the time, she had believed it was her fault. He said it was. Said that he hated to punish her, but she made him do it. That it was for her own good and the good of their marriage. But sometimes she'd wondered . . . Did Pete keep changing the rules? Did he try to make her feel stupid and incompetent? To feel— to *be*—dependent?

And if so, what was wrong with her, that she'd let him do it? What had he seen in her that had made him believe she'd let him do it?

She'd had no one to talk to, to offer perspective. No one to ask for support even if her embarrassment, insecurity, and self-doubt would have allowed her to.

Pete had been dead for three years now, and she still hadn't figured out what to believe.

Something nudged her sock-clad left foot. She jerked her head up and saw Ben watching her with an expression of concern.

Cassidy, Dave, and Robin had unlinked hands and returned to their food.

"That's enough of a serious subject," Cassidy said. "It's a good day, I feel great, and it's wonderful having you guys here for dinner." She focused on Ben. "This is because of you. We've asked Sally over so many times, but she always has some excuse."

"She does, does she?" He gave Sally a teasing grin.

She made a face at him.

Under the table his sock-clad foot nudged hers again.

Her pulse kicked up and she drew her foot away as Cassidy said, "So, thank you, Ben."

He put his fork down on the plate he'd emptied, and leaned back. "Not sure what I did, but you're welcome. I'm happy to be here. Great company, great food, and it's nice seeing the inside of the inn."

"You should try the restaurant some time," Cassidy said. "Mitch is an amazing chef. And the Western bar is so much fun." She eyed his sling. "Guess you're not up to line dancing?"

"Not for another few days. You have line dancing in the bar?"

"Sunday nights," Cassidy said. "It's fun even if you don't dance. Why don't you come this Sunday and check it out?"

"Love to," he said promptly. "Sally, why don't we see if Heather's available Sunday to keep an eye on Ryland Riding?"

What was up with this "we" business, and him trying to make plans for her? Though she had to admit, she sure used to like hanging out at a Western bar listening to country music and dancing with cute cowboys . . . But that was in her Sally Pantages days. "I'm sure the bar is great. But you all know I'm not big on socializing."

"Mom and Evan will be there this Sunday," Robin said. "And Gramma Brooke and Jake. You know them. They're nice, right?"

She was being ganged up on again. "They're nice," Sally admitted. "But I don't have anything to wear."

"Days of Your," Cassidy reminded her.

The thrift shop. She had been tempted when Cassidy mentioned it earlier. It could be more fun and economical than ordering generic clothes online. One day, maybe she would come into town and check it out. The next time she had a little cash. "Saturday's booked. No way do I have time to come into town and shop."

"Hmm." Cassidy rose to clear the plates. "We're about the same size. You could come here Sunday and I'll lend you something."

"I couldn't do that."

Cassidy tilted her a smile. "What did I say earlier? Friends like to help each other out. It'd be fun."

Watching Sally's face, Ben wondered when she'd last done something as totally girly as hanging out with another woman, trying on clothes. Maybe gossiping about guys. He kind of liked the idea of Sally gossiping about him. Hopefully, she'd have good things to say.

Though maybe not. If she compared him to Dave or to Ty Ronan, men barely older than he was, he'd surely come up lacking. That was the kind of guy who'd be a good match for Sally.

Cassidy and Dave exchanged glances. Cassidy said, "Sally, Robin, would you mind helping me clear the table and get dessert and coffee going? Robin, we'll see if we can persuade Sally to come into town Sunday and have some fun."

Robin bounced to her feet and Sally rose more slowly. Ben knew she'd be all too happy to help in the kitchen, but figured she'd rather not face a double dose of female persuasiveness. He gave her an encouraging grin and got a scowl in return, which made him smother a chuckle.

"So," Dave said when the three females had left the room.

Ben looked at him where he sat at the opposite end of the dining room table, and wasn't sure whether to let out the chuckle or to feel terrified. Dave's elbows rested on the table, his hands were clasped, and his eyes were narrowed. Bad enough that he'd hassled Ben about not having a goal or plan in life. What was coming next?

"You and Cassidy had this planned." Ben reached for his wineglass.

"She knew I wanted to talk to you alone."

Ben took a sip of bubbly wine, though a slug of beer would be better suited to this conversation. "I get that Sally's your friend. She's my friend, too." Deliberately, he added, "From way back." In other words, from long before Dave even met her.

"Cassidy and Robin say I can be overprotective when it comes to the people I care about." Dave looked solemn and older than his years. "I don't think it's such a bad quality."

"I don't either. I'm the same way with my family and friends."

"Then you won't be offended if I ask what's the deal with you and Sally." His level tone made it clear that he didn't give a damn whether Ben took offense.

"Nope. I think she's lucky to have such a good friend. I want to be that kind of friend to her as well."

"Friend? That's all? You're staying out at her place."

Ben drummed the fingers of his right hand against the place mat, deliberating. "Seems to me you should be asking Sally about this. But I'll tell you anyhow. I have a trailer with my own sleeping quarters, kitchen, bathroom. That's where I live." Not that he wouldn't happily share Sally's bedroom, but she'd yet to invite him past the kitchen door. "My horse is in Sally's paddock and we've got a place to exercise and train. In return, I assist Sally with whatever my shoulder lets me do. That's the deal." He repeated Dave's word.

"Hmm."

"Let me guess. You want to ask what my intentions are."

"Well?"

Because Ben appreciated the way the other man cared for Sally, he told him. "I like Sally and I respect her. A lot, on both counts."

He glanced toward the open dining room door and caught a murmur of voices from the kitchen down the hall. Turning back to Dave, he leaned forward and said quietly, "I'll be honest and tell you I'd be a happy man if it turned into something more. But all I've got to offer is short term, and that might not suit a woman like her who deserves so much more. Besides, Sally's got her boundaries, her defenses. She's . . ." He hunted for the right word. "She's vulnerable."

Dave's brows rose. "Don't let her hear you say that." His voice too, was low.

Ben gave a short laugh. "I'm not that stupid. She's strong, proud, too independent. But there's something beneath it." He studied the other man. Did Sally trust

Dave enough to tell him a truth she refused to reveal to Ben?

Dave's hazel eyes gazed steadily into his. "Grief can knock you back a long way. Make you wary about ever jumping in again."

"I saw that with my grandma after Granddad died. But . . ." He drummed his fingers again. "Look, I don't want to gossip about Sally. But we both care about her and . . . I think there's something wrong. She's too nervous around men."

Dave blinked once, slowly. "A widow. A young, attractive woman living alone. Makes sense she'd be cautious." His tone was neutral. If he knew Sally's secret, he wasn't divulging it. At least not yet.

"Sure. But you didn't know her before she got married. She was sassy, feisty." He gave a quick grin. "Hell, she had no trouble putting cocky cowboys like me in our place. Now all that sass is gone and she acts . . . afraid. I think some man scared her. Maybe hurt her."

Dave let out a long sigh. He rose, thrust his fingers through his hair, and paced the length of the room. "Cassidy and I wonder about that, too. It was part of the reason we were so surprised to hear she had a man staying at her place, and we wanted to meet you."

So Sally hadn't confided in Dave either. Relieved that the other man had accepted him, Ben turned sideways in his chair to look up at him, "If she didn't know me from the old days, she wouldn't have let me stay."

"She knew you well enough to trust you."

"She trusts me up to a certain point, but she has strict boundaries. And she's skittish. Like a horse that's been mistreated. D'you know what I mean? Are you a rider?"

"I sure am. And yes, that's a good description." His

jaw tightened and he shot a glance out the open door. "I hate to think of someone hurting Sally."

"I know." Ben realized he had fisted his right hand. Stretching his fingers out again, he said, "I've tried to talk to her. She won't admit that something happened. But I did get her to tell me that, if there had been some problem, the guy was no longer a threat."

Dave's face lightened. "I'm surprised she'd say that much. And relieved."

Ben rose to stand beside Dave. He checked to make sure that the female murmur was still safely distant. "Wondered if it might be Pete."

He frowned. "Surely not. He and Sally were crazy about each other."

"You saw them together?"

"No. But everyone said so."

"Did Sally say so?"

Dave opened his mouth to reply, then closed it. After a moment, he said, "No. But she let me believe it." He frowned. "Did you know Pete?"

"No, but I was around when he swept in and courted Sally. It was fast, romantic. He was like a freaking tidal wave carrying her along with him."

"Sometimes love hits like that." A shadow in Dave's eyes suggested that he might be thinking of his deceased fiancée.

"I guess. They did really seem to be in love." Ben had put a lot of thought into this over the past day or so, and now he shared what he'd been thinking. "But looking back, it was almost too intense. The guy was obsessed with her. She gave up rodeo, suddenly they were getting married, then they moved to B.C. Did you know she cut off connections with her family? And all her rodeo friends? That sure as hell wasn't like the gal I used to know."

Dave gave a low whistle. "I didn't know all of that. She doesn't talk about personal stuff. Here, she and Pete kept to themselves."

Ben swallowed, and then spoke words that grated in his throat. "Abusers isolate their victims, right? If something bad had been going on, Sally'd have had no one to turn to for support."

"I hear what you're saying. But he's been dead three years and she's still skittish."

"Maybe because he gave her reason to mistrust men. Damn, Dave, you should've seen her the way she used to be. So happy and vibrant."

The other man's eyes warmed. "You do care for her. More than a little."

Gruffly, Ben said, "Hard not to. Maybe I'm wrong, and it wasn't Pete. But the fact remains, she's messed up."

The female voices grew louder and Robin cried, "No, Merlin! Stay in the kitchen."

Dave said under his breath, "Then help her, Ben, but don't hurt her. She can't take being hurt again." He strode over to meet his wife, relieving her of a platter with a chocolate-iced cake.

Sally followed with a tray holding four coffee mugs and a glass of milk. Robin carried dessert plates and a carton of ice cream.

As Ben resumed his seat, Cassidy said, "Guess what? We talked Sally into coming on Sunday. So, Ben, you make sure she doesn't back out."

As Sally handed him a mug, he gave himself the treat of brushing his fingers against hers. "Hah. This woman has a mind of her own. But I'll use my best persuasive powers. I'll tell her she'll break your heart if she doesn't let you play dress-up with her."

Sally snorted, but her eyes danced with humor as she

gave him a mock glare. "You think you're pretty clever, don't you, cowboy?"

He winked, happy that she was joking with him. "I have my moments."

"I suppose you do." Her eyes softened with an expression that made his heart give an unexpected throb.

Oh, man, Sally Ryland was getting to him.

Dave had warned him not to hurt her. But it occurred to Ben that, just possibly, he might be the one who was in for some pain.

Chapter Eleven

Early Saturday evening, after a day packed with lessons, Sally was tired but full of a sense of achievement.

"Busy day," Ben commented as they led the last two horses out to the large paddock. "You're a great teacher. You enjoy it, don't you?"

"Very much." She unbuckled Melody's halter and gave the buckskin a final pat on the neck before stepping outside the fence and latching the gate.

"Not as exciting as barrel racing."

"It's exciting in a different way. I find it really satisfying to share my love of horses and to help riders develop their skills."

"Watching you, I can see what you mean."

Without discussing it, their footsteps turned toward the foaling paddock where Song and Moon were both flourishing. She and Ben settled side by side, his right forearm next to her left one on the top rail of the fence. Hers was covered by a cotton shirt, buttoned at the cuff. His was bare below the short sleeve of his shirt. The heat of midday had worn off, thankfully. Earlier, it had been a scorcher. Out in the ring, sweating under the triple layers of bra, tee, and shirt, she'd seen Ben working Chauncey's Pride in the neighboring ring, his shirt unbuttoned down the front. She'd caught tantalizing glimpses of firm pecs and six-pack abs. It hadn't helped her concentration on the lesson—and she'd been amused and irked to notice that the moms in the bleachers had paid more attention to him than to their young riders.

But at least it normalized her own distractedness. It wasn't slutty to enjoy looking at a handsome man.

"Best entertainment in the world," Ben said.

She gave a guilty start before realizing he meant the colt playing with its shadow. "I could watch foals forever." Or, it seemed, Ben's fine body. Moon made her smile with affection and amusement; Ben's physique aroused more—well, *arousing*—sensations. Around him, she felt like a woman again. She was beginning to think that might not be such a bad thing.

He turned to her. "Want to put something together for dinner?"

Much as she enjoyed being around him, she shouldn't get used to it. Besides, she needed her personal space. Even more than that, she needed him to respect her boundaries. "Not tonight, thanks. I have some housework and other stuff to do." Her pulse quickened. Going against Pete had never worked out well.

"You still need to eat. I could make something and bring it over."

She swallowed, unable to distinguish between kindness and pressure. "That's nice of you but, uh, I'd kind of like to be alone."

"Sure." He said it easily, without any undertone of hurt or anger, at least not that she could hear. "Just promise me you'll eat."

Tension eased from Sally's shoulders. "I'll eat. After

that amazing meal last night, I think it may just be salad and hard-boiled eggs tonight."

"I hear you. That was some food, eh?"

Leaning on the fence beside him, she glanced at his profile. Ben likely wouldn't want to hang around Ryland Riding on his own on Saturday night. "Feel free to go into town."

He glanced at her. "I'd rather pack up some sandwiches and a bottle of beer and take Chaunce out for a long ride. Go to the lake, or up that hill you took me to, and have a picnic."

That sounded nice.

He cocked an eyebrow. "You're welcome to come."

Had she looked wistful? "Maybe some other time." She did need some space, some time away from Ben, and something had been nagging at her all day that she wanted to do.

"I hope so."

They walked to the barn, then went their separate ways.

Sally made herself a quick, light meal, did an hour or two of housework, and then went into the spare room. This had been her and Pete's bedroom. After he died, she'd called Goodwill and donated the furniture, along with his clothes and personal possessions. Online, she'd bought an inexpensive bedroom set and had it delivered and set up in a different room.

Now the old bedroom was empty but for storage boxes. After some rummaging, she found the one that contained her tooled cowboy boots, the one nice pair she'd kept from the old days. Not that she'd ever worn them again, but sentiment wouldn't let her toss them. They were well broken in from two-stepping and line dancing in lots of bars along the rodeo circuit.

She eased her foot into one. To her surprise, the boot fit like her foot belonged in it. The leather, the shade of dark honey, was dry, but leather conditioner should restore it. If she went to the Wild Rose tomorrow night, her feet would be dressed in appropriate style.

Next she found the box that held her trophy buckles. Pete had said it was egotistical to flaunt a flashy belt buckle, but Sally had always taken pride in these. It wasn't the "I'm the best" thing as much as the sense of how she and Autumn Mist had worked hard and achieved something special together. Sally took out the last one she'd won, from the Calgary Stampede just before Pete proposed to her.

It symbolized the end of her old life. Could wearing it again symbolize the start of a new life, one where she freed herself from Pete's influence? Maybe she could become a new Sally, one who acknowledged her past accomplishments, her present strengths, and her femininity.

From a shelf in the closet, she took out her old jewelry box. Her best friend had given it to her for her twelfth birthday. Made of pale wood, it had a rearing horse carved on the top. She opened the lid. Inside, there were only a few items.

She picked up the engagement ring with the big, sparkly diamond solitaire. She hadn't been able to wear it when she was working around Ryland Riding, but she'd had to remember to put it on whenever she was in the house.

Pete came through the door from the mudroom, a smile widening as he took in the attractively set table, her demure dress, the pot bubbling on the stove. "Now there's a fine sight to greet a man after a hard day's work."

Sally let out a breath. Her last lesson had run late, and

she'd dashed into the house in a panic, trying to remember all the things she needed to do before Pete came in. It seemed she'd got it right.

He held out both hands. "Come here, my pretty wife."

She stretched out her arms, then gazed in horror at her left hand. Her ring finger bore only the simple gold band. Her sparkly engagement ring lay in a dish on the bedroom dresser.

"What the hell?" Pete's voice went from sugar to icy steel. "Where's your ring? What's this mean, Sally? You don't want to be married to me?"

"I'm sorry, I'm sorry. Of course I do." It had been the early days, and she'd meant it then. "I'm wearing my wedding ring. I never take it off. But—"

He grabbed her wrist and dragged her toward the stove. One swipe of his other hand sent the soup pot flying. And then he forced her fingers down on the hot element.

The burns hadn't been deep. She'd applied antibiotic lotion and worn gloves, and they'd healed fairly quickly.

But she had learned that there were no "buts," no excuses.

Next, Sally picked up the gold wedding band. She'd worn it all the time, even for a year after Pete died. She'd been too scared to take it off. Scared of crazy things. Like that he wasn't really gone but was faking her out, setting a trap, waiting to catch her betraying their marriage.

After all, how could he really be dead? One minute he'd been gripping a pitchfork, yelling at her, red-faced and furious, raising his hand to strike her.

She backed away, tripped, turned, and started to run even though she knew it was futile, it would only make him angrier.

And then he made a sound. A tortured, startled, disbelieving sound. One she'd never heard from him before.

It made her freeze, glance back, and watch as, in slow

motion, the pitchfork fell. His raised hand groped toward his chest. And he went down. Heavily, solidly.

Still frozen, she watched and waited. Waited for him to get up. To come after her, madder than ever.

Instead, lying on the floor of the barn, he stared toward her, his face contorted. "Sally," he gasped. "Sally, I . . ."

She should run to him and start CPR. But she'd as soon try to help an injured grizzly bear. He could smash her with one swipe of his hand. He could be faking.

Or he could be dying, in answer to her desperate midnight prayers.

She should pull the cell phone out of his shirt pocket and dial 911.

Instead, she turned and walked away. She went into the house and vacuumed the downstairs. Then she went back out to the barn and yes, he was still lying there, his eyes shocked and furious, staring at nothing. Now, she carefully picked the phone—the only phone they owned—out of his pocket and called 911.

"I came out to the barn and I found my husband lying on the floor. I think maybe he's had a heart attack or a stroke."

The dispatcher asked questions and she stumbled through answers: no, she couldn't find a pulse, didn't think he was breathing.

An ambulance arrived and the paramedics pronounced Pete dead. They gazed into Sally's stunned face, wrapped a blanket around her shoulders, and held her frozen hands. They said that even if she'd found him earlier, there was nothing anyone could have done to save him.

That didn't assuage her guilt. She knew that, even had there been a way of saving Pete, she wouldn't have done it.

Now her hand clenched around the cold metal of the two rings. The edges of the diamond stabbed into her palm. Until death do us part. A life sentence.

But even after Pete's death, she hadn't been free. He'd left her not only a heavily mortgaged piece of land and a business loan on a shaky enterprise, but a manure heap of self-doubt, shame, and guilt.

She opened her hand and stared down at the rings. How had something that had started with such promise so quickly turned dark and scary? How had she let it happen?

So many times after his death, when she'd worried over how she could possibly make the next mortgage payment, she had thought of selling these rings. Yet something had held her back. Now, maybe it was time to get rid of these reminders.

But the rings weren't the reason she'd opened her jewelry box tonight.

She lifted out a couple of the half dozen pairs of dangly earrings: etched silver feathers and gold hoops strung with turquoise stones. She'd loved to wear them to the bar, along with a fancy shirt with an embroidered yoke and pearly snap buttons.

The earrings would look good with her tooled boots and the clothes Cassidy was going to loan her. When Sally was thirteen, she and a couple of friends had pierced each other's ears. The holes in her ears had grown over, but the Internet would remind her how to do it. She could imagine the expression on Ben's face.

She grinned, then shook her head and put the earrings back. That was just plain foolish. If she decided to get her ears re-pierced, she'd have it done professionally.

At the bottom of the box, she found the silver chain with the dangling horseshoe. This was the item that had been on her mind all day. Her parents had given her the necklace when she had signed up for Little Britches rodeo. It became her lucky charm. She'd worn it every single time she competed. When she took it off after that last Calgary Stampede, the night Pete had proposed, she'd had no idea she would never wear it again.

She walked into the bathroom and stood in front of the mirror, then undid the clasp of the chain and held the necklace up. Automatically, her fingers did what they used to do and fastened the clasp behind her neck. She stared at her reflection.

Her face was thinner, her cheekbones more pronounced. Her long hair was now much shorter, a mess of wavy curls that she whacked off when they got annoying. The freckles across her cheeks and the bridge of her nose were the same. The neckline of her T-shirt was higher than anything she used to wear. The horseshoe, which used to dangle on display in the notch of her collarbone, now tangled in the neck of her tee.

She lifted the pendant free, straightened her shoulders, and imagined herself without the tee, wearing a snug-fitting Western shirt with the top three snaps undone.

She'd told Ben she couldn't find her way back to the carefree woman she used to be, and that was true. But she didn't like the woman she'd been when she was with Pete, nor the one she'd become after he died. Could she find a new Sally whom she did like?

She touched her lucky horseshoe and knew where she had to start.

With her family.

Sunday at a quarter past six, Ben opened the screen door into Sally's mudroom. Freshly showered, he wore jeans, boots, and a black Western shirt with cinnamon stitching. The door from the mudroom into the kitchen was open, but he knew better than to take that as an invitation. Instead, he knocked on the frame and called, "Ready?"

A few seconds later, Sally stepped into the kitchen, looking uncertain. "As ready as I'll ever be, I guess." She had a purse over her shoulder and toted a big bag. Other than that, she looked the same as always. No, there was one thing different: a silver necklace.

"I recognize that horseshoe," he said as he took the bag from her. "You used to wear it."

"It was my lucky charm. My parents gave it to me."

"Your parents?" And she was wearing it now, even though she'd been estranged from her family? "Does this mean you talked to them?"

"No, I . . ." She started down the back steps and he walked beside her. "I need to. But I'll start with my sister. Do you still have Penny's phone number?"

"Sure do." He gave her back the bag and then, one handed, pulled his cell from his pocket, located the number, and handed her the phone. He took the bag back and they stopped walking while Sally input the number into her own phone.

They stopped at the barn to say good-bye to Heather, who was again looking after Ryland Riding. When the teen told them to have fun, Ben almost chuckled at the doubtful expression on Sally's face.

As for him, he was looking forward to the evening. When he and Sally climbed into his truck and he started the engine, Blake Shelton's "Honey Bee" was playing on the radio. Ben tapped his fingers on the steering wheel, the catchy tune giving him an urge to dance with the pretty lady beside him, and without his sling. He stretched his shoulders. "It's a week since I bust my shoulder, and I'm sick of this damn sling."

"How's the shoulder feeling?"

"Way less painful. It's definitely healing."

"You're doing the exercises Monique gave you?"

"Yes, Mother." Still, he liked the way she wanted to look after him.

After that, they drove in silence, listening to a succession of country classics and newer songs. He might not be able to line dance with this shoulder, but he was damned well taking off the sling and at least getting in a couple of slow dances. That is, if Sally was even willing to dance that way, given how jumpy she was about letting a man touch her.

In the parking lot at the back of the Wild Rose, he noted a silver SUV with RIDERS BOOT CAMP and a logo of boots on the side. "Looks like Robin's mom and stepdad are here."

Sally didn't respond, just clenched her fingers around her big bag and climbed out of the truck. He ushered her in the back door of the inn and they took the elevator to the fourth floor. When she stepped out into the hall, he moved up close behind her.

She scowled at him over her shoulder. "Don't herd me."

"Just making sure you don't cut and run," he teased. Feather-light, he touched her shoulder and, to his relief, she didn't jerk away. "Sally, it'll be fun if you let it. Don't stress out."

She ducked her head. "I feel silly being so nervous over something so . . ." She considered, and he waited. Finally, she said, "Normal."

He squeezed her shoulder gently, enjoying her warmth and firmness through her shirt. "I'll be here. If it gets to be too much, let me know and we'll leave. But give it a fair shot, okay?"

She glanced up at him. "Thank you." Then she squared her shoulders, stepped toward Dave and Cassidy's door, and knocked firmly.

Cassidy answered promptly. "I'm so glad you're here. This is going to be fun, dressing up together." At the moment, she wore a turquoise tank over skinny black yoga shorts, and her feet were bare. Ben sure wouldn't mind seeing Sally dressed that way.

When the three of them walked past the living room, Robin was on the floor with two cute toddlers, playing with colored blocks. "Hi! I'm babysitting tonight. This is my little brother Alex and my aunt Nicki."

Ben and Sally said hi, then as Cassidy led them into the kitchen, he said quietly to their hostess, "She means her niece, right?"

"Nope. To Robin's chagrin, that toddler is her step-dad's baby sister. Brooke, Evan's mom, had her babies at fifteen and forty-three."

"Man." He shook his head. "She sounds like quite a woman."

"She's amazing. You'll meet her tonight. She and her husband—her second husband—are down in the restaurant having dinner with Jess and Evan. They'll come over to the bar later."

Dave walked into the kitchen, dressed in jeans and a blue-on-blue Western shirt, and offered drinks. Since Ben was driving, he decided he'd stick to one or two beers at the bar, so he accepted a Coke instead. Sally took a glass of ginger ale, then let Cassidy tow her away.

Dave and Ben went into the living room and talked about this and that—the Wild Rose, the rodeo, Ryland Riding—while Robin and the toddlers played. Then

Robin said, "It's almost bedtime for these two. Dad, will you watch them while I get the crib ready in my room?"

"Sure." As his daughter scooted down the hallway, Dave went over and hoisted Nicki into his arms. "Can't resist cuddling a baby." He came over to Ben, offering him the girl. "Or will you be able to hold her, with that sling?"

Ben had a soft spot for little kids, too. "I can manage."

Dave eased the girl over to him, and went to lift Alex.

Ben gazed down at dark-haired Nicki, whose eyes studied him curiously. "Hi," she said.

"Hi there," he murmured. She was a warm bundle, cute in her flowered tee and miniature jeans. A sweet smell rose from her, some kind of baby shampoo or soap. "I'm Ben and I'm told your name is Nicki. I hear it's almost your bedtime."

"Sto-ry," she demanded.

Dave chimed in. "Robin will read you and Alex a story, Nicki." To Ben he said, "You like kids? Figure on having some?"

"Sure do. Down the road when I find the right woman and I'm ready to settle down."

"Sally loves kids too, and she's great with them."

"Yeah, she always has been. I was surprised she and Pete never had any. Although if he was an—" He broke off, not about to say "abuser" while he and Dave held two innocent kids.

Dave's solemn gaze met his. "I hear you."

From down the hall, female voices broke the serious mood. Expectantly, Ben turned. Cassidy appeared first, clad in snug, figure-flattering jeans, a white Western shirt with turquoise trim, and turquoise cowboy boots. She made a "ta da" flourish with one hand. "Come on, Sally. Don't be shy."

A moment later, Sally walked into the room. Ben let out a whistle of appreciation, keeping it low so as not to hurt Nicki's ears. Sally looked very much the way she used to, in a close-fitting light yellow shirt with blue stitching tucked into a snug pair of jeans. The top snaps of the shirt were open and her pendant hung around her neck. On her feet were tooled, honey-brown boots and around her slim waist was a leather belt with a Calgary Stampede buckle.

If he wasn't mistaken, she even wore a subtle bit of make-up around her eyes as well as pink gloss on her lips. Aside from her more mature features, the only thing different from the way she looked in the old days was her hair, the short, coppery-gold curls gleaming in the light. "Sally Pantages, look at you. Take a look, Nicki. That's what a barrel racing queen looks like."

The little girl babbled something that sounded like speech, but without real words.

Sally said, "Ben, you're being silly." Despite a flush of embarrassment on her cheeks, there was pleasure in her greenish gray eyes.

"Which is pretty much the same thing you always used to say to me."

She actually laughed. "I suppose it is. You were so full of yourself, and so young."

"I'm older now, and it's hard to be full of myself when I'm wearing evidence that a bronc got the best of me. So what do you say to giving me a dance?" He cocked his head toward the sling. "I'll shuck this stupid thing and—"

"You will not! I won't dance with you if you take it off."

"Ha. That means you'll dance with me. You heard her, Nicki. You're my witness."

"That's not what I said!"

"As entertaining as this discussion is," Dave said dryly, "I'd like to dance with my wife. Let's take the little ones in to Robin, and then head down to the bar."

Ben started to rise, juggling Nicki and trying not to jar his bad shoulder. Immediately, Sally was there, reaching for the toddler. "Let me take her." He passed Nicki over. His heart gave a tender throb at the glow on Sally's face as she smiled at the child.

Murmuring to Nicki, Sally followed Dave down the hall. Ben enjoyed the feminine sway of her hips in those borrowed jeans. He realized Cassidy was watching him.

"I'm glad you're doing that girl stuff with Sally," he said. "Her life's pretty much all work, no play."

"I know. Dave and I've tried to get her to do this kind of thing before, but she always resisted. Guess there's something about having you here . . ." She studied him inquisitively.

"A reminder of old times, perhaps."

"Oh, I'm sure that's it." There was humor in her tone.

Seemed maybe her female intuition told her there was something going on between Sally and him. He only hoped Sally was starting to feel the same way.

Sally and Dave returned then. Cassidy linked her arm through Sally's and steered her toward the door. Ben and Dave followed.

Down on the ground floor of the inn, they walked through the lobby and into a nearly full dining room decorated like a ritzy old-fashioned saloon, and then on to the bar. Ben glanced around, immediately feeling at home. He'd been in dozens—more like hundreds—of Western bars, and the Wild Rose's was one of the nicest.

Three or four dozen patrons sat at tables or along the bar or stood chatting. They ranged from late teens to white haired. Most were dressed like Ben and his companions, though a couple of girls wore denim miniskirts with their cowboy boots and another couple had long skirts.

Tim McGraw was singing about how he was looking for "that girl," and the clack of pool cues hitting balls sounded from a back corner. A slight, pleasant scent of beer and freshly cooked French fries hung in the air. Ben's stomach growled.

The dance floor was empty, but likely the place would get rocking later. He sure hoped he could hold Sally to that semi-promise of a dance or two.

Chapter Twelve

Sally kept close to Ben as the four of them entered the bar and Dave and Cassidy exchanged greetings with numerous people. Her heart fluttered. So far, tonight had been a little overwhelming: the girly fussing with Cassidy, Ben's teasing flattery, the sight of him snuggling that adorable child so comfortably, then the absolute rightness of holding Nicki in her own arms.

While Cassidy went to speak to the bartender, Dave snagged a table for four and Sally sank into a chair. She gazed around, trying to settle her nerves. She'd been here recently, for Dave and Cassidy's wedding reception. The room had been done up fancier; now it felt more like the kind of place where she used to hang out. The wooden furniture was rustic but comfortable, light glinted off bottles of alcohol behind the bar, cowboy-style paintings decorated the walls, and country music played on a jukebox.

A smile teased at her lips. A Western bar. If she was going to practice being "normal," what better place? There was no reason that tonight, being here with her friends, should be scary.

When a brown-haired waitress in a pink Western shirt and bolo tie came by, Dave said, "Beer? We have a nice pale ale." He looked first at Ben, then cocked an eyebrow toward Sally.

Ben said, "Sounds good."

Sally pressed her lips together, deliberating. But really, how could she be in a Western bar and not drink beer? "Sure. Me, too."

"And I'm starving," Ben said. He opened the bar menu that sat on the table, laying it so she could read it, too. Neither of them had eaten dinner, both working up until the time they'd needed to shower and dress.

Her gaze lit on something she loved and hadn't had in years. "Nachos with the works."

"And I'll have a steak sandwich with mushrooms, please," Ben said. "Cooked medium rare. And fries." He made a rueful face. "I try to watch my carbs, but those fries smell so good."

"They are," the waitress promised.

"How about you add an extra order for the table," Dave said to her. "If Ben has some, Cassidy's going to want them, too."

"Sure thing, boss."

After the waitress left, Sally took her cell from her shirt pocket and double-checked that she'd set it to vibrate.

"Does this take you back to the good old days?" Ben asked her.

She smiled at him. "Yeah, it does." Her gaze lingered. The black shirt set off his dark skin, and the cinnamon stitching echoed the color of his eyes and the highlights in his dark hair.

Cassidy returned bearing a tray with four beer bottles. "Want a glass, Sally?"

"No, the bottle's good."

Cassidy took the empty chair on Sally's right. It was reassuring having her there. Though the other woman was bubbly and outgoing, she also had a sensitive, supportive side.

Ben raised his bottle in a salute to Dave. "You've done a great job with this hotel."

"Thanks. She's a gorgeous old building. She deserves it."

Sally had just tasted her beer when two couples approached the table. Though she had only met them twice before, they'd been friendly. Besides, Dave, Cassidy, and Robin spoke about their relatives so often, Sally felt like she knew them pretty well.

When they greeted her, she smiled back. "Hi, folks. I'd like you to meet my old friend, Ben Traynor. Ben, this is Robin's mother, Jess Kincaid, and her husband, Evan." Jess was an adult version of her daughter, an attractive woman with a nice figure and glossy chestnut hair about the same color as Ben's eyes. Evan was a tall, handsome man with sun-streaked brown hair.

"And this is Brooke Brannon," Sally went on. "She's Evan's mom, though you'd never believe it to look at her." Brooke, with her fit body, serene face, and wavy blond hair, looked way too young to be the mother of a thirty-year-old. "And this is her husband, Jake." He was a striking, muscular man with black hair.

After they all exchanged greetings, Cassidy said, "Would you guys like to join us?"

They agreed, and Evan and Jake pulled up another table. Everyone shifted closer together.

Ben's sleeve brushed Sally's. A simple touch of fabric against fabric, yet her skin heated with awareness. A week ago, she'd have jerked away in anxiety. Now it wasn't fear that made her move her arm. It was that disconcerting tug of attraction.

The sensation of being female, sensual, aware of a man was hard to resist. The last time she'd been attracted to a man, it had gone horribly wrong—but Ben wasn't Pete. He'd leave in a week or two. At most, what he wanted from her was sex. He wasn't going to fall in love with her, marry her, and want to possess and control her, to shape her into his notion of the perfect wife.

The others were talking about the food at the Wild Rose, which Sally had only sampled at the wedding reception, when she'd been too socially uncomfortable to do more than nibble.

But now she'd have her chance, because their waitress was here, delivering their order. The nachos looked delicious, served with cheese, salsa, black beans, guacamole, and sour cream. Using her fingers, Sally dug in. The combination of flavors was perfect.

Ben inhaled a couple of fries. "Taste as good as they smell." He turned to Jess. "Robin mentioned your Riders Boot Camp. Sounds like a great place. How long has it been running?"

Enthusiastically, Robin's mother filled him in, with others in the family chipping in information. Though the intensive riding program had been Jess's idea, it was obvious that everyone else at the table was involved and enthusiastic.

Sally, listening as she ate nachos and snagged an occasional fry, was reminded of the way her family and friends had supported and cheered for her when she'd been barrel racing. After that, it had been just her and Pete. He'd been so adamant that they be self-sufficient.

When he died, she'd been determined never to

depend on anyone again, for fear of losing control of her life. Hiring Corrie as an assistant had made a big difference in lightening her load, but Sally hadn't depended on her. She could still handle Ryland Riding on her own.

As for Ben, he'd done more than lighten the load. He turned the dreariest chores into teamwork, praised her teaching skills, and cheered for her when she and Melody raced around the barrels. She didn't depend on him. But when he headed back to the rodeo circuit—

His good shoulder bumped hers, interrupting her train of thought. "You okay?" he murmured close to her ear, his breath stirring her hair. His closeness sent one of those disconcerting sensual ripples through her blood.

"Yes." And she would be okay after he left, too. She'd grown used to being alone. But she'd miss him in so many ways.

"By the way, Sally," Brooke said, "I had a client at the salon today whose seven-year-old daughter is interested in taking riding lessons. I suggested she call you."

"Thanks. That's nice of you." Brooke worked at a salon called Beauty is You, and was kind enough to not make snide comments about Sally's do-it-herself haircut.

"Something I've learned about Caribou Crossing," Brooke said, "is that if you're a decent person and you try hard, folks are more than willing to help you out."

"Very true," Jess said. She turned to Ben. "I want to hear about the rodeo. That's a career I thought about when I was a girl."

"One of the many careers you thought about," Evan teased. "If it involved horses, you considered it."

She made a loose fist and popped her husband lightly on the arm. "Says the man who thought he wanted to be a hot-shot investment counselor in New York. Now here you are, back in Caribou Crossing, advising people on how to plan for their retirement."

"What can I say?" he said easily, reaching for her hand and weaving his fingers through hers. "In the end, it was all about a woman."

"It's always about a woman," Jake Brannon said with a wink at his wife.

"Or a man," Cassidy put in with a wink of her own at Dave.

That was how it had been for Sally. She'd moved to Caribou Crossing because Pete had found the spread here. And, she now guessed, because he'd wanted to separate her from her family and her old life.

"Not that Caribou Crossing isn't worth falling in love with all by itself," Cassidy said. "It gets into your blood."

"True," Sally agreed. Even though her marriage hadn't worked out, and she now regretted being estranged from her family, she did love the splendid countryside.

"It does seem like a terrific place," Ben said.

But, Sally thought.

Sure enough, he went on. "But what's in my blood is rodeo. It'll be a few years before I'm ready to give it up and put down roots."

Sally toyed with a tortilla chip. For some people it was a place, for others it was a person, and for some, like Ben, it was a way of life. She'd enjoy this short time with him, then wish him well when he returned to the circuit. After he'd gone she'd check his standings now and then, and see if there were any new videos on the Internet. Maybe they'd e-mail occasionally.

She really would miss him. As a friend. Only a friend. A male friend who sent tingles of sensuality through her, awakening her female, sexual side. Not that she was convinced she wanted that side to stir to life. Sexuality, love, those things led to relationships. She'd been there, done that, had the scars to prove it. Being alone was safer.

Yet since Ben had re-entered her life, safety was seeming a little dull. . . .

The waitress came to clear the table. "What else can I bring you?"

Ben said, "One more beer, but that's my limit. Sally?"

To her surprise, her beer bottle was almost empty. "A glass of ginger ale, please."

When the waitress had gone, other patrons of the bar drifted by the table, saying hi to the people there and getting introduced to Ben, and often to Sally as well. It was embarrassing that she'd lived here seven years yet knew so few people. Still, they did seem friendly, and three even said they'd be in touch regarding lessons or boarding.

After the third, Sally said to her friends, "I've run ads in the *Caribou Crossing Gazette* and online. People should already know about Ryland Riding."

"People like to do business with someone they've met," Jess said. "Hang out at the Wild Rose every now and then, and you'll get more clients for sure. Get your hair done by Brooke at Beauty is You and chat with the other customers."

"Come to Days of Your with me," Cassidy chimed in.

Fortunately, someone else came by the table, which saved Sally from having to respond. She reached for her beer bottle and took one final sip. Become part of the community? Could she do that? She was so out of practice. Could she be friendly, yet still portray a professional image?

Even tonight, what were people thinking, seeing her here with Ben? He was her old friend, her volunteer assistant; the two of them knew that's all there was to it.

But were people speculating, gossiping? She had to be careful of her reputation, as Pete had always told her.

Her heartbeat speeded with anxiety. She'd been enjoying herself, but now she felt overwhelmed again.

Ben leaned close. "You're overthinking again. Go to the thrift shop with Cassidy. Get yourself a couple of pretty shirts. What can it hurt?"

Watching the stress lines ease from around Sally's eyes, Ben smiled. "There you go. Relax and take it one step at a time."

Though hanging out with friends on Sunday night was a totally normal thing for Ben, he knew that for Sally it was a big step. A step away from her hermitlike existence. He hoped no one pushed her too hard, or she'd retreat back into her shell.

On the subject of pushing too hard, he wondered how she'd react if he suggested a dance. Several couples had been dancing the two-step and slow dancing to music playing on the jukebox. Right now, Kenny Chesney was singing the tug-the-heartstrings song, "Come Over."

Making sure his gesture caught Sally's eye, Ben started to undo the wrist cuff of his sling.

"No," she cried. "Ben, you can't take off the sling!"

He stopped. "I'll leave it on if you dance with me."

"I don't want to dance." Her eyes belied her words, flicking a yearning glance toward the dance floor.

"Then I guess I'll have to take off the sling and find someone else to dance with."

Her lips pressed together in a tight line. "I'm sure you'll have no trouble finding someone. And if you want to take off the sling and delay your return to the circuit, then far be it from me to stop you."

A chuckle burst from his lips. "Not that you give a damn about any of that."

"Of course I don't." She said it huffily, but a moment later her lips twitched with humor.

"Well, I do. I want to heal as fast as I can." He paused. "And I don't want to dance with anyone but you." He stood and held out his right hand. When she didn't take it, he said, "Aw, come on, Sally, this is embarrassing, being rejected in front of all these people."

By now, most of the others at the table were listening. Cassidy chipped in with, "Poor Ben, that is pretty humiliating. Sally, why not take pity on the guy and give him one dance?"

The Kenny Chesney song ended and a catchy rhythm started up.

"Oh!" Sally's eyes lit. "Keith Urban. 'Somebody Like You.' I love this song."

"Me, too," Jess said, leaping to her feet. "C'mon, Ev, let's dance."

"Keith Urban," Cassidy said, "is seriously hot. You ever seen that guy play the guitar? Dave, dance with me."

Jake stood up and said to Brooke, "Let's go, babe."

Ben said, "Sally?"

Finally, she reached out and put her hand in his, and let him tug her to her feet. This felt so good, having her small, strong hand with its calluses and work-roughened skin grasped firmly in his. It felt good that she'd voluntarily taken his hand and that she'd opted into the physical closeness of a dance—even if there would be an awkward sling between their bodies.

On the dance floor, he released her hand and gently put his right arm around her upper back, just under her arm.

She was stiff, yet her left hand crept up to rest light

as cottonwood fluff on his shoulder. "How do we do this?" She gestured with her right hand.

Because of the sling, he couldn't hold her hand, so he suggested, "You could hook your fingers in my belt loop." He'd rather she reached around and slipped her hand into the back pocket of his jeans, but he knew that wasn't going to happen.

Gingerly, she curled her fingers into the belt loop, not letting her hand rest on his waist.

Music like this, your feet just had to move, so he set their bodies in motion. After a first couple of stumbling steps, old habits and her natural athleticism took over and Sally was right there with him. The quick steps didn't bother his shoulder much, though he'd best not try line dancing.

His left arm, sandwiched between them, prevented their chests or hips from touching. It was one hell of an unsatisfying way to dance, but she'd probably be more at ease than if their bodies brushed and pressed the way he'd have liked. Ben also figured that the catchy beat was more comfortable for her than a clutch-and-shuffle tune.

Not that this one wasn't romantic, with those lyrics about the guy wanting to love someone like his special woman. Romantic didn't have to mean candlelight and champagne, especially for country folk. Sunshine and that new wind blowing, like Keith Urban sang, worked fine if a man was with the right woman. And so did the sparkling green lights in Sally's eyes, the flush on her cheeks, and the flash of her smile.

The song ended all too soon, but another tune promptly followed. Kenny Rogers with "The Gambler." Ben didn't stop, didn't ask, just kept dancing and Sally stayed with him. Under his hand, her back was supple, her muscles flexing as she moved fluidly. He wished he could yank off the damn sling and pull her snug up against him so their hips brushed with each step.

Her curls weren't tangled tonight as they so often were, and they gleamed golden under the light. He caught an occasional whiff of a fresh, outdoorsy scent. Not flowery and sweet, more like sunshine on August hay. The perfect scent for Sally.

When Kenny Rogers hit the famous chorus, voices rang out as most of the people in the bar sang along. Ben joined in, and a moment later so did Sally.

When the song ended, she laughed and shook her head, sending her curls tossing gently. "I'd forgotten how much fun this was."

The sight of her so happy, the feel of her slender body under his hand . . . Something panged in his chest. With the words of the song echoing in his head, about knowing what to throw away and knowing what to keep, a bizarre instinct told him that this was a decision point in his life. He cared about Sally's happiness. He cared about Sally Ryland.

Maybe he cared a lot about her, and could care more. But she was a woman with issues and boundaries. She was also a woman with a settled life and a business she'd worked hard to establish. He might fit in here for a little while, but soon their lives would go their separate ways.

The next song started. Lady Antebellum's "Just a Kiss," a slower number.

Someone slammed into his bad shoulder. "Shit!" He bit out the curse.

Sally's eyes widened in dismay. "Ben, are you—"

A harsh voice cut across her words, a man saying, "Katy, cut it out. You've had too much to drink and—"

Sally jerked away from Ben and he swung around to see one of the miniskirted girls, fists planted on her hips, confronting a tall, broad-shouldered guy. Shrilly, she cried, "I haven't! I'm having fun!"

The man grabbed her by the shoulders. "You're making a fool of yourself. And a fool of me. We're going."

"I don't want to!" Flushed-cheeked, she tried to pull away but he didn't let go.

"Hey, folks," Ben said in a low, even tone. "Maybe you both need to cool down a little. Why don't you—"

"You stay out of it, asshole." The guy let go of the girl and squared off against Ben.

The other dancers had stopped moving and were watching, and the bar had gone silent.

Suddenly, Dave was at Ben's side. "Toby, Katy," he said calmly, "you're disturbing my patrons. Like the man said, you need to cool down. Katy, you go wash your face and I'll get you a big mug of coffee. Toby, take a walk around the block, then take another. When you can be civil to Katy, you can come back."

The guy glared at Dave for a long moment, and Ben was aware of a collective breath-holding. Then Toby cursed under his breath and stalked out. A brown-haired woman in jeans came to put an arm around Katy and steer her away.

Dave called out, "Okay, folks. Is everyone ready for some line dancing? What d'you say we get Jimmy B and Bets up to call it out?"

A collective cheer was his answer.

Ben said, "I'm afraid that lets me out." Especially after that blow to his shoulder, which had left him aching. "But Sally, you go ahead if you want to."

She shook her head. "I want to go home."

"Aw, it's early. Don't let those two spoil the fun. Let's watch the dancing and—"

"I really want to go home. Please, Ben." Her voice was strained, pleading.

He took a closer look, seeing that her rosy cheeks had gone white, her shoulders were hunched, and she'd wrapped her arms across her chest.

A light clicked on for him. He had seen a squabble between a boyfriend and girlfriend who'd had too much to drink. Something that could have escalated if no one had intervened. But he'd bet his Canadian Finals Rodeo buckles that for Sally there was a more personal resonance.

"Sure. I'll take you home now." He desperately wanted to put his arm around her, to tuck her into the sheltering curve of his body.

But he suspected that would be exactly the wrong thing to do right now.

Chapter Thirteen

Monday morning, Sally gave up on the hope of getting any more sleep, and rose earlier than usual. She turned on the coffeemaker and waited impatiently, needing that hit of caffeine after a night spent rehashing her evening at the Wild Rose.

She'd been doing okay, hanging out in the pub. At times she'd felt overwhelmed, but she'd followed Ben's advice and tried to think in terms of one step at a time, and then she'd relaxed again and had a good time. Especially when she'd danced with Ben. Even though the sling had been in the way, she'd been physically closer to him than she'd been to a man since Pete died.

She'd felt the flex of his powerful shoulder muscles beneath his shirt and the warm firmness of his arm around her. She hadn't felt confined, threatened, or intimidated. His touch, while confident, had been gentle. He had guided her in directions her body naturally wanted to move, so it felt like the two of them were in sync. She'd had to exercise self-control to keep her fingers curled into his belt loop and not release them to rest on his hip or lower back.

She'd been thinking that it wasn't such a bad thing

to feel like a woman and to be attracted to a man. That maybe it was time to stop playing it so safe, to stop letting Pete have so much influence over her.

Her mellow mood had been shattered when that Toby jerk accused his girlfriend of making a fool out of both of them, and grabbed her. Sally had flashed back to being with Pete. She'd frozen, unable to breathe, afraid she was going to faint.

Later, as she'd lain in bed listening to the gentle patter of rain and smelling the scent of cool drops hitting dusty earth, she'd thought that maybe the flashback had been inevitable. But she was mad that she'd let it get to her the way it had. She had been taking steps toward the normal life and the new Sally she'd decided to pursue when she put on her lucky pendant. And then she'd let Pete chase her back to her safe cocoon.

Sally poured steaming coffee and sipped gingerly, then went through the mudroom to stand at the railing on the back deck, her mug beside her. The first rays of sunlight glinted off drops of water left by last night's shower, and the world smelled fresh.

A fresh day, a fresh chance to be the woman she wanted to be. For some reason, she thought of her student, Amanda, with the prosthetic leg. Ben had commented that she was a gutsy girl, and it was true. Amanda wouldn't let pain or fear hold her back from living a full life.

Sally only hoped she had the same courage. And she wished she had a better picture of what a full life would look like, for her.

She'd learned one thing from last night: she wanted a life that included friends and an occasional trip into town. But what about men? A special man? Her marriage had been messed up, but how much of that had been Pete and how much had been her? Even if he was an abuser, she'd let him do it. How could she prevent the same thing from happening again? It wasn't like he'd hit her when they were dating. He'd courted her, flattered her, been romantic. Seemed like a nice guy, and she'd taken his tendency toward possessiveness as a compliment. She'd been attracted to him and he'd swept her off her feet.

She was attracted to Ben, and he seemed like a nice guy. Pete had, as it turned out, wanted to transform the confident rodeo star into an obedient wife—and she'd let him. Ben wanted to transform the introverted businesswoman back into the old Sally Pantages. Or did he? She sensed that with Ben, it wasn't about him; he wanted her to have a richer, more confident life. But since when could she trust her own judgment when it came to men?

Coffee finished, she took the mug into the kitchen. Why was she even thinking this way? The most she could ever have with Ben would be a very short-term fling, and she wasn't that kind of woman. Was she? She certainly didn't want the townspeople of Caribou Crossing thinking that she was.

How had life gotten to be so confusing?

Her hens wouldn't have answers, but at least they'd offer comfort. She went to the coop and exchanged morning greetings with her flock. After going through the regular routine and collecting five eggs, she sank down on the step of the shed. Cordelia, a Buff Orpington, clambered onto her lap and settled as Sally stroked her lovely apricot-colored feathers. A couple of the others pecked busily around Sally's booted feet.

"I may not know what I want to do about Ben," Sally told them, "but there's one thing I do know." She slid her phone from her shirt pocket, took a deep breath, and placed the call.

It was only an hour later in Alberta. She hoped her sister was still an early riser.

After two rings, a female voice said, "Hello." A cheery voice, familiar but older.

"Penny? This is Sally."

"Sally . . ." There was a pause, as if she was trying to place the name. Then an ear-splitting squeal. "Sally? Sally! Oh my God, it's you!"

"Hey there."

"I'm so glad you called!" She was still at high volume. "How are you?"

"Aside from deaf in one ear? I'm fine." And near tears at hearing Penny's voice and the pleasure in it.

"You saw Ben Traynor? He told you we'd talked?"

"Yes, and he told me you're married and expecting. Congratulations."

"Thanks." There was a pause, then she went on, subdued now. "This is weird. The last time I saw you I wasn't even twenty-one. So much has happened since then."

"I know."

"I don't know what all happened between you and our parents, but Sally, was it really so bad that you never wanted to talk to us again? Even when Pete died?"

She sighed. She had wanted to, but been too embarrassed, guilty, and messed up. Settling for a partial truth, she said, "I didn't know if you wanted to talk to me. I know none of you were happy about me marrying Pete."

"It happened so quickly, the two of you meeting and then getting married, and you giving up rodeo. Yeah, it was super-romantic, but I thought Mom and Dad were right that you should've taken more time to be sure. About Pete and about your career, after all the work and passion you'd put into it."

Of course they'd been right.

Penny went on. "And no one understood why you guys couldn't start Ryland Riding closer to home. Folks knew you, and they'd have been happy to do business with you."

"Pete found this great spread at a reasonable price. I know it was hard, me moving so far away. But if they'd tried to understand rather than criticizing and then cutting us off—"

"Oh, come on, Sally. They tried. I tried. We called, e-mailed, wrote. For a year."

"What?" Her sister was reinventing history. Sally's family had cut off contact a few months after she and Pete had taken possession of this place.

One of the Barred Rocks, Lucille, was apparently tired of not getting attention. She flew up to settle on Sally's shoulder. Sally leaned her head gently against the black-and-white body.

Penny said, "But after the first few weeks, you stopped answering. You didn't return our calls and Pete sure wasn't friendly to us. He finally told us you didn't want us in your life. And you never so much as sent a birthday or Christmas card."

"No," Sally whispered disbelievingly. The mail came to and went from a bank of boxes a mile down the road. Pete had always dealt with it. They'd had only one phone, a cell, and he'd hung on to it because he handled the business end of their operation. For the same reason, he had controlled the computer. She'd let him. He'd had firm ideas about his responsibilities and hers, and she'd gone along—after learning that to do otherwise had painful consequences.

She hooked a finger into the silver chain around her neck, pulled the horseshoe free of her T-shirt, and held it gently. She'd come to suspect that Pete had wanted to

separate her from her old life, but had he deliberately
cut her off from her family? And lied when he'd said it
was the other way around? "Penny, I have to go. I . . ."
Need to think, to try and sort this out. "I have students
coming. But I'll call again."

"Please call Mom and Dad, too," her sister said.
"They're getting older and it broke their hearts what
happened with you. And think about your niece, who'll
arrive in a month and a half. What am I going to tell
her about her aunt? Whatever the hell went wrong with
this family, we need to fix it, Sally."

Her sister's words and the emotion in her voice sent
a ray of hope into Sally's heart. Penny seemed to believe
the situation was fixable. Sally might find her way back
to her family.

"I'll think about it, Penny. Give me a little time."

"Okay." She put on a school-teacherish tone. "But if
I don't hear from you in a few days, I'm calling you
back." Her voice softened when she added, "Bye for
now. I love you, Sally."

Before Sally could respond, Penny had hung up. "I
love you, too," she whispered, and Lucille clucked in
response.

Overwhelmed, Sally gently removed Lucille and
Cordelia from their comfy spots. She'd love to tell Ben
about the call, yet she was so embarrassed about last
night, so confused by her feelings for him, that she
couldn't face him yet.

She stalled by going back to the house for breakfast.
She scrambled two fresh-from-the-bird eggs and
ate them with toast and strawberry jam. Then, having
only postponed the inevitable, she turned her steps to
the barn.

Ben was grooming Madeleine's horse, Star of Egypt.
He glanced up with a warm smile. "Morning, Sally."

"Morning." Diving right in, she said, "I'm sorry about dragging you away so early last night." And for barely speaking on the way home, then hurrying off with a quick good night, not even a thank you. "It was a nice evening but it got to be too much for me. I'm sorry if I spoiled it for you."

He was usually so easygoing, and she hoped he'd say something like, "No problem." Instead, as he moved around to the palomino's other side, he said, "You can make it up to me."

Warily, she asked, "How?"

"Come for dinner tonight. At my place."

"Your place? You mean your trailer?" She stroked Star's glossy neck and breathed in the comforting aroma of horse, considering the offer. The idea of sharing that confined space with Ben made her uneasy. So far, he hadn't done anything to make her mistrust him, but nor had Pete until after they were married—or, at least, she'd been too in love to recognize the warning signs. Besides, there was the disconcerting effect Ben had on female instincts and urges she'd thought had died long ago. Sitting at that little dinette, their knees would bump. His presence would be too much. Too physical, too . . . Okay, too sexy.

Apparently oblivious to her turmoil, he had bent to run a soft brush down Star's legs. "The trailer's cramped," he said. "I thought we'd sit outside. I've got folding chairs and a table, and a million-dollar view."

She couldn't help but smile. It was indeed a million-dollar view. Too bad that her equity in it was so tiny. Musing on his offer, she thought that the picture he'd painted was appealing, but why would he put himself out to fix—or buy—a meal for her? What did he want? "Why?"

"Jesus, woman. D'you have to make everything so

damned complicated?" He straightened and scowled at her over the horse's back. "I thought it'd be nice. That's why. Stop thinking about it and say yes. Okay?"

She actually liked that he expressed his annoyance so openly. It reassured her that he was neither setting a trap nor about to hit her. She was coming to believe that with Ben, what you saw was what you got.

She wanted to accept his invitation. Eating a meal she hadn't lifted a finger to prepare was such a treat. But more than that, she enjoyed his company. She'd tell him about her phone call with Penny and see what he thought. He could be pretty perceptive.

"Yes. With thanks, Ben."

Ben helped Sally ready horses for her new clients, who were coming at nine, then hung around to greet them. He shook hands with Andrew, the guy he'd met at the physiotherapist's office, and introduced him to Sally. Andrew, stocky and redheaded, introduced his husband, Terry, who was Asian and more slender. Both men were around Ben's age, in decent shape, and clad in jeans and boots.

Leaving them to get on with the lesson, Ben did the exercises and stretches Monique Labelle had given him, along with some of his regular strength and flexibility training. He'd gone for a run earlier, before the day began to warm. His shoulder still ached, but it was improving. As a right-handed roper, surely he'd be in shape to compete with Dusty this coming weekend.

Monique, whom he'd seen twice, had warned of dire consequences if he went back too soon, and it was hard to discount the opinion of a former Olympic athlete. He'd see what she said on his next visit, and if he had to, then he'd just bite the bullet and wait another week. Not that it was any hardship spending more time with Sally.

When the lesson ended, he went to help out. The two guys were enthusiastic and wanted to learn how to take off the saddles and bridles and groom the horses.

Sally worked with Terry, and Ben instructed Andrew. As he showed him how to undo the cinch, he asked, "What brought you two to Caribou Crossing?" Ben spoke loudly enough that Terry could hear as well.

"We came for my granny's wedding," Andrew said, "and fell in love with the place."

"Your grandmother's wedding?" Sally said. "That must have been fun."

"Especially since she was marrying the love of her life, a woman she hadn't seen in almost sixty years," Andrew said, clumsily removing the saddle and dragging the pad off with it.

One-handedly, Ben caught the pad before it hit the ground.

Terry said, "Isn't that just the sweetest thing you've ever heard?"

"It is pretty sweet," Sally said. She guided the two men to the tack room and showed them where to put the saddles.

When they were back, working on the bridles, Ben said, "Yeah, it's sweet. But man, think of those wasted years. If they loved each other when they were young . . ."

"I know." Andrew paused in undoing the throat latch to gaze at Ben, his expression serious. "But times were different. To admit even to yourself to being gay was hard. Besides, they were really young. At that age, you can't really be sure it's a forever kind of love, can you?"

"If I'd met you when I was that young," Terry said, "I'd have known."

"Maybe. But society told them it was wrong. Granny Irene and her girlfriend Daphne figured that if they split up they'd, you know, move on. And they did, and had full lives, but they never found that same kind of love again."

Ben helped Andrew juggle getting his horse's bridle off and the halter on. Curious, but not wanting to be rude, he said, "Your grandmother obviously had kids."

"She married, but it wasn't a happy marriage. They split up. Granddad remarried, but she didn't, not until she and Daphne got back together." He said, "Sally, you might know Daphne Haldenby. She taught fourth grade here for decades."

"No, I only moved here seven years ago. But I do hope the two of them are happy. They certainly deserve it, after all that time."

"They're totally adorable together," Terry said. "They're another reason for us to move here. We're all, like, bosom buddies."

"Nice," Ben said.

"It is," Sally said, a little wistfully. Was she thinking about her own family?

"Now we'll take the horses out to the paddock," she said.

She and Ben gave the students the lead reins and guided them. Then the four humans leaned on the top rail of the fence, watching the dozen or so horses as they grazed and socialized. Ben could tell from the contented expressions on the two men's faces that they'd be coming back for more lessons, and likely would end up owning horses of their own.

He nudged Sally's elbow with his. When she turned, he cocked his head toward the guys and gave her a smile. Her return smile and slight nod told him she was thinking the same thing.

When the men had left, Ben said to Sally, "I need to make a trip into town. Is this a good time?"

"Sure. In fact, you should have a couple of days off. Corrie took Mondays and Tuesdays."

Amused, he shook his head. "What would I do with days off? You think I'm going to laze by the pool and suntan all day?"

Her eyes twinkled. "There are lakes you could laze by."

"Maybe I'll take a picnic lunch and ride out to one of them, spend an hour or so. That's all the lazing I can handle. Of course, if you want to come along . . ."

"Ben, you already talked me into having dinner with you. Let's not overdo, uh . . ."

"A good thing?" he teased.

Her lips twitched. "Whatever."

"Okay, then I'll head into town. Need anything?"

Of course self-sufficient Sally turned him down.

Once he got to Caribou Crossing, he parked off the main street and strolled through the small, picturesque downtown. He noticed Days of Your, the thrift store Cassidy had mentioned. The window display was bright and interesting, and one mannequin sported a Western shirt that would look good on Sally. It was a casual, daytime shirt in blue and green checks, not one of the dressier ones with fancy stitching on the yoke and pearly snaps. He wandered into the store.

A curvy redhead greeted him with a friendly smile. "Hey there. Thanks for dropping in. It's been lonely here this morning. I'm Maribeth."

"I'm Ben. I saw that checked shirt in the window. Thought my friend might like it."

"What size does she wear?"

How the hell would he know? "Uh, I think you know

Cassidy Esperanza?" That shirt of hers had looked just right on Sally.

"You bet! She's one of my best friends."

"My friend's more or less her size."

"Then you're in luck, Ben." She selected a pink shirt off a rack and climbed into the window. She unbuttoned the checked shirt and handed it to him. "Don't want the poor girl flashing her wares in public," she said cheerfully as she dressed the mannequin in pink. She backed out of the window. "What do you think? Is this for someone I might know?"

"No, I don't think so. Listen, if it doesn't fit"—or if Sally reamed him out for being presumptuous—"can I return it?"

"Sure. No problem."

She folded the shirt and stuck it in a bag.

Whistling, he set off to shop for dinner. He decided on barbecued ribs, then dropped into the liquor store and asked the woman there to recommend a good red wine. He chose one with a name he liked: Jackpot Syrah from Road 13 Vineyards.

In no rush, he drove a different road back, a longer route that looped into the foothills. With the window open, he sucked in the scent. Light green; that was how the air smelled. Hay, a hint of cottonwood, a touch of cedar. He slowed to let two mule deer cross the road, and again a few minutes later to watch a bald eagle soar across the blue sky.

Oh yes, this was a fine place. He'd ride out here on Chaunce one day. See if he could persuade Sally to come along. That field of wildflowers on his right would make her smile.

Impulsively, he pulled to the shoulder of the road and got out. He hopped a ditch and leaned on the split-rail fence. The scent now was green plus flowers, sweet and a little spicy. Butterflies flitted here and there and the hum of bees made him think of wildflower honey.

After a glance around to make sure he was alone, Ben hopped the fence. No one would notice the loss of a dozen or so white daisies, spikes of orangey-red Indian paintbrush, blue lupine, and bright yellow flowers he didn't know the name of. The brilliant copper-colored hummingbirds that darted and whirred from blossom to blossom still had plenty to choose from.

Climbing back into the truck, Ben had to laugh at what he intended to offer Sally tonight: messy spare ribs, a forty-dollar bottle of wine, and a straggly bunch of wildflowers. But hell, he was a cowboy, not some urban sophisticate.

He arrived back at Ryland Riding just before noon, put away his groceries, and stuck the flowers in a glass of water. Carrying the shirt, he went in search of Sally. He found her in the barn office at the computer, with file folders and papers beside her and a frown on her face.

He tossed the bag down beside her. "Got you something."

She gazed up curiously, but didn't touch it. "What? Why?"

"Saw it in the window of that shop Cassidy was talking about. It made me think of you."

Her eyes widened, and she took the shirt from the bag. "Oh! Ben, that's . . . You shouldn't have."

"D'you like it? I hope it fits."

Hesitantly, she held it up. "It's really nice, but I can't let you do this."

"Sally, it's used clothing. It cost a whole eight dollars. Don't make a big deal out of it."

She stood, her chin lifting. "I'll pay you for it."

He gave a disbelieving snort. "D'you realize how

ridiculous that sounds? It's eight freaking dollars, Sally."
His voice was rising, so he took a breath and strove for
a lighter tone. "Could you just say thank you and stop
arguing?"

Her mouth softened. "Maybe I could."

God, she was irresistible when she looked like that.
"Go on," he coaxed, "give it a try."

She gave in to a smile. "Thank you, Ben. I really like it."

He grinned, wanting so badly to hug her. "Now was
that so hard?"

"Kind of."

It was progress. He hoped that tonight, over dinner,
he could get her to relax and finally open up to him.
He needed to know what had happened to make her so
wary of men. And he figured she needed to talk about
it before she could move ahead and heal.

Chapter Fourteen

It had been a relatively slack day, but all the same Sally took a shower before dinner. These days, it was so warm that she got sweaty wearing her usual garb of a T-shirt under a long-sleeved cotton shirt.

Ben had been hot, too. He'd had his short-sleeved shirt unbuttoned for much of the afternoon, hanging loose over his jeans. After they'd turned the last of the horses out into the paddock, he'd hauled up the hem to wipe his sweaty face.

Making her already-dry mouth go even drier.

"How can you stand wearing so many clothes in this heat?" he'd asked.

"I'm perfectly comfortable," she had lied. For years, she had layered clothing a size too large, to make sure men didn't look at her in "that way" and think she was coming on to them. Long sleeves, the cuffs done up, to hide the Pete-inflicted bruises.

Now, fresh out of the shower, she studied her reflection. One bruise on her forearm, from banging into the corner of a stall door. Her body was slim, maybe too slim, but her shoulders and arms were even more toned than when she'd barrel raced.

In the bedroom, she put on a plain beige cotton bra and reached automatically for one of her well-worn tees. She stopped, bit her lip, and instead picked up the checked shirt that lay on the bed. She slipped her arms into the sleeves, buttoned up the front, and looked in the mirror.

This shirt was the correct size and it skimmed her breasts then narrowed at her waist. The open neck framed her horseshoe pendant. She rolled the cuffs a couple of times, baring her wrists and the bottom of her forearms. What she saw was an okay-looking woman in a nice, gently worn shirt. Not a seductress. "Stop over-thinking," she muttered.

On the way out of the house, she collected three of this morning's eggs from the fridge. Outside, the air had cooled slightly, so the temperature was pleasant. A warm, dusty scent lingered, a reminder of the day's heat.

Ben had parked his trailer on a flat patch of stubbly grass with the entrance facing the view. A portable barbecue rested on a crate, a tempting aroma drifting from under the closed lid. Barbecue sauce? Two folding chairs sat on either side of a card table. The table was bare but for a water glass filled with a vivid bunch of wildflowers.

When Pete had brought her flowers, they were carnations or roses wrapped in plastic. Sally loved these wildflowers, so casual and outdoorsy.

"Ben?" she called.

"In here." He came to the door.

His hair was damp and tousled. He must have forgotten to comb it, but she liked it this way. He'd buttoned his blue short-sleeved shirt, and she tried to convince herself she was glad.

She held up the small bowl of eggs. "I brought these

for breakfast." Quickly, she corrected herself. "I mean for *your* breakfast."

His lips twitched as he took the bowl. "Thanks. I'll enjoy these. I'll get you a drink."

Tonight it might be safer to avoid beer. "Water will be fine."

"Coming up." He disappeared, and a few seconds later returned to hand her two glasses like the one that held the flowers, these full of cold water.

She put them on the table and when she turned back to him, he was passing her two more water glasses half filled with what looked like red wine. "Ben, I—"

"It's called Jackpot Syrah. Taste it and see what you think."

Since he'd already poured it, it would be rude to say no. She took a sip. Back in the days when she drank alcohol, she'd mostly had beer, and sometimes a shot of tequila. Champagne for a really big celebration. She was no connoisseur of wine, but hmm . . . She sipped again. Was that a hint of cherry? "I don't know those fancy words they use to describe wine, but it sure does taste nice. Kind of, uh, rich, if that makes sense."

He stepped outside, took the other glass, and tasted. "'Rich' sounds right to me. Think it'll go okay with barbecued ribs?"

"Mmm, I thought I smelled barbecue sauce. Yes, I'm sure it will."

Ben opened the barbecue to turn the ribs. "Almost done. I have potatoes in foil cooking too, and I pillaged your garden for salad veggies."

She sat on a folding chair. "I told you you're welcome to anything from the garden. If you can get it before the deer and bunnies."

"You need a fence."

"I know. When Corrie planted the garden, we didn't

think about the hungry critters. She was embarrassed, since she'd worked in a garden center. But they don't get a whole lot of deer roaming around Vancouver where the center was located."

"I could build you that fence."

Every time she turned around, the man was finding something nice to do for her. That habit was almost as disconcerting as his physical appeal. "That's a kind offer. But even if I took you up on it, you'd be wasting your time. I'll be too busy to garden after you're gone."

"You need a new assistant."

"I know." Glancing at his clean shirt, she said, "You can also help yourself to the washer and dryer in the mudroom. You must be running low on clean clothes."

"I am. Thanks, that's great."

She gestured at the makeshift vase. "Where did you find the flowers? They're so pretty."

"I drove through the foothills. Nice country up there. Hopped a fence and stole these. Didn't figure anyone would notice. Don't go telling anyone, okay?"

"I can keep a secret." The words slipped out teasingly, before she thought. They sent a dark echo through her mind. Oh yes, she had kept secrets. Bruises, cracked ribs, harsh words. The miscarriage Pete had caused when he punched and kicked her in the belly.

"Sally? Are you okay?"

She forced air into her lungs. "Fine. A little tired, I guess."

"Relax, drink some wine."

"Let me help with dinner." She started to rise.

"Sit. You're my guest."

Slowly, she sank back. This was a first: being waited on by a man.

Ben brought out a big bowl of salad, two plates,

knives, forks. A roll of paper towels. Butter, in the wrapper. Salt and pepper shakers.

Automatically, her mind tallied the mistakes: no place mats; no proper napkins; no butter dish, and the butter would start to melt. Any one of those things would have earned her a slap from Pete. She eyed the wildflowers, so casual and vivid. The wine, a gorgeous purplish red in the sunshine.

Pete was wrong.

Oh, maybe it was good, as a general rule, to take the care to set a nice table, to not waste butter, even to avoid alcohol. But not all the time. There was a lot to be said for a casual, picnic-style meal with a glass of wine.

Pete had been wrong about her family, too. Maybe they had pried and offered unwanted advice, but they'd done it because they loved her.

He'd been wrong to punch her when she confirmed she was pregnant. Wrong to burn her fingers when she forgot her engagement ring. Wrong about so many things.

She felt as if blinders had fallen from her eyes and she could see her marriage clearly.

What was wrong with me that I let it happen? And whatever that was, how do I make sure it never happens again?

Ben had taken the plates to the barbecue and was dishing out foil-wrapped potatoes and ribs slathered with sauce. He put a plate in front of Sally. "Look okay?"

He was waiting on her. Cooking for her. Caring about what she thought. He hadn't tried to sweep her off her feet with a fancy restaurant meal, as Pete had done. He'd put this together himself and everything was a reflection of him. He wasn't like Pete. She was sure—as sure as a woman whose judgment had failed her once could be—that Ben wouldn't go from romantic flattery to the smash of a hand in an instant.

"Sally?"

She glanced down at the meaty, spicy ribs and giant potato, and then beamed up at him. "Everything's perfect." And she didn't mean just the food; she meant the handsome, generous, considerate man, too. "Thank you, Ben."

"Taste it before you say that."

"I can tell by the smell that it's delicious." Gingerly, she unwrapped the hot potato, sliced it open, and added a dollop of butter, then salt and pepper.

They both dished out salad, and ate hungrily. After a few bites, she shared some good news. "Can you believe, I've already had some e-mails and phone calls about lessons and boarding from people I met at the Wild Rose last night?"

"Your friends are right—in a community like this it pays to mingle." He studied her across the card table. "I'm surprised you and Pete didn't do that."

She wouldn't give Ben the old excuse about how she and Pete had wanted to be their own self-contained unit. Standing, she picked up the empty wineglasses. "Why don't I get us some more wine?" She'd give Ben a refill and herself a splash more, and then she'd find a safe topic of conversation.

Ben stretched back as much as the folding chair would allow. He hoped another glass of wine would help Sally share some of those secrets she seemed so determined to keep.

A shattering crash came from inside the trailer, followed by, "Oh, no!"

He leaped to his feet and dashed in. The wine bottle lay on the floor, red wine streaming over the dark fake-wood laminate. The two glasses had shattered and Sally flung herself down on the floor amid the spilled wine and shards of glass, grabbing at the wine bottle.

"No!" he shouted. "Sally, no, stop!" He gripped her shoulders and hauled her to her feet, pulling her away from the mess.

She jerked away and cringed back, eyes full of terror, raising her hands as if to ward off a blow. "I'm sorry, I'm sorry, I didn't mean to," she babbled. "The bottle slipped and I grabbed for it and knocked over the glasses. I'll clean it up, let me clean it up!"

Oh, shit. Now Ben was sure it was Pete who had abused her.

Keeping his voice calm as he would with a terrified horse, he said, "Sally, it's okay. I only grabbed you because I don't want you getting cut by broken glass." He stepped back.

For a long moment, she didn't respond. Was she in shock, so that his words hadn't penetrated? Then her hands lowered slightly and she eyed him warily, "I'll clean it up. I'll buy new glasses and another bottle of wine. Let me fix this."

"It was an accident. Don't worry about it. We can clean it up together, but we need to be careful of broken glass. I'll get a broom and dust pan."

Her gaze was fixed on his face, anxious and disbelieving. As if she suspected a trap. "You're not mad?"

"Of course not." He tried a small joke. "It's not worth crying over spilled wine."

She didn't smile. Her taut muscles didn't relax.

"You don't trust me," he said. "You don't believe what I'm saying, do you?"

Slowly, she shook her head and whispered, "I want to."

He swallowed, aching for her and furious with the man who'd turned her into this fearful, cringing person. "I'm not him. Whoever did this to you, I'm not him. I'm not mad. I'm not going to hit you. You have nothing to fear from me." God, he hated seeing her stricken expression. Softly, he asked, "Who was it? Was it Pete?"

Tiny muscles in her face quivered.

"Sally, you need to stop keeping secrets. They're hurting you. Tell me. Let me help."

Tears welled in her eyes. She choked back a sob.

He took off the inhibiting sling and cautiously reached out to capture a tear that had overflowed. She tensed. He put his good arm around her and eased her stiff body closer to his own. "Let it go, Sally. Let go of the fear, the secrets. You're safe with me."

"I don't cry." She spoke so low he could barely hear. "When I cried, he hit me."

It took all of Ben's willpower to keep his body from clenching with anger. "Cry all you need to, sweetheart," he whispered. Not that he liked to see a woman cry, but she had a lot of tears and pain bottled up that needed to come out before she could begin to heal. "I'm never going to hit you."

A shudder wrenched her body, as if something was letting go. Releasing, or maybe breaking. She made a choky, hiccupping sound. And then she clung to him, her arms tight around his back, her head on his chest, sobbing.

"Let it out, Sally. Let it all out." He wrapped his arms around her and stroked slow circles on her back.

She cried for a long time as they stood in the hallway of his trailer. Wrenching, body-wracking sobs that made him wish Pete Ryland were still alive so Ben could show him what it felt like to be beaten and terrified. Then quieter, whimpering sobs, and eventually sniffles and shudders. She cried hard enough that his shirt was soaked, long enough that his shoulder ached from supporting her.

Finally, she muttered against his chest, "I'm s-so em-barrassed."

"Oh, sweetheart, no. Don't be embarrassed." He bent his head and kissed the top of her head. The gesture was unthinking, but the softness of her curls against his lips made him realize it was the first time he'd kissed her. Although he hated the circumstances, he was glad she'd finally opened herself to trusting him. "You needed to cry."

She eased out of his arms and he let her go. Head down, she raised an arm and wiped the sleeve of her shirt, the one he'd given her and had delighted in seeing her wear, across her eyes and runny nose. Slowly, as if it took huge effort, she lifted her head and gazed at him. Her eyes, her nose, even her forehead, cheeks, and chin were blotchy. Her lips wobbled. "Did I need to b-break your glasses and spill your wine?"

The fact that she felt comfortable enough to try for a joke made him smile and say gently, "I think you did. Or you'd have kept all the pain inside, eating away at you." He touched her arm and she didn't flinch. "Tell me what he did. You won't be free until you do."

She did the so familiar thing of crossing her arms over her chest. "It's humiliating."

"You think getting thrown off a bronc and busting your shoulder isn't humiliating? Hell, Sally, shit happens; you deal with it; you move on. Shit happened to you and I need to know what it was so I can help you deal with it and move on."

Her brow furrowed. "Why? It's not your problem."

Because he cared about her. Maybe more than was sensible for a rodeo cowboy who had no plans for settling down. "I'm your friend," he reminded her. "I want to see you confident and sassy again. Not afraid, not hiding out here like a hermit, but having a full life." A life that could—should—include another husband one day, an established man who respected and loved her. Who gave her the kids Ben knew she yearned for.

That thought hurt a little. But he wasn't the guy for her, and he wanted Sally to be happy.

Guessing she'd feel more at ease outside than in his cramped living quarters, he said, "Let's go out and watch the sunset. Talk. Have a drink." Teasingly, he said, "Happens that I'm out of wine. . . ."

She gave him a small, rueful smile.

"But I can offer you beer or water."

"I'll take water." She paused. The smile grew. "If you trust me with a glass."

He laughed. "I'll take my chances. My stuff's not exactly fine crystal."

"I'll clean up the mess."

"No, I'll do it later. You go on out. I'll be right there."

She nodded and obeyed. He guessed she could use a couple of minutes by herself.

Avoiding the spilled wine and broken glass, Ben got a beer from the fridge and ran a fresh glass of water for Sally. He also fetched a damp washcloth and a few tissues from the bathroom. When he went out, she was leaning back in a chair, her face tipped up to the evening sky and her eyes closed.

Not opening her eyes, she said, "I love how the air smells here." Now her puffy eyes opened and she gazed at him. "Despite everything, I like it better here than in Alberta. The scenery, the air, it speaks to me."

"It's lovely country all right."

When he handed her the glass, she drank thirstily, almost draining it. He gave her the washcloth and tissues, and went back inside to refill the glass, taking the dirty plates with him. He put the sling on and returned. "Tell me about him," he said quietly.

She pressed her lips together. "You'll find out who I really am. It's not a pretty picture."

"I don't care about pretty pictures." Though he suspected that, for him, Sally would always be pretty, inside and out. "I care about you. Start at the beginning and tell me the story."

Chapter Fifteen

Sally gazed at the handsome cowboy with his tear-soaked shirt. If she told Ben the truth, he'd think less of her. Or would he? Did it even matter? If he could help her makes sense of it all, wouldn't that be a good thing?

She wanted this man to think well of her. But it was probably too late for that anyhow. She'd wasted good wine, broken two glasses, and cried all over him. She must look like the total mess she truly was. He was a friend. Not a prospective boyfriend, despite his disconcerting appeal. If he'd felt attraction to her, her behavior tonight would have destroyed it.

The sun dipped toward the horizon, painting the sky with streaks of orange. The sight was beautiful, but her eyes ached and so she closed them. Hiding behind closed lids, not seeing Ben's face, made it easier to talk. Words slipped out. "He swept me off my feet."

Behind her lids, she saw the images. "It was romantic and exciting. Pete took me to fancy restaurants, he had a sports car, he flattered and courted me. He was only a year older, but he had a real job and he made good, steady money. He bought me dresses—not slutty ones, actually quite conservative—and he said a woman should look feminine, not always wear jeans and boots. He made me feel prettier and more feminine than I ever had."

Maybe there'd been warning signs, but she hadn't recognized them. "It was like he put me on a pedestal, and yet"—as she realized now—"the *me* he put there was one he was creating. It wasn't Sally Pantages, cowgirl and rodeo performer, daughter and sister, friend. It was his vision of the perfect Sally. His future wife. His idea of a perfect wife."

"I thought you were pretty perfect the way you were," Ben murmured.

"I was too—" She stopped. "After we were married, Pete started to criticize me. He said I was too loud. He said I was a tease who flaunted my body and led men on, especially when I drank. I was immature, and alcohol made me act like a fool." Just like Toby, yelling at Katy last night. "After our wedding reception, he said he didn't like the person I became when I drank, so for the sake of our marriage we would ban alcohol from the house."

Ben made a guttural noise in his throat. "The asshole. I never once saw you act like a fool. You laughed, you danced, you had fun. Damn it, Sally, there's nothing wrong with any of that! I loved seeing you like that."

She shrugged. "I believed him. He told me I was naïve, that I didn't understand men and how easy it was to mislead them, to seduce them. He said that if I loved him, my femininity and sexuality should be reserved for him. It seemed to make sense at the time."

"I buy in to fidelity, but that doesn't mean you have to dress and act like a nun."

"Pete said that from the day he laid eyes on me, he didn't have the slightest interest in another woman.

He was pleasant to our clients, but he never flirted. He dressed plainly. All he expected of me was to behave the same way he did." She opened her eyes, picked up the water glass and sipped, then closed her eyes again, still hanging on to the glass.

"Flaunting yourself and leading guys on is way different from wearing flattering clothes and being outgoing."

Of course they were. How had she let Pete persuade her otherwise? "He kind of, well, brainwashed me, Ben." And she'd let him do it.

"He was an asshole. You're single now. You can dress and act however you want."

As if it were that easy. "I don't know what's appropriate. I don't trust my judgment."

"Just look at Cassidy, Jess, Brooke. Attractive, bright, interesting women."

That did make sense. Why had she let Pete rule her even after his death? "I guess you're right. I've been so isolated. . . ." She had another sip of water. "That was Pete's doing." But she was getting ahead of herself.

She picked up the story. "When I accepted his proposal, he wanted to get married right away and start our life together. He liked the world of horses and riding—he was a weekend rider—and said his job with the construction company was boring. He wanted us to start a business. It was so exciting. Exciting enough that I didn't mind giving up rodeo. Besides, I wanted to be with Pete, not traveling the rodeo circuit. I really was crazy, head-over-heels in love with him. Stupid in love. So eager to listen to all his advice."

She opened her eyes and glanced at Ben, his strong-featured face even more striking in the sun's fading rays. "I had no business sense. Mom had always organized my rodeo career. She booked everything and told me where and when to show up. She banked my earnings and gave me, like, an allowance or paycheck, otherwise I probably wouldn't have saved anything. Pete, though, he had a degree in business and was a site manager with that construction company."

"I can see that you'd listen to his business savvy," Ben admitted in a grudging tone.

"We did discuss it. What we could do with our skills and our love of horses, and what we could finance based on the money we'd both saved. We came up with the idea for Ryland Riding together. He hunted for properties and found this one, with all the basic stuff we needed."

"In British Columbia."

"He said he'd hunted in Alberta too, but this was the best deal. Besides, he said it would be good for our marriage for it to be just the two of us. He made it sound so romantic. My parents were upset, though. They said we should take more time and think things through. They didn't want me to move away." She sighed. "I should have listened to them, but I was young and in love. Besides, I had no idea that they'd cut me off completely."

Remembering what her sister had told her, she said, "Though now I'm not sure they did, or whether Pete did that." She told him about that morning's phone conversation, and how Pete had controlled their e-mail, mail, and only phone.

Ben whistled. "Sounds to me like the guy deliberately isolated you from your family. From your old friends, too?"

She nodded. "After we got settled here, I finally had a chance to write thank-you notes to everyone who'd given us wedding presents. I wrote something personal to most people too, like how I hoped distance wouldn't keep us from staying in touch. I expected at least some of them to respond. But no one did."

His dark brows had pulled together. "Pete took those thank-you notes to the mailbox."

She nodded. "He dealt with all the mail." She pressed her fingers to her temples. "I was so stupid. But he loved me. He always told me how much he loved me. When he said my parents had cut us out of their lives, he said it was better this way. Him and me against the world. He said we didn't need anyone else."

Ben leaned over and rested his hand on her jean-clad knee. "You see what he did, right? By isolating you, he not only bound you tighter to him, made you dependent on him, but he took away your chance to get other people's perspective. They would have criticized him, made you doubt him. He couldn't have that."

"You're probably right." She bit her lip. To this day, she didn't understand Pete. "Or maybe he just really loved me. He said that thing from that *Jerry Maguire* movie, about how we completed each other. He said we were two halves that made a whole. He didn't need anyone else and didn't see why I should." She'd felt cut off and lonely, and disloyal for feeling that way.

Ben shook his head. "Seems to me, if you love someone, you don't tell them what they need. You ask them."

"He did, sometimes. But he always had some reason why I was wrong. Like, I wanted a radio because I love country music, and a TV, just because I'd always had one. He said our life should be about our marriage and our business, and that radio and TV were frivolous distractions. I admit, I still don't have a TV because there'd be no time to watch it. So, you see what I mean? He was kind of right."

"But you always have the radio on in the kitchen."

"I do. And here's another thing. I wanted us to get

chickens. We had them on the ranch where I grew up, and I loved them. But he said they were messy, noisy, and time-consuming, and it was easier to buy eggs."

"It wasn't about the eggs, though. Not for you." He patted her leg. "If your chickens never laid another egg, you'd still keep them because they're your friends."

"Yes." Her emotions were so close to the surface, she felt tears rise. Not just at the thought of her hen friends, but because Ben understood. And he didn't seem to think she was foolish. She puffed out a breath and struggled for composure. "Pete was old-fashioned about what a husband should do and what a wife should do. His parents had had that kind of home."

"Speaking of his parents, did he cut off contact with them, too?" Ben let go of her leg to reach for his beer.

She missed his touch. "They died in some horrible car accident when he was in his late teens. And he had no siblings. I was it. His entire life." She'd felt sorry for him, that he had no one but her. All the while, he'd been scheming to ensure she had no one but him.

"Anyhow," she said, continuing with the story, "he worked hard building the indoor arena, doing maintenance, handling the business. When he absolutely had to have help, he let me assist, but he didn't like to. He wanted me to concentrate on the horses, the lessons, and the house. The house had to be clean and tidy. A hot dinner had to be on the table when he got in from work, and I had to have showered and changed into a dress." She'd given all those dresses to Goodwill after he died.

"I tried," she said quietly. "I tried so hard. But I kept messing up. I'd be positive that he'd said he'd be back for dinner at six-thirty, but then he'd come in at six and I'd still be in jeans and the meal wouldn't be ready." Remembering, she shivered. "He'd be mad."

Ben was glad it was almost dark now. It meant Sally couldn't tell how tightly his hands were clenched into fists. Trying to keep his voice level, he said, "And then he'd hit you."

Her head was down and she swallowed audibly. Breathed, "Yes." A moment later, she went on. "He'd slap me, or grab my arm and fling me across the kitchen. Or force my fingers down on a hot stove element."

Anger coursed through Ben's body so forcefully that it was all he could do to stay in his chair.

Sally drank the last of the water and put the glass on the table. Still not looking at Ben, she said, "He'd berate me. Say I made him do it."

"No," he said flatly. "You didn't."

"When he hurt me badly, he'd apologize. He's say he was sorry, but that it was his job as my husband to help me be a good wife so that we'd have a strong marriage. If he went into town, he'd bring back flowers." She gulped. "Female clients told me how lucky I was to have such a romantic husband who clearly adored me."

"Shit. How could people not see him for what he really was?"

She gazed at him, her eyes huge in the dusky light. "He really did adore me."

"If so, it was in a sick, perverted way. The man was an abuser, Sally. Pure and simple. There's no excuse for what he did."

Her sigh was weighty and tired. "I'm not totally stupid or inexperienced. I knew about domestic abuse. A few times, I stood up to him. I said I wouldn't forgive him, and I was going to leave him. But he'd tell me how much he loved and needed me. He said I needed him, too. That I couldn't walk out on Ryland Riding; I'd have no way to make a living. He said I'd be all alone, there was no one I could turn to. That he was the only one who wanted me and appreciated me."

Ben's jaw was clenched so tightly he couldn't speak. He forced himself to relax the muscles. "Emotional abuse. He isolated you and undermined your confidence."

"It's easy for you to apply labels." There was a small flash of spirit in her voice, and he was glad to hear it. "You weren't there, Ben. You didn't live twenty-four-seven with the man."

"I'm sorry, sweetheart. I know that labels don't explain what it was really like. I've heard about that kind of abuse and I know you can get trapped so it doesn't seem like there's any way out. So you even think you deserve to be treated that way."

She ducked her head again. "Sometimes I wished he would die," she confessed in a barely audible whisper. "And then he did."

"You didn't cause it. Not that I'd blame you if you had."

After a long moment, she said, "Maybe I did cause it. He was mad, yelling at me, coming after me when he had the heart attack."

"Then he deserved it."

She gave a small gasp. "Ben, I . . . I didn't try to help." She wrapped her arms across her chest. "He fell and he was conscious. I didn't call 911. I ran away. I l-let him die. Later, the paramedics said there was nothing anyone could have done, but I didn't even try. And I lied to everyone. I said I'd been in the house when it happened. That I found him later, already dead." Her eyes searched his face. "Does that make me a horrible person?"

"God, no." Gently, he tugged one of her hands free from its grip on her upper arm. Cradling it in his, he said, "It makes you an abused woman who was terrified of her abuser."

She didn't pull her hand away, but nor did she return the pressure. "And that makes me sound like a victim. Which I guess I was. But I hate to think of myself that way. Maybe that's why I was in denial."

"He messed with your mind. No wonder you couldn't sort things out."

"Even after he died. At first I couldn't really believe he was dead. That this wasn't one of his traps to make sure I obeyed his rules. And then, well, my mind was still such a muddle. I couldn't sort it out." She wove her fingers through his. "Until now. Until you helped me."

He squeezed her hand. "I'm so damned glad you dropped that bottle and broke those glasses."

She gave a small, surprised laugh. "I am, too. I never thought I'd be glad to break something, but it brought everything to a head. Pete would have hit me, but all you cared about was that I didn't hurt myself on broken glass. You know those times when you said I could trust you, that you weren't like him? Well, it finally truly sank in. And it's sunk in that Pete really is gone and I never need to be afraid like that anymore."

They sat in silence as darkness fell around them. A shrill whine near Ben's ear had him slapping his cheek, hoping he got the mosquito before it got him. "It's cooling off and the skeeters are out. Hang on a sec." He went into his rig and came back with a couple of lightweight cotton hoodies. When he gave her one, she took it hesitantly, then put it on as he did the same. They both pulled up the hoods to protect their necks and ears.

He hadn't turned the outside light on, but enough light came through the windows of the trailer that he could see how small and feminine she looked, dwarfed by his overlarge hoodie. She brought out his protective instincts, yet he knew the best thing he could do for her was help her believe in her own strength.

"You're free of Pete." He made it a statement, hoping that she'd accept its truth. "That means you really can move on. What do you want your life to be like, Sally?"

"Whew. That's a big question. I do love it here: the scenery, the climate, my horses and hens, my students. Once, I'd assumed I'd have a happy marriage, a home." She paused. "Children." Another pause and then, "Pete didn't want children. I got pregnant, and when he found out, he beat me and I miscarried."

"Oh shit, Sally. That's . . ." He was so shocked and horrified, he didn't know what to say. "God, I'm so sorry." He paused, but had to ask. "Do you think it was intentional? Did he want you to lose the baby?"

She blinked back tears. "I don't know. I hate to think it, but . . ."

"Why didn't he want kids?"

Her shoulders straightened. "Looking back, I'm starting to see the forest, not just the trees. Maybe Pete did love me, but he was possessive and jealous. He didn't want me giving affection to anyone, or anything, other than him. Not my family, not my horse, much less my own baby."

Ben nodded. "And if he'd ever hurt your child, you'd have left him. Loving your kid would have given you the strength to go." He had to wonder whether Pete came from an abusive family, and his mom hadn't found a way to leave.

"God, I hope so." The self-doubt in her eyes almost did him in.

"I know so." She would do anything to protect her child. How could he know this woman better than she knew herself?

Her eyes were glazed with tears again. "Thank you, Ben."

For a few minutes, they were quiet. Then he said, "That was then. How about the future? What do you want now, Sally?"

She sighed, picked up her water glass, and then put it down again when she saw it was empty. "I guess . . . I'd still like all those things—love, a family—but how can I trust my judgment when it comes to men? How can I know if a relationship will be healthy? I let Pete control me. I let myself become dependent. I let myself be abused and didn't walk away."

He wanted to argue with her, yet it was a fact that she'd done those things. If she met another man like Pete—a thought that roiled his blood—might she do the same again? He sure as hell hoped not.

She sighed. "This morning, Andrew, the new student, said that young people are too inexperienced to be sure if the love they feel is the forever kind. I think I'm even less confident now, past the age of thirty, that I'd have the sense to recognize the right kind of love."

"I hate it that Pete did that to you."

"I hate it that I let him do it."

"Then don't let him keep doing it. Oh, I'm not saying to leap into the arms of the first man who comes along, but why not get your feet wet? Socialize; have coffee with some guys." Damn, it was painful forcing those words out. The next ones came much easier. "If you want to try your wings, feel free to use me as a guinea pig."

After a pause, she said, "Aren't those mixed metaphors, or some such thing?"

"You know what I mean. I like you a lot, Sally. I sure

hope by now you know you can trust me." He badly wanted to touch her, but figured she might hear his message better if he didn't. "You must also know that I'm attracted to you."

She sucked in a breath. "How could you be? I'm such a mess."

"You're strong and beautiful. And sexy."

"Ben, I can't . . . I don't . . ." She sounded confused and exhausted.

"Hey, I'm not gonna push. I'm just saying, when you're ready to test your wings, I'd be mighty happy if you took that first flight with me." He rose. "We need to get some sleep. I'll walk you to your door." Ben took the wildflowers out of the glass and handed them to her, then held out his hand. He liked that she didn't pause before putting hers into it.

He tugged her to her feet. "I know you've got a lot to think about. Just, while you're thinking, don't forget about me."

Chapter Sixteen

Sally woke on Tuesday feeling kind of spacy. Light, like she'd been drained. Tired, yet exhilarated. She thought of the well-worn expression: today is the first day of the rest of your life. For years, she'd assumed that each day would be much like the previous one. Since Pete's death, those days had been pretty darned fine. Yet now she had a sense of possibility, of hope and a new self-confidence. Life could be more than pretty darned fine; it could be fabulous.

It was all due to Ben.

In the kitchen, she admired the bouquet on the table. Whatever her life might look like, she'd make sure it included wildflowers.

Out in the chicken coop, she sat on the top step with her half-finished mug of coffee beside her. Gertrude, a Barred Rock, clambered onto her lap. "What happens next?" Sally murmured as she stroked the hen. "Aside from the wildflowers?"

The creature clucked contentedly and Sally smiled. She had followed her instincts when she got her flock, and they hadn't steered her wrong. Maybe her judgment wasn't as bad as she thought it was. "At least when it comes to chickens, eh, Gertrude?"

Shortly after, when Sally entered the barn and saw Ben in a stall, his back to her, doing the utterly prosaic task of mucking out dirty straw, something stirred inside her. He'd proved to be a true friend, from shoveling manure to helping her start healing from the psychological damage Pete had inflicted. He'd heard her deep, dark secrets, he'd seen her at her worst, and still he supported her. What's more, he was attracted to her. This amazing man wanted *her*. Not because she was a convenient female and he was horny, but because he really saw her and cared about her. Chapped skin, baggy jeans, touchiness, hang-ups, and all.

Was she ready to consider being with a man? The only one she could imagine trusting that much was Ben. The only one she could imagine being attracted to was Ben. He made her aware: physically aware of him and of her own body, aware of sensuality and sexuality. Aware of possibilities. It was seductive, and yet . . .

Could she even imagine having sex again?

That act had become so fraught. With Pete, lovemaking had at first been romantic and he'd showered her with compliments. But over time he'd become critical. Sometimes he hurt her. It got to the point that she couldn't lose herself in physical pleasure because she never knew when he might pinch or slap, or pound into her so hard she was afraid he'd damage her insides.

If she'd been tired or not in the mood, he didn't care. He had said a good wife was always there for her husband. Sometimes he'd used rough sex to punish her. Other times he'd wanted make-up sex after he'd hurt her—and even if he was gentle, her body and emotions were so wounded that all she wanted was to be alone.

Since he'd died, she had owned her own body. Could she ever imagine sharing it with, opening it to, another man?

But she was getting ahead of herself. Ben had suggested she take things slow. There were lots of steps before that intimate, irrevocable deed. He'd said he'd like it if she tested her wings with him. Maybe that was something she could do.

He turned and a smile spread across his face, warming his eyes. "Hey, you. Good morning. How you feeling?"

"Better. Much better. Thank you." She squeezed her eyes shut against a surge of emotion. "Those words seem s-so inadequate." Her voice quavered.

"Aw, Sally." Distress shadowed his eyes. The poor guy must be afraid he was in for another shirt-soaking.

She sniffed, shook her head. "No, I'm fine, really. Happy, hopeful." Hoping to make him smile, she said, "Did your floor survive my accident?"

And she won that grin again. "Good as new. It's indestructible."

That flashing smile, those dancing chestnut eyes . . . If she wanted to test her wings with Ben, how would she make the first move, to let him know she was interested?

She'd muse on that. "I'd better get to work."

They fell into their normal morning pattern, but as she went through the familiar activities, she saw herself in a new light. Not only was she great with horses and a pretty fine teacher, she was a strong woman. She'd held Ryland Riding together by herself for three years.

In the late morning, she asked Ben, "Would you be okay holding down the fort for a couple of hours if I went into town?"

His brows rose, but he quickly responded, "You bet."

Immediately, she had second thoughts. "Or did you want to take Chaunce for a ride?"

"I'd rather practice in the ring. Exercise my roping arm. I can do that and keep an eye on things. If anything important comes up, I'll call your cell."

"Thank you."

"Maybe I can run a load or two of laundry?"

"Of course. Help yourself."

She went into the house and changed into her newest jeans, frowning at how shapeless they were. She picked the nicest of her old shirts, wishing the one Ben had given her wasn't in the laundry basket. At least she could wear her good boots and brush her hair, though it too was a shapeless mess.

Pete had liked it long. One night, a few months after he died, she'd been brushing her hair and remembered how he'd sometimes pulled it so hard that tears sprang to her eyes. She'd taken scissors and hacked it mercilessly. The last time she'd had hair shorter than her shoulders, she'd been a kid. It surprised her to find it still had that girlish curl. Thank heavens it did, or her do-it-yourself cut would look appalling. She did love the practicality of it, though, and couldn't imagine ever going back to long hair. Certainly not to please a man.

Grabbing her purse and keys, she went to see if her rarely used truck would start. Fortunately, it did. When she reached Caribou Crossing, she parked at the end of town and continued on foot, admiring the attractive storefronts of shops. How could she have lived twenty minutes from town for seven years and know almost nothing about this place?

But that was the past. She was a new woman. Back straight, chin up, she set about accomplishing her various tasks.

It took her a couple of hours and more than an ounce

of courage, but she was smiling as she drove home. Window open, elbow resting on the sill, she enjoyed the breeze in her hair and remembered those days on the road, chasing the next rodeo. When the radio played the Waylon Jennings version of "Mamas Don't Let Your Babies Grow Up to Be Cowboys," she sang along.

Her thoughts turned to Ben. Was he that kind of cowboy, the kind who was always on the road, always alone? Not that it mattered to her, because she wasn't aiming to be a serious girlfriend. But for Ben's sake, she hoped that when he was ready to quit rodeo, he'd find a ranch or some other horsey place to call home. And, of course, a loving wife and two or three kids. He'd been such a natural, cuddling that sweet toddler, Nicki.

It had tugged at her heartstrings. For a moment, she'd imagined herself and Ben with a baby of their own. That was an absurd fantasy, but maybe it wasn't so ridiculous to think that one day, she might find a man who was . . . well, who was a lot like Ben. Not only strong and capable, but kind, gentle, and supportive. A man she could trust. But, unlike Ben, a man who was available, not itching to return to a different life. Perhaps she might one day realize the dreams she thought she'd given up on, of a happy marriage and children.

As for right now, it gave her great pleasure to drive this country road and see the sign for Ryland Riding, to turn down the driveway and think that this piece of heaven was hers. Well, mostly the bank's, but hers as long as she kept up with the mortgage payments. It also made her surprisingly excited to think of future trips into Caribou Crossing to spend social time with the friends she was making and to further explore all that the charming town had to offer.

Her little kids' lesson would start in less than an

hour, and as she drove into the barnyard, she saw Ben leading a pair of haltered horses in from the paddock.

He flashed a welcoming smile and she waved a hand as she drove to where she parked her truck. She hopped out and gathered her bags. Though she hadn't eaten a proper lunch, she'd devoured a giant, gooey cinnamon bun from a lovely bakery.

When she stepped into the barn, Ben had one of the horses in a stall and the other in cross ties as he groomed it. He stopped work to eye her from head to toe with an appreciative gleam in his eyes. "You went shopping. The results look mighty fine."

"Thank you." Armed with a new sense of herself, plus the knowledge that new clients meant a modest uptick in income, she'd had herself a little splurge.

At Days of Your, with the assistance of Cassidy's friend Maribeth, she'd chosen two pairs of jeans, one plain and one a little fancier. Both were her size, not painted on but definitely not baggy. She'd purchased an embroidered snap front shirt, two nice but less dressy shirts, and three tees that were more flattering than her loose, high-necked ones. She now wore the plain jeans and a pale blue tee, with a darker blue shirt over it.

He cocked his head. "Your hair . . . It's the same but it's different."

"Brooke squeezed me in." The stylist had trimmed split ends, evened everything out, and thinned Sally's thick hair to give it more body and bounce. She had also shampooed and conditioned with products that smelled herbal and wonderful.

"I like it," he said. "What else did you get up to in the big city?"

She handed him the liquor store bag.

He drew out the bottle of Jackpot Syrah, which had

cost an unbelievable forty dollars. "Aw, Sally, you shouldn't have done this."

She screwed up her courage. "I thought that if I invited you over for dinner, you might bring it."

A smile grew. "I just might. When did you have in mind?"

"Why not tonight?"

The smile widened. "Why not indeed?"

"It won't be anything fancy," she warned. "Do fajitas sound okay?"

"Delicious."

He was so easy to please. Even in the beginning, when Pete was wooing her, he'd been picky and demanding. He'd said it was because they both deserved the best. For Sally, the best was a man who was happy with simple things.

Ben whistled as he dressed for dinner. Sally was a more free-spirited woman today. He didn't fool himself that last night had banished all her Pete ghosts, but she'd turned a corner and was traveling a new path. Was there any chance that, a few hours from now, that path might lead to a good night kiss?

He had to laugh at himself. In bars after rodeo performances, all he had to do was wear a trophy buckle and flash a smile if he wanted to hook up with a buckle bunny who'd ride him all night long. Now here he was, feeling like an adolescent at the prospect of winning a first kiss.

Truth was, the buckle bunny thing had worn thin a few years back. Sure, he liked sex, but when that's all it was about, his own hand worked almost as well. He liked a woman he could talk to. One who was interested in him, Ben Traynor, not in collecting a notch on her tooled leather belt. Hell, he wanted to be respected in the morning—and he wanted to respect the gal in the bed, too.

Even if he didn't get a kiss from Sally, he'd rather spend the evening talking to her than doing bedroom acrobatics with some anonymous female.

Not that he didn't want that kiss.

He grabbed the bottle of wine and a corkscrew, and sauntered over to Sally's house. Summer was heating up and he wore cargo shorts and sandals. During her lessons this afternoon, Sally had tossed her shirt over the fence, wearing just a short-sleeved tee. It was the first time he'd seen her bare arms. They were slim and toned, strong yet graceful, pale from not having seen the sun. That delicate skin made him think of baring the other covered-up parts of her body, and his own body stirred with arousal.

He forced his thoughts to something else: the e-mails and texts he'd answered before he left the trailer. His mom had wanted to know how he was feeling and to give him a little guilt for not spending his recovery time in Alberta. Dusty had reported on the weekend rodeo in Coronation, Alberta. He'd come third in tie-down roping. As for team roping, he said the wannabe heeler had potential, but Dusty doubted they'd be pulling in prize money anytime soon. He'd told the kid their partnership was temporary, a chance for him to gain experience.

Dusty hadn't tried to give Ben any guilt, but he felt it anyhow. His injury was costing his partner prize money. He could easily push through the pain and get back in action. Yet harsh experience told him that going back too soon could cost him, and Dusty, big-time. Some years back, Ben had done that, and it had resulted in a more serious injury that made him lose the rest of the season and his chance at the Finals.

He had a physio appointment tomorrow. Maybe he'd be lucky and Monique would clear him for this weekend's rodeo. If not, he was damned well going to be ready for the weekend after.

Walking past the vegetable garden, Ben scared off a rabbit. He wished Sally would let him put up a fence, but she said she wouldn't have time to garden anyhow. It bugged him to think that, after he was gone, she'd go back to wearing herself out doing everything. The woman needed to hire an assistant.

Hmm. The idea of some guy living in the apartment in the barn, out here all alone with Sally . . . No, he wasn't keen on that. Unless it was an older guy, a grandfatherly type. That'd be good. It'd be better still if Corrie came back.

He went up Sally's back stairs and into the mud-room. The kitchen door was open, the radio playing Miranda Lambert. "Hey there," he called.

"Hi, Ben." Her voice floated out. "Come on in."

Earlier today, he'd used the washer and dryer in the mudroom, but this was his first invitation to enter her house. Smiling, he kicked off his sandals and went inside. Sally was at the counter, slicing vegetables, and tossed him a smile over her shoulder.

"Want me to open the wine?" he asked.

"Sure. Oh, I don't have a corkscrew."

"Figured you wouldn't, so I brought one along."

"Thanks. There are glasses in that cupboard." She gestured with her head, her fingers occupied with slicing peppers.

After getting down two juice glasses, he glanced around, smiling to see the wildflowers on the table. The kitchen was old-fashioned, the appliances in that seventies harvest gold. People scoffed at the color, but he found it cozier than white or stainless steel.

This room wasn't exactly homey, though. It was functional, not unattractive, but the walls and ceiling could use a coat of paint in a lighter shade than the dull green, and the cracked lino needed replacing. More than that, the kitchen lacked personal touches. There were no photos stuck to the fridge, no artwork on the walls, no crocheted tea cozies or quirky salt and pepper shakers. It seemed as if Sally spent no more time in this room than she had to. Bad memories?

Tonight, it would be nice if they could create some pleasant ones.

He poured wine and put a glass beside her where she was now dicing tomatoes.

"You trust me with that?" she asked dryly.

He chuckled, pleased that she could joke about last night. "It's your own glass." He had a swallow of wine, hoping that tonight none ended up on the floor. "How can I help?"

She shot him a surprised glance. "It's under control. Why don't you sit outside with your wine and relax?"

"Because I'd rather be here helping you. Come on, make me feel useful." He wasn't the kind of guy who wanted to come home at the end of the day and have a meal put in front of him. He'd rather share the cooking—and Sally's company.

"If you're sure. You could grate some cheddar, and put the sour cream, guacamole, and salsa into bowls." She told him where everything was, and he got to work. As he grated, she tossed strips of beef into a cast iron frying pan. They sizzled, giving off a tantalizing scent.

"You marinated the beef? What do you use?"

"Garlic, lime juice, chili flakes, cumin, salt, pepper.

I haven't made fajitas in a long time, so I hope they come out okay."

"Smells terrific."

"Good. Cassidy reminded me how much I enjoy Mexican food."

Ben scooped grated cheese into a bowl. "Pete didn't like it?"

"Lord, no. He was your classic Alberta meat and potatoes guy."

He spooned the other condiments into little bowls as she'd asked, though it would have been way easier to just put the store containers on the table. "Want me to take these outside?"

"Yes, please, and the tomatoes."

He did as she asked, and added the wildflower bouquet to the table.

She scooped the beef out of the pan and tossed in sliced onion and red and green pepper.

"Want me to get out the tortillas?" He'd seen the package in the fridge.

"Oh! I forgot." She turned a startled, wary gaze on him. "I should have warmed them. I'll put them in the microwave. It won't be as good as the oven, but—"

"Sally, I don't care if they're warm." He took out the package and opened it. "But if you want them heated, I'll put them in the microwave. How close are we on the filling?"

"Less than a minute. I'll just toss the beef back in and finish it off."

He put a few tortillas into the microwave and set the heat for thirty seconds. While waiting, he topped up the wine in his juice glass and added a splash to her mostly untouched glass. The microwave dinged, so he put the warmed tortillas on a plate and took them and the glasses out to the deck. Sally followed, holding the cast-iron pan full of steaming filling, which she put on a hot plate. They sat down to eat.

"What a feast," he said happily, spooning meat and vegetables onto a tortilla, adding a liberal sprinkling of condiments, and rolling the whole thing up.

She watched him take a bite, waiting until he said it was delicious before serving herself.

While they ate, he asked about her trip into Caribou Crossing. Then they discussed a new client who'd come by. Ben didn't tell her about his mom's nagging e-mail but did fill her in on Dusty's news. He told her he'd be seeing Monique tomorrow, and would see when she thought he'd be fit to compete.

He'd been here only a week, yet it felt strange to think about going. About leaving Sally alone. "Any luck finding a new assistant?"

"No. I sure wish Corrie would come back."

"Have you heard from her?" he asked as he assembled a second fajita.

She nodded. "I e-mailed to ask how she was and to tell her about Moon Song. She replied and said she really misses this place. She never said exactly why she had to go. I sure hope it's nothing too awful." Sally picked up her glass and swirled the wine, staring into it.

Ben assumed she was reflecting about Corrie, so it was a surprise when she put the glass down and said, "I need to call my parents. It's going to be hard."

"Did you used to get along with them?"

"Sure. We were close. They supported me in pursuing rodeo as a career."

"I'm lucky that way, too." He considered. "Your parents loved you. I bet that hasn't changed. They were hurt by being cut out of your life, but if you explain, they'll understand."

"I hope so. I sure owe them an apology. I am going

to call, just as soon as I get up the nerve." She lifted her glass again, and this time took a hearty swallow. "They were right, but I didn't listen. Why didn't I? I wasn't some foolish teenager, trying to rebel against them. I was a grown-up. Twenty-five years old. I'd traveled on the rodeo circuit for years, looking after myself on the road. I shouldn't have been so naïve."

"First love?" he suggested.

"First serious one. But . . ." She scowled into her glass. "Why did Pete pick me? Did he really love me, or did he see something in me? Something that made him want to . . . tear me down, to deconstruct the woman I was and create a new one. A woman he'd bend to his will." She gazed at Ben beseechingly. "What did he see in me that made him believe he'd be able to do that?"

"I sure didn't see anything like that, Sally. Don't blame yourself. He was twisted and he used what he called love to manipulate you."

"Why did I let myself be manipulated? Why did I always believe him?" She shook her head. "Why did I let him set the rules and punish me for breaking them even when half the time I just *knew* he'd changed them? Why did I believe him when he said my parents and sister wanted nothing to do with me? Why did I believe him when he said he loved me and that I was nothing without him? Why didn't I walk away?" She wrapped her arms around herself, this time not across her chest but lower, over her belly.

The belly that had once held the beginnings of her child. A child she'd have loved with all her heart and protected with her life. A child Pete had taken away from her.

Hunching forward, she rocked back and forth.

Ben's heart ached for her.

Chapter Seventeen

Sally hugged herself, feeling the emptiness in her womb. Why hadn't she left Pete after he made her miscarry? Those things he'd said to her, they were like a spider web he spun around her, holding her in place, powerless. While little by little he devoured her spirit, her personality, her soul.

"Sally, don't let him get to you." Ben moved closer and his hand stroked circles on her upper back the way he'd done last night. "There's nothing wrong with you. Sure, like anyone else you had weaknesses. We all do. Things that people can exploit if they're mean. Pete beat you up, physically and emotionally. Don't beat yourself up, too."

She loosened the tight grip of her arms. "How do I know it won't happen again?"

"You're older and wiser," he said bluntly. "Don't be isolated. Get back in touch with your family, make some friends. Build your confidence. See a counselor."

She cocked her head. "A counselor? The macho rodeo cowboy is suggesting therapy?"

He touched his sling. "A fractured shoulder might heal by itself, but it'll do better with the help of a physio."

"Hmm. I'll think about it." It would mean spilling her guts to a stranger, but she'd done that with Ben and felt better for it. "Okay, that's enough of my issues for tonight. I know you watch your carbs, but could I tempt you with warm peach pie à la mode?"

"Oh, man, that sounds great."

"It's bakery pie, not homemade, but it looked good." It was a sign of how much she trusted Ben that she'd done this. The first and only time she'd served store-bought baked goods to Pete, he'd thrown the chocolate cake across the kitchen.

"Sally, I know you're too busy to bake pie."

They both gathered up plates and leftovers and he followed her into the kitchen. She didn't protest when he rinsed the dirty dishes. This was companionable, the two of them working together rather than her waiting on him. Her kitchen felt like a warmer, nicer place.

Soon they were back on the deck with pie and ice cream, and mugs of coffee. It was dusk now, and she lit the citronella candles to discourage the mosquitoes.

She savored her pie while Ben wolfed his down. Then he moved his chair from behind the table so he could stretch back in it and rest his bare feet on the low railing that ran around the deck. Balancing his coffee mug on his flat stomach, he said, "Terrific dinner. Thanks, Sally."

"Thank *you*, Ben. For everything."

"My pleasure." His smile warmed his eyes, telling her he really meant it.

Tonight he wore shorts that ended a few inches above his knees, showing off well-shaped legs dusted with dark hair. Though he was naturally dark-skinned thanks to his Native Canadian heritage, his legs were lighter in color than his tanned arms. She was so used to seeing him in jeans and boots that his bare legs and feet seemed particularly naked. Physical. Masculine.

Appealing.

She kicked off her old flip-flops and wiggled her own bare toes. Maybe the next time she went into town, she'd buy shorts from the friendly Maribeth.

Shedding clothes was liberating. Wearing nicely fitted ones was, too. Pete had made her feel like she needed to hide her femaleness from the world, but Ben had suggested she look at Cassidy, Jess, and Brooke as role models.

She liked that. He didn't issue orders the way Pete had. He gave her suggestions and things to think about so she could make up her own mind.

They sat in easy silence as she finished her pie and he sipped coffee. Then he said, "I keep meaning to ask, whatever happened to that pretty silver grulla mare you used to ride? I remember how you used to dress to match your horse."

Silver grullas were rare, and Misty'd been gorgeous with her silvery body and dark sepia brown points and face. Sally had worn a silver shirt teamed with brown pants and a brown hat. Rodeo was, after all, a performance for an audience.

"Autumn Mist," she said nostalgically. "I hope she's enjoying a happy retirement. When I quit rodeo, I sold her to a breeder who specializes in rodeo horses." The mare could breed winners: she'd had the quickest legs, the tightest turns, the fire in her belly to round those barrels cleanly, race down the stretches, and bring it home in the fastest time.

"I'm surprised you sold her. You were such a team. When a rider has a bond like that with their horse . . ." He shrugged.

"I know." Ben had it with Chaunce; it was obvious when she saw them together. "I still miss her. Pete said we needed all the money we could raise to buy this place and get the business started." She lifted her chin. "I see now that making me sell Misty was another way he cut me off from my past, from everything I cared about, and made me emotionally dependent on him."

"Bastard."

"Yeah." It felt good hearing Ben say that. Even better would be saying it herself. "He was a bastard. An asshole." She swallowed. "An abuser. He was sick and he was mean." Power flooded through her as she spoke each word.

"Good for you," Ben said gruffly. He cleared his throat. "It kills me that he isn't still alive so I could beat him up and give him a taste of his own medicine."

That notion shouldn't give her a thrill, yet it did. Still, she said, "It's the past, Ben. I'm in control of my life now." And she knew what she had to do. "I'm going to call my parents." After this conversation, she had the nerve to do it.

"Good." He paused. "You mean now?"

She checked her watch, and added an hour. "They've probably gone to bed. I'll do it first thing in the morning."

"Speaking of which." He dropped his feet to the deck. "Morning comes early."

They took the dishes to the kitchen. She hadn't left a light on, so the room was dim. On the radio, Kip Moore started to sing "Hey Pretty Girl," one of those songs that made a relationship sound like a lifelong romance. When she had married Pete, she'd actually believed that was how it would be. She laid her plate and mug on the counter, but when she reached to click the light switch, Ben's hand stopped hers.

"Hear what he just said?" he asked.

"He asked her if he could have the next dance."

"Seems like a real good idea to me." Deftly, he undid

the cuff and collar of his sling. "Don't tell me I shouldn't take this off. It's just one dance."

She tensed, uncertain, as he held out his arms to her. And then, because this was Ben and because she wanted to, she stepped closer. She put one hand in his and rested the other on his uninjured shoulder.

When he set their bodies in motion slow and easy, she closed her eyes and let herself simply enjoy being with this man. Enjoy being a woman dancing to a romantic song with a man she liked. Not a woman without baggage, but a woman making a fresh start.

Ben's body was so strong but he held her as if she was as special as a wildflower. Her hand rested in his as if it had come home. This close, she could smell his scent, like sunshine on pine needles. He hummed along to the music, a little off-key, which struck her as endearing.

Kip Moore had reached the verse where the woman in the song had their baby. It always brought tears to Sally's eyes and made her click off the radio. But not tonight. She remembered how right little Nicki had felt in her arms. Maybe one day she'd be a confident woman and she'd meet the right man—a kind, trustworthy man a lot like Ben—and they'd fall in love, marry, and have children. How amazing it was to feel hopeful. Perhaps even optimistic.

The song ended and, still within the circle of Ben's arms, she looked up at him. She owed everything to this man. The one gazing down at her with warm eyes, eyes that held affection and—her breath caught—desire.

Her body tightened in response, every cell tingling with awareness. With an instinctive craving for his touch. And yet she'd learned to be scared of touch. Learned that a caress could so easily do a one eighty and become a blow.

His head lowered.

She tensed. She wanted him to kiss her, yet memories of being hurt made her afraid.

As Ben's lips touched her forehead, she kept utterly still. He held her loosely; she could pull away if she chose to. Yet she didn't. She waited and, as his soft lips lingered against her skin, she slowly relaxed and enjoyed the sensation, gentle and warm as the kiss of the sun. She closed her eyes and tilted her head up to him.

He kissed the space between her eyebrows, the tip of her nose.

Her breath quickened and her lips parted slightly to let air in and out.

His lips touched hers, feather-light. Not pressing, just resting there as she breathed against him. Did she want more? Could she handle more?

Before she could decide, his mouth left hers and he was stepping away from her with a sigh of regret. "Night, Sally. It was a fine one."

And he was gone, leaving her with her lips still open a crack, unable to find the right words. Maybe there were no words for how wonderful this felt.

Lying in bed, Sally listened to the resident birds vying to see which could give the most vibrant welcome to a new day. She felt like adding her voice. She had so many things to look forward to, including new clothes and attractively cut hair. And Ben.

First, though, there was something she needed to do. Now, while the day beckoned, before she could have second thoughts.

It was an hour later in Alberta. Her parents, country folk, rose with the dawn. She sat up in bed and called the old, familiar number. Two rings and a male voice answered, "Morning."

"D-dad? It's Sally." Had Penny mentioned that they'd spoken or was this coming as a complete surprise?

The long pause told her it was a shock to her father. She imagined his jaw dropping, and hoped that, when reality sank in, the expression on his face would be pleasure rather than anger. "Sally? Is that really you?" His normally vigorous voice faltered as hers had.

"It is. I'm sorry for not calling before, but I wasn't sure . . . I didn't know if you'd want to hear from me."

"Not want to hear from you? You're our daughter." He must have turned his head slightly, because he didn't burst her eardrum when he yelled, "Marge, get in here, it's Sally!" Then, into the phone, "Are you all right? You're not sick or anything?"

"No, I'm fine. Just—"

"Wait a minute. I'm going to put you on speaker phone so we can both hear."

A moment later, her mother's voice said, "Sally, is it really you?"

"Mom, I'm so sorry—"

"I thought we'd never hear from you again!" Sally heard tears in her mother's voice.

Blinking back moisture in her own eyes, she said, "I wanted to talk to you but I thought you were so mad at me for marrying Pete and moving away."

"We weren't exactly happy," her dad said gruffly. "But we sure didn't mean to drive you away from even being in touch with us."

"You didn't. I think . . ." It was Pete. "I talked to Penny and she said that for the first year after Pete and I moved here, you e-mailed, phoned, and wrote."

"Well, of course we did." Her mom sounded confused.

"But you didn't reply," her dad said. "Then Pete told us in no uncertain terms that you didn't want any contact with us, and we should stop harassing you."

There it was: the truth. Her parents would never lie to her. Unlike the husband who had promised to love, honor, and cherish her. "There's something I need to tell you."

And she let it spill. All of it. How Pete had cut her off from them, isolated her from the world. The emotional abuse. The physical abuse. Even the miscarriage. Sometimes she could barely force words out, she was crying so hard.

Her mom sobbed too, and Sally thought that even her dad shed a tear or two. He said that if Pete was still alive, he'd rip him to pieces and her mom said, "Not if I got to him first."

It was messy; it was honest; it was loving. She only wished she were with them to feel their arms around her.

Finally, her mother said, "I really wish you'd known you could always come to us."

Sally wiped tears away. "He messed with my mind. But I'm thinking for myself now."

"What happened, honey?" her dad asked. "I mean, why did you call us now?"

"Penny met an old friend of mine who's still riding in the rodeo. He was coming to B.C. and she asked him to look me up. She said enough time had gone by, and that you all missed me. That made me think, and I called Penny, and—"

"She didn't say anything!" Her mom sounded outraged.

"It was only a couple of days ago and I was confused. That was when it started to sink in, what Pete had done. I cut the call short. Penny probably wasn't sure what I'd do and didn't want to get your hopes up. I need to call her again."

"Would it be easier for you," her mother asked, "if we told her what you said, so you don't have to go through it again?"

She considered. "I think it would. And then would you ask her to call me?"

"Of course," her mom said. "Oh, Sally, I wish you could come for a visit."

"Or just come back," her father said. "Why don't you come home?"

"I'd really like to be close to you guys, but I do love it here." Now it wasn't only the appeal of the countryside, and the business she'd built, it was also the sense that she might have friends, even become part of a community. Of course in Alberta there'd be some of the kids she'd gone to school with, but she was a different person. Too much had happened. "Maybe you could come here for a visit?"

"We for sure can do that," her dad said. "Penny can't travel for a while, though. Did she tell you she's expecting?"

"She did. That's so wonderful. I'd love to see her, and the baby when it arrives. And to meet her husband. But I really can't leave Ryland Riding." Even if Corrie had been here, it was too much responsibility to hand over to someone else. Nor could Sally afford to cancel lessons.

"We'll work something out," her mom said.

Sally recognized that determined tone. When Marge Pantages used it, things happened.

Ben, at work in the barn, kept glancing at his watch. Usually, Sally was here by now. Had he offended her— or even worse, scared her—with that kiss last night?

When she finally appeared, her eyes were puffy and

red. Damn. "You've been crying," he said gruffly. "If I did something to upset you—"

"No!" She shook her head, her tossing curls bright in the barn's dim lighting. "No, not at all. I called my parents and it got pretty emotional."

He peeled off his work gloves and caught her hand. "Oh, man, was it bad?"

Another head-shake, less vigorous. "No, it was really good. I told them everything. They forgave me, said they understood." Her lips twitched. "They both wanted to kill Pete."

"They can get in line behind me."

"I think they're going to come out for a visit."

"They'll be proud of what you've built for yourself here."

"You think?"

"This is damned impressive." It impressed the hell out of him. Made him very aware of how little he'd accomplished at going-on thirty. What did a bunch of trophy buckles and a few thousand dollars in a savings account count for compared to what Sally had achieved?

"It's strange to think that I wouldn't have all of this but for Pete. I think in his own way he did love me and want a good life for us. But he was . . ."

"Twisted. And an asshole."

"Yes." She smiled and freed her hand from his.

"I need to know something. Is it okay that I kissed you last night?"

Her eyes widened, then she blinked slowly, lashes fanning down, staying there for a couple of beats before they rose again. Something knowing and female touched the corners of her mouth. "You call that a kiss, cowboy?"

It was his turn to be surprised. He gulped, but quickly

recovered. "I can do way better than that, ma'am," he drawled. "If you give me a second chance."

She gazed into his eyes, not blinking now or looking embarrassed. "I just might do that."

Heat surged through him, making his heart thud and tightening his groin. "Sally, I like you and I want you. You know I'll only be around for a little while. But while I am, I want whatever you're willing to give me. You get to set the boundaries. Always. Tell me what they are, and I'll never overstep."

"I believe you. Right now, the boundaries are a moving target. Let's take it one step at a time and see where we go."

"Fair enough. How about we see if Heather's available to come out for the evening? We could ride into town, pick up some picnic food, and find ourselves a pretty spot to eat dinner." He imagined the two of them stretched out on a blanket, maybe by a scenic lake. Romantic and secluded, yet other riders might pass by, which would help Sally feel safe.

Chapter Eighteen

The late-afternoon sun felt good on Sally's bare arms. The aroma of fresh cut hay made her breathe in deeply and smile as she and Ben trotted their horses side by side along a dirt-and-grass farm road. A red-wing blackbird sent a serenade trilling from a fence post.

Her long-sleeved shirt was stuffed into the cantle bag she'd tied onto the back of Campion's saddle, and she felt free and easy in her short-sleeved green tee. She'd need to buy sunscreen, though. It was something she hadn't needed before, since she'd always been so covered up.

She gazed over at Ben, looking so at home on the back of his Paint despite the sling he wore. "Good thing you ride Western." English style riding involved holding reins in both hands.

"If I rode English, I wouldn't have been on a bucking bronc," he reminded her, and they both laughed.

A lot of folks thought people were crazy to compete in rodeos, but she'd always said it was no more crazy than most jobs. For her and Ben, crazy would be sitting inside at a computer all day, not breathing fresh air or exercising or challenging their bodies. Despite the temporary glitch of a fractured shoulder, his body, clad now in a short-sleeved blue shirt along with his usual jeans, boots, and hat, certainly showed the benefits of all that exercise. No question he was a fine-looking man. A man in his prime.

As for her, she'd thought she was past her "best before" date, yet in the past few days she'd begun to think maybe that wasn't true. Look at Brooke Brannon. The woman was more than ten years older than Sally, a grandmother and new mother. She looked young, vibrant, sexy, and her handsome husband, Jake, was obviously head over heels for her.

Maybe what mattered was attitude, Sally thought. If you *felt* vital and attractive, then you could be those things. Right now, that was how she felt. She tossed her hat back so it dangled by the cord, and urged Campion into a gallop. The bay gelding loved to run. Fingers of breeze combed through her curls, making her feel free and a little wild.

Ben's laugh sounded from behind her, then Chaunce raced up beside her, keeping pace.

How much better this was than spending her evenings cleaning tack, doing housework, or paying bills. Having Ben around had, among other benefits, lightened her workload. She'd even found an hour to work in the garden, though it was frustrating to know she was helping feed the deer and rabbits. She hadn't mentioned that to Corrie, not after all the effort the younger woman had put into that garden.

Corrie had asked, in her e-mail, whether Sally'd found a new assistant. Sally had fudged and said she did have someone helping her. She hadn't wanted Corrie to worry. She, on the other hand, was concerned about Corrie and whatever problems had called her away.

Riding into a patch of woods, Sally slowed Campion

to a trot and leaned forward to pat his neck. As the trail narrowed, Ben eased his horse in behind.

What would she do when he left? And not just because he was such a helpful assistant. His cheerful company brightened each day and his insight and support helped her regain her confidence. The attraction that sparked between them made her not only remember she was a woman, but be glad of it. If Ben hadn't dropped by to visit, she might well have been stuck in the same old rut for the rest of her life.

And wasn't that a sobering thought? Not that she'd been miserable by any means, but now her eyes had opened to how much more life had to offer.

When they came out of the trees and onto a dirt road, Ben drew up beside her again.

"I owe you so much," she said.

"What?" He glanced over, frowning. "What are you talking about?"

"For helping me break out of the prison I'd stuck myself in."

The frown lifted. "Aw, Sally. That's about the nicest thing anyone ever said to me. Thank you."

Her mouth opened in disbelief, then she had to laugh. "Ben Traynor, you're really something. I start out thanking you, and somehow you turn it around so you're thanking me."

"Seems like you and me are lucky to be together."

"I guess we are." And how flattering that was, that he counted himself lucky to be with her rather than with some hot young buckle bunny.

As they rode on, she told him about her sister's phone call this afternoon. Penny had been in tears over what Sally'd gone through. They'd sworn not to let anyone or anything ever again drive a wedge through their family.

Entering the outskirts of town, Sally asked, "Where will we put our horses?"

"There's a place called Westward Ho!"

"I think that's where Dave and Cassidy board their horses."

"I checked it out the last time I was here."

She followed him and they arrived at a nicely maintained barn and paddock. Because they only figured on being half an hour, they chose to tie their horses to a hitching rail in the shade. After loosening the horses' cinches and giving them a couple of sips of water, they provided the cheerful teen staff person with their cell numbers and the animals' names. Then they strode along the sidewalk leading downtown.

Ben reached for her hand and it felt like the most natural thing in the world to let him take it. Such a simple thing, but how wonderful it felt, being connected to him that way. His fingers entwined with hers in a perfect fit.

But when she saw Madeleine, the owner of Star of Egypt, step out of a store, her habit of privacy returned and she slid her hand free. Madeleine turned and walked in the other direction, not even noticing Sally and Ben.

"Sally?" Ben questioned.

"I'm not comfortable with holding hands." Bad choice of words. She felt very comfortable with her hand in his. Trying to clarify, she said, "I don't want people gossiping about me."

He glanced at her and she sensed there was something he wanted to say, but he settled for "Okay."

It was late enough that the specialty stores like the bakery and deli were closed, so Sally and Ben went into the grocery store.

"I packed bottled water in my cantle bag," she told

Ben, "and I put what was left of last night's wine in a plastic bottle. I picked some baby carrots from the garden, and I packed a couple of pieces of peach pie."

"A good start. Let's get a loaf of French bread, some cheese and cold meat, and some olives. I brought a knife. No plates, though."

"I have paper towels. They'll do. I didn't bring glasses because I was afraid they'd break. I've been responsible for enough broken glass. Want to buy plastic ones?"

"I'm good with drinking out of the bottle. If you are."

Passing a plastic bottle and both drinking out of it? She loved the informality and the intimacy. "I'm good with it."

It didn't take long to make their selections, and she remembered to add sunscreen.

Back at Westward Ho!, Ben stuffed the groceries into their saddlebags and she borrowed the restroom to slather on sunscreen, then wash her hands.

As they rode out of town, Ben said, "Want to go to that lake with the beaver dam?"

"Sure. It doesn't have a beach, so it's less likely to attract local teens who want to party."

Her logic proved right. When they arrived, they had the lake to themselves except for the ducks, dragonflies, and a pair of noisy kingfishers. Ben unfastened a plaid blanket that he'd had rolled and tied to the back of his saddle, and spread it on a sunny patch of rough grass. They tugged off their boots and socks and couldn't resist rolling up the legs of their jeans and dipping their feet into the cool water.

Refreshed, they heeded their growling stomachs and unpacked the goodies. Using Ben's knife to slice the bread and cheese, they dug in. As they ate, they passed the plastic bottle of wine back and forth. An older couple rode by and exchanged greetings, and then a teenage girl who was texting as she rode.

As contented and lazy as one of her hens basking in the sun, Sally didn't feel any pressing need to make conversation. Either Ben felt the same way or he picked up on her mood, because he mostly kept quiet too, except to make an occasional comment about the food or to offer her more wine.

Though they didn't talk, she was totally aware of him. He was large, taking up more than his fair share of the blanket, but he was also just so physical and masculine. The tanned skin of his forearms, the press of his strong thighs against the faded denim of his jeans, the relish with which he ate, they made her not only aware of his body but also of hers. And of the slow warmth of arousal rippling through her blood, far more intoxicating than the wine.

After polishing off the peach pie, they packaged up everything but the wine and water. Ben stretched out on his side, using his good arm to prop his head up. "This is the life."

The air had cooled slightly and Sally pulled her shirt on over her tee, but left the sleeves rolled up her forearms. She sat cross-legged on the blanket beside him. "You're easy to be with," she told him shyly. "I feel like I can be myself, and that's okay with you."

"It's more than okay. That's how I want you to be." He studied her face. "Who's 'yourself'? I mean, how do you see yourself?"

"Um . . ." No one had ever asked her that. She reflected, taking an absentminded sip of wine. "A country girl, obviously. Hardworking. My parents taught me that things that come too easily often don't have much value. There's a lot of satisfaction in old-fashioned hard work."

"True. But life's got to be about more than work."

"Sure. So, to add to my list: nature-lover, horse-lover, chicken-lover. Those things give me joy. So does teaching, especially teaching children. I love country music. Wildflowers. Fresh veggies from my own garden. I guess I'm a woman of simple tastes and pleasures."

"Those are all good things you're listing. Anything more that you see in yourself?"

Thinking about that, she uncurled her legs and stretched out on her side, facing him. "Being a daughter and sister used to be a big part of my identity. A friend, as well. I value those things and I care about people. I'm . . . rusty when it comes to relationships, but I'd like to rebuild some and also pursue some new ones."

He sat up. "How about man-woman type relationships?"

"That's a really good question." She lay still, watching him. He was such a tempting man.

"Is there a really good answer?" he teased as he slipped off the sling.

She tensed slightly, not with fear as much as anticipation and desire. Was he going to kiss her? Come on to her? Her body craved him, yet the idea of sex made her anxious. What a mess she was. Slowly, she said, "I didn't think I'd ever want to be with a man again. I didn't think I could ever trust one. Or trust my judgment."

"But?" He took her bare foot in both his hands, startling her.

Again she tensed but then, as he began to massage her foot, she relaxed and shifted to lie on her back, giving him better access. Oh, that felt good, his warm fingers kneading firmly, finding aches she hadn't been aware of. Putting her hands behind her head to pillow it, she closed her eyes. "I'm only now realizing how badly Pete messed me up. And that I can be a different person—I already am—but it's going to take time."

"But it was okay when I kissed you? Did you like it?" His thumbs worked the top of her foot and his fingers rubbed the bottom, strong enough to cause a delicious sensation as knots of tension softened and released.

"Mmm. Ben, that feels so good. And yes, I liked it when you kissed me, and I liked dancing with you. It made me . . ."

His hands paused. "Yes?"

"Want more," she confessed, her eyes still closed, the words barely more than a breath.

He captured her other foot and started to work it. "Me, too. Sally, I won't hurt you and I won't try to control you. I like you all feisty and strong and independent. Do you believe me?"

"I think I do. You make me feel . . . safe." Here they were, on a picnic blanket out in the middle of nowhere, and was he trying to jump her? No, he was massaging her feet. Which, actually, felt more than a little arousing.

"Safe is good. Sexy is good, too."

She couldn't help but grin. "I guess it could be." The sensations traveling from her foot up her leg to her feminine core were pretty darned sexy, and definitely good.

"You know I'm going back on the rodeo circuit, right?"

Surprised, she opened her eyes and looked up, to find him gazing at her. "Of course."

"After I go, I hope we'll stay friends. Keep in touch. I want you to know that if you ever need me, you should let me know."

"O-kay," she said slowly. "But, um, it kind of sounds like you're saying good-bye now. I thought Monique said today that you'd need to wait at least another week."

"She did. Sorry, that's not what I mean." He released her foot and gazed earnestly at her. "I want to be clear about where I stand. Most important, I want us to be friends. And like I told you, I'm really attracted to you. If you're looking to, uh, try out the male-female thing with someone safe, then, uh . . ." He broke off, made a rueful face. "Oh, man, I'm messing this up."

A giggle spluttered out and she sat up, hooking her arms around her bent knees. "You're volunteering to have sex with me out of the goodness of your heart?"

He grinned back. "Like I said, messing up totally. I'm trying really hard not to sound like some lust-crazed monster, and I promise I won't act like one."

She leaned over and touched his bare forearm, so strong and warm. "I think I get it."

"No expectations. No demands. No strings. If it never gets past a kiss, that's fine."

"You're not going to force a wedding ring on my finger and move me to some distant province?" she asked dryly, proud that she could attempt a joke about her experience with Pete.

"Somehow I don't think that's in the cards."

In truth, she knew Ben would never do anything like that. Not only wasn't he that kind of man, but he had no interest in leaving rodeo and settling down, not for some years yet. Even if he had, he should find a younger, less damaged woman, one who had more to give him than she did.

He had said he was safe. That was true in so many ways. Safe, in that he'd respect whatever limits she set. Safe, in that he wouldn't sweep her off her feet and try to take over her life. Safe, in that he'd already helped her start on the path of healing. He'd helped her feel like a woman, an attractive and sexy woman.

And she was attracted to him. Right now, she couldn't imagine even contemplating sex with any other man.

The evening sunshine turned Sally's eyes a deep mossy green. "You know what I'd like?" she asked.

"No idea." Though he could hope.

"Another dance. In my kitchen. And after, when you kiss me, maybe you could"—mischief glinted in her eyes—"ramp it up a little?"

He was on his feet, extending his right hand to pull her up. "Race you home."

They loaded up their gear and, despite his joking words, took their time riding back. It was a perfect July evening and Ben liked hanging on to the anticipation of that dance and ramped-up kiss. The ride, with the sun slipping from the sky and the only sound the creak and jingle of the horses' tack and the soft thud of their hooves against hard-packed ground, seemed like part of the slow, teasing sense of foreplay.

He had to be careful, to bank down on the desire that threatened to rage through his body. Yeah, in part he felt like a lust-crazed monster, but he'd rather die from blue balls than do anything to scare Sally.

Back at Ryland Riding, they greeted Heather and a couple of owners who'd just returned from a ride of their own and were turning their horses out to pasture. Heather left and Ben took care of Chaunce and Campion while Sally tended to her chickens. He then made a pit stop in his trailer to splash water on his face, brush his teeth, and comb his hair. He left the sling on the table and deliberately did not put a condom in his pocket. It wouldn't be right for things to go that far tonight, even though his body hungered for release.

Man, he was as nervous as a teen on his first date.

Mary-Jane Kowalski. Brown hair, blue eyes, and the cutest impish grin. They'd been twelve and he'd taken her to the movies. She'd wanted to see *Free Willy 3,* so two ranch kids who'd never seen the ocean had watched boys rescue an orca from whalers. He'd held her hand, their fingers greasy from eating buttered popcorn. Grinning at the memory, he sauntered toward the house, admiring an indigo sky full of stars.

The kitchen door was open and he heard music playing. After knocking lightly on the doorframe and calling a quiet "Hello," he took off his boots and stepped inside. The room was dark and there was no sign of Sally. On the radio, a Carrie Underwood song ended and the announcer said, "And now I'm gonna play something for all the lovers out there. Grab your honey for Keith Urban singing about 'Somebody Like You.'"

"Sally," Ben called, "they're playing our song."

Footsteps thumped lightly on the stairs and she appeared in the kitchen doorway, illuminated by light from the hallway behind her. "We have a song? Oh, that one." She'd taken off the long-sleeved shirt and now wore only the tee with her jeans. She was barefoot and her hair was freshly brushed.

He held out his arms to her and she stepped into them with no hesitation. Ignoring the pain in his shoulder, he gathered her close but not too close, holding her firmly but gently. Taking care with her. Leading her so that their bodies found a harmony in tune with each other and the music. Her hand was warm and relaxed in his, her waist supple under his other hand. His sock-clad foot brushed her bare one a time or two.

He struggled to control the arousal that tightened his groin.

As Keith Urban sang about letting go of the lonely days and forgiving himself for his mistakes, Ben hoped that Sally could do all of those things too. If she did, what would she want? Would she want, as the guy in the song did, to love somebody?

Ben wanted that for her. He wanted her to have all the things she'd ever dreamed of. A man who respected and loved her, who deserved this amazing woman. One day Ben would drive though Caribou Crossing, stop to visit, and she'd have a husband and a couple of kids. And he'd feel . . . well, he'd feel what he felt right now. A pang he couldn't put a name to, something poignant that sent an ache through his heart.

And that was just plain crazy when he was holding this sweet-smelling, gently curved, strong yet vulnerable woman in his arms. He eased her a little closer so his hip brushed hers.

She rested her head against him, her cheek turned into his shoulder so that her soft breath caressed his neck.

Now no amount of self-control could will his growing erection to subside. He murmured against her soft hair, "Don't get nervous, sweetheart. I told you I want you, but nothing's gonna happen unless you want it to."

She didn't answer. Nor did she move away.

The song faded away and Brad Paisley's "She's Everything" came on. Another good one to dance to, but instead Ben eased away from Sally, keeping her hand in his. "Come on outside."

When they were on the deck, he said, "It's a night full of stars."

She gazed at the sky, her eyes huge and her face luminous in starlight. "It's beautiful."

"Not half as beautiful as you." He rested two fingers under her chin to keep her head tilted upward, and then he stepped in front of her and bent to touch his lips to hers.

She closed her eyes and angled her head so their mouths matched up perfectly.

He ran his fingers through those soft, soft curls to lightly cup the back of her head, and he kissed her gently.

Her lips softened, parted slightly, and she kissed him back. Lightly, tentatively, her breath smelling of mint.

He didn't push, didn't try to part her lips or take the kiss any further, just focused on the moment, on the wonder of having Sally kiss him.

Her arms crept under his and around him and she came up on her toes. Her lips pressed harder, her breasts brushed his chest, and her hips snugged up against his. The hard-on that distended his fly didn't seem to faze her.

With the tip of his tongue, he tasted her lips.

She made one of those uniquely feminine sounds, like a sigh and moan combined, and her tongue touched his, shyly at first then growing bolder.

He teased her tongue with his until finally she darted hers inside his mouth. After she'd explored, he took his turn. As they kissed, he slid one hand down her back, cupped her firm butt, and squeezed.

She wriggled her hips against his erection, her restless movements telling him how turned on she was.

Cautiously, he reached between their bodies and caressed her breast through her clothing.

She pressed into his hand, making that hungry sound again.

He eased his mouth from hers. "You feel amazing. Are you okay, sweetheart?"

"Yes." And then, softly, "Nervous."

"We're not gonna have sex tonight, so don't be nervous about that, okay?"

"We're not?"

"I didn't bring a condom because it's too soon."

She cocked her head. "You decided that?"

"Uh, yeah." Not wanting her to think he was bossing her around, he tried to explain. "You haven't been with a guy in a long time, and the way things were with Pete, I know you're carrying some pretty heavy baggage. I don't want us to, you know, get carried away and end up doing something you might regret in the morning."

Something sparked in her eyes, or was it the reflection of starlight? "You figure I'd regret having sex with you?"

"Not because it wouldn't be good," he clarified. "But because it happened so fast."

"Because I got carried away? Because you're so irresistible that I'd just get carried away?"

He groaned. "Sorry. You know that's not what I meant. Jeez, Sally, I didn't mean to be obnoxious. Believe it or not, I was trying to be considerate."

She gave a soft, forgiving laugh. "I do believe you. You maybe could've phrased it better, but I hear what you're saying and you're right. I admit I'm relieved to not have to worry about whether I'm ready for sex Whether I'll be able to handle it." The corners of her mouth tucked up with a hint of mischief. "Though I'll also admit to a little sexual frustration."

"Hey, sweetheart, I never said I was gonna leave you sexually frustrated."

Her eyes widened. "Now you've definitely got my attention, Ben Traynor."

Chapter Nineteen

For a cocky cowboy, Ben could be endearingly awkward. And very sweet. Not to mention sexy. He'd certainly made her hot and twitchy. But he was right, that even as she enjoyed the slow build of arousal in her body, anxiety hovered.

Where did they go from here? More fooling around? That was what he'd seemed to suggest.

With Pete, sex had been intercourse, usually in the missionary position. When she had her period, it was her giving him a blow job. Ben made her remember how seductive foreplay could be. More so, though, when it wasn't accompanied by the whine of mosquitoes. "Shall we go inside?"

"Sure."

This time, she took his hand and led him into the kitchen. The radio was still playing. They could dance again, but she wanted something more intimate. Because of that, and because she believed Ben when he'd said nothing would happen unless she wanted it to, she led him into the hallway and up the stairs. In the bedroom, enough light came from the hallway and through the uncurtained window to reveal the shapes of the furniture.

Quivering with nerves, she sat on the edge of the bed. Ben stood in front of her. "No sex," she said, reminding both of them. His fly bulged with a sizable erection, tempting her to unzip him and fondle him. But warring with that impulse were bad memories of Pete's hands holding her head in an unrelenting grip as he forced his swollen dick down her throat and she tried not to choke. When Ben said they wouldn't have sex, what did that mean? Would he want her to bring him to release with her mouth? Once upon a time, she'd enjoyed doing that, but—

"I won't even take my clothes off," he said. "Does that make you feel safer?"

His desire to take care of her warmed her heart. "Yes," she admitted. "I hate being like this. So . . . fragile and pathetic."

"You're neither of those things, Sally." His voice was firm. "Now lie back on the bed."

When she complied he lay beside her, rolling on to his left side to face her. He winced. "Ouch. Wrong side."

She gasped. "I forgot about your shoulder! Ben, we shouldn't be doing this."

"Shh." He rose and walked around the bed. "Can't imagine we're going to get so acrobatic that it hurts my shoulder." He said it dryly, which for some reason eased her nerves.

She rolled over to face him and when he lay on his right side, there was no wince. He stroked his hand gently down her arm, starting at the shoulder and moving over the sleeve of her T-shirt then onto the bare skin above her elbow, then over her elbow and along her forearm to her wrist. "This is nice, lying here together," he said.

What did he expect her to do? What did she want to do? Tentatively, she reached out to explore his face. With trembling fingers she caressed his strong cheekbone, thinking about his striking male beauty. "I know you're part First Nations. From what relative?"

"Mom's mother was Blackfoot." He stroked the inside of her wrist. "You really want to talk about that now?"

"I was just thinking how it makes you so distinctive. So handsome."

"Okay, maybe we can talk about it."

She gave a soft giggle. He had such a way of relaxing her even as he turned her on. With a more confident touch, she traced the line of his jaw, then moved up to touch his lips with two fingers. "Kiss me again, Ben."

Resting his hand on her shoulder, he leaned forward and did, slowly and thoroughly. Her blood sang with sweet pleasure as she kissed him back. Never had a man made such a lazy, sensual feast of her mouth. Arousal throbbed between her legs and her nipples hardened, craving his touch. Her clothes were too confining, yet she didn't have the guts to take them off.

He cupped her breast. Even through the cotton of her bra and tee, she felt his heat. Her flesh tingled. When he squeezed gently, she pushed into his hand, wordlessly asking for more.

He leaned closer, pressed his mouth against her nipple through her tee, and moistened the fabric with his tongue. Her already-taut flesh tightened further as need became an ache. When he sucked her with moist lips, she couldn't suppress a moan of pleasure.

His hand slipped under the hem of her T-shirt and caressed her skin above the waist of her jeans. The slight abrasion from his calluses enhanced his every touch. "So soft," he murmured. He lifted the bottom of her tee away from her body, kissing a trail that followed where his fingers had stroked her. When he slid his fingers under her bra and eased it upward, away from her breasts, she tensed in anticipation. The good kind of anticipation.

"Okay?" he asked.

"Oh, yes. Don't stop."

Now his seductive mouth was on her bare nipple, laving it, caressing it, sucking it. Oh, Lord, how good it felt. Her hips twisted restlessly as arousal pulsed between her legs. "Don't stop," she murmured again.

"It'll feel better if I take off your tee and bra."

She raised herself so he could peel off her shirt, undo the back clasp of her bra, and slide it off as well. Her first instinct was to throw an arm across her chest to hide her nakedness. Her second, when she saw the appreciative smile on his face, was to lie back and let him admire her. And, hopefully, to touch her.

Which he did, suckling the other nipple.

The need between her legs sent her hips forward, seeking contact. She pressed her jean-clad front against him, hooking her top leg over his thigh, seeking the right angle so she could rub against his erection. Once, sex had been a joyful, satisfying act. Back when she'd been a whole, vital, confident woman. Ben, with his mouth and hands, his patience and care, was bringing that woman back to life.

He took his time with her breasts but he also kissed her chest, her shoulders. He moved her horseshoe pendant out of the way and pressed kisses to her neck and throat. His caresses made her aware of every inch of her nakedness, making her feel feminine and beautiful.

When he put his hand on her shoulder and gently urged her to lie on her back and untwine their lower bodies, she murmured a protest but complied. He touched the waist of her jeans, slipped the button free, and paused. "Is this okay?"

She squeezed her legs together, pressing against the ache between them, imagining what it would feel like if he touched her there. If he entered her . . . But he'd said there'd be no intercourse tonight, so she didn't have to worry if he'd be gentle, or if it would hurt. If she'd be afraid—and if all these wonderful sensations would die as memories flooded back. "Yes, it's okay." She lifted her hips to make it easier for him to slide her jeans off.

And then she was naked but for a pair of blue panties. Plain cotton, bikini style; no fancy lingerie. Panties with a very damp crotch.

But Ben didn't go straight for her crotch, nor attempt to strip off her panties. Instead, still clad in his own jeans and shirt, he moved down the bed and caressed her feet and ankles, his fingers teasing and sexy. Slowly, he made his way up her legs, adding kisses, licks, and nips that made her realize her legs had some surprising erogenous zones.

When he reached her upper thighs, she knew he must smell the musky tang of her arousal. What would he do? He'd said he wouldn't leave her sexually frustrated.

He sat back, studying her from head to toe. "You're a treat to look at, Sally, and to touch." Sliding up the bed, he gazed into her eyes. "How you doing, sweetheart?"

"Good." The word came out breathy, on an exhalation. "Very good."

"Not scared?"

"I'm . . ." She examined her feelings. Knowing he wouldn't enter her, she didn't have to worry what it would be like. She could simply enjoy. "No, I'm not scared."

"I'm glad." He dropped a quick kiss on her lips, then moved down her body. More light kisses landed in her navel and along her panty line, but he didn't peel her panties off or even slide his fingers under the cotton.

Maybe she wouldn't have minded if he had. . . .

His big hand spread over the front of her panties, covering her mound. His fingers slipped lower. On a needy sigh, she parted her legs, hoping he'd touch her where she most needed it. Through damp cotton, he cupped her sex, his hand so warm and firm. It felt wonderful, but she craved more. Tension of a purely sexy kind coiled inside her, a tension he'd promised to satisfy.

He stroked back and forth with two fingers, the sensation so delicious that she whimpered and pressed against him. She thrust her head back against the pillow, closing her eyes to better focus on the sensations, tilting her hips upward and widening the spread of her legs.

Would she climax? Even back in the days when she'd enjoyed sex, orgasm hadn't come easily for her. She'd feel the build-up, but often not quite get to the peak.

Even reaching this point with Ben was a triumph. She shouldn't be greedy. And yet, it had been so long since she'd felt that blissful sense of physical release.

If he stroked with just a bit more pressure . . .

As if he'd read her mind, he did, and his thumb pressed her clit. Need tightened, heated. She reached, reached . . .

And he was gone. What? He was going to leave her like that?

But no, now his hands were on her thighs, gently spreading them farther. His mouth pressed against her where his fingers had been. He breathed hot air through the crotch of her panties, then his fingers were back, stroking, and now his lips found her clit. As he'd done with her nipples, he sucked the tiny bud, while pressing firm finger strokes against her swollen labia.

Needily, she thrust against him, her hips lifting off the bed. His hands gripped her butt, supporting her and holding her against his mouth, making her his personal feast.

Pleasure gathered, sharpened. Everything in her centered, focused, climbed toward the peak that beckoned.

And he took her to the top.

She cried out as something inside her shattered in surging waves of ecstasy. Of physical release, but also of relief. She wasn't irretrievably broken. Even at the height of orgasm, she was aware that the climax that made her come apart so powerfully was also healing her and restoring her confidence in her womanhood.

Ben held her through it, until the ripples of aftershock faded. Then he eased her lower body back onto the bed. Her eyes were still closed, tears of happiness seeping from under the lids. She was utterly drained, absolutely exhausted, and totally content.

The bed shifted as he lay beside her again. A finger brushed her damp cheek. "Sally?"

She forced her heavy lids open. "I'm good. So good." She sighed and lifted a limp arm to touch his face. Only now did she realize that, all through this, she'd lain on the bed accepting the pleasure he gave her, and giving nothing back. "Oh, Ben, thank you. That was amazing."

"I'm glad."

"I'm a terrible lover. It was all about me."

"You're crazy, sweetheart. Touching you gave me pleasure. Making you feel good was"—he shook his head as if he couldn't find the right word—"one of the best things ever."

"But you . . ." She glanced down and verified that he was still hard beneath his fly. That had to be painful. "Do you want . . ." He'd given her so much. And she honestly did want to touch him, to see his body naked, to explore and enjoy him. Though at the moment she barely had the energy to keep her eyes open.

"I got everything I wanted, and more." He brushed the moisture off her other cheek. "No, that's a lie. There's one other thing."

"What's that?"

"A good-night kiss." He touched his lips to hers, feather-light. "Sleep tight, Sally."

Ben would have loved to spend the night with Sally, but he sensed that would have been too much for her to handle. She needed time alone to process what had happened. Besides, he already had the worst case of blue balls in his life. Lying beside her sweet, sexy body in the hours until dawn would probably kill him.

So he hauled his aching body back to the trailer and took matters into his own hands, which was a damned poor substitute for burying himself in her lovely body. He didn't feel a single ounce of resentment, though, as he lay in bed waiting for sleep. What he'd told her was true. Helping her enjoy her own sexuality, having her trust him with her body, had been as big a high as winning a championship.

But, greedy man that he was, he wanted more. He sure hoped, for Sally's sake and his own, that tonight had given her the confidence to engage in a full sexual relationship. With him. With that seductive thought in mind, he drifted off to sleep.

When he woke with the birds, he showered and dressed quickly, eager to see Sally and make sure she was all right. Rather than wait for her to appear in the barn, he took his first mug of coffee to the chicken coop. Sure enough, she was sitting on the step, her head bent over one of the blond Buff Orpingtons, which had settled on her lap. She was stroking it, murmuring so softly he couldn't catch the words. A woman with a chicken. It was a pretty, domestic picture.

He leaned against one of the coop's fence posts, sipping coffee and enjoying the moment. Then into his mind flashed a replacement image: Sally in a rocking chair, cuddling a baby to her breast. His heart gave a mushy throb.

Until reality hit. The baby and the lovely woman with the copper-gold hair and greenish eyes would belong with some other man. With that well-established Caribou Crossing guy who would earn and deserve Sally's love.

Frowning, Ben told himself that sometime down the road, after his rodeo days, he'd have a wife and a couple of kids. He and Sally would still be friends. They had become close ones, and he wasn't going to lose that.

"Ben?" Sally's voice drew his attention and he realized she'd looked up and seen him. "Are you okay? You're frowning. Was last night—"

"Perfect." He changed the frown to a smile. "For me, it was perfect. How about for you?"

Her face brightened. "It was wonderful. But hmm . . . I have to wonder about you if your idea of perfect sex is keeping your clothes on the whole time."

He let loose with a laugh. She was okay, so okay that she could tease him about sex. "It was perfect for our first time," he clarified. "Have to admit, my jeans did get a little confining."

"I noticed." She gazed boldly at him across the few yards that separated them. "Next time, I think those jeans need to come off." She eased the hen from her lap, stood, and brushed her hands on the thighs of her pants. She was wearing her new jeans, the ones that showed off her figure, along with a pink and blue checked shirt he hadn't seen before. A fitted, Western-cut one that showed off her curves.

She came through the gate, latched it, and stood in front of him. "Good morning."

"Good morning." He leaned down and she tilted her head to meet him.

Too bad he had one arm in a sling and was holding a coffee mug, so he couldn't hug her. Still, they shared a leisurely, thorough morning kiss that had an immediate effect south of his belt. He couldn't wait to get those jeans off and feel her bare skin against his. Pity there was a day's work to put in first.

"Mmm, you taste like coffee," she said.

He offered his mug and she took it and sipped. "Excellent coffee, too," she said.

"I like my coffee, so I buy the good stuff." He eyed her with amusement as she slugged back some more. "Feel free to finish that. I can make more."

Her eyes widened over the rim of the mug, then she said slowly, "This is how much I trust you. If you were Pete, I'd rush into a frantic apology." Deliberately, she took another swallow of coffee. "But with you, I'll hog your coffee and know you won't get mad."

Pleased that she understood that, he said, "And if I do get upset about something, I'll tell you. We'll talk about it. I'll never hurt you, threaten you, or bully you."

Slowly, she nodded. "I really do believe you."

In the interest of being totally honest, he said, "I might wheedle, beg, and try to persuade you. . . ."

Humor glinted in her eyes as he went on, dead serious himself. "But you can always say no. I never want you to feel pressured to give in. I need you to believe that because I don't want to have to always pussyfoot around you." He peered deep into her eyes. "Okay?"

She held his gaze and gave a firm nod. "Okay." The glint came back as she said, "Be warned, I might try some wheedling myself."

He grinned. "I'll let you in on a secret. Promise me a kiss, and I'll do just about anything you want."

She chuckled. "I'll bear that in mind." Then she handed the mug back, almost empty now, and opened the gate. "Nice as it is to hang out and share—or hog— coffee, Madeleine will be here soon."

"Ah yes, the delightful Madeleine."

She bumped her elbow against his good arm. "She likes you. She flirts with you."

"I don't flirt back." He shifted the mug to his other hand so he could slide his fingers through hers. He swung their clasped hands up. "Speaking of which, how d'you want to, uh, play this? You and me? You've said you don't like people gossiping about you." It had irked him when they were in town and she wouldn't hold his hand. He was so damned proud to be with her, he'd be happy to tell the world.

"I don't. Ryland Riding is my business. I want to be professional."

He guessed he could see her point, but decided to tease her. "So no PDAs? I can't do this?" He raised their clasped hands and kissed the back of hers. "Or this?" He bent to press another kiss to the top of her head, enjoying the silky tickle of her curls against his skin.

"Mmm, that's so nice. But no, I don't think so. After

all, you'll be gone in a week or two. I don't want people thinking I had some quickie fling with, um . . ."

"Your stable hand?" He tried to keep the bitterness out of his voice. He was just her stable hand, a rodeo cowboy lending a hand—literally, because he only had one good one—to the owner of this impressive operation. It was a blow to his ego; pretty much the opposite of having buckle bunnies chase after him.

"My old friend," she corrected. "Maybe I'm too sensitive about what people think, but I've spent years being totally private. I had so many secrets to hide."

"So we're a secret to hide?" Trying to put ego aside, he guessed he could see that hooking up with a rodeo cowboy she hadn't seen in seven years, who vanished after a couple of weeks, wasn't exactly going to enhance her professional reputation.

"I don't know. This is new to me. Let's just see how things go."

"Sure." He tried to make it sound casual, easy. "How about dinner tonight? Not in public, so we can do DAs without worrying about the P part?"

"Sounds great. Let me think what I've got in the fridge and freezer."

"Leftover salsa, guacamole, and sour cream, right? I have a big package of tortilla chips and a bit of cheddar cheese. If you have some more cheese, we could make nachos. If you don't mind eating nachos again so soon."

"Not at all. I have years of deprivation to make up for." The gleam in her eyes made him think she might be thinking of more than nachos.

"Then it's a plan." He raised her hand and kissed the back again. "I'm gonna grab a bite to eat then I'll get Star of Egypt ready for Madeleine. But first . . ." He kissed her.

Her return kiss tasted not only of coffee, but of hunger and promise.

Whistling, he headed off to get on with the day, already looking forward to tonight. It couldn't come fast enough.

And that of course meant that the day moved particularly slowly. Ben did steal a moment every now and then when no one else was around to put an arm around Sally's shoulders or waist, and to drop a kiss on the top of her head, her freckled nose, or her full lips. Those near-innocent touches fired him up as much as the most explicit foreplay would have.

When their work was finally done, they put together a heaping plate of nachos and ate them hungrily. As they finished, Ben, who wore shorts, realized the temperature had dropped a few degrees and gray clouds were rolling in. "Rain's coming. Maybe even a thunderstorm."

They blew out the citronella candles and went inside to do the dishes. On the radio, Willie Nelson had Georgia on his mind. Ben had Sally on his. As they moved around in the kitchen, he bumped his hip against hers and let his bare forearm slide against hers. When he gave her firm butt a squeeze as she stood at the sink washing dishes, she said, "You're getting awfully touchy-feely, cowboy."

"Is that an objection?"

"No. It's nice." She shut off the water and turned to him. "Lets me know you're attracted to me. And it makes me . . . aware of you."

"Makes *me* horny," he admitted. "All day, I've been thinking about what you said, about my jeans coming off."

Green glints of mischief sparkled in her eyes. "But you're not wearing jeans."

"Shorts are even easier to take off. In case you're interested." Frustrated by the sling, wanting to hug her properly, he undid the collar and cuff. "Don't say anything," he warned. "My shoulder's feeling better every day. And it'll feel a hell of a lot better if I can do this." He put his arms around her and snuggled her body up close to his.

"Oh well, if it helps your shoulder then," she teased, looping her arms around his neck. "Anything else that would help?"

"You could kiss it and make it feel better."

Her lashes swept down, paused, then came back up and the green in her eyes was deeper. "You're talking about your shoulder?"

His cock throbbed with need and he groaned. "The thought of your lips pretty much anywhere on my body is enough to drive me crazy."

She tugged gently on his neck, urging his head down. "Let's start with lips on lips."

"Anything you say, ma'am."

His mouth was still getting to know hers, an exploration he couldn't imagine ever tiring of. They kissed teasingly, with nips and darts of the tongue that hinted at passion waiting to explode. He banked down his need, refusing to get carried away and move too fast for her. He couldn't conceal his erection, but he needed her to know he could use restraint.

Chapter Twenty

Ben sure did get to her, Sally thought as she lost herself in the kiss. He was so sweet, so patient, and so damned sexy. How far did she want things to go with him?

All the way.

Could she? Or would fear paralyze her? She wasn't afraid of Ben, but her body had such scary memories of sex.

If she stopped now, she'd be letting Pete ruin things. No way would she give him that kind of power, not with Ben here to support her. She eased back in the circle of his arms. "If I'm going to kiss your shoulder, that shirt's going to have to come off."

"Help yourself. See how considerate I was, wearing a buttoned shirt rather than a tee?"

"Hah. You wear buttoned shirts because it hurts to lift your left arm over your head."

"You got me."

"Good thing you're a right-handed roper." She undid the top button, below the couple he'd left undone. Her fingers brushed his skin, so warm and firm. The pads of her fingers tingled, itching with the desire to touch more of him. All of him.

"Sweetheart, right now roping is the last thing on my mind."

She undid a couple more buttons and studied the powerful chest she was uncovering. Amazing musculature, marred by fading, purplish green bruises radiating out from his left shoulder. Resting her face against his skin, she breathed him in, that tangy, outdoorsy scent. Felt the rise and fall of his chest; heard the rapid thud of his heart.

He brushed a hand through her curls but didn't take hold of her head, didn't try to control her movement.

She pressed a kiss to his chest, then another, the bruised part and the unbruised alike. Then she undid the rest of the buttons and pushed back the sides of his shirt. Lord, but he was fine—except for a long scar on one side near his waist. "Ben! Ouch. What happened?"

"Got nicked by a horn."

"More than nicked." She ran a gentle finger along the ridge of scar tissue. "You did some bull riding?"

"Not since I was a teenager and realized it wasn't for me. No, I was nearby when a bull went crazy in the arena. Turned on the rider; sent the bullfighters flying. Me and a couple other cowboys jumped the fence and went in to help."

A hero. Rodeo was like that, in terms of both the danger and the support. "I'm glad you lived to tell the tale." She stretched up to press a kiss to his lips. "Want to take your shirt off?"

"You're in charge, Sally. Do what you want, and stop when you need to."

The idea was reassuring and a little intoxicating. Her fingers brushed across his pecs lightly, experimentally. "You're too good to me."

"There's no such thing as being too good to you."

Realization had been coming to her in pieces, last

night and today, and now it crystallized. She stared into his eyes. "I know what you're doing."

"How d'you mean?"

How to phrase it? "Pete took control away from me. You're giving it back."

"Yeah. Is that okay?"

"It's good, but . . ." She admitted the truth. "I'm not sure what to do with it."

"Follow your instincts."

"I stopped trusting them. For years. But with you . . ." She'd give it a try. With trembling hands, she slid his shirt off his shoulders.

It dropped to the floor and she retrieved it and hung it over a chair. With her back to Ben, she said, "Maybe we should go upstairs." Her voice came out breathy and high.

"If you want."

She turned and had to stare in wonder at his naked torso. Pete, a man who'd done a lot of physical labor, had been muscular, too. At first she'd found him sexy, but then his size had become one of the weapons he used against her. Ben's body was beautiful even with the bruising and scar. His musculature was lean, athletic, and graceful. Powerful, but she trusted that he wouldn't use his strength against her.

She splayed her hands, fingers spread, on his pecs. Not pressing, not caressing, just resting there, appreciating him. "Yes, Ben. I want."

As they walked up the stairs, she heard a heavy drumming on the roof. "It's pouring."

"The horses will be okay, won't they?"

"They will. It'll be Moon Song's first real rain." It had sprinkled a couple of times since he was born, but nothing like this. "I hope he has fun with it." She could picture the colt's puzzlement at this strange deluge from the sky, then she bet he'd frolic and play.

"Do you want to go out and watch?"

Yes, but no. "I'd rather be with you."

"Now that's a mighty fine compliment."

"It is," she agreed.

Tonight, with the clouds and rain outside the window, her bedroom was dark. She turned on a reading lamp by the bed. Quietly, she said, "This isn't the room I shared with him. Or the bed." It was important to her that Ben know this. "I changed everything after he died."

He didn't respond, and her words echoed in her brain. What a lie. She had changed her bedroom, but she hadn't changed *everything*. Not her habit of privacy nor her wariness of men. But now, thanks to Ben, she was stepping out of the emotional prison Pete had trapped her in.

"Lie down," she invited Ben.

When he lay on his back toward the center of the double bed, she sat on the edge and leaned sideways to stroke his chest. The denim of her jeans confined her and chafed, so she stripped them off. Tugging down her tee to cover her panties, she climbed onto the bed and curled on her side beside him, propping herself up with one arm.

His upper body—the unbruised part—was golden brown in the lamplight, tempting her to explore. She pressed her fingers into his firm muscles, taking it easy with the injured shoulder. She brushed her fingers through a scattering of wiry hair, tested the firmness of his pecs, teased his nipples with a fingertip. "What feels good?" she asked softly. For her, every touch made her hunger more for him.

"All of it. Feeling your fingers on me."

Lips would be even better. She leaned over him, bracing herself with a hand on the other side of his body, and bent to taste his skin. Tentatively at first, she kissed and licked his chest. At his sounds of pleasure, she grew bolder. When she sucked his nipple, she felt a corresponding tug in her breast, an aching desire to be touched. The same need throbbed between her legs.

Outside, thunder rolled with a long, deep grumble. A few seconds later, lightning cracked, sending a strobe of light into the bedroom. For a moment, she felt disoriented, like she and Ben were in a movie.

His voice drew her back. "What do you want, Sally? Do you want me to touch you?"

She wasn't used to asking for what she wanted. She wasn't used to anyone caring. Straightening, she said hesitantly, "Would you touch my breasts?"

A grin split his face. "That would be my pleasure."

As thunder and lightning sang a dramatic duet outside, Ben helped her peel off her tee and bra. That left her in only her panties, but she didn't feel self-conscious as she leaned over so he could fondle her breasts. Her horseshoe pendant dangled as he teased her nipples until they were hard buds. Arousal spilled from them, pulsing through her with anticipation and need.

She found the confidence to say, "I think it's time your shorts came off."

With unsteady fingers, she fumbled with the button. His erection strained at the fabric and her mouth was dry when she slowly pulled down the zipper. "Just so I know," she said nervously. "Did you bring a condom tonight?"

"In my pocket. But we won't use it unless you're sure."

The assurance gave her a boost of courage, enabling her to tug at the waist of his shorts as he raised his hips.

Being careful to leave his underwear in place, and not yet daring to glance at his groin, she tugged his shorts down and off. Kneeling on the bed, she sucked in a breath and gazed up his body.

He wore tight-fitting black boxer briefs, short-legged and low on his hips. The soft, thin fabric showcased the bulge of his balls and the thrust of a barely confined erection.

She ached to rub against him. And he'd told her to do what she wanted. Straddling his hips, she lowered herself, quivering with anticipation. When his rigid length pressed between her legs through the layers of both their underwear, she moaned at how delicious it felt.

He raised his hands to cup her breasts. "So beautiful, Sally, and man, do you feel good."

She did. She felt sensual, sexy, and hungry for more. He rubbed her nipples gently, sending darts of arousal through her. The crotch of her panties was soaked; her sex pulsed with need. Outside, the thunderstorm raged passionately. Inside, the lamp bathed the bed in warm light and Ben gazed up at her with passion too, but with more than that. With tenderness, appreciation, affection.

And she knew. She was ready. Ready to have intercourse with this amazing man. She wanted to feel him inside her, banishing all the pain of the past and creating pleasure together. "I want you, Ben. All of you. Now."

His chestnut eyes gleamed. "Then take me, sweetheart. Take everything you want."

She scrambled off him, found his discarded shorts, and pulled the condom package from his pocket. With eager, trembling fingers she pulled off his boxer briefs. His erection sprang free, bold and beautiful. Hers. To be used for her pleasure, not to hurt or control her.

Somehow, she managed to open the condom package and sheath him. Then she yanked off her panties.

When she started to lie down on the bed, Ben said, "Why don't you take top? That'll give you more control."

Top? Pete had never wanted to have sex that way.

"Go on, sexy cowgirl," Ben invited. "Take me for a ride."

When she straddled him again, she realized he was right. This way, she wasn't afraid of being threatened or overpowered. She reached between their bodies, curled her fingers around his firm, hot shaft, and carefully eased the tip inside her. Her body clenched for a moment, then pleasure rippled through her and she relaxed, opening to let him slide in slowly, inevitably.

When they were fully joined, she began to lift up and down, getting used to him. To the wonderful feel of him. Exhilarated, she bent to kiss him. "Oh, Ben, this feels perfect."

"Sure does, sweetheart." He thrust gently, matching the pace she set.

She arched her back, thrusting out her breasts in a clear invitation. When he fondled her nipples, they were so achy and sensitive that his caresses made her shiver with pleasure.

For long minutes she moved on him, learning about him and learning things about her own body she'd never known before. The thunder and lightning had stopped, but rain drummed steadily on the roof. Inside, she and Ben were in a blissful cocoon. She wanted this to go on forever. Yet the tension of arousal climbed within her until it clamored with a demand she could no longer deny. She wanted—needed—to come now.

But to do that . . . "Ben, I need . . . Please, touch . . ." She couldn't bring herself to say "my clit," but when his fingers drifted down to caress it gently, she moaned. "Oh, yes."

She threw back her head, glorying in his touch, focusing totally on the place where their bodies joined, where his fingers and his erection created magic. There was one more thing she wanted, to make this moment perfect. Bending her head to gaze into his dark-lashed eyes, she said, "Come with me. Please come with me."

He thrust harder and she whimpered with pure pleasure. His thumb tapped and stroked. She shuddered as she felt her climax begin, deep in her core, rising, growing—and then it exploded so powerfully it made her cry out with release. The release of so many things, both physical and emotional.

In her ears there was a roaring, rushing sound like a river in flood. Penetrating it came Ben's guttural cry. And a moment later, "Oh God, Sally."

The pulsing waves of his release joined the aftershocks of her own, merging with them and prolonging them so that their two separate climaxes became a single mutual experience.

When the shudders inside her finally stopped, she felt drained, yet light as air. Exhausted, yet free. Blissful. Slowly, she eased herself down on the bed. When he'd removed the condom, she curled against him and his arm came around her. "Thank you, Ben."

Thinking that this was pretty much heaven, Ben lay flat on his back with Sally curled against him. Her head rested on his good shoulder; her right arm lay across his chest; her leg was flung over his thighs. Like she wanted to hold on to him and never let him go. Which, at the moment, sounded like a mighty fine idea to him.

"That was really great," she said dreamily.

He squeezed her shoulder. "Freaking fantastic, sweet-heart. You feel okay?"

"I feel good. Wonderful." She pressed a kiss to his skin then sucked gently, not enough to leave a hickey but with a teasing sensuality that stirred his blood. "You know what I feel like?"

"No idea."

Pushing up to rest her weight on her left elbow, she gazed intently into his eyes. "More."

Did she mean more sex? His cock pulsed with inter-est. But this was the first intercourse Sally'd had in years. He shouldn't jump to conclusions. "More, uh . . . ?"

"Sex. I want to do it all, try it all." Her eyes gleamed.

"Oh, man." Talk about an instant erection. "I only brought one condom, so—"

"Damn."

Her frustrated tone and the furrow in her forehead made him chuckle. "So I'll have to go out to my trailer and get more."

"It's pouring outside."

He let out a disbelieving laugh. "You think a little rain's gonna stop me?" He was out of bed in an instant, seeing her gaze drop from his face to his hard-on. "Back in a flash."

As he sprinted out the door, her voice followed. "Aren't you going to put clothes on?"

"Waste of time. They're only gonna come off again." A little water never hurt a guy.

The cool rain did, however, take care of his erection as he ran down the back steps and sprinted toward his trailer. The rough, muddy ground wasn't the easiest stuff to run on, not in bare feet. Especially when he passed out of the dim circles of light cast by the house and barn lights. It was almost pitch black by his trailer.

But he made it, grabbed the box of condoms, and started back. As he neared the house, the ball of his right foot came down hard on a stone. "Shit, shit, shit." He hopped around on one foot.

"Are you okay?"

Startled, he looked up to see Sally at the open bedroom window, naked in the pale golden light from the room.

"Yeah," he called back, the pain forgotten as he dashed for the house.

By the time he made it up the back steps, she was on the deck. Out in the rain, still naked, she raised her arms and shimmied in a sensual dance. Like a woman under a tropical waterfall, not in a cool, Cariboo rainstorm. When he came up to her, she stopped dancing and grinned. "That was about the funniest sight I've ever seen, you naked in the rain, hopping around and cussing, hanging on to a box of condoms. I'm never going to forget it."

He brushed wet curls back from her forehead even as more raindrops landed on her skin. "You dancing naked in the rain was about the prettiest sight I've ever seen, and you can bet I'll never forget it." He circled his arms around her and moved close so the fronts of their bodies touched. Cool, rain-washed flesh quickly heated with the contact. "In fact, I'm never gonna forget a minute of tonight."

"Me either." She stared up at him, blinking against the rain. The outside light showed him that all traces of laughter had gone from her face. "Ben, you've made me whole."

His heart melted, but before he could speak she went on. "I promise I will never let anyone break me again."

"Aw, sweetheart." It shattered his heart, thinking about how that man had hurt her. "I know you won't.

And if anyone ever tries, you let me know. I'm guessing you're not prone to violence, but I have no qualms about throwing a punch when it's warranted."

"Let's not even talk about violence, okay?"

"Yeah. Sorry about that. Now let's go in before you catch a chill."

"I bet you can warm me up."

"I bet I can at that."

She stepped back, out of his arms, and took the box from him. "I bet you can even warm me up in the rain."

"Uh . . ." What did she mean?

She pulled out a wrapped condom and tossed the box into the shelter of the roof's overhang. "I've never been kissed in the rain."

As she opened the wrapper, his erection grew. Sex in the rain? "Hey, sweetheart, when you said 'try it all,' you really meant it."

Her eyes danced. "Is that a complaint?"

"Never." Laughing, he pulled her into his arms and kissed her as rivulets of rain dripped down both their faces.

Morning sun warmed Ben's face and he opened bleary eyes, squinting against the light. The sound of a long, loud yawn made him yawn reflexively and roll over in bed with a good morning smile. What a night it had been. Sally had wanted to do it all, try it all, and he'd done his best to oblige until sheer exhaustion sent them both to sleep.

His smile widened when he took her in, then he started to laugh.

Her eyes popped open. "What are you laughing at?"

"Sally, you will always be beautiful. But this morning you look a little, er, tousled." Her uncombed curls had dried every which way, messed by his hands and her pillow. Her cheeks and chin were rosy with beard burn. She looked adorable and sexy.

He rubbed a hand across his stubbly jaw, then touched a gentle finger to her chin. "I shaved before I came over last night, I swear."

She gave a humorous grimace. "You marked me?"

"'Fraid so."

She was quiet for a moment. "Marks from pleasure. That's something new for me." Another pause. "The demons are gone. We chased them away, Ben. I'm free."

"That's something to celebrate. Want to give me a kiss and say good morning properly?"

She wrinkled her nose. "Two sets of morning breath? A fresh case of beard burn? Not to mention, I'm already going to be walking like I spent the night bull riding."

"You sayin' I'm hung like a bull, little lady?" he said in a John Wayne drawl.

She gave a burble of laughter and put on a drawl of her own. "Pardner, I'm not touchin' that one with a ten-foot pole. No, wait, you're the one with the pole, though I'm not sure it's even ten inches." Giggling, she climbed out of bed and yeah, she didn't exactly bounce out. It was more like the way he moved the morning after a rough fall.

"Want to measure it?" he challenged as she walked across the room with him admiring her shapely rear view.

"Later. Right now, I need a shower. And no, you're not joining me." She went through the doorway, then peeked back around the frame. "Not this time. Tonight, though . . ." And she disappeared from sight.

Leaving him grinning his fool head off. Whistling despite the pain in his shoulder, which had been exacerbated by a night of bedroom acrobatics, he clambered out of bed and set about finding his clothes. How many hours until tonight?

And how many more tonights, he wondered a few minutes later as he made his way to his trailer and his own cramped shower.

Though the selfish part of him was glad Dusty's new heeler was no phenom, every rodeo Ben missed not only cost him money and standings, but cost Dusty as well. Ben roped with his right hand, using his left on the reins to guide Chaunce. His horse was a natural and the communication between the two of them was almost intuitive now, so Ben's left shoulder and arm didn't need to do much. Monique's adamance had kept him from driving to Peace River to compete this weekend, but for sure he'd be up for roping the weekend after—even if he had to hold off on bronc riding for a while longer.

Every other time he'd been sidelined by injury, he'd champed at the bit wanting to get back to rodeo. Now, he was torn. Life at Ryland Riding was pretty nice, and being with Sally—especially now that they were lovers—went way beyond nice. Too bad she'd settled down and had so many responsibilities. If she'd still been barrel racing, they could have had one mighty fine time riding the circuit together.

Instead, he'd soon be back doing what he loved, and she'd be here. Doing what she loved too, but by herself, working herself to exhaustion. That didn't sit well with him. Business was picking up: not only did she have Andrew and Terry, but in the past week she'd acquired two other new students and a new boarder. Sally had to find an assistant.

After he had dressed, Ben made coffee and had a quick breakfast. He filled his thermos with the rest of the coffee and got to work. When Sally arrived, he had a chestnut gelding in the cross ties, grooming it for the owner who'd soon be in for a prework ride. He smiled at Sally. "Do I get my good morning kiss now? Can I bribe you with some of the coffee you like?" He picked up the thermos he'd set on a bench and handed it to her.

"That's definitely worth a kiss." She leaned in for a lingering one, then opened the thermos and took a swallow. "Mmm. This could be addictive."

She went to the tack room and returned with the horse's saddle pad, saddle, and bridle.

As the two of them readied the horse, Ben said, "Why don't you get in touch with Corrie again? See if there's any chance you can sweet-talk her into coming back."

"I don't feel right about asking, not when she's got some personal thing going on."

"Being asked is flattering. What's wrong with letting her know what a great job she did and how you miss her? And how business is growing and you'd love to have her back. Maybe she's sorted out her personal issues by now. Maybe she thinks you've replaced her."

"Hmm. That makes sense."

"Do it now," he urged. He wanted to know that Sally would have time to commune with her chickens, grow fresh vegetables, go riding just for pleasure, and build herself a social life.

And what about dating? Sharing her wonderful, generous body and heart with a man. Falling in love, getting married, and having children. He ground his teeth.

"Okay, okay," she said. "Don't scowl at me."

"I'm not—" All right, he was scowling, and he couldn't tell her the real reason: that he was jealous as hell of the man who would prove himself worthy of Sally and win her heart.

This was crazy. He'd never been possessive about any other woman he'd slept with.

He shoved that thought out of his mind as he bridled the horse, and then helped another owner with her horse. Andrew and Terry arrived next. In addition to taking one-hour lessons on Mondays, they'd also booked two-hour trail rides with Sally on Fridays.

After Sally and the men had ridden off, Ben cleaned the barn then tacked up Chaunce and did some work in the ring. He guided his horse this way and that, making quick turns and stops as he roped bales of hay and fence posts. Really, he hardly used his left shoulder—at least as long as nothing unexpected happened.

A blue minivan drove into the yard. There'd been no one listed on Sally's schedule until after lunch. Ben slid off Chaunce and left him inside the ring as a tall, black-haired woman dressed in jeans and a gray T-shirt jumped out of the driver's side. She went around to slide open the side door on the other side. A ramp came down and, as Ben approached, he saw she was helping a boy who was seated in a wheelchair up front on the passenger side. She unfastened whatever secured the chair in place, and the boy powered it backward, sideways, then carefully down the ramp, with the woman standing close by. The kid, who looked to be about eight or nine, was frail and had a mop of dark hair and wide, curious brown eyes. He was dressed in jeans, a T-shirt, and sturdy shoes. Ben wondered what disability kept him in that chair.

"Hey there," Ben greeted them. "Welcome to Ryland Riding."

The woman held out her hand. "I'm Lark Cantrell and this is my son, Jayden." She studied Ben's face. Recognizing his First Nations blood, he guessed, just as he saw the same in her light brown skin and strong features. She was fit and definitely had presence.

"Nice to meet you." He shook her hand, not surprised that her grip was firm. "I'm Ben Traynor." He extended his hand to the boy, who met it with a weak shake. "Hi, Jayden. How can I help you two?"

"Is Sally Ryland around?" the woman asked.

"Sorry, she's out with students. I'm her assistant."

"I should have called, but Jayden and I were talking at breakfast and he got excited, so I took a half day off work and we took a chance."

"She'll be back in less than half an hour if you want to wait. Or maybe I can help?"

"Jayden has cerebral palsy and he's keen on horses. Yesterday we met with his physiotherapist, Monique, and—"

"Monique Labelle? I see her, too. Sorry, please go on."

"She says that therapeutic riding could be helpful for Jayden. There's no program around here, but Monique says Sally's been helping one of her other patients. We wondered if she'd be willing to work with Jayden, too."

"I really want to ride," the boy said. His speech was quick, the words slurring together a little, and his eyes were bright with excitement and hope.

Bringing the kid was a clever strategy. Who, much less a softhearted, child-loving person like Sally, could resist the boy's enthusiasm? "I'm afraid you will have to talk to Sally about that." He didn't say that he was pretty sure she'd bend over backward to accommodate young Jayden. "Why don't you wait? I'll introduce you guys to my horse, Chauncey's Pride." He gestured toward the ring.

"Are you a cowboy?" the boy asked.

"I'm a rodeo cowboy," Ben told him.

"Cool!"

"And Chaunce is my roping horse."

"He's pretty," the boy said.

"He prefers 'handsome,' but he'll appreciate the compliment."

Lark gave a soft laugh. "Is he gentle? He won't hurt Jayden?"

"He's a gentleman and he loves kids." Glancing at the rough dirt surface of the parking lot, Ben said, "I'm not sure how the chair's going to handle this ground." He started to take off his sling. "May need to be pushed."

"That's okay," Lark said. "I'll do it. I'm plenty strong."

"My mom's a frfr," the boy said proudly.

"Sorry, I didn't quite catch that."

He gave a frustrated scowl. Slowly, more clearly, he said, "Firefighter. She's the chief."

"Really? Wow." He glanced at the tall woman again, knowing better than to comment on her gender. "That's even cooler than being a rodeo cowboy."

She flashed a smile. "Toss up, I'd say."

Chapter Twenty-One

It was seven-thirty that night when Sally put a bowl of salad on the table on the deck and sat down with a sigh of relief. "I'm tired and starving."

"Me, too." Ben, who'd been manning her barbecue, came to join her, bringing three juicy burgers.

Unlike last Friday when they'd taken off early to go to dinner at Dave and Cassidy's, today she'd had a couple of new clients and the very welcome business had extended the workday. She and Ben had postponed their shared shower, to have a quick meal first.

As he took his usual chair across from her, she asked, "You don't mind about not going into town for dinner?" Earlier, he'd asked if she'd like to see if Heather could tend Ryland Riding so they could eat out.

As she dished out salad for them, he shook his head. "This works fine, too." Under the table, his bare foot caressed the top of hers.

Arousal rippled through her, reminding her of why she'd turned down the dinner invitation. "I admit there's something appealing about the idea of putting on my one nice dress and sitting across from you in a fancy restaurant, having someone wait on us, and eating something I'd never cook at home."

Ben put down his burger. "But?"

"Now that we've, uh . . . Now that we're . . ." Maybe she hadn't lost all her inhibitions last night. She ducked her head and started in on her own burger.

"Lovers?"

Lovers. She liked that term much better than "sex buddies" or "friends with benefits." It sounded gentle, affectionate, almost romantic. Not that her relationship with Ben was a romance. In truth, they really *were* only friends with benefits—but he was such an amazing friend and the benefits went so much deeper than a few, albeit wonderful, orgasms. "It would be hard to act like we were just friends, and I'd rather not publicize our relationship."

He drank a long, slow mouthful of beer. "As you said yesterday morning. Before we really became lovers."

She nodded and sipped her own beer.

"You don't want people knowing you're sleeping with me." There was a slight edge to his voice. Almost as if she'd hurt his feelings.

Probably she'd misread him, but she'd hate to hurt Ben so she said, "You can understand why someone like me, who's always been so private, wouldn't want to broadcast that I'm having this . . . fling, or whatever they'd think it is. Can't you?" She couldn't bear it if people saw her very special, very intimate relationship with Ben as a tawdry hook-up.

"Guess I can." He bit into his burger. A minute or two later, he said, "One day you're gonna start dating again. Right?"

"I . . ." Would she? It was hard to imagine being with anyone other than Ben. But soon he'd be back to the rodeo life he loved. For years she'd believed that it wasn't her destiny to have a happy marriage and children, but now she was a different woman, thanks to him. "I suppose one day I might."

"Not every guy's gonna want to keep the relationship behind closed doors."

"No, I guess not." If she was dating someone seriously, if they cared for and respected each other, there'd be no reason to hang on to her habit of privacy.

"When you find the right man"—he spoke slowly, deliberately—"you'll want to broadcast it to the world."

Would she? Into her mind flashed an image of her and Ben, strolling the streets of Caribou Crossing holding hands. Feeding each other bites of dessert across a table. Slow dancing in the bar at the Wild Rose and sharing a kiss on the dance floor.

Ben. He was the man she'd be proud to be with. But only if their relationship was for the long term, which it wasn't. She had to be wary about letting herself care too much about this man who'd made her rediscover that being a woman could be a wonderful thing.

Would she ever find a man to love? If so, he'd have to be someone a lot like Ben.

"Sally?"

"What? Oh, broadcast it to the world? I suppose you're right."

He rose. "I'm getting another beer. Want one?"

"No, thanks."

While he was gone, she finished her burger and split the remaining salad between their two plates. When Ben sat down again, she chose a more comfortable subject. "It was interesting talking to Lark and Jayden this morning."

"The kid's a charmer, isn't he?"

"Oh, man, you can say that again. Who could resist?" The boy was spunky, smart, and loved horses.

He chuckled. "I figured you'd take him on."

"Lark's already scheduled a meeting for all of us with Monique." It would be interesting to finally meet the physiotherapist she'd spoken to on the phone over the past months as they helped Amanda adjust to her prosthetic leg. "I'm looking forward to working with Jayden. I'm sure riding will help him."

"It will." He laughed again. "I'm remembering Robin Cousins spouting off about the benefits of learning new skills and connecting with horses." His face sobered. "Those are two very different kids, aren't they? It must be a tough proposition, raising a child like Jayden."

"He's totally worth it." She'd happily have a child like Jayden.

"For sure." Ben touched her bare forearm, his fingers a warm caress. "I'm just saying that special needs mean a big investment of money and time."

She nodded and took a sip of beer. "And Lark's a single parent. Fortunately, they have financial assistance from a charity for kids with disabilities."

"That's terrific." Ben raised his hand to tweak a curl of hair off her cheek and tuck it behind her ear. He lingered to stroke her earlobe and her neck, sending delicious tingles rippling through her.

"New clients mean more work," he said. "Have you heard back from Corrie?"

"Not yet." Ben would be gone soon. What would she do without him? Not only without his help, but without his company? She gazed at him solemnly. "You looked good in the ring, roping on Chaunce." When she'd returned with Terry and Andrew, Ben had been giving Jayden and Lark a demo, moving in graceful, athletic sync with his white-and-bay Paint. "How did your shoulder feel?"

"Not bad."

"Uh-huh?" she said skeptically.

"It's healing. I don't need my left arm that much. Chaunce has all the right instincts and he's really responsive to my signals."

"You're a team." How well she remembered what that was like. "It's like you read each other's minds."

"Exactly."

Ben had his life and he needed to get back to it. For some reason—probably because he was such a good guy—he felt responsible for her. But he wasn't. She had to make him realize that. Needing to touch him, she ran her fingers lightly over the back of his hand.

"If Corrie doesn't come back," he said, "and you can't find another assistant, I wonder if Heather might be interested in doing some stable work?"

"That's a good idea. I'll ask her." She narrowed her eyes in a semi-serious warning glare. "And this is my problem, Ben. Having you help out is wonderful, but your life is on the rodeo circuit. I won't have you staying here out of some . . . chivalrous instinct."

"Chivalrous?" He gave a quick laugh. "Sally, damn it, we're friends. We're lovers. I care about you. I don't want you working yourself to the bone."

"Well, I care about you, too." More than she should. "I'll find a solution." With the pick-up in business, she could afford to pay a decent wage to a part-time person. Not a live-in again; not unless she could find another woman. But she felt more confident about dealing with men. She could imagine hiring a guy to come and put in some hours. One with excellent references and a compatible personality. Maybe older, semi-retired. Or maybe a gay man. "The ad I posted was for a full-time live-in, but I'll post another for part-time. There might be a local person who'd work a couple of hours a day, more on weekends. Even that much would be a big help."

"Then start looking, okay? Tell your friends. Jess must know a bunch of horsey people."

"Good idea," she agreed. "I'll tell my students' parents, and the owners. Someone might know someone." Someone had to, because she wouldn't hold Ben back. "You need to qualify for the CFR." The Canadian Finals Rodeo was at the beginning of November. "And I'm sure you want to make as much as you can before the season ends."

"Right." Ben frowned down at his beer bottle, annoyed at the reminder that he wasn't in the same financial league as land and business owner Sally.

Rodeo was seasonal work unless you competed on the American circuit. That option was open to Canadians and he'd tried it back when he just rode broncs. But the costs and hassles—especially when you drove and toted your horse along with you—didn't make it worthwhile. So he stuck to Canadian rodeo and each year hoped to make enough to tide him through the off-season. Then whatever he earned working for the horse trainer was gravy.

Most years, it worked out. He had some money put away. Not a lot, though. He remembered what Dave Cousins had said, about how a goal motivated you. Ben's goal each year was winning at CFR, not saving to buy a ranch or start a horse training business.

He sure didn't have anything to offer Sally.

Her voice interrupted his musings. "I'll do the dishes then e-mail a few people and put the word out."

"Good." As he drained his beer, he wondered why he'd gone off on that weird train of thought. He had years to plan his second career, organize his finances, and find the right woman.

If there was another woman as special as Sally Ryland. . . .

"Can you do the barn chores?" she asked. "We'll be finished quicker. After all"—she rose, giving him a shy yet mischievous smile—"there's that shower waiting."

The shared shower. A jolt of arousal brought him to his feet. Why the hell was he contemplating the future when he was with Sally now? Before long they'd be steaming up her bathroom—and then her bed. He circled her waist with his good arm. "Now that's an incentive."

He kissed her. Only a taste, a promise of more to come. Then, whistling, he set off to do his chores.

He was cleaning tack when Sally came into the barn and headed for the office. She'd be sending those e-mails. He sure hoped they produced results, and soon.

A few minutes later, she dashed into the tack room. Her face was as bright and excited as he'd ever seen it. "Ben! Corrie's coming!"

He pulled her into a one-armed hug. "She wants to come back? Sweetheart, that's great."

"It's wonderful." She kissed him, a darting kiss on his mouth. "I can hardly believe it."

"What did she say?"

"That she's been missing country life. That working here is what she really wants to do. She says she can be here next weekend. Isn't that perfect? That's likely when you'll be ready to go back on the circuit, isn't it?"

"You're right. Her timing's perfect." Everything was working out and he was relieved. So why did he feel kind of flat, rather than sharing Sally's excitement? "She'll live here again?"

Sally nodded vigorously.

"So between her and Heather, you can get some time off now and then."

"I can. And now I have a reason to take it. I don't want to live like a hermit any longer."

"That's good, Sally." He forced enthusiasm into his voice. It was more than good, it was great. Man, he was in a strange mood. "I'll get that deer and rabbit fencing up before I leave, so you and Corrie can have your garden to yourselves."

"That would be wonderful. Oh, Ben, your coming here was the best thing that could ever have happened to me. In so many ways."

He gave a half smile. "Thank your sister for that one."

"I have, and I will again. We've been talking every day. But I thank you, too." Again she stretched up to kiss him, and this time it was a slow, lingering kiss.

She drew back in the curve of his arm. "Where and when can you catch up with Dusty?"

"Next Saturday and Sunday, we're entered in the rodeo in Kennedy, Saskatchewan." He and Dusty had discussed the possibility of Ben driving out to join him. Now, with Corrie coming that same weekend, Ben didn't need to worry about leaving Sally on her own. So why was he hesitating? "That'd mean leaving next Friday." They'd have just under a week more together.

"Or Thursday. It's almost a twenty-four-hour drive, isn't it? You should break it up, overnight. Otherwise, even if you take frequent exercise breaks, it'll be a lot of strain on your shoulder and on your poor horse, standing in that trailer."

"Guess you're right. And Mom would like it if I overnighted with them in Calgary. So she can see for herself that I'm all in one piece."

"So you'll leave next Thursday," Sally said softly. "That means we have almost a week." She smiled, but the expression in her eyes seemed a little sad. The light in the barn was dim, so he couldn't be sure. Still, he hoped that she too had regrets about saying good-bye.

"We should make the most of that time." His voice was gruff. He cleared his throat and tried to lighten things up. "Starting with that shower."

Now he saw a spark in her eyes, and she wriggled her pelvis against his. "That sounds like an excellent place to start."

Chapter Twenty-Two

It wasn't dawn light, bird song, or her alarm that woke Sally the next Thursday morning. It was Ben's kisses on her shoulder, his erection nudging her butt, as she lay spooned in his arms.

She kept her breathing slow, feigning sleep. Putting off the moment when she had to confront this day.

She loved lying this way with Ben. His arm holding her close, the warm solidity of his chest against her back, his legs bent to mirror the shape of hers all the way down to their feet. It was almost as intimate as when their bodies were joined. He was so *there*. Where she wanted him to be.

But this was the last time he'd be there. Today, he would drive to Calgary, where he'd spend the night with his parents. Then he'd go on to Maple Creek, Saskatchewan, and pick up Dusty and his horse. They'd been competing in a midweek rodeo. After that, Dusty could do the lion's share of the driving as they headed east across the province to Kennedy.

Though she hated to think of Ben going, Sally was relieved that the time had come. She wasn't sure she could survive another day with him.

She'd faced the truth in her heart. For her, love wasn't about one day finding a man a lot like Ben Traynor. It was Ben himself. She loved him. For his sexy cowboy ways; for his chivalry; for the gentle heart that cared about horses, disabled kids, and women with wounded souls.

There would never be another somebody like Ben.

Yet again, her heart had chosen the wrong man. But at least this time she'd chosen a good one. One who had helped her heal, to become a strong enough woman that she could handle letting him go. She wouldn't hide away after he was gone. She'd shop at Days of Your and wear pretty clothes; invite Dave, Cassidy, and Robin to come out for a ride and a barbecue; accept the next invitation someone extended to her. She'd get to know Corrie better, if the young woman was open to it.

Yes, Sally had her plan all worked out. And the first part of it was to smile for Ben and not let him know how much she was hurting. He needed to get back to the life he loved, and he needed to do it with the knowledge that she'd be okay. The last thing he needed was a clingy woman whimpering that he'd break her heart if he left.

They would be friends. They'd keep in touch. She'd have memories of all the wonderful time they'd spent together. It would be enough. It had to be.

She took a deep breath, gathering her strength, then sighed and wriggled against him. "Mmm, nice alarm clock." Collecting the hand that lay across her chest, she brought it to her lips and kissed it, then placed it on her breast.

He toyed with her nipple. "You're awake."

Her nipple hardened. "More awake every minute."

She wriggled again, adjusting her position so she trapped his erection between her legs.

Slowly, he pumped back and forth, his shaft caressing her tender flesh. Drawing arousal and moisture from her. Brushing her clit.

This was how she wanted to make love this last time. Not face to face. She wasn't sure she was strong enough not to cry if she gazed into his eyes. Better to do it like this, spooning, almost as if it were a dream. The final scene in an amazing dream that had transformed her and taught her she was a sensual, confident, loving woman.

"Condom?" she murmured.

Maybe he felt the same way she did, because he didn't attempt to change their positions, not even to give her the first orgasm with his mouth and fingers as he so often did. In fact, he didn't say a word, only stretched over to get a condom package, which he handed to her.

She opened it and reached down between her legs to sheath him. A large part of her didn't want to do it. She wanted to create a baby with Ben Traynor. But it wouldn't be fair, not to him and not to their child.

Protection in place, she tilted her hips and guided him into her.

"Sally," he whispered as he slid in.

"Ben," she murmured back. An affirmation that this was the two of them, lovers, joining their bodies. And their hearts. For she knew, deep inside, that at least a small part of Ben's heart belonged to her.

Shutting her eyes tight, she forced back tears and concentrated on the physical sensations, every single one of them. The building arousal, yes, but everything else as well. The soft brush of his breath against her sleep-tousled hair. The fresh aroma of morning air coming through the open, screened window to combine with their bodies' scents of sleep and musky sex. The gentle creak of the bed, a rhythmic counterpoint to the sexy sounds of slick flesh coming together.

Outside, the birds gave their usual exultant welcome to a morning that Sally felt anything but exultant about.

No, she didn't want to get emotional, at least not in a sad way. She *should* be exultant—grateful for everything Ben had given her and happy that they would remain close friends even if only by e-mail and an occasional phone call.

Slowly, he stroked in and out, one hand cupped around her breast. The movements were small, restrained compared to some of the passionate lovemaking they'd engaged in over the past days. Yet their very smallness made the sensations so focused and intense. Sally almost didn't want to come, not for the last time, but he didn't leave her a choice. Arousal mounted inevitably and she whimpered.

"Come with me, Sally," he whispered against her hair.

Her heart stopped. For a moment, she thought he was asking her to come on the rodeo circuit with him. To be with him—but to leave everything she'd built here.

Then she realized what he meant, as his hand moved from her breast down across her ribs and belly, and gently he fingered her clit. Orgasm. Not a major life change. Not an attempt to control her life the way Pete had done. Not a desire to be with her a while longer. She didn't know whether to be glad or sorry, but she had to laugh, silently, at herself.

Then his deft fingers demanded her full attention and she pressed against him, helpless. Wanting, needing what he could give her.

And he did, driving the two of them slowly, relentlessly, to climax.

She shuddered in his arms, waves of pleasure rippling through her body as pain constricted her heart.

Lying with Sally in his arms, their bodies still joined, post-orgasm lassitude seeped through Ben's veins. He couldn't give in to it; he needed to get up and on the road. He'd prepared everything last night. All he had to do was make coffee, fill his thermos, and load Chaunce. The thought of the old routine—the call of the near-empty open road, the exhilaration of competing, the easy pleasure of sharing a beer with Dusty—sent a jolt of adrenaline to counteract the lassitude.

How many hundreds, if not thousands, of times had he packed up at or before dawn and pulled onto the road, more than a few times leaving a warm, willing woman behind in bed? But never a woman like Sally. Hell, he was going to miss her.

It was really too bad she wasn't still a barrel racer. But she wasn't, and he wasn't some settled-down established guy like she'd be looking for, and those were facts.

He eased away to deal with the condom, wondering how to say good-bye.

With her back still turned to him, she said, "You should get going, Ben. It's a long drive."

"Yeah."

Her body tensed, then she rolled over and gazed into his eyes. "Promise you'll drive safely? And stop and rest?"

"Promise you won't work yourself into the ground?"

A soft smile touched her mouth. "I'll promise if you will."

"Deal." He smiled back at her. God, but he cared about this woman. "I'll e-mail or call to let you know how things are going. You'll do the same, right?"

"Absolutely."

"Well . . ."

"You know I can't thank you enough. For everything."

Her tone was too serious, her eyes too solemn. Gratitude wasn't what he wanted from her. Affection, yes. "Yeah, you got a deer fence out of it," he teased.

"I got a lot more than that. It doesn't seem fair, everything you did for me and all I did was give you a place for you and Chaunce to stay."

"You gave me . . ." He trailed off, searching for the right way to describe everything she'd given him. Her warm, generous body; the best slow dances and lovemaking he'd ever experienced. A bunch of great shared times: riding at sunset, throwing together meals at the end of a hard day's work, even mucking out stalls. Doing things with Sally turned chores into enjoyment. She'd given him her trust, sharing secrets she hadn't told another soul.

"Yes?" she asked.

"You. You gave me you. You let me into your life and I let you into mine. And we're stuck there now." Man, he really wasn't good with words. "I mean, we'll always be friends. Always be there for each other." God, he hoped she felt the same way.

"Yes. Oh, yes." Her eyes glistened and she sniffed. "I'm going to miss you."

Oh hell, was she going to cry? "I'll miss you, too. But we'll stay in touch. All the time." It was hard to imagine a day going by without talking to Sally.

"Well," he said awkwardly, "I should get going."

She pushed herself to a sitting position, shoved an extra pillow behind her back, and pulled up the sheet to cover her breasts. "And I need to do the morning chores.

Let's just say good-bye now and"—she swallowed—
"go our separate ways."

He slid out of bed and quickly pulled on his clothes,
then gazed down at Sally.

She crooked a finger. He sat on the bed and leaned
over to kiss her. When their lips touched, she closed her
eyes. Her fingers sifted through his hair. They parted
their lips and deepened the kiss. She gripped his head
tightly for a moment, then released it. Opening her
eyes, she broke the kiss. "Bye, Ben," she murmured on a
soft breath, her eyes shimmering with tears.

"Bye, Sally." He straightened and gazed at her for
one last moment. Not memorizing her face because
he'd done that long ago. Just capturing one final image
to hold in his heart.

Then he turned and, without looking back, left the
room. He wasn't going to take the time to shower, nor
to brew coffee. Leaving was hard. Best to just do it.

Chapter Twenty-Three

Late Saturday afternoon, Sally was slicing grilled beef, onions, and green peppers for fajitas when her cell rang. A glance at the screen had her grabbing it. "Ben! How did it go?" He'd called last night to let her know he, Dusty, and their horses had arrived safely in Kennedy. Today, they'd been scheduled to compete in team roping.

"It wasn't our best time by a long shot, but we made it into the short round tomorrow." His voice was as welcome as cold, pure water on a hot summer day when her throat was parched.

She sank into a chair at the kitchen table. "That's terrific." The short round was the finals of the event. "How's your shoulder?"

"Fine."

She grinned. "Yeah, cowboy, I know. Now tell me the real truth."

His chuckle, warm and low, made her shiver with need, just as if he'd run his callused fingers across her skin. "Can't put one over on another rodeo rider, can I? It's fine, really. The okay kind of hurt."

Tiredness and a little strain, but no further injury.

"I'm glad. But no bronc riding until you're cleared by a doctor or physiotherapist, promise?"

"Yes, Mom."

"Ha ha."

"Corrie get there okay?"

"She's unpacking now, and then she'll come over for dinner. I'm making fajitas."

"I'm envious."

"I guess you and Dusty will be having dinner and a couple of beers?"

"Yeah, we'll hit a bar tonight. Haven't had a chance to shop for groceries yet."

She imagined the pair of them at a Western bar with buckle bunnies flirting. She didn't figure Ben would be going home with any tonight, but he was a virile guy. He wouldn't want to go too long without sex. The thought of him with some other woman, doing the things he'd done with her . . . She shuddered. She had no right to be jealous, but that didn't stop her.

"I'm real glad Corrie's there," he said. "Not just to help with the work, but so you've got some company."

It was his company she wanted. But of course she wouldn't say that. Trying to sound happy and carefree, she said, "Yes, it'll be great. I want to get to know her better."

Out the window, she saw Corrie walking toward the back steps. In denims cut off at midthigh, a cotton tank top in sage green, and sturdy sandals, the young woman looked healthy and fit. "In fact, she's just arriving. I'd better go. Good luck tomorrow. Let me know how you do."

"You bet. Take care, Sally."

"You, too." She put down the phone.

Corrie came into the mudroom, took off her sandals, and stood tentatively in the open kitchen door. "Hey."

"Come on in. Help yourself to a beer. They're in the fridge."

"Uh, thank you." Corrie almost tiptoed into the room, quite a feat for a strapping woman of five feet ten. She took a bottle from the fridge and twisted off the cap. "Can I help?"

"Not tonight. You're the guest." To celebrate Corrie's return, Sally had driven into town and bought the ingredients for one of her own favorite meals. She'd also picked wildflowers for the table as well as for Corrie's apartment.

It seemed everything she did: the shopping expedition, the flowers, the meal she'd chosen—one she'd shared a couple of times with Ben—reminded her of him. But then everything did, since he'd gone. She'd shed some tears as she sought comfort with her hens, but life went on and hers was busy, not allowing time for melancholy. Except when she was alone in bed at the end of each long day. Tonight, she'd replay that phone call over and over, not so much for the words as for the sound of Ben's voice.

She forced away the sadness. She'd been in a horrible marriage, then she'd been alone and had led a constrained existence. Now she was alone again, but her life was richer. She should be happy for what she had, not depressed over what she didn't.

Corrie propped a hip against the kitchen table. "Thanks for cleaning the apartment and putting some groceries in the fridge. And for the flowers."

"You're welcome." In all meanings of that phrase. Sally tossed the onions into a heated cast-iron pan. A few stirs, add the peppers, add the beef to quickly reheat it. "We're all set. Condiments are on the deck table. I'll bring the filling. Could you bring the plate of tortillas?"

A couple of minutes later, they were both seated,

Corrie in Ben's usual place. As they dished out food, Corrie said, "This looks great. It's really nice of you."

"You had a long drive on a hot day. And I'm happy to see you." Sally smiled. "I know I've said this before, but I'm so glad to have you back."

"I'm so glad to be here." She gazed out at the view, beaming. Her oval face, framed by the pulled-back walnut-brown hair she wore in a long braid, bore no make-up. She wasn't conventionally pretty, but there was an understated beauty about her regular features, clear skin, and gray eyes. Sally guessed that if someone who was skilled with make-up and hair styling got their hands on her, they could make her look like a movie star.

Corrie turned her attention back to her rolled fajita, and took a bite. "Mmm, delicious." After another bite, she said, "I took a quick tour around the place. It's looking great. I saw new names on the schedule, new horses in the paddock, and wow, that deer and rabbit fencing around the vegetable garden is awesome."

"Things are going well. Fingers crossed." She raised her hand, the middle finger crossed over the index one.

"Fingers crossed." Corrie mirrored the gesture. "Your last assistant was obviously great."

"He was. But Ben wasn't as much an assistant as an old friend."

"Oh?" She slanted Sally a curious gaze, then quickly refocused on her food, obviously remembering how Sally valued her privacy.

"Yes, from my rodeo days. He dropped by to say hi. He had to take a couple weeks' break from rodeo because of an injury, so he offered to help out in return for a place to park his trailer and keep his horse."

"A nice deal for both of you."

Corrie had no idea how nice, and that information was too personal to share. "It was."

"You look great, too," Corrie said. "Younger and, uh, not stressed out."

"I feel better, for sure. Having business pick up has taken a weight off my shoulders. But how about you, Corrie? You left because of some urgent personal thing. Now you're back, so I hope it got resolved okay."

"Yeah." Corrie fidgeted with her beer bottle. "It's fine."

"Good." But not good enough for the new Sally. "I don't mean to pry, but I care about you, Corrie. If you want to talk about it, I'd like to listen."

"Oh. Uh . . ." The younger woman lifted the bottle and drank deeply. Finally, she said, "Back when I was a kid, I was shy; I stuttered; I was taller and bigger than my classmates, including the boys; and I liked animals better than dolls. Kids teased me and I didn't have many friends. When Bill asked me out in high school, at first I thought it was a joke."

"Oh, Corrie." Sally'd been the opposite as a girl: always pretty, confident, popular.

"But it wasn't. We've dated ever since. He's the only guy I've ever gone out with. We both went to college, then he went to law school. I didn't really know what I wanted to do, and I took the job at the garden center because I like physical work, and being outside."

Sally nodded. Corrie's former employer had provided a glowing reference.

"Last year, when Bill graduated and we both turned twenty-five, he proposed." Her mouth twisted. "Actually, he said it was time we got married." She raised her bottle and took another long swallow.

"Not the most romantic proposal," Sally ventured.

"No, but then I'm not the kind of woman who inspires romance."

"I'm sure that's not true. You've grown into a lovely woman."

Corrie gave a disbelieving snort. "Anyhow, when I thought about us being married, living in Vancouver, him being a lawyer and me keeping working at the nursery, I just . . . well, I didn't exactly feel happy. Then I was online and happened across the job you'd advertised. It was exactly what I wanted to do. So I told Bill I needed some time to think, to decide about my future. He wasn't happy. At all." She scrunched up her face. "But what could he say? Besides, he had an articling position at a big downtown firm and they were busting his balls making him work insane hours."

"So you came to work at Ryland Riding, and made yourself indispensable. And then?"

"Bill said my time was up. I needed to grow up and do the sensible thing. Come home and marry him. He wasn't going to wait any longer."

"Hmm. Again, that wasn't the romantic way to do it, but I admit I can kind of see his point. He needed to know if you really wanted to be with him."

"I know. I wasn't being fair to him. And I did want to be with him. Well, sort of. I mean, he was the only man I'd ever been with. Not just sex, but, you know, cooking a meal together, going to a movie. Me hanging out at his place reading while he did some work. Besides, he was the only guy who'd ever shown interest in me. If I didn't marry Bill, I'd probably be alone for the rest of my life."

"No." Sally shook her head. "That's not true, Corrie." If it had been the other way around—that he was the only man Corrie could ever imagine loving—then she probably would be alone. As Sally expected that she herself would.

"Well, whatever. That was what I thought, so I went home. My parents were happy to see me and, like Bill, happy I'd finally come to my senses." She frowned, gazing at the beer bottle she rotated between her hands. "It was surreal. Being the old Corrie, living in the basement suite at my parents', spending time with Bill. Like a time warp. Or like my time here at Ryland Riding had never existed; I'd just dreamed it. But it was sure a great dream. Yeah, I was lonely sometimes—"

"I'm sorry. I should have been better company."

"No, not at all. I'm shy and an introvert. And self-sufficient. I figured you were the same way, and that was fine. I had the horses, this amazing countryside, and a job that I enjoyed every minute of." She nodded thoughtfully. "That's what I remembered when I was back home. I missed it so much. I didn't feel really alive."

Sally nodded. That was how she felt about this place, too.

"Then I read your e-mail. It was like, you know, that cliché 'click,' the light bulb moment. It hadn't all been a dream, and I could have it again." A smile lit her mouth, then it faded. "It was the hardest thing in the world, telling Bill. After years together, after him being so patient, I hurt him. And yet in my heart I knew it was the right thing for both of us. When you see the truth, you have to honor it, don't you think?"

"I do." Sally's truth was that she loved Ben Traynor. And the way she honored that truth was by not telling him. By respecting the life he'd chosen, wishing him the best of luck, and being a good friend. Even if she longed to be so much more.

* * *

"This is the life, eh?" Dusty said. He hoisted his beer bottle toward Ben. "Good to have you back, man."

They sat at bar stools in a bare-bones Western bar in Kennedy on Saturday night. Ben clicked his bottle against Dusty's. "Good to be back." It had felt damned fine being out in the arena again. He grinned, remembering how he and Chaunce had chased after the steer as Dusty roped its head and tugged it to the side, then Ben let fly with his rope and neatly captured its hind legs. Chaunce and Paddy, Dusty's horse, had done their part, backing to face each other, pulling the ropes taut. Teamwork, the four of them moving smoothly together.

Life was back to normal. He and Dusty were sharing the rig again, their horses keeping each other company in the back.

He shifted position, trying to ease the ache in his injured shoulder. When he'd been roping, he'd forgotten about it, but that workout on top of the long drive had been rough. Still, he was used to this. The healing process took time. He'd wear the sling when he needed to, keep up with the exercises Monique gave him, and he'd be fine.

His heart, though . . . There was an ache in it that was getting worse hour by hour. He missed Sally. Sure wished she was sitting here tilting back a beer bottle with him and Dusty. Sure wished she'd be sharing his bed tonight, and breakfast in the morning.

Talking to her on the phone only made the ache worse. But it was pretty darned clear that she was doing okay without him. He was glad she was reaching out to Corrie. Making friends. Last night she'd mentioned having plans to get together with Cassidy Esperanza and two or three other women in town, since Corrie'd be there to look after Ryland Riding.

Before too long, Sally would meet a man. One with

a serious job who wanted to marry and start a family. He took a healthy swig of beer. "Yeah, it's good to be back," he said again, reminding himself of that fact.

"So how's Sally Pantages anyhow?" Dusty asked. "Still as purty and feisty?"

Ben had told him he'd looked her up and stayed to help out, but that was all he'd said. "Yeah, in a more grown-up way."

"It's a pity that gal quit the circuit, but if you're gonna do it, hers was the right way. Goin' out on top, not like some busted-down old-timer who don't have the sense to know his time's over."

"You ever think of quitting, Dusty?"

His partner shoved back his shaggy hair, a light shade of brown that matched his name, and gave a crooked grin. "Maybe after we hit the top and stay there for long enough that it's time to give some younger guys a chance. You?"

"Sounds about right." Wasn't it every rodeo rider's dream? "Ever thought what you'll do when that day comes?" For the first time, it struck Ben as strange that, after years on the road together sharing the cramped quarters in the trailer, drinking beer, and shooting pool, they'd never talked about this stuff. Always, their conversation had focused on the immediate. And didn't that just point out the huge difference between Ben and Sally?

"Can't say that I have. Something'll come along. Be a rodeo judge, maybe, and stay on the circuit." Dusty flagged down the waitress, flirted a little, and ordered another round of beer. When she'd gone, he said, "How 'bout you?"

"Been starting to think it might be time to make some plans. Lay some money by. Have a goal to work toward." Here he was, parroting Dave Cousins.

"Guess that makes sense. What you got in mind?"

"Something outdoors, where I get to ride. Maybe buy a ranch of my own, or go in as partners with someone." He decided to run his new idea by Dusty, see if his partner figured he was nuts. "Or it could be fun to run a rodeo school."

A slow grin spread over Dusty's face. "Sure as hell would. Train the next generation." He winked. "Let 'em idolize you."

Ben laughed.

"Maybe we'll do that together," Dusty said.

"Maybe we will."

"After we been on top for a few years," he drawled, giving Ben another wink.

"Yeah. After that."

Chapter Twenty-Four

Early on a Wednesday evening toward the end of August, Sally was saying good-bye to Lark and Jayden Cantrell after the boy's lesson. He'd been coming twice a week and was showing steady progress, which had all of them excited.

Brooke Brannon drove her Toyota into the yard, parked, and came over to say hi. In a short khaki skirt, a sleeveless pink shirt, and sandals, she looked summery and pretty.

"Hi, Sally and Lark," the blonde said. "And this must be Jayden." She held out her hand to the boy in the wheelchair with his riding helmet on his lap. "I'm Brooke, and I hear from Sally that you're turning into her star pupil."

The boy's face glowed. "I'm trying."

"You're smart to start riding early," Brooke said. "I didn't learn until I was . . . well, let's just say many years older than you."

As Brooke chatted with Jayden, Lark took Sally aside. "It's so great to see my son more confident, as well as stronger and better coordinated."

"He's a great kid. You're so lucky."

Lark beamed. "I know. Thanks for realizing that."
She lowered her voice. "Can you believe that some
people feel sorry for me?"

Sadly, Sally could believe that, but she sure wasn't
one of them. "Well, I envy you. I'd give anything to have
a son like Jayden."

"It'll happen for you one day."

"Maybe. I hope so." She'd actually begun to think
about adopting. It was likely to be the only way she'd
ever have a child. Ben had been gone for more than
five weeks, but she was no closer to imagining herself
being attracted to another man, much less falling in
love with one.

Lark went to rest a hand on Jayden's shoulder. "We'd
better get going. Your grandmother will have supper
waiting." Sally had learned that Lark's mother lived
with them, and they all helped each other out in whatever ways they could. It made her a bit envious, though
she now spoke to her own mom, as well as her dad and
sister, several times a week.

Expertly, Lark and her son used the van's side ramp
to load Jayden and his chair, and Lark secured the chair
in the area that a passenger seat normally occupied.

When the pair had driven off, Brooke said to Sally,
"That boy's a keeper."

"Isn't he?"

They exchanged a smile, then the blonde said, "Did
our friends get off for their ride?"

"Cassidy and Maribeth arrived about an hour ago,
and Corrie went out with them."

Over the past weeks, Sally and Corrie had become
friends with a few other women. Several of them got
together at least once a week. Sally had become
comfortable leaving teenaged Heather in charge of
Ryland Riding.

For the first time since Sally had arrived in Caribou Crossing more than seven years ago, she had friends and a social life. It was wonderful and made life even richer. And yet friends couldn't fill the aching void in her heart created by Ben's absence.

Sally walked over to the hitching rail and collected the reins of Pookie, the placid gray mare she used for her work with Jayden. "I need to get Pookie untacked and put her out."

"I'll help, then we can get dinner going."

They walked toward the barn with the horse following behind. Quickly, they removed her tack and then both began to groom her.

"Heard anything from Ben lately?" Brooke asked.

"He and Dusty won team roping last weekend in Lethbridge and qualified for the Canadian Finals. He hasn't had as good luck in saddle bronc. He hasn't been drawing the best stock. He said the one in Lethbridge bucked like a rocking horse."

"But that would make it easier to stay on, wouldn't it?"

"Staying on for eight seconds is only part of it. With a dink—a horse or bull that doesn't buck well—the score's not going to be great. What you want is stock that's rank."

"Rank?" Brooke wrinkled her nose. "That sounds nasty."

Sally laughed. "Yeah, that's exactly what rank means. The tougher the animal is to ride, the higher the risk and the better the opportunity for the cowboy to exhibit his skill. The animal gets a score, too; the ranker it is, the higher the score."

"I'll trust you on that. How is Ben's shoulder?"

"Holding up well, he says."

"You talk often?"

"Pretty regularly." By phone, video chat, or e-mail.

She tried to act like a good friend while all the time her heart cried out to him.

She and Brooke took Pookie out to the paddock and released her. Moon Song, the rapidly growing colt, pranced over to the fence and Brooke lavished him with pats and praise.

"We'd best get going on dinner," Sally said. "The others will be back soon."

"I have a mint-chocolate cake in my car. It's been sitting in the fridge at the salon all day."

"That sounds decadent. Thanks, Brooke." The woman was an awesome cook. As they fetched the cake, Sally said, "Where's Nicki tonight?"

"At home with her dad. Jake has the night off."

"A night off, and he's okay with you being here with us?" Although she'd seen numerous examples of her girlfriends' husbands seemingly being fine with their wives heading out for an evening without them, it still surprised her.

Brooke, balancing the cake as they strolled toward the house, said, "Sure. Just like I'm okay with him and his buddy Jamal wanting some guy time now and then. Different people satisfy different needs, right? Much as I love Jake, his eyes glaze over if I start talking girl-talk."

"I suppose."

"Marriage means partnership," Brooke said firmly. "It's not being bonded at the hip. That's conjoined twins, not husband and wife. Seems to me that if you look to your spouse to meet all your needs, you're going to be sorely disappointed. And it's not fair on them."

No, it wasn't fair. Pete hadn't been fair on her.

Sally had taken Ben's advice and started seeing a therapist, and now had a much better understanding of the dynamics of her and Pete's relationship. Pete might truly have loved her, but he was a damaged man, probably incapable of loving in a healthy way.

"You and Ben really get along," Brooke said.

"We do."

"Sometimes I get the impression there's, you know, something more." Brooke's tone was tentative, giving Sally every opportunity to toss off a quick denial as she'd always done in the past, even when it was her mom or her sister Penny doing the hinting.

Sally sighed. She'd really come to like the older woman. To trust her. It would sure be nice to have one person she could talk to, really talk to, about Ben. "He's special, and yes, I care for him a lot. But he has his life and I have mine and it was time for him to move on."

"Hmm."

They stepped into the mudroom. Sally pulled off her boots, a bit relieved that Brooke wasn't going to pursue the topic, but mostly disappointed. The two women went into the kitchen. Brooke put the cake in the fridge and cooed over the latest pictures of Sally's brand-new niece which were tacked to the door, right beside the photo of her mom and dad on the porch of their ranch house.

Then she faced Sally. "I've heard that before, you know. The 'I've got my life, he's got his' line."

Maybe the conversation wasn't over. "Where? In a country song?"

"No, from me. After Jake and I first got together, he went back to his job in Vancouver. We decided not to stay in touch. Even though I loved him with all my heart."

"But he loved you, too. Didn't he?"

"It took him a while to figure things out. Thank God

he did, and that he came back to persuade me. Not just once, but twice."

"Good for Jake. I'm so happy for the two of you."

"Me, too." The blonde flashed a satisfied smile. "But someone needs to be the one who has the guts to go after it, or it may never happen."

Sally crossed her arms over her chest. "What are you saying, Brooke?"

"That you need to examine your heart. If you love the man and want to be with him, maybe you should tell him. I was a coward. That could have cost me so much."

Sally shook her head. "It's not the same. Ben loves rodeo. He's not ready to give it up."

"Maybe there's something he'd love even more, if he knew the offer was on the table."

"All he wants from me is friendship."

"You're one hundred percent sure of that?"

"I—" About to say "I am," Sally stopped as her heart jerked and raced. Damn Brooke for making her think there might be a possibility, when she was sure—okay, almost sure—there wasn't. "Ninety percent?"

"Jake proposed to me and I turned him down."

"Seriously? Even though you loved him?"

"Yes. I thought he only wanted to marry me because I was pregnant. But he came back. He convinced me that he truly loved me. Listen, my friend, it doesn't always have to be the man who has the sense to recognize the worth of what he had, and try to win it back."

"So you think, even if there's only a ten percent chance . . ."

"It's worth going for." Brooke nodded emphatically. "What's the worst that could happen? Right now, you believe that the two of you can only be friends. If he confirms it, are you any the worse off?"

Sally reflected. "I might be. And not just because my pride would take a beating. It would change things between us. He'd be aware of how one-sided things are. He might not be as open with me. It could damage our friendship."

Brooke pressed her lips together and nodded slowly. "I hear you. Maybe I should have kept my mouth shut. I guess I'm not very good at giving advice."

"I appreciate that you care enough to try and help—" Sally broke off as the sound of female laughter carried through the screened kitchen window. "The others are back."

Maribeth's cheerful voice said, "Corrie, you need to jump back in the dating pool and swim around some."

"I'm not ready, and I wouldn't know where to start," Corrie replied.

Boots clomped up the steps. "I'll introduce you to some guys," Maribeth said. "I've dated pretty much every unmarried man in Caribou Crossing."

"Jeez, Maribeth," Cassidy said as the screen door to the mudroom creaked open and they entered. "Corrie deserves better than your rejects."

"Hey, I wouldn't do that," Maribeth said in an injured tone. "These are really good guys. But there wasn't that click. You know that click?"

"You bet I do," Cassidy said as the three of them came into the kitchen, sock-footed. "Yeah, you gotta wait for the click."

"You do," Brooke agreed.

But what did you do when you felt that click with a guy whom you were sure—or at least ninety percent sure—didn't reciprocate the feeling?

Sally pondered that question, and Brooke's well-intentioned but confusing advice, all through dinner. She discussed it with the hens when she settled them for the night. It was still on her mind as she prepared for bed and wondered if the phone would ring.

Around ten o'clock, it did. More nights than not, she or Ben got in touch around this time. It was casual chat, sharing tidbits about their days. Tonight, as she lay between the sheets of the bed she'd shared with him, it was hard to achieve a breezy tone, but she did her best. She listened for any hints in his voice that he felt something more for her than friendship, but didn't catch a thing as he told her about the drive to Armstrong. He was back in British Columbia, only a half-day's drive from Caribou Crossing. He hadn't suggested dropping by.

Trying to sound upbeat, she told him that her family was planning a visit to Caribou Crossing in October. She filled him in on Jayden's lesson and tonight's dinner party. She of course omitted her conversation with Brooke, but said that Maribeth was trying to get Corrie to start dating.

"Is Corrie thinking about it?" he asked.

"She says she's not ready."

"Hmm." There was a pause. "You haven't mentioned that new boarder lately."

"Which one?" There'd been three in the past few weeks.

"That lawyer. What's his name? Randy?"

"Oh, Randy." She laughed, thinking of what she'd done, something that would never even have occurred to her in the past. "Didn't I tell you? This is kind of fun."

"Fun?"

"I told you he recently moved here? He's looking to

meet people and he actually asked me out." It had been flattering, as had the times she'd been hanging out with her friends at the Wild Rose bar and men had asked her to dance. Of course none of them compared to Ben.

"He asked you out?" Ben struggled to keep his voice even as he surged up from his seat on the floor of his horse's stall at the back of the trailer. Chaunce shot him a questioning look. Damn, Ben had known this would happen. Sally starting to date. He should be happy for her, but instead felt hurt and pissed off as she babbled on about how nice, smart, and successful this lawyer was.

Ben had reached for the door handle, to go out and pace in the fresh night air, when she said, "And it occurred to me that he and Madeleine might be perfect for each other."

"Huh?" Had he missed something? "He asked you out, so you tried to matchmake him with someone else?"

"He's not my type."

Relieved, yet wondering what more she wanted than nice, smart, and successful, he again sank back down beside Chaunce. The Paint had been witness to a number of late-night calls. Better the horse than Dusty, who was in the living quarters section of the trailer. "Why not?"

"There's no click."

No what? Baffled, he shook his head. "Sorry, what did you say?"

"Oh, nothing. But it's like, well, he has his own horse and loves riding, but he's happy to have Corrie and me do the heavy lifting. I can't imagine him using a hoof pick."

A chuckle escaped Ben. "So if you put up a profile

on an Internet dating site, it'd say 'must be handy with a hoof pick'?"

"Pretty much."

"Ah." He was a mighty fine hand with one himself, which he had proved to her once his shoulder had healed enough. If that were all it took to win Sally's heart, he'd be set for life.

Wait a minute? Was that really what he wanted? To be with Sally for the rest of his life? Was that what the ache in his heart was trying to tell him? He knew he cared for her, cared a lot, and that the idea of her dating someone else pissed him off. He'd have to think about this some more. In the meantime, she was carrying on about why she'd thought Randy and Madeleine might get along.

"Anyhow," she said, "they'd been riding at different times and had never met. I suggested he come one evening when she'd be there. They flirted in the barn, went riding together, and went for dinner after. They're now officially dating."

That was one prospective suitor out of the way. How many more would there be? "I guess there's someone out there for everyone." He almost groaned. He sounded like a talk-show pseudo shrink.

"I guess there is." She paused. "I wonder how you know if you've found them?"

Maybe when your stupid heart hurt worse than a broken shoulder? "Uh," he stumbled around, "I dunno. I guess you just know."

"I guess you do. Well, it's late. We both need to get some sleep."

"Sure. Night, then."

In fact, he didn't need to go to bed now. Tomorrow was a free day. He and Dusty'd been in Lethbridge,

Alberta, last weekend and there hadn't been any rodeos midweek that they could reasonably get to. So they'd taken a leisurely couple of days to make the drive to Armstrong. The Interior Provincial Exhibition and Stampede was a huge event that ran for five days over the Labour Day long weekend. Neither he nor Dusty was scheduled to compete until Friday, which was the day after tomorrow.

They wanted to do well here. There were two ways to qualify for the Canadian Finals Rodeo in November. One was to be in the top ten money earners in your event—which meant competing in every damned rodeo you could get to. The other was to place first or second in one of the last ten rodeos of the Canadian Tour season. He and Dusty had done that for team roping, winning last weekend in Lethbridge. But he hadn't qualified in saddle bronc yet, nor had Dusty in tie-down roping. If they could achieve that this weekend, it'd sure take some pressure off.

"I could visit Sally," he told Chaunce. In fact, he could have been with her right now. It was a four-hour drive. He could've left Dusty to look after the horses, and taken the truck. "But she knew I'd be in Armstrong," he muttered, "and she didn't suggest I visit."

Chaunce tossed his head.

"Yeah, and I didn't suggest it either. Maybe it isn't a good idea."

Another head toss, this time more demanding.

Ben hauled himself to his feet and fed his horse a carrot, then gave one to Dusty's horse Paddy, a powerful chestnut gelding. "Right now, the one thing that seems like a truly fine idea is to have a beer. Or two. Night, guys."

At some rodeos, he and Dusty put their horses in the

barns on the rodeo grounds, but often they kept them in the rig where the cowboys could control the environment and keep a close watch on their equine partners.

Now, Ben went through the connecting door to the living quarters. Dusty was watching a baseball game on TV. Ben checked out the score: the Blue Jays were getting their butts kicked.

"Beer?" Ben asked, heading for the fridge.

"Wouldn't say no." Dusty clicked off the TV. "Game sucks."

"Sit outside?" Without waiting for an answer—how many times had they done this over the years?—Ben handed two cans of beer to Dusty, then got the folding chairs from a storage compartment.

They sat down outside the door and popped the tabs on their beers. For a few minutes, they drank in companionable silence. Around them were parked other contestants' vehicles: trucks, horse trailers, people trailers, rigs like his and Dusty's. A couple of cowboys walked by and they all exchanged a "Hey."

Eventually, Dusty said, "How're things with Sally?"

"Good."

"You two sure do a lot of talking for a guy and a gal who're just friends."

Ben shrugged. They drank some more, then he said, "I been thinking some more about that rodeo school idea." He'd been doing a lot more than that. Much of his spare time over the past couple of weeks had gone into researching the various rodeo schools in Canada and the States. He'd e-mailed a few owners with questions and spoken to a couple of others on the phone, finding they were invariably happy to discuss their work with another rodeo cowboy.

"Yeah?"

"You think anyone would come?"

"Hell, yeah. We're already on the way to making names for ourselves. Give it a few more years, win the CFR a couple more times." Dusty'd won tie-down roping once and Ben had won saddle bronc twice. "We'll have serious cred."

Ben rotated his beer can back and forth. "I was wondering about, maybe, now."

"Now?" Dusty cocked his head. "What the hell? You're not thinking about quitting rodeo?"

"I dunno." Was he? "Maybe."

"Well, shit. I don't know what to say."

Ben rubbed a hand over his jaw and hunted for words. "There's only one reason I'd quit after this year. And shit, yeah, I'd feel bad about breaking up our partnership, leaving you in the lurch. But the thing is . . . it's about Sally."

For a long moment, Dusty didn't react. "Oh, man." He hooted, then whacked a hand against Ben's shoulder. Luckily, he was sitting on Ben's right side, so it was the shoulder he hadn't injured. "I knew you were more than friends. You've gone and fallen for her."

"I guess I have."

Dusty was grinning so widely he could barely speak. "You wanna do all that white picket fence stuff."

"Well, more like a split rail, but I guess I kind of do." In fact, he couldn't think of anything much better than life with Sally, raising a couple of kids, working with horses, and living on that pretty piece of land she owned. And there it was: the big hitch. He groaned. "But I don't really see it working."

"No? Hey, she could do worse than you. Not a lot worse, mind you, but—"

Ben shut him up with a light punch to the biceps. "Thanks for that."

"You don't think she has feelings for you?"

"Friendly ones." And sexy ones, a thought that tightened his groin. "She needs a different kind of guy. She's gonna start dating someone else—"

"She isn't dating? That says something."

"Maybe." Ben hadn't told Dusty about Sally's reasons for being wary of relationships.

"What kind of guy you figure she needs?"

"She owns this big chunk of land, runs a business. She's successful. She needs—"

"Hey, you're successful. You've won saddle bronc at the CFR a couple times, and you could do it again this year. Not to mention, we got a chance at team roping."

"Yeah, but I'm not exactly getting rich. Sally needs, oh, more like a doctor or lawyer or someone who owns his own business."

"Huh." A pause. "She say that?"

"Uh, no." Ben's lips twitched. "She wants a guy who's good with a hoof pick."

"There you go."

"But seriously, I don't have much to offer. Yeah, I've saved up some money, but not a lot. If I do well at the CFR, I might have enough to buy some horses and set up a rodeo school—on her land, if that was okay with her."

"So this is about macho pride? Needing to be the one who owns more property and makes more money? Dude, I know we're cowboys, but it's the twenty-first century. Didn't anyone ever tell you that women are equals?"

"Hell, yeah. I just want to be an equal, too."

"And equality's about money? That what Sally thinks?"

"Uh . . . I don't know," he admitted.

"Then you gotta ask." Dusty had a swallow of beer,

then grinned. "And you knew that all along, right? That's why you started talking about rodeo school."

Ben hadn't consciously known it. But now he realized that, ever since the day he'd driven away from Sally's place, his heart had been doing its damnedest to lead him back.

Tomorrow, he'd make some more calls to folks who ran rodeo schools. This weekend, he'd draft a business plan.

And as soon as this rodeo wound up, he was going to follow his heart all the way back to Caribou Crossing.

Chapter Twenty-Five

"Corrie," Sally said, "how do you feel about being left in charge Saturday and part of Sunday if Heather comes in to help?" It was Thursday evening and they were in the office reviewing the schedule for Friday and the Labour Day weekend. "The classes and private lessons that are scheduled are all beginner ones." Because it was the last long weekend of summer, a lot of people were out of town or occupied with family stuff, so the schedule for Saturday, Sunday, and Monday was lighter than usual.

"Sure. Heather and I can manage fine."

"Great. I'll call her to confirm." The teen had already offered to help out this weekend.

"So you're taking a little holiday?"

"It's the weekend of the Interior Provincial Exhibition and Stampede in Armstrong. I thought I'd drive there and see part of the rodeo."

"Cool. But why don't you stay over Sunday? Take the whole long weekend?"

"Hmm." Worrying her lips together, Sally mulled it over. She didn't plan to tell Ben she was coming. That way, she could scope out the situation and decide how and when—or if—to approach him. She might spend an hour at the rodeo and come straight back without ever letting him know she'd gone. Or . . . she might talk to him, find that he returned her feelings—

Oh, Lord, what was she thinking? Was such a thing the least bit likely?

"Sally, I can handle it. Have confidence in me."

It wasn't Corrie she lacked confidence in; it was herself. And that, damn it, was Pete's doing. She hadn't had a flashback since the altercation at the Wild Rose, but she was still letting Pete influence her behavior. She knew better than that, thanks to her therapy sessions. "I do have confidence," she said strongly. "Let's call Heather and set it up."

After they did, Corrie went up to her apartment to run a bubble bath and read before bed. Sally did an Internet search for motels in Armstrong, made a few calls, and found that every place was booked up because of the IPE. Damn, so much for her brave idea. Maybe this was a sign that she shouldn't chase after Ben.

Yeah, right. Amanda hadn't taken the loss of a leg as a sign that she should curtail her full life. Jayden wasn't letting cerebral palsy stop him from growing stronger. The lack of motel rooms wasn't a sign Sally should quit; it was a test of her resolve.

She called Cassidy. "I was hoping to get to the rodeo in Armstrong this weekend."

"Cool! You'll see Ben? Say hi from Dave, Robin, and me." Cassidy might have suspected the truth about Sally's relationship with Ben, but she'd never pried.

"I just found out that all the motels are booked. Do you have any ideas?" Who better to ask than the assistant manager of a hotel?

"Leave it to me. You want Friday, Saturday, and Sunday?"

"Just Saturday and Sunday. If you find me something, I'll be forever in your debt."

"Don't be silly. That's what friends are for."

Feeling more hopeful, Sally left the barn and made her nightly visit to her hens. On the way back to the house, her cell rang and she grabbed it out of her pocket.

"You're all set, at a nice little hotel," Cassidy said. "I'll e-mail you the confirmation."

"Thank you so much!" If she were to believe in signs, this had to be an excellent one.

Sally's Friday passed in a busy, blurry daze, capped by a phone call from Ben to say that he and Dusty'd done well in team roping and qualified for the short round on Sunday. She had congratulated him, but cut the call short, uncomfortable about her secret.

And then it was Saturday morning and she was saying good-bye to her hens and asking them to wish her luck. She spent a few minutes with Corrie and Heather, going over details they'd already discussed three or four times, and then finally drove away.

She kept the radio on all the way, determinedly singing along rather than letting herself think. Too bad that so many country songs were of the lost love variety.

When she located the hotel Cassidy had booked, she let out a whistle. It was charming with its green paint, white trim, and window boxes full of late-summer flowers. She'd expected a run-down motel along the highway, given the bargain basement price quoted on the confirmation. Obviously one person in the hospitality industry had extended a courtesy to another, and Sally was the beneficiary.

After checking in, she took a quick shower. She'd made the drive in loose-fitting jeans and a tee. Now she put on good jeans and boots and her best Western shirt, pale yellow with green stitching on the yoke and pearly snap-buttons. A few weeks ago she'd had her ears re-pierced and she wore the etched silver feathers from her rodeo days. And of course her lucky horseshoe pendant. She completed the outfit with a pretty straw Resistol hat with a vented brim, a treasure recently acquired from Days of Your, which she wore only on special occasions.

All decked out in her finest, driving to the IPE grounds in the early afternoon, she could no longer resist the "what if's." What if Ben was with another woman? But how likely was that, given that he talked to her most nights at bedtime? Even if he wasn't, what if Sally declared her undying love and saw a look of stunned horror on his face?

She took a deep breath and tried to calm her frantic nerves. This was way different from her rodeo days, when the nerves had been an exciting thrill of anticipation combined with the hope that she and Autumn Mist would have a good race.

The memory, and the familiar happy energy of a big country fair as she paid and went through the admission gate, lifted her spirits. This felt like coming home, though she'd almost never gone to a rodeo as a mere attendee rather than as a competitor.

She could probably talk her way into going back into the contestants' area—some of the older folks would likely remember Sally Pantages—but she didn't want to distract Ben. Competitors had their prep routine, and she wouldn't interfere. It was simply being considerate, not that she was a coward.

After purchasing a hot dog and a soda, she found a spot in the rapidly filling bleachers. One end of the arena had the bucking chutes for the broncs and bulls. The other end was where the timed events—roping and steer wrestling—would originate. She of course chose the end by the bucking chutes.

Listening to country music on the loudspeaker and eagerly drawing in the familiar scents of dust, cattle, horses, and concession food, she ate her meal. Around her, hundreds of fans, many dressed in Western gear, settled in the bleachers and chatted about the day's events.

She checked the program. Dusty'd be competing in the first event: tie-down roping. Ben would ride in saddle bronc roughly an hour after that.

Then she turned to the "Top Cowboys" pages and found Ben's handsome, smiling image. She skimmed the information provided. As she knew from their conversations, he'd won saddle bronc at the CFR twice. Last year he'd finished third and, with Dusty, ninth in team roping. He wasn't making a fortune at rodeo, especially not when you took into account all the expenses like entry fees, gas, and maintenance of the rig. Still, he was ending up well into the black, which was better than most competitors did.

She flipped to the "Ladies Barrel Racing" pages and studied the photos. Four of the dozen women featured had been around back in her day. It was a career that could last for decades. Just like roping, Ben and Dusty's event. Saddle bronc riders could go a fairly long spell, too; the wear and tear on the body was harsh, but not as bad as with bull riding.

Was there any way that Ben might consider retiring

early, or at least cutting back considerably on the number of rodeos he attended? If not, could she imagine them being a couple, yet spending more than half the year apart? She sighed. It sure wouldn't be ideal, but better that than to give him up, or to ask him to prematurely quit the career he loved.

But she was getting ahead of herself. There was a good chance Ben couldn't imagine ever loving her as more than a close friend.

On the loudspeaker, Vince Gill was rocking "Ridin' the Rodeo," firing up the crowd. When the song ended, the announcer's voice boomed out, "Everyone ready for some rodeo?"

As the audience yelled and whistled a raucous affirmative, a buzz of adrenaline surged through Sally's blood. It didn't feel right to be out here in the stands, rather than back in the readying area with Autumn Mist.

The rodeo had opened earlier in the week, so today there was no introductory Grand Parade. After introductions and announcements, it was right down to business with tie-down roping.

Taking deep breaths, she watched the first competitors. Dusty would ride fourth. When his turn came, she recognized the lanky guy with dusty brown hair and an easy smile. He and his horse, Paddy, a powerful chestnut, pulled in an excellent time and nailed down a slot in the short round.

She watched the next event, bareback bronc, then a trick rider who took her breath away. After that, it was steer wrestling. Saddle bronc was scheduled next. Ben would be putting on his chaps, checking over his saddle and bronc rein one final time, doing his stretches. Talking to the other contestants, exchanging tips about the animals each had drawn.

Finally, steer wrestling ended and the broncs were

loaded into the chutes. The cowboys' adrenaline would be pumping, and her heart raced just as fast.

Ben would ride sixth and he'd drawn an animal named Sidewinder. The fencing of the chutes made it hard for her to see inside, but the black horse reared up, trying to climb or batter its way out. She crossed her fingers that Sidewinder was as rank as it looked, so Ben had a chance at a good score. *If* he held on for eight seconds and rode with all his skill.

The event started and she paid little heed to the first competitors, except to note the scores of the three who made it to eight seconds. Instead, she kept an eye on Sidewinder's chute.

And then there was Ben, climbing the side of the chute. Her heart jerked to a dead stop. She sucked in air and stared hungrily. He looked so healthy and fit, so handsome in his sky-blue shirt, protective vest, and fringed chaps. It didn't seem that he'd had a haircut since she last saw him and her fingers itched to twine through the dark locks that curled past his collar below his hat. He looked completely in his element as he and Dusty, who was perched on the other side of Sidewinder's chute, carefully saddled the restless horse.

How could a man who rode broncs ever be content with the uneventful routine at Ryland Riding? And yet she loved that routine as much or more than she'd loved barrel racing. . . .

The fifth bronc burst out of captivity, the rider stayed aboard for five seconds before tumbling over the horse's head, and then it was finally Ben's turn.

"Please, please, please," she whispered under her breath. Make the animal a good bucker; help Ben ride well; keep him safe.

Even at this distance, she could see his look of intense concentration as he measured the braided rein, got a

firm grip on it with his right hand, and said something
to the bronc. Slowly, he lowered himself, sliding onto
the saddle and into the stirrups as the animal twitched
and jerked.

She held her breath.

With his left hand, Ben tugged his hat down low,
then he gave a quick nod. The gate swung open, and
Sidewinder exploded into the arena.

As required, Ben's boots stayed over the break of the
horse's shoulders until the animal completed its first
jump out of the chute. The bronc bucked forward and
back, twisted sideways, and Ben matched its rhythm. His
form was perfect. His bad shoulder didn't seem to give
him any problems as he held his left arm up for balance.
He spurred down from the neck in a long, seemingly
easy swing. Sidewinder leaped up, all four feet a yard or
more off the ground, and came down twisting. Ben's hat
flew off, but he stuck on.

Eight seconds could feel like forever. If they did for
her, she could only imagine how they felt for Ben.
"Hang on, hang on," she muttered. The bronc reared,
so high that she feared it would go over backward. But
it didn't; it plunged down again, its front feet hitting
the ground with a bone-jarring jerk. But Ben was still
there, the burr on its hide that it just couldn't shake.

The buzzer sounded. Eight seconds. The crowd
cheered, whistled, and applauded, Sally right along
with them. He'd done it; he'd ridden one of the ranker
broncs she'd ever seen.

But it wasn't over yet. Ben still had to get off safely.

Sidewinder hadn't stopped bucking, but he'd settled
down a little as if he knew his job was almost done.
Ben lowered his left hand to the rope, pulled his feet
from the stirrups, and vaulted off the horse to land
bent-kneed and on his feet. Grinning widely, he waved

to acknowledge the audience's applause while the pickup riders guided the bronc out of the arena.

As Ben collected his hat, his score came up. It was 91, which elicited another grin, along with more cheering from the audience. It was an exceptionally good score, and well deserved. No question he'd be in tomorrow's short round.

Ecstatic for him and proud as all get-out, she realized her view of his departing back was blurred by tears. Blinking to clear her eyes, Sally pulled out her phone and texted him.

Congrats! An amazing ride and a wonderful score! Call me when you get a chance.

When she'd driven here, she hadn't been positive she'd actually contact him. Now, whatever the outcome, she had to see him.

His phone would be in his trailer. He'd take his saddle back there, but would he check for messages? Even if he did, what if he didn't call back until later tonight? Should she have said she was in the arena? If she didn't hear from him in a couple of hours, she might text or call again.

Trying not to let nerves ruin her enjoyment of the rodeo, she watched the next events, but the only one that truly held her attention was the barrel racing. As each horse dashed into the arena, Sally's muscles flexed and she leaned forward, her body attuned to that of the cowgirl, urging the horse on as it flew to each barrel, hustled around it, then dashed onward. It pleased her that the leader was one of her old competitors—not the bitchy Mandy Kilpatrick, but Emmy Crandall, a woman she'd always respected.

She was watching bull riding when her phone vibrated

against her thigh. She grabbed it, saw Ben's name, and answered. "You were fantastic!"

Ben, sprawling on the dinette seat in the open-doored trailer, an ice pack on his bad shoulder and a heating pad in the small of his back, beamed. This was a great sign, Sally caring enough to check scores on the Internet. "Thanks. I can't believe you've seen the results." He took a long drink from the glass of cold water on the table.

"That was one rank horse."

Someone must've posted a video on YouTube. "Sure was," he said with satisfaction. "That was the horse and the ride I've been looking for."

"I bet. Can I buy you a beer to celebrate?"

Yes! That was a clear invitation. Wasn't it? Trying to keep the jubilation from his voice, he sought clarification. "You're inviting me to come visit after the rodeo's over?"

"No, I mean I'm inviting you for a beer right now."

Right now? That could only mean . . . "You're here? Really?"

"I'm in the stands watching bull riding. I'd rather be drinking beer with you."

Yes! "Meet you at the entrance to the beer garden in five minutes." He was on his feet, unplugging the heating pad, going for clean socks. Thank God he'd washed up after his ride, and put on a fresh shirt.

Sounding amused, she said, "You must really want that beer, cowboy."

"It's not the beer I'm craving, Sally." He hung up, pulled on the socks and his boots, and grabbed his hat.

He went to the back of the trailer where Dusty was

cleaning Paddy's bridle. "Guess what? Sally's here. I'm gonna get a beer with her. Don't know when I'll be back."

The other man studied him with a big, goofy grin. "Or *if* you'll be back. Want me to clear out for the night? I can find a bed somewhere."

"Uh . . ." He hadn't thought past the need to hold Sally in his arms again. "I dunno. How about I give you a call or text later?"

"No sweat." Having taken off his hat earlier, Dusty now tipped an imaginary one. "Y'all have fun now."

"You'll keep an eye on Chaunce for me?"

"You bet."

Ben wasn't going to do anything as junior high as run, but his strides were long as he hurried toward the beer garden.

There she was, waiting, glancing around. She hadn't seen him yet, and he paused to drink in the sight. But only for a moment, because he needed to get his arms around her.

He strode toward her, she saw him, and her face lit up. He lifted her off her feet, wrapped his arms tight around her waist, and kissed her as if she was the only thing in the world that he wanted. Which, at the moment, was entirely true.

Her hat fell off; her thighs gripped his hips; she met his kiss full force. In fact, after she devoured his mouth, she planted breathless, laughing kisses over every square inch of his face.

Finally, she stopped kissing him and, with her arms circling his shoulders, leaned back in the cradle of his arms. "Hey there, cowboy. I missed you."

"I missed you, too." He eased her down until her boots landed on the ground.

She bent to retrieve her hat. Straightening, putting

the hat back atop her copper-gold curls, she said, "That was one incredible ride. I'm so glad I saw it."

"It felt pretty damned good. I'm glad you saw it, too."

"So it's okay that I came? I wasn't sure if surprising you was a good idea."

"Best surprise of my life. But damn, woman, you stole my idea. I was gonna drive to Caribou Crossing as soon as the rodeo was over."

"Great minds think alike, I guess." But she said it with a touch of uncertainty. Probably she was wondering what he'd intended, in planning a visit.

Just as he wondered about the reason for this surprise of hers. It had to be more than a hankering to see the rodeo, or she wouldn't have given him such an enthusiastic greeting. Would she? "Let's get that beer and catch up."

"Let's."

They stepped toward the entrance to the beer garden, and an excited boyish voice said, "You're Ben Traynor!"

He turned and saw a kid of thirteen or fourteen with a middle-aged couple, all of them in Western clothing. The boy's eyes were wide with that "I'm a big fan" expression. Normally, Ben loved talking to kids who were into rodeo, but now all he wanted was to be with Sally. Still, he smiled. "So my mama tells me."

"It's so cool to meet you! That ride on Sidewinder was sweet! Will you autograph my program?"

"Sure, and it's cool to meet you, too. You look like you're a cowboy. Am I right?"

"I want to ride broncs like you." The boy held out his program, saying, "Mom, you got a pen?"

The woman rooted in a large shoulder bag and said tolerantly, "That would be, 'Do you have a pen?' and Yes, I do." She produced it and handed it to Ben. "Nice to meet you. We saw you in Williams Lake back in June as well."

"That was a sweet ride, too," the boy said with relish.

"Yeah, until the bronc tossed me." Ben opened the program to the page with his photo and info. "What's your name, son?"

"Dirk. But hey, you stayed on for eight seconds and you won! That's all that counts."

There was no reason to tell the kid about the fractured shoulder, pain, rehab, missed rodeos. It was all in a day's work. As the boy would learn, if he got into rodeo himself.

Ben said good-bye to Dirk and his parents. He was turning back to Sally, who'd stood aside watching quietly, when another voice, female this time, cried, "Sally Pantages! Oh my God, it really is you!"

Emmy Crandall, one of the top barrel racers, caught Sally in a hug.

Sally returned it. "Emmy, hi! Nice to see you. And nice to see you ride this afternoon. That was a great run. You have a new horse since back in the day."

"Yeah, I had to retire Jasmine. But Caballero's a doll, too. Took us a while to find our rhythm, but we're pulling in fast times now." She flashed a cheeky grin. "Sure helps that *you're* not competing. So what are you doing these days anyhow, you and that guy you married?"

"I'm in Caribou Crossing. He died and—"

"Oh, man, Sally, I'm sorry. That blows."

Sally shrugged. "Stuff happens. Anyhow, I have my own place and I'm teaching riding and boarding horses. It's fun."

"Huh. Well, whatever fires you up, I guess. I sure never thought you'd give up rodeo."

"It's nice to be settled in a beautiful place rather than

on the road all the time." Sally flicked a quick glance in his direction.

Emmy's attention shifted from Sally. "Hey there, Ben. Good to see an old friend, eh?"

"Sure is." Although he hoped that before long he and Sally would be much more than just friends.

Emmy refocused on Sally. "I'm meeting up with a couple of the other gals in the beer garden. Why don't you come?"

"Actually, Ben and I were just going to"—she paused infinitesimally—"get a bite to eat."

A bite to eat? Weren't they getting a beer? This woman could get him so confused.

"Sure," Emmy said. "Well, if you're around later, or tomorrow, it'd be fun to catch up."

"I'd like that." The wistful expression in Sally's eyes attested to the truth of her statement. Would she rather talk to the barrel racers than be with him?

But then she turned to him, and wistful was replaced by something sparkly and intense that sent a fresh jolt of excitement through his blood. "Ready to go?" she asked a touch breathlessly.

"Sure."

He was all set to go into the beer garden when Sally caught his arm and tugged him in the opposite direction. Bewildered, he asked, "No beer?"

She dropped her hand from his arm and gazed up at him, amusement kinking her lips. "Are you that desperate for a beer, cowboy?"

Her. He was desperate for her. "Uh . . . I thought that's what we'd planned."

"Does it have to be here? Where it's pretty clear we're both going to get recognized, and we won't be able to talk?"

Enlightenment dawned and with it relief and pleasure. "You want to be alone with me," he teased.

Uncertainty flickered on her face. "If you'd rather stay here—"

"No way," he cut her off. "We should definitely go someplace where we can be alone and, uh, talk." Sex would be better. Or no, maybe it wouldn't. Well, of course it would, but he did have things he needed to say to her. Maybe after she heard them, she wouldn't want to make love with him. And that was a sobering thought.

Damn. Thrilled as he was to see her, he almost wished Sally hadn't come. Wished he'd been able to follow through on the plan he'd been putting together in his head. About how he'd ditch Dusty somewhere—maybe put him up at the Wild Rose Inn—and drive out to Sally's wearing his best clothes, with a bouquet of wild-flowers, a bottle of champagne, and a rudimentary business plan for opening a rodeo school.

He'd wanted to get all his ducks in a row. He knew she was attracted to him, so he'd planned to look as good as he could, not like a guy who'd barely managed to put on a fresh shirt after getting sweaty and dusty riding a bronc. He knew her feminine side appreciated wildflowers and an occasional extravagance like good wine. He also knew she was a practical businesswoman, so he'd figured on pulling together the information he'd gathered, so he could show her a realistic business plan.

Now here he was, off guard and unprepared. Did he have any hope of winning his lady's heart?

Chapter Twenty-Six

Nerves jangling, Sally wondered what Ben was thinking as they walked to where she'd parked her truck. He'd seemed so glad to see her, but now he didn't take her hand and he hadn't said a word since commenting that they should be alone and "uh, talk."

Had she done the wrong thing, coming here and catching him by surprise?

When they reached her parking spot, she said, "Do you want to drive?"

"It's your truck. D'you want me to drive?"

"I'd rather you navigate." She unlocked the passenger door. "I don't know Armstrong."

He climbed into the seat as she went around and took the driver's seat. After finding her way out of the huge parking lot, she followed Ben's directions to the small downtown area, which reminded her of Caribou Crossing with its heritage buildings and cute storefronts.

Suddenly, Ben said, "Hang on. Pull over when you get a chance."

Half a block along, she found a spot and parked. Assuming he had seen a bar or restaurant, she was about to pull the key out of the ignition when he said, "Wait here a minute. I'll be right back." And then he was gone, the door slamming behind him.

Puzzled, she settled back and tried not to worry.

It was more than five minutes until the passenger door opened again. A sizable bouquet of flowers was thrust inside.

"Oh!" Sally stared at the mixed blooms in all colors imaginable. A heady scent drifted toward her. "Those are gorgeous."

Ben climbed in, juggling the bouquet. "The florist didn't have wildflowers, so I had to go with second best." He peered at her anxiously. "I figured you weren't a dozen red roses kind of gal. Hope I'm right."

"You're so right." A dozen red roses, that conventional gift, was what Pete had brought when he apologized for hitting her. "Thank you, Ben." This was a good thing, wasn't it? He wouldn't give her flowers if he wasn't glad she'd come. From him, flowers had never carried a mixed message. "Now, where shall we get that beer?"

"I hope you meant it about getting food, too. I asked the florist for a restaurant recommendation."

"Great." This was another good sign.

He recited the directions as she drove, and they arrived at a restaurant called Sundown.

They climbed out of the truck and he handed her the flowers. "Yours, my lady."

Was she his lady? She sure wanted to be. Accepting the armful, she buried her nose in the sweet-smelling blossoms. "Mmm. I'll ask the restaurant to put them in water."

Clad in their Western garb but leaving their hats in the truck, they walked toward the door. Ben took her free hand, interweaving their fingers. Such a simple gesture, but it felt so good and meant so much. She squeezed his hand.

Sally had been expecting something akin to a Western bar, but instead, when they stepped inside, she saw that the place was fancier, with interesting art on the walls, pale yellow linen, and candlelight. It was actually pretty romantic. And, fortunately, not pretentious, or she'd feel out of place in her Western garb.

The young woman who greeted them smiled at the flowers. "Lovely. I'll put them in a vase." Then she led them to a quietly situated table for four in the half-full restaurant, and carefully scooped the bouquet from Sally's arms. When Sally and Ben were seated across from each other, the waitress asked if they'd like a drink.

"We'll take a look at the wine list," Ben said.

When the woman had left, Sally said, "You don't want that beer I promised you?"

"Not tonight. This is my treat, and I think we need wine. That okay with you?"

"I won't complain. Just bear in mind that one of us has to drive."

The waitress returned with the flowers in an attractive ceramic vase. She set them down on the unoccupied side of the table rather than between Sally and Ben where they'd have blocked their view of each other.

They both thanked her, then Sally opened the menu. While she perused the intriguing selections, she was vaguely aware of Ben pointing to something on the wine list.

She was still deliberating when the waitress returned with an ice bucket on a stand, the top of a bottle poking up from the ice, and two flute glasses. Sally's mouth opened as the waitress deftly eased the cork from a bottle of Veuve Clicquot and poured bubbly golden liquid into both glasses. "Enjoy." She departed with another smile.

Sally stared across the table. "Champagne?"

"Seems to me it suits the occasion." Despite the words, his tone was tentative.

Champagne was for major events. The last time she'd tasted it was at her wedding reception, when Pete said she'd gotten drunk and foolish. Damn Pete, anyway. He wasn't going to spoil her reunion with Ben. Unsure whether "the occasion" was his amazing ride or the two of them being together again, she raised her glass. "It does suit the occasion." Hedging her bets, she said, "To your great ride on Sidewinder, and to seeing you again."

He lifted his own glass. "To seeing you again, Sally. And to us." There was something challenging in his chestnut-eyed gaze, almost as if he dared her to drink that toast.

Which she would, very happily. She clicked her glass firmly against his. "To us."

His eyes softened, warmed, and he raised his glass to his lips as she mirrored the gesture.

The liquid slipped into her mouth, a chill fizz that exhilarated her, as did that warmth in Ben's eyes.

When she put her glass down, the waitress reappeared to ask if they were ready to order. They gave her their selections, and then were alone again.

"Thank you for the flowers and champagne," Sally said. "And for finding such a lovely restaurant."

He gazed down and fiddled with his glass, the slim flute looking impossibly graceful and fragile in his large, calloused hand. "You never wanted to go out for dinner with me in Caribou Crossing." His gaze lifted, and the challenge was back. "You didn't want people thinking we were a couple."

Had she hurt his pride? His feelings? "I was too touchy about privacy. I'm sorry if"—no man wanted it suggested that his feelings had been hurt—"if I was obnoxious."

He sighed. "I guess I understood. After what you went through with Pete, you were used to keeping your personal life to yourself. And you had your business reputation to consider."

"Thank you."

His gaze again dropped to his glass. Either the bubbles fascinated him, or he was avoiding looking at her. "But I wondered if you were, you know, embarrassed to have your name linked with mine."

She cocked her head. "I'm not sure what you mean. I didn't want the town gossiping about me, saying I was slutty."

Now he did glance at her. "Why's it being slutty to date someone and sleep with them?"

"It's not. But that's not how people were likely to view it. They'd just see me having a fling with a passing cowboy."

His brow furrowed. "So was it the temporary nature, or that it was me, or both?"

Unsure what he was asking, she rested her forearms on the table and was about to ask for clarification, but the waitress arrived with their appetizers. Sally removed her arms and sat back, waiting impatiently. Though her shrimp and avocado salad and his wild mushroom soup looked scrumptious, she was more interested in the baffling conversation.

As soon as the waitress left, Sally said, "Ben, I'm not sure what you're asking."

"If you'd been sleeping with someone like Dave or Evan, would you have been so concerned about keeping it a secret?"

"What?!" Aghast, she gaped at him. "I would never sleep with a married man."

He groaned. "Jesus, sorry, that's not what I meant. I mean, a guy who's successful, has his own business. Versus a guy who tries to scrape out a living as a cowboy."

How many times had her mouth fallen open tonight? She'd lost count, but it did it again. "You think I care about a man's status? His income?"

"Well, I mean, look at you. You deserve a guy like you."

"I haven't a clue what you're talking about." And if he hadn't softened his comment with the word *deserve*, she well might have upended the bottle of bubbly over his head. "What does 'like me' mean?" Did he think she was status-conscious? Good Lord, did he know her at all?

"You own this huge chunk of beautiful land. You operate a thriving business and—"

Her disbelieving laugh stopped him. "You think I'm rich and successful?"

"Well, not exactly rich, but—"

"Ben, you idiot."

"Uh . . ."

She'd always been too embarrassed about her financial situation to share it with anyone. But she loved Ben, and she had to come clean. "That land I own? It's really the bank that owns it. My equity in it is tiny. Things have improved in the last weeks, but before that I often had to scramble to make the mortgage payment. Often, it's been an insane, sleepless-night juggling act to keep my bills up-to-date enough that no one cuts off services."

She stared straight into his eyes. "I've always worried that one day the bank would foreclose and my horses, hens, and I would be homeless."

"Shit, Sally," he breathed. "I had no idea. You never told me any of this."

"There was no reason to. My financial issues are my problem."

"I wish you'd shared them. But I know you value being self-sufficient."

"Because Pete made me dependent on him. Thanks for understanding. And Ben, I'm getting used to the idea that friends enjoy helping friends."

"That's good to hear."

For the next few minutes, they ate their appetizers in silence, taking occasional sips of champagne. Finally, she said, "Ben, I hope you know that I don't care if a man is wealthy. It's who he is inside that counts. What kind of a man he is. Decent, hardworking." She smiled a little, thinking of all Ben's wonderful qualities. "Supportive. Good with horses and children."

His lips quirked up. "Handy with a hoof pick?"

"That one's essential." Did he realize she'd been describing him? Did she dare carry on and tell him that he was her image of the perfect man—and not only because of all his attributes but because of the way he made her heart and body sing?

As the waitress cleared the empty appetizer plates, served the main courses, and topped up their glasses, hope surged in Ben. He was all those things Sally wanted, wasn't he? Of course she'd left out what he figured was the single most important thing: love. His ex-girlfriend Jana had had loads of positive attributes, but he'd never felt anything more heart-tugging than affection. Though she'd wanted him to leave the rodeo and get a steady job at home, being with her hadn't made *him* want to do that.

Sally tasted her salmon dish. He sampled his beef

stroganoff. They traded tastes. The food was great. So was the champagne and the restaurant. The bouquet of flowers smelled just fine.

He'd done all these things—the fancy restaurant, champagne, and flowers—to set a scene that was as close as possible to what he'd planned to do when he went back to Caribou Crossing. To make it romantic, to show Sally how much she meant to him, to prove he was more than a burgers and beer guy.

How was he doing? "Those qualities you were listing off," he said. How to phrase this without sounding swelled-headed? "They, uh, sound kind of like me."

"Yes, they do." She pressed her lips together and worried them around.

But he had more to offer her than just being a hard-working guy. He had a business concept, even if it wasn't a fleshed out plan yet. Afraid of what she might say when she finally stopped twisting her lips together, he blurted out, "What do you think of rodeo schools?"

She stared at him. Blinked. Shook her head slightly, making her silver feather earrings dance and brush her slender neck. "What do I think of them?"

"Do you think they're a good idea?"

"Sure. There aren't enough places for cowboys and cowgirls to get proper training."

He nodded. "You can do all sorts of things with a rodeo school. For example, train the kids who are just getting into it." He took a bite of beef.

"Yes, they need a place where they can get started on the right foot."

He nodded. "And a rodeo school can take amateurs who've started out on the circuit, and help them hone their skills."

"Even pros go to rodeo school. When they're in a

slump, or working on a particular problem, or after an injury. Or to get a fresh perspective, move to the next level."

"I've done that a time or two," he said. "But there aren't enough schools. And it costs a lot to travel all the way across the country to attend one. Especially if you compete in a timed event and need to bring your horse." He polished off the final bites of his meal.

"True," she said.

"Some schools take complete beginners," he mused, thinking about the websites he'd visited and owners he'd contacted. "Even people who've never been on a horse. I'm not sure I agree with that."

"I know. It's like, is the school for training serious riders or for pandering to total dudes?" Sally finished her salmon and picked up her champagne flute.

"Exactly." It was encouraging to find they thought the same way.

Their waitress cleared the table and offered dessert. Sally said she was too full and Ben agreed. They turned down coffee in favor of finishing the champagne.

When the waitress left, Ben said, "A good rodeo school's gotta be about more than the technical skills." He was eager to show her how serious he was about this, and to convince her he could make it work. "It's about attitude and discipline, developing a physical fitness and training regime, getting the proper equipment and taking care of it. Learning how to—"

"Ben, why are we talking about rodeo schools?" Sally looked puzzled, maybe a little unhappy.

Oh-oh. What had he done wrong now? "Uh, well . . ." How to explain that he was making a sales pitch—on him being a guy she could build a future with?

"I mean, the topic is interesting," she said, "but here

we are at this lovely restaurant, we haven't seen each other in a month and a half, and we're talking about rodeo schools?"

"Yeah." And he was blowing it. "Damn, I'd really intended to have a draft of a real business plan."

"Business plan?" She stared at him like he wasn't making sense, which he had to admit was pretty much true. Then she said slowly, "Business plan for a rodeo school? Are you saying you're thinking of starting a rodeo school?"

He nodded, his pulse jackhammering. Would she think he was insane? Or would she believe he could actually make a go of it?

Still speaking slowly, measuring out each word, she asked, "When were you thinking of doing it?"

"After this season. I hope to win some decent money. I've got some put by already, and if I can add a chunk to it, I should have enough to buy some stock, get a start on building the facilities I'd need." Thanks to his research, he had a good idea of the figures involved; he just hadn't had a chance to put them into a spreadsheet. "If I put together a decent business plan, I ought to be able to get a bank loan for the rest."

She looked confused, and he realized he'd left out something important. "Of course I'd pay for use of the land and any shared facilities. The whole idea's for me to contribute, not to take advantage."

"What land?" Again she weighed out each word. "Take advantage of who? Whom?"

He frowned. Hadn't he made that clear? "Sally, I'm talking about combining forces. Ryland Riding and Traynor Rodeo School. Together."

Sometimes her pretty face could be so expressive; other times she could be impossible to read. The latter, he was sure, came from her experience with Pete. He hated that right now she'd put on the impassive face. He had laid his future, his heart, on the line and she was giving him nothing back.

Something flickered in the green depths of her eyes. Something that looked like vulnerability. "Why?" she breathed. "Why would we do that?"

Well, hell. If she had to ask, then obviously she didn't feel the same way.

He knew when it made sense to back off. Like when he'd been a crazy kid and thought bull riding would be cool, then realized it scared the shit out of him and he was wiser sticking to broncs. The wise thing now would be to tell Sally he'd thought it might make good business sense, but if she didn't agree then that was fine. He'd always figured on spending another five or ten years rodeoing, so it wasn't like he'd have lost anything.

Except that he would have. He'd have lost Sally. Damn it, he wasn't going to lose the woman he loved without first laying everything on the line.

"We'd do it because"—he'd never said the words before, and he had to swallow before he forced them out—"because I love you. And if there's any hope you might one day . . ." The look of utter shock on her face brought him to a stumbling halt.

Appalled, he watched as her eyes went a bright, glittery green and then tears spilled down her cheeks. He grabbed for her hand. "Oh hell, Sally, I didn't mean to make you cry. I'm not trying to pressure you." Belatedly, it occurred to him that maybe she thought he was like Pete, trying to impose his wishes. "I'd never ask you to do something you don't want to do."

The tears still flowed freely.

"Please stop crying. I'll do anything. I'll take it all

back. We can pretend we never even mentioned rodeo schools, and—"

"Would you just"—she sniffled—"shut up?"

He closed his mouth.

She freed her hand and used both hands to brush tears from her cheeks. She gave a big sniffle, then said, "Do *not* take it back." Sniff. "Did you really say . . . you love me?"

He nodded, not sure if he was still supposed to keep his mouth shut.

"Did you mean it?"

"Yes," he dared to say. "But I didn't want to make you cry."

"You big idiot." She shook her head, coppery curls tossing. "You total, utter idiot!"

"I'm sorry." Just what he'd done that was so wrong, he wasn't entirely sure. But if he could, he'd take it back, redo it, whatever she wanted.

She shook her head some more. Her cheeks were drying; her eyes gleamed but this time not with tears; and her mouth formed a grin. She let out a chuckle.

"Sally?" he said warily.

She gave another snorty-sounding chuckle. "You know those broncs that come out of the chute ass-backward?"

"Yeah?"

"The judges award a re-ride. Cowboy, you might want to take that re-ride." Her voice held dry humor but her eyes were telling a different story, all soft and melty.

She was saying he'd approached things ass-backward. But he'd respected her feminine side with flowers, a nice restaurant, and champagne, and he'd respected the practical businesswoman by discussing business ideas with her. He'd even told her he loved her.

At the very end. Was that what she meant?

The last time their waitress had offered to refill their champagne glasses, they'd both waved her off. Now, he lifted the neglected bottle out of the ice bucket and poured half a glass for Sally and another for himself.

Chapter Twenty-Seven

Tension made Sally's entire body tremble, not so much that anyone would notice yet enough that she felt like she might fly apart in a zillion pieces. Trying to calm her breathing, she gazed at the golden liquid, not as fizzy as it had been when the bottle was first opened, but still bubbly. Celebratory.

Ben had poured champagne. He'd said he loved her. This was going to be the happiest night of her life. Wasn't it? Or had she completely misunderstood the situation?

"Sally?"

She raised her gaze from the glass to his face. Did her hopes and dreams, and the love she felt for him, show in her eyes?

"Sally Pantages Ryland, I love you."

He'd said it again. He was taking his re-ride and starting with the most important thing. Again moisture filled her eyes, hazing her vision. She blinked, wanting to see every detail of his striking, beloved face.

"You're the only woman I've ever loved," he went on. "The time I spent with you—working side by side, going for rides, sharing meals, making love—that was the best time of my life. When I got back to the rodeo, it was good riding Chaunce after a steer, hanging out with Dusty. Having a ride like the one this afternoon is a real high. But none of it's been as good as it used to be, because I kept missing you."

No matter how fast she blinked, happy tears overflowed. "I kept missing you, too."

"I realized I loved you. I want to spend my life with you."

To spend his life with her? Oh my God, this was really happening.

"But I wasn't sure I was good enough for you. Hell"— he gave a rough laugh—"I know I'm not good enough for you."

"You are, Ben." She reached across the table and grabbed his hands, holding on to him and never wanting to let go. "You're perfect for me."

"I want to offer you something. I want to *be* something, something more than your assistant. That's Corrie's job now, anyhow. I want a thing of my own, like you have with Ryland Riding, but it needs to be something I can share with you. Something we can build together. Does that make any sense?"

"Yes." She nodded firmly. "A lot of sense."

"With a rodeo school, I could step back from the circuit, but still do some local rodeos to keep my hand in. I'd still live in the world of rodeo. I could pass along everything I've learned, and keep learning more. Watching you, I saw how rewarding it is to teach."

"It sure is. But do you think you could be happy, not competing full-time?"

He gave a wry grin. "I'm pretty damned sure I won't be happy if I'm not with you. But yeah, I think running a rodeo school would make me real happy. Along with helping you and Corrie with Ryland Riding."

Her heart was so full, it felt like it was overflowing, the same as her damp eyes.

"I've been doing a bunch of research and I was gonna draft a business plan this weekend," he said. "Then I was going to come see you after this rodeo."

"You were?" While she'd been gathering her courage to come to him and tell him she loved him, he'd been doing the same thing.

"I wanted to have all my ducks in a row. Lay it out all neat and tidy." He laughed. "But it was still gonna be ass-backward, I guess."

She couldn't help but smile. "If you'd led with the 'I love you,' you'd have saved yourself a lot of effort."

He smiled back. "That would've done it?"

She nodded, then suddenly realized she hadn't told him how she felt. He wasn't the only one who was doing this clumsily. Squeezing his hands, she said, "I love you, Ben. With all my heart. With or without a rodeo school. Even if you stay full-time on the rodeo circuit."

Watching his face, she read his reaction. Saw when his own eyes moistened. His voice was choky when he said, "But that'd be no fun. I want to wake up with you every morning and go to bed with you every night."

"I want that, too. More than anything."

He freed his right hand and raised his champagne glass. That big hand, so confident when holding the rein on a bronc or roping a steer, actually trembled. "To us, Sally. To our love."

She raised her glass, amazed to find that her own hand was steady, and clicked it against his. "To us, our love, and to building a future together."

"Those are the finest words I've ever heard."

Epilogue

On a balmy June evening the next summer, Sally came out of the chicken coop. Her evening chores were finished, but there was one thing more that she and Ben needed to attend to tonight, if she could work up the courage.

Speaking of her husband, there he was now, easing the door of the bunk house closed. Seeing her, he raised a hand in greeting and strode toward her. At his heels was Zeke, their blue heeler.

She leaned down to stroke the dog, then straightened and asked Ben, "Get the kids settled for the night?" It was the second night of a weeklong bronc riding course at the newly minted Traynor Riding and Rodeo School.

"Yeah. They're out like lights. They're not used to working this hard." Ben put his arm around her and she reciprocated as they strolled toward the house with Zeke following them. "You get your ladies settled?"

"I did." She'd also asked her hens to cross their wings for her and Ben.

"No more putting it off." He hugged her tighter against the reassuring warmth of his muscular body.

"I know. But what if it's negative?"

"Then we'll keep trying. I like the trying."

"Me too, but I want a baby, Ben."

"Sweetheart, there's time. It'll happen when it's meant to happen."

She knew that his words, like his hug, were meant to be reassuring. But she also knew that Ben yearned as much as she did for a child—or, even better, two or three.

At the bottom of the back stairs, they said good night to Zeke, who was an outdoor dog. Then they went up to the mudroom, shucked their boots, and entered the kitchen. The room was so much brighter now with light yellow paint and terra cotta tile, so much homier with photos stuck to the fridge and a couple of Robin's drawings on the walls.

Sally's husband patted her on the butt. "Go upstairs and pee."

"How romantic," she said in a mock grumble.

She took the stairs steadily, one foot after the other, not letting herself stop. Her period, which had always been regular, was a week late, and she felt like she'd been holding her breath for every minute of those days. Yesterday, she'd tempted fate by buying a pregnancy test, figuring that for sure she'd wake up today and find that her period had started. But she hadn't.

Until the moment she took that test, she could hope. Once she read the results . . .

Resolutely, she went into the bathroom and fished the package out from under the sink. She'd already opened it and read the instructions, but now she did so again. She couldn't help but remember the other time she'd been pregnant. How happy she'd felt, and yet she'd been wary of Pete—and she'd been right to be wary.

Thank God for Ben. Thank God for second chances.

This time, she'd found a man who loved and supported her, who respected and honored her.

After she peed on the stick, she checked her watch. "Three minutes," she murmured, knowing it would feel more like an hour.

When she went into the bedroom, their song was playing. Keith Urban sang about how, when his special woman hugged him, he could do anything in the world. Ben stood at the window, his back to her. The music had masked the sound of the bathroom door opening.

She studied him for a long moment. His straight back, strong shoulders, lean hips and legs. So strong, so handsome. But more than that, he was the finest man she'd ever known. Sometimes it was hard to believe that he was hers. But he was. She hadn't had to find someone *like* Ben; she had the real deal. And together they could do anything. Whether it was this month or next, they would create a baby, a family.

She just really, really hoped the time was now.

"Honey?" she said.

He turned and strode over to her. "Well?"

"Still waiting." She put the stick down on the dresser and stepped away from it. "I'm not going to look until it's been three minutes."

He clasped her hand and she held up her other arm to display the face of her watch. "Another forty seconds," she told him. "There'll be two pink stripes if I'm pregnant. One if I'm n-not." She stumbled over the last word.

They both stared at her watch in silence as the second hand moved unbelievably slowly. Finally, she said, "Now. But I'm not sure I can look."

"Want me to?"

"Yes. It's two pink stripes if—"

"I know." He stepped toward the dresser.

Time stood still. Sally didn't breathe.

Then Ben turned to her, grinning from ear to ear.

"Oh my God!" she cried.

"We're having a baby!" he affirmed.

He dropped the stick as she leaped into his arms and he caught her. Her thighs locked around his waist, his arms circled her shoulders, and he whirled the two of them around and around. She laughed and cried at the same time, gazing down into his beaming face.

When he finally stopped spinning, he staggered to the bed and eased her down as if she were a fragile doll rather than a strong cowgirl.

She caught his head between her hands, pulled him down to her, and smothered his face with kisses. "I'm so happy, I'm going to burst."

"I'm so happy, I'm going to make love to you all night long." He winked. "I've never made love to a pregnant woman before."

"I'm delighted to hear that."

He raised up and peeled off his tee, revealing his sexy muscled torso with the scar from where he'd risked his life to save another cowboy's. He pulled his belt through the loops, then started in on her shirt buttons. "This is going to be so cool, watching your body change."

"And gradually turn whale-sized," she said contentedly.

"You're gonna be so beautiful, Sally Traynor. Even more beautiful than now." He peeled the sides of her shirt back. "Hey, I think your breasts are bigger already."

She laughed, the movement jiggling her B-cup breasts. "Wishful thinking."

"Lovely breasts, whatever size they are." He sucked her nipple through her bra, making it pucker and sending a tug of arousal rippling through her. "Responsive breasts. Breasts that turn me on something fierce."

As he turned his attention to her other nipple, he

was doing a fine job of turning her on, too. Eventually, he reached behind her to snap open the clasp of the bra, then he helped her struggle out of her shirt and bra.

"Naked is better," he confirmed, working the button at the waistband of her jeans.

Obligingly, she shifted position so he could strip off her jeans and panties. His gaze focused on her belly, flat and toned.

She rested a hand on it. "Our baby's growing in there. Our little boy or girl."

"Little cowboy or cowgirl," he corrected. His hand cupped hers. "It's the most natural thing in the world, yet it seems miraculous, doesn't it?"

"Everything seems miraculous. Ever since the day you stepped back into my life."

Author's Note

When I first pitched the idea for the Caribou Crossing Romances to Kensington, I didn't even dream about the day I'd be finishing title six, but here it is. Wow! I love writing this series; I love visiting the small Western community in British Columbia's scenic Cariboo; and I love exploring the lives of strong yet vulnerable heroines and heroes.

Sally Ryland is definitely one of those women. The widow has survived domestic abuse and runs her own Western riding school/horse-boarding operation, but like many abused women, she has difficulty trusting men—and trusting her judgment. For Sally to heal and be able to love again, she needs a very special man, and that's exactly what I give her in rodeo cowboy Ben Traynor. He knew her from her barrel racing days, before she was swept off her feet by the man who later abused her. He knows how vibrant and gutsy she used to be—and will do anything to help her rediscover her confidence—and her sexuality.

I've been asked if people need to read the Caribou Crossing Romances in order. No, not at all. Each is a stand-alone story. You can dive in at any point. If you're interested in reading the romances of other characters from *Love Somebody Like You*, take a look for Robin's grandparents Miriam and Wade in *Caribou Crossing*, Jess and Evan in *Home on the Range*, Brooke and Jake in

Gentle on My Mind, Karen and Jamal in *Stand By Your Man*, and Dave and Cassidy in *Love Me Tender*. Lark's story is coming up, in *Ring of Fire*, and Maribeth's will follow.

I'd like to thank my editor, Martin Biro, for being such a delight to work with, and Kensington Publishing for taking a chance on a new author way back in 2005. We've been together ten years now! Thanks also to my agent, Emily Sylvan Kim at Prospect Agency, for a terrific eight years of collaboration. I am a strong believer in the critiquing process, and for this book I'd like to thank Mary Ann Clarke Scott, Lacy Danes, Shelley Bates, and Nazima Ali for their invaluable input.

This is a work of fiction and I've taken artistic license with a number of details, particularly some bending of the facts with respect to the Interior Provincial Exhibition and Stampede in Armstrong—an event I would be thrilled to attend one day.

I love sharing my stories with my readers and I love hearing from you. I write under the pen names Susan Fox, Savanna Fox, and Susan Lyons. You can e-mail me at susan@susanlyons.ca or contact me through my website at www.susanfox.ca, where you'll also find excerpts, behind-the-scenes notes, recipes, a monthly contest, the sign-up for my newsletter, and other goodies. You can also find me on Facebook at facebook.com/SusanLyonsFox.

If you enjoyed LOVE SOMEBODY LIKE YOU,
be sure not to miss Susan Fox's

LOVE ME TENDER

Dave Cousins, owner of the Wild Rose Inn, is known
throughout Caribou Crossing as the nicest—and
loneliest—guy in town. He's had his heart broken
more than once, and he's determined not to let it
happen again. So it's no wonder he's wary when a
free-spirited drifter leaves him longing for more than
just a steamy fling . . .

Like the wild goose tattooed on her shoulder, Cassidy
Esperanza goes wherever the wind takes her. For her,
a new day means a fresh start. And yet something
about her days in Caribou Crossing—and nights with
its handsome hotel owner—makes her think about
staying a while. But when life takes an unexpected
turn, her first instinct is to take flight once more. Is
Dave strong enough to help them both face their fears,
come to terms with the past, and believe that sometimes
love truly can last a lifetime?

Also includes the bonus novella "Stand By Your Man."

A Zebra mass-market paperback and eBook on sale now!

Turn the page for a special excerpt.

At five-thirty A.M., Dave Cousins eased open his daughter's door to check that all was well. Eleven-year-old Robin didn't stir from what he'd be willing to bet was a horsey dream. Merlin, their black poodle, raised his head from where he lay curled on the rug beside the bed. At Dave's silent gesture, his head went back down. Robin would take the dog out once she rose. Until then, it was Merlin's job to guard her while Dave, the owner of the Wild Rose Inn, went downstairs to do some work.

He cast one more loving glance at her face, so sweet and relaxed in sleep, and the tumbled chestnut hair that by day was always pony-tailed. He sure did like the days Robin stayed with him, rather than with Jessie and Evan. His ex-wife and her new husband lived outside town, surrounded by horses. In many ways, they had so much more to offer Robin. So far, luckily, that fact didn't seem to trouble the girl. Dave loved her to pieces, and she seemed to reciprocate.

When Robin wasn't around, his life, no matter how busy, felt empty. Lonely.

If Anita hadn't died, things would be so different.

The thought brought a surge of pain, anger, guilt, and desolation, that nasty thundercloud of emotions. He swallowed against the ache that choked his throat, and forced back the feelings.

This was why he tried not to think of the fiancée who had been the love of his life.

Briskly he walked to the door of the two-bedroom owner's suite on the top floor of the Wild Rose and pulled on his cowboy boots, then let himself out. As he ran down the four flights of stairs, he was already looking forward to returning in a couple of hours to have breakfast with Robin.

When he entered the lobby, lit by early morning sun, the Wild Rose worked her—he always thought of the inn as "her"—magic on him, and he felt a sense of peace and satisfaction. He had rescued a lovely but ramshackle historic building that was destined for destruction and restored her, creating a haven for travelers and a gathering place for locals.

The décor featured rustic yet comfortable Western furniture accented with photographs and antiques honoring Caribou Crossing's gold rush history. Behind the front desk, Sam, the retired RCMP officer who handled the inn overnight, frowned into space through his horn-rims.

"Morning," Dave greeted him. "Words not flowing?" Sam was writing a mystery novel and it came in fits and starts.

"Got distracted." Sam scratched his balding head. "By the woman in twenty-two."

"Someone who checked in last night?" Twenty-two had been one of only three empty rooms at the beginning of the man's shift. "I take it she's pretty?" Sam had never married and had an eye for the ladies, which translated into a rough charm that suited the Wild Rose's ambience.

"For sure. Once she got some color back in her cheeks." Sam paused, a born storyteller confident that he'd hooked his audience.

"Go on."

The night manager leaned forward, his pale gray eyes bright even after a night awake. "It's past eleven when she staggers into the lobby. Mid- to late twenties, slim build, some Latina blood. Jeans and a top that's too light for the nights this time of year." June in Caribou Crossing featured warm, sunny days but the temperature cooled when the sun went down.

"Staggers?" Pale and staggering; that didn't sound good.

"Those white cheeks of hers, they weren't just from the cold. It's more like she's done in, on her last legs. She stumbles across to the desk, backpack weighing her down. I get up to go take her pack, but before I reach her, what does she up and do?" His shaggy gray eyebrows lifted.

"What does she up and do?"

"Faints dead away."

Dave frowned, worried. "Did you call nine-one-one?"

The storyteller was probably incapable of giving a simple yes-or-no answer. "I bend down, make sure she has a pulse, and by then she's stirring. So I whip into the bar and fetch a shot of rye. The Caribou Crossing Single Barrel. Figure if our hometown drink doesn't fix her up, I'll call for help."

Dave didn't know whether to groan or grin. "Did she drink it?"

"I wave it under the gal's nose, and she snorts and jumps back like a horse when it sees a snake. She sits up, grabs the glass, downs it in one swallow, and says, 'Damn, that's good.'"

Surprised and relieved, Dave laughed and Sam joined in.

"I did offer to call a doc," Sam assured him, "but she says no, she's just exhausted and hungry. Been hitch-hiking all day, up from Vancouver, hasn't had much to eat. Says she came in to ask if there's a hostel in town. That whisky put some color back in her cheeks and she's trying to be all bright and cheery. But under all that, she looks like a nag that's been rode hard and put up wet. I tell her she'll stay here; she starts to argue; I tell her I won't take no guff. Give her a key, carry her pack up to twenty-two, then I heat up some beef stew and biscuits from the kitchen and take it up." He shrugged. "After that, I don't hear another peep out of her."

"Hmm." Dave glanced at the ceiling, still concerned. "I'd feel better if a doctor had taken a look at her." A few of the doctors had an arrangement through an an-swering service: one was always on call, and they made house calls.

"She said she wasn't going to waste a doctor's time. The gal was pretty damned firm about it." He gave his balding head a shake. "Put me in mind of old Ms. Haldenby. You know?"

The retired schoolteacher was a fine—and intimi-dating—woman who definitely knew her own mind. "There's no arguing with someone like that," Dave agreed. "It sounds like you did all you could. Good work, Sam."

"See if you still say that when I tell you I didn't get a credit card or even a name. Figured it could wait till she was feeling better."

"Yeah. Even if she skips, it's no big loss." Dave was more worried about the woman's health. But Sam was a smart, observant guy. If he'd thought their visitor really was sick, he'd have overridden her objections, as he had when he'd given her a room.

"Anyhow," Sam said, "the damned woman took my mind right out of my book. Got me thinking about her story, and I bet it's a good one."

Dave rolled his eyes. "You and your overactive imagination. She's a hitchhiker who didn't have the sense to rest when she needed to. She'll be up and on the road, hopefully paying her bill before she goes."

Around eleven, Dave was at the front desk relieving Deepta, the receptionist who worked weekdays from six-thirty to two-thirty. He was trying to book opera tickets in Vancouver for guests who were heading there tomorrow, but the online system kept glitching. Frustrated, he took a deep breath, unsnapped the cuffs of his Western shirt and rolled them up his forearms, and gave the system another go. It stalled again.

"Hi there," a cheerful female voice said. "Anywhere around here I can get a good capooch?"

He looked up and his eyes widened in appreciation. This had to be the guest in twenty-two, and yeah, she sure was pretty. Medium height, slim, nice curves shown off by shorts and a purple tank worn over something that had pink straps. He saw the Latina in her olive-toned skin and the shiny black hair cut in a short, elfin cap. Her black-lashed eyes were blue-gray and sparkling, matching her white smile. She was the picture of health, he was relieved to see.

And that smile was irresistible. He smiled back. "That translate to cappuccino?"

Humor warmed her eyes. "What else?"

"Thought maybe you were talking about some weird mixed-breed dog," he drawled.

Her burble of laughter was musical and infectious. "No, it's caffeine I need right now." She yawned widely without covering her mouth.

It should have been unattractive but he had trouble imagining that anything this woman did would be unattractive. Something stirred inside him, a warm ripple through his blood. "Caffeine does come in handy now and then."

"A double-shot capooch sure would." She stuck a hand out. "I'm Cassidy. Cassidy Esperanza."

With guests, he aimed for the personal touch, so he came out from behind the desk and extended his hand. "Dave Cousins."

He spotted a tattoo on the cap of her right shoulder: a Canada goose flying across the moon. Striking, almost haunting.

Cassidy's hand was like the rest of her: light brown, slender, attractive. Her shake was full of vitality. He shook a lot of hands in the course of a day, but this one felt particularly good in his—and now the ripple in his veins was a tingle of awareness. No, more than awareness; he was *aware* of lots of appealing women. This was attraction.

His heart—the part of it that could fall in love—had died three years ago. His body hadn't, but he had zero desire to follow up on any hormonal stirrings.

So why was it so difficult to free his hand from his guest's? "Best coffee in town's right here." A couple of the coffee shops did a fine job too, but for some reason he wanted to keep Cassidy Esperanza at the Wild Rose. "Good food too, if you're hungry."

"Cool." She gave another of those huge yawns, stretched her arms up, and raked her fingers through that cap of hair, ruffling it. Normally, he preferred long hair on women, but the pixie cap suited Cassidy's slightly exotic face.

"I'm awake," she said with a quick laugh, eyes dancing as she studied his face. "I swear I am. Got a good sleep too. Don't know why I'm yawning." Her face sobered. "Before I do anything, I need to have a talk with the manager."

"Let me guess, you're twenty-two."

"Twenty-two?" She shook her head slightly, looking confused. "No, I'm twenty-seven. What a weird question."

"Sorry, I mean room twenty-two. The woman who came in last night and . . ." He paused, curious to see what she'd say.

"Did a face plant?" She raised her brows ruefully. "You heard about that? Yeah, that's me. Totally embarrassing. But the guy on the desk was great. Only problem is . . ." She pressed her full, pink lips together, then released them. "Can I confide in you? Maybe you can give me some advice."

He dragged his gaze from her lips. "Uh, sure."

"The nice guy gave me a room last night, and food, but the thing is, I don't have the money to pay. I came in to get warm and see if someone could point me toward a hostel, and next thing I knew I was on the floor and this guy was"—she broke off and grinned with the memory—"waking me up with a whiff of whisky. Which tasted delicious, and I guess I owe for that too, now that I think of it."

"Look—"

"No, I realize I owe for the room and everything, and this is a classy place so it won't be cheap. But the thing is, I'm pretty much broke."

Oh, great.

He opened his mouth, but she rushed on again. "I

swear I won't cut out on you. I was going to look for a job in Caribou Crossing anyway, and as soon as I get one and have some money, I'll pay up. But it might take a few days and I'd sure understand if the manager was mad. So if you could give me any tips on how to deal with him, I'd really appreciate it."

As best he could tell, she was sincere. "Tell him the truth. And you did. I'm the owner of the Wild Rose."

"Oh! My gosh, I didn't realize. Wow. You don't look old enough."

He'd heard that before. "Just turned thirty."

She studied him again, lips curving. "Gotta love a hotel where the owner wears jeans and cowboy boots."

"It's part of our ambience."

She glanced around the lobby. "Yeah, it's kind of a cool blend of Old West and Santa Fe. That room— twenty-two—is awesome. That four-poster canopy bed with all the ruffles and flounces, the stool to climb up into it. I worried when I saw the chamber pot, but then I realized it was for decoration and there was a real bathroom. Claw-foot tub and all."

Canopy bed. Claw-foot tub. Slim, vibrant, sexy Cassidy. Physical stirrings below the belt had him giving a mental head-shake. He would never fool around with an inn guest. In the past three years, he'd pretty much figured he'd never fool around again. If he wanted female companionship, he had platonic friends. Casual sex wasn't his thing, and love wasn't going to happen. Anita had been the love of his life. His heart belonged to her, and always would.

And there he went, thinking of her again. The familiar sense of desolation threatened, but somehow the grin Cassidy tilted toward him countered it.

"So, Dave Cousins, Mr. Owner, want to have breakfast

with me? I'll run my tab even higher and you can tell me where I might find work."

Though he liked being friendly and informal with guests, he kept it professional. Occasionally, he joined them for a drink or a coffee, but not often. This time he was tempted—against his better judgment. There was something about Cassidy that made him feel . . . lighter.